Through the Gate of Ivory

To: Dónal,

Have -a good

read Reta

For Cheryl, Clare, Catherine,
Deirdre, Aileen and Conor,
who were there from the inception

Through the Gate of Ivory

Patrick Devaney

*Sunt geminae Somni portae; quarum altera fertur
cornea, qua veris facilis datur exitus umbris,
altera candenti perfecta nitens elephanto,
sed falsa ad caelum mittunt insomnia Manes.*

(There are twin Gates of Sleep, of which one is said
to be of horn, allowing an easy exit for shadows
which are true. The other is all of shining white
ivory, perfectly made; but the Spirits send visions
which are false in the light of day.)

Virgil, *The Aeneid*, Book VI

THE LILLIPUT PRESS
DUBLIN

First published 2003 by
THE LILLIPUT PRESS LTD
62–63 Sitric Road, Arbour Hill,
Dublin 7, Ireland
www.lilliputpress.ie

A CIP record for this title is available
from The British Library.

1 3 5 7 9 10 8 6 4 2

ISBN 1 84351 016 2

The Lilliput Press receives financial assistance from
An Chomhairle Ealaíon / The Arts Council of Ireland.

Set by Marsha Swan in 10 on 12.5 Sabon
Printed in Ireland by ßetaprint of Dublin

Contents

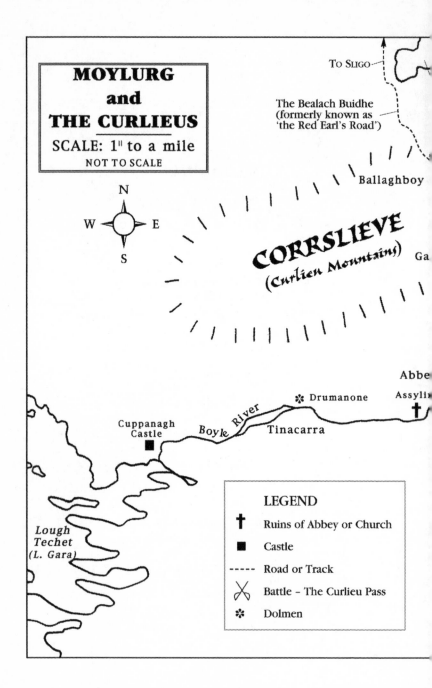

MOYLURG
and
THE CURLIEUS

SCALE: 1" to a mile
NOT TO SCALE

N
W — E
S

To SLIGO

The Bealach Buidhe
(formerly known as
'the Red Earl's Road')

Ballaghboy

CORRSLIEVE
(Curlieu Mountains)

Ga

Abbe

Assyli

Drumanone

Cuppanagh
Castle

Boyle River

Tinacarra

Lough
Techet
(L. Gara)

LEGEND

✝ Ruins of Abbey or Church

■ Castle

----- Road or Track

✗ Battle – The Curlieu Pass

❋ Dolmen

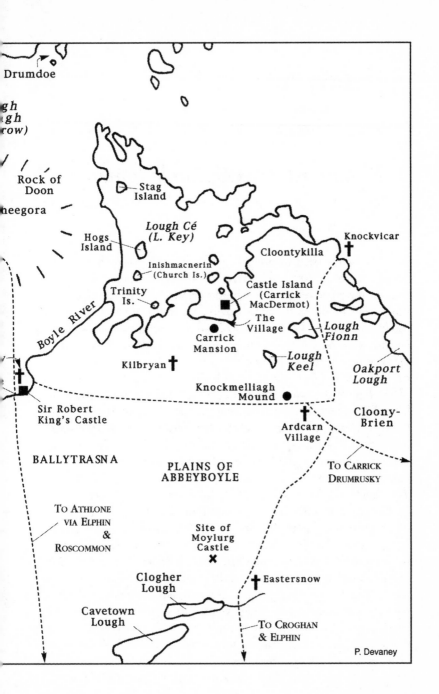

Drumdoe

gh
gh
row)

Rock of
Doon

heegora

Stag
Island

Lough Cé
(L. Key)

Hogs
Island

Cloontykilla

Knockvicar ✝

Inishmacnerin
(Church Is.)

Castle Island
(Carrick
MacDermot)

Boyle River

Trinity
Is.

The
Village

Lough
Fionn

Carrick
Mansion

Kilbryan ✝

Lough
Keel

Oakport
Lough

✝
■

Knockmelliagh
Mound ●

Sir Robert
King's Castle

Ardcarn ✝
Village

Cloony-
Brien

BALLYTRASNA

PLAINS OF
ABBEYBOYLE

To Carrick
Drumrusky

To Athlone
via Elphin
&
Roscommon

Site of
Moylurg
Castle
✕

Clogher
Lough

✝ Eastersnow

Cavetown
Lough

To Croghan
& Elphin

P. Devaney

vii

Foreword & Acknowledgments

WHILE I have tried to preserve accuracy when dealing with historical figures in this novel, I have occasionally, where the imperatives of the story required it, altered details. My treatment of Úna Bhán MacDermot is the most obvious example of this licence, yet the researches of scholars such as Marcus MacEnery show that the legend as we now have it is itself inaccurate and Sir Dermot Mac-Dermot has established that there are two contenders for the role of the tragic heroine, one of them belonging to the Dungar branch of the family, the other belonging to the Loch Cé branch; it is the latter Úna I have chosen to portray as the object of Tomás Láidir Costello's love. Nevertheless, it can be argued that there is too much difference between the character and fate of the traditional Úna and my own, but if Virgil can alter legends – as he does when dealing with the punishments of some condemned souls in Book VI of *The Aeneid* – I feel that I may safely follow in his footsteps.

Other facets of the novel may seem inaccurate but are the result of physical changes in the landscape (Monksland was designated "bog" on seventeenth-century maps and is now cultivated land) or the alteration of county boundaries (the eastern portion of the Barony of Costello, where Tomás Láidir's family lived, was once in Co. Mayo and is now part of Co. Roscommon). Finally, the hero, Charles Stanihurst, is recalling events that occurred one third of a century prior to the time of writing so, despite his concern to be truthful, lapses or distortions of memory are to be expected, especially in one who has suffered so many vicissitudes and whose journey back to the Upper World was through the Gate of Ivory.

Among the people I am indebted to for assistance in writing this novel are: Sir Dermot, The MacDermot (now deceased), for his letters on the MacDermots and the Úna Bhán legend; Muireann Ní Bhrolcháin for translating a poem by Tomás Láidir Costello; John Flynn of Armagh Planetarium for information on the Julian and Gregorian Calendars and phases of the moon; Eamonn Bourke for clarifying details of Burke history; Marguerite O'Conor Nash for information on the O'Conors; Michael Holland for printed material on Ballintober Castle; Laura Burke for making available her researches on the King Family; Richard McGee and Canon Garrett for help with some aspects of Boyle and Ardcarn history; John Joe Costigan for explaining the difficulties in growing apricots; Eamonn McCann for information on traditional building and roofing materials; Michael Ó Comáin of the Heraldic Office for investigating the date of Hugh O'Conor Don's knighting; the Director of the Meteorological Service, Glasnevin, for articles on Irish weather in past centuries; the Penguin Group (UK) for permission to quote extracts from *Virgil: The Aeneid*, translated by W. F. Jackson-Knight (Penguin Classics, 1956); Lynne Whittaker, Mary Cullen and Tadhg Ó Dúshláine of St Patrick's College, Maynooth, for reading the MS, and Colm Lennon for pointing out some historical inaccuracies in it; Declan Kiberd of University College Dublin for reading the MS; Sheila O'Hagan for checking style and presentation; my colleagues, Kathleen O'Leary, Ciaran Dockery and Michael O'Donnell, and my sister Christina for reading the MS; my wife Cheryl for typing the first fifteen chapters, making corrections to the three books and reading proofs; my daughter Catherine for typing two chapters and the epilogue and revising family trees; Catherine Heslin for typing the remainder of the novel, as well as the revised copy; my son Conor for running off floppy disks; my daughter Clare for typing the back cover text; my sister Mary for providing a map of the Boyle area; the staff of the library of NUI, Maynooth, especially Étain Ó Siocháin, Maynooth Library and the Church of Ireland Representative Church Body Library, Dublin, for obtaining books; the editors of *Books Ireland* and the *Roscommon Association Yearbook 2002* for publishing extracts from the novel; Antony Farrell, Sarah Deegan and Liam Carson of The Lilliput Press for their editing and advice; the EBS

Building Society for financial assistance; Nicola Sedgwick for completing the Moylurg map and Dermot Nangle for completing family trees and the main map and preparing the typescript. Finally, I would especially like to thank Cyril Mattimoe, who patiently answered my queries on Roscommon history and read the MS, and Mike Lennon of the Roscommon Association, who gave invaluable assistance with the publication.

I

SOWING

Hinc via Tartarei quae fert Acherontis ad undas

(From this place is a path which leads to the
waves of Tartarean Acheron)

Virgil, *The Aeneid*, Book VI, l. 295

Chapter 1

THERE IS a phrase which the Gaels of this country use to denote the upheaval the great founder of the Commonwealth, Oliver Cromwell, wrought in their lives: "To hell or to Connacht". Thirty-three years ago I myself went to hell *and* to Connacht.

When I first attempted to set down an account of that journey I took as my starting-point the day in the year Thirty-Nine that the Lord Deputy, Black Tom Wentworth, magnificent in his robes of state, came striding through the quadrangle of Trinity College with the Provost, Dr Chappell, trailing a peacock's train of fellows and resident masters behind them: this opening entailed such a close examination of my profligate student life that, overcome by shame, I was unable to proceed. Finally, on recalling that Homer and Virgil begin *in medias res*, I decided to be guided by the ancients, for in truth my journey was a journey into the past, a past almost unknown to our people in the Pale. I have taken, therefore, as my new starting point that fatal moment when I first set foot on the soil of Connacht.

There was nothing obviously hostile in the demeanour of the three men opposite me, yet I felt my whole body tense as I watched them. Maybe it was their great, shaggy, woollen mantles; hard, moustached faces and long, unkempt hair that alarmed me, either that or their wolflike strides and keen, unsmiling eyes. One of them was leading a saddleless garron by reins fashioned from strips of rawhide and all were carrying staffs. With assumed nonchalance I pulled Nell's leather reins and pretended to be searching for something in my saddlebags. Should they make the slightest move in my direction I would jerk Nell around and make a dash for the town of Athlone, which, enclosed in massive walls, straddled the Shannon not more than a furlong behind us. The three hesitated, called out something in Gaelic, then, catching sight of a company of mounted soldiers approaching, continued on their way westward. The soldiers, who were armed with swords and pistols, wished me "Good evening" in strong provincial accents. I had an almost overpowering impulse to ride back with them to the familiar world of cobbled streets, close-packed houses and fire-lit taverns. Unfortunately, I could not, for I was a fugitive from that world, and before me lay the Gaelic-Norman world of Connacht, *ultima Thule*, separated from the east by the broad, smooth-flowing Shannon.

Unwrapping the last of my provisions, I gulped the stale bread and cheese without dismounting. What would I not have given for a tankard of ale to wash it down! The need to husband my few remaining coins, however, meant that I would have to endure being thirsty till I encountered a stream – and it was all because of my own gullibility that I was in such straits, for I had been robbed the previous evening outside Maynooth.

The incident had occurred almost within sight of the Earl of Kildare's great castle. Four ruffians, whom I took, from their age and bearing, to have been soldiers, approached me under pretence of asking for alms and when I foolishly yielded to compassion, they dragged me from the saddle. One of them would have knifed me on the spot if his leader had not ordered, "Unhand the gentleman or, by God, I'll do for you." It was almost with a sense of gratitude that I surrendered my purse – though not the money I had hidden inside my shirt – and begged them to leave me my horse. This their leader, who acted like a man of some breeding, consented to do, and I thanked him sincerely as I remounted.

"If Strafford were still in Ireland, we wouldn't be preying on gentlemen like yourself," he apologized, "but people must survive."

And that's true too, I reflected as I galloped away, grateful to have come out of the affair so lightly. Black Tom Wentworth, Earl of Strafford, had made himself a thorn in everyone's side from the moment he had been appointed Lord Deputy but at least he had imposed order and peace on the country. Now the pack, Protestant as well as Papist, had turned on him and from the rumours coming out of London, he would be lucky to escape with his life.

The three woodkernes – for such I took them to be – were by this time far ahead. Maybe they were just curious after all and I had mistaken their intentions. Nevertheless, when I came to a junction, I waited till they had disappeared out of sight along the western road; then took the road leading north. From my recollection of Mercator's map this would bring me through Roscommon town and on to Sligo, where with any luck I would find a ship to take me to Galway, my original destination. From Galway, I would be able to sail to Spain or the Spanish Netherlands or even, perhaps, to the New World.

"*Trathnóna breá, buíochas le Dia.*" A stout, red-faced woman enveloped in rags with a half-naked child in tow approached me from the side of the road. The little girl looked so frail that I hadn't the heart to ignore the plea for alms, as I took the woman's guttural words to be. Throwing a penny on the ground, I was repaid with a flood of invective punctuated with the words *Sasanach* (Saxon) and *Diabhal* (Devil). Recognising my mistake, I dismounted, retrieved the penny and with a smile offered it to the girl, who shrank back behind her mother. Then, recalling an expression of my mother's, I said, "*Tóg é, a stóirín*" (Take it, little pet), at which the woman's demeanour changed. Curtseying slightly, she inundated me with blessings, among which "*Beannacht Phádraig agus Bhríde ort, a dhuine uasal*" (The blessing of Patrick and Brigid on you, sir) was the first complete sentence of Gaelic I had comprehended since encountering the Wild Irish. Pleased with my success, I prevailed on the woman to accept a shilling and asked directions by pronouncing the words "Roscommon" and "Sligo" carefully. At first the woman did not understand, then her dark eyes lit up and she said, "*Ros Comáin,*" pointing in the direction I was going and adding, "*An Sheriff,*" by which I understood that the Sheriff lived there. Since I lacked sufficient Gaelic to elicit further information, I bade her goodbye; then continued on my way.

It was now late evening, with the sun dropping down towards the western hills. Despite my black frieze jerkin, a chill breeze penetrated my doublet. Anxiously I urged Nell forward but she was flagging and barely managed a trot. "Good girl," I encouraged her, trying to keep the anxiety out of my voice. If I were caught out in open country after dark I had every expectation of being set upon by robbers. Connacht, with its half-wild Papists, was reputed to be especially dangerous, though here in Roscommon County there were surely sufficient garrisons to keep the main road to Sligo safe. Or were there?

Suddenly Nell sidestepped to avoid a puddle, almost throwing me across her withers. Cursing, I righted myself by grabbing the pommel. If I allowed the tiredness that was lurking at the edges of my mind to lessen my attention, sooner or later I would take a fall. One and a half days of riding, broken only by six hours sleep in a barn near Clonard, had turned my thighs to lead and filled my back with pain. How I longed for the warm bed with its straw mattress and clean linen I shared with my brother Thomas. The hour that had thrown me into the company of that English officer when I should have been attending a lecture on Copernicus was the bitterest in my young life. Even now I could see the moist red lips between the neatly trimmed beard and moustache and smell the nauseating, wine-scented breath. God, what a fool I had been!

There we were, ensconced in the Black Raven in Winetavern Street, discussing Marlowe's 'Hero and Leander' and Shakespeare's sonnets over tankards of claret and it had never occurred to me that the erudite, polished stranger with an accent which I could imagine resembled that of my beloved bard – "Ah, Charles Stanihurst – what a delightful name!" – was more interested in my person than in my opinions – not until he attempted to embrace me as we were walking in broad daylight down St John's Lane and I shoved him so violently that he banged his head against a nearby wall and slumped to the ground. While I was desperately searching his wrists and neck for the least sign of a pulse beat, a crowd of revellers approached and immediately began to bawl, "Stop! Murder!" so that I was obliged to take to my heels, my hands sticky with the blood of my erstwhile drinking companion.

It occurred to me as I fled back into Winetavern Street and raced down it, dodging hawkers, carters, beggars, housewives and strollers, that the stranger might by some miracle have regained consciousness – for I had not intended him any serious harm – but even if he had, I would, at the very least, be thrown in Newgate gaol for assaulting an officer in His Majesty's Navy. Worse still, my family would have been subjected to investigation, something unthinkable, not only because of its effects on my father's business but because it would have uncovered the fact that he had married a native who had refused to abjure her Popish ways. True, my mother did not attend Mass but neither did she accompany my father to Divine Service and in the present religious climate that would have been enough to brand her a recusant. It was one thing to waste my parents' hard-earned money by neglecting my studies but another to jeopardize their security by bringing them to the attention of the Castle authorities. The only course open to me was to flee Dublin at once.

Reaching Prickett's Tower, I swung left into Wood Quay, walked quickly past the Crane and the home of Lord Justice Parsons, then bounded like a deer down Merchant's Quay, slowing down before I came to Bridge Gate. From there I strode across the bridge to the echoing cobbled streets of Oxmantown and my home beyond St Michan's Church.

Borrowing a handful of my father's crowns and sovereigns and Thomas's mare, I assured my mother that I was only riding out to Chapelizod to get a copy of Virgil's *Aeneid* from John Crofton, a fellow student, and kissing her like a Judas, I hurried away before she could question me. To salve my conscience, I did indeed call to John's home, where I penned a hasty letter to my parents, informing them that due to a misfortune I couldn't explain at present, I was forced to leave Dublin. As soon as circumstances permitted, I would give them a full account of my actions but they could rest assured that I had not behaved dishonourably. John, who was a great favourite with my two sisters, Margaret and Bridget, promised to deliver the letter that very evening. He did not ask what had happened but, like the true friend he was, gave me provisions for the journey as well as the *Aeneid* and a Bible, declaring that a traveller without a Bible was like a pilgrim without a staff.

The countryside through which I was now riding was not calculated to lift my spirits, though it was not without a certain desolate grandeur. On either side stretched a flat, brown bog covered with mosspools and heather and in the distance, to my right, I could glimpse a great expanse of water that must have been Lough Ree. Two or three times I decided to turn back to Athlone, but then the recollection of those woodkernes with their rapacious eyes and shaggy cloaks which might conceal a dagger or pistol changed my mind. There was also the image of a frightened man to dissuade me. This fellow, who was only a few years older than myself, had been waiting to pass through the gate on the Connacht side when the guards, after a whispered consultation, pounced on him.

"Why are you arresting me?" he cried. For answer a sergeant hit him with the butt of his musket in the stomach. The look of anguished appeal in his eyes as he was being dragged away pierced my heart but I was too afraid of attracting attention to intervene. Anyway, I told myself, he was probably only some common thief or miscreant. Now I realized with a pang of guilt that he might well have been arrested in mistake for me.

Whatever the truth of the matter, I must avoid Athlone. If the worst came to the worst and I was followed, I would make a run for it and hope that Nell, tired as she was, would carry me to safety but, as if fate were determined to thwart my escape, at that very moment she stumbled and lurched, then, to my horror, refused to move another inch. Dismounting, I examined her hooves but could find no stone or cut, yet when I tried to urge her on she limped. Clearly there was something the matter with her right front foot but whether it was a broken bone or simply a sprain I couldn't determine. How I regretted not having taken more interest in the horses instead of leaving their care entirely to Thomas. What use were Marlowe and Shakespeare to me now, unless to provide me with words for my predicament.

"A horse! A horse! My kingdom for a horse!" I declaimed to the red disk of the sun poised above the western horizon. In reply something that might have been a fox or a wolf emitted a thin, plaintive howl, sending a shiver through my body. Despite my frantic scrutiny, I could glimpse neither house nor cabin anywhere. Nothing except the crude road on which I stood and some half-wild cattle and sheep grazing on the fringes of the bog testified to the existence of man.

"So this is how your life will end," I told myself. "You will freeze to death in this uninhabited wilderness, and wolves will eat your corpse." The contemplation of such a quietus had the desired effect: I resolved to go on living. Yet, what was the best course of action?

As I stood there watching Nell graze, I felt like a mariner caught between the Scylla of Athlone and the Charybdis of the unknown country ahead. Finally, I resolved that if no help came by twilight, I would tramp on without Nell till my strength gave out.

Chapter 2

INEXORABLY the sun sank below the horizon, causing the breeze to grow chillier. If only I hadn't met that Englishman I would now be at home in my warm room studying Caesar's *De Bello Gallico* or Virgil's *Georgics* – not that I always kept my mind on the classics. For the past two years I had taken to writing poetry, in particular a long, sententious piece in which the hero, Colin Scott, describes life at the university. On the day that Strafford visited Trinity, I had been sitting in the library opposite Hugh O'Rourke, composing more verses, while ostensibly reading the *Dialectica* of Ramus. Suddenly a crowd of senior sophisters descended on us; the poem was snatched away and, despite my protests, read aloud by my arch-rival, Michael Hamilton:

> *"The academic mirror clears*
> *Like quiv'ring shadows in a river massed*
> *The blended colours separate to form*
> *One undistorted scene, enchanting, vast.*
> *A rustic concept Colin finds untrue:*
> *The students are devout.*
> *Their days are not in Godless revels passed.*

"Listen to that, my uncouth comrades. Spenser here believes we are devout. How gracious of him! Wait! There is more:
   '*Not here the gay, disordered life –*'"
   "Stop jeering, Hamilton," O'Rourke interposed, "and give Stanihurst back his verses."

"Hark!" Hamilton declaimed. "A benighted son of the Whore of Babylon."

"If you Puritan dawcocks weren't so assured of your place in heaven, we whoresons might have a little more peace on earth," O'Rourke remarked affably.

A section of the listeners applauded, for it was because of Puritan agitation that Strafford had passed a law to prevent Catholics such as O'Rourke from graduating unless they first took the Oath of Supremacy. Strafford had also aroused the ire of Puritans by his insistence that the Irish Church accept the Thirty-Nine Articles of the Church of England: as a result, most of the students had decided to ignore his visit that day.

"Are you going out to greet the Lord Deputy?" I asked Hamilton with a show of innocence.

"Not I," he retorted, "but I expect that dyed-in-the-wool royalists like yourself and O'Rourke are." The "dyed-in-the-wool" epithet was a jibe at my father, who was a wool merchant, and at O'Rourke's, who raised sheep.

"I'm pleased to welcome a man who accepts Catholics into the army," O'Rourke said, "even if he also denies them the Graces."

"And I'm pleased to welcome a man that has appointed God-fearing bishops and cleared the sea of pirates, even though he has suppressed the wool trade," I added, knowing that the reference to bishops would irk Hamilton.

"It's hardly surprising that a relation of the Archbishop of Armagh should defend bishops," Hamilton observed with a mocking smile, "but answer me this: do you regard our Provost, Dr Chappell, as one of those God-fearing bishops?"

Now I was trapped, since by the new university statutes, to which he had sworn, Dr Chappell should have resigned the provostship once he had been appointed Bishop of Cork and Ross. "'Judge not, that ye be not judged'," I cautioned lamely.

"Hamilton would judge his own mother," O'Rourke commented. "Aye, and find her guilty as well."

"You are evading the question, Stanihurst." Hamilton refused to let me escape.

"If Archbishop Laud is satisfied with him, why shouldn't we be?" I tried another tack.

"So you believe that the Chancellor also has the right to ignore the statutes, do you?" Hamilton persisted. By this time the Assistant Librarian was calling for silence.

"Farewell," Hamilton spoke loftily. "Your attitude, O'Rourke, I can understand, though not approve. As for you, Stanihurst, your judgment of leaders is no better than your verse." With a contemptuous gesture, he threw the poem on the table; then walked away.

That afternoon, Hugh and I stood among the small crowd of cheering students that greeted the Lord Deputy, little realizing that his downfall and Dr Chappell's resignation were so near. Neither did I even dimly conceive that within the span of eighteen months I myself should be a wanted man, though as the following poem, written at that time, shows, I did foresee that, unless I studied more diligently, academic failure was inevitable:

> *I knew that on this task would rest*
> *The future life, the further goal;*
> *I knew but shirked the fateful test.*
> *Through secret fear I let the bowl*
>
> *Of earthly bliss topple and break*
> *And scarcely paused to see*
> *Its bright contents their shards forsake,*
> *Soaking the clay of revelry.*
>
> *I knew, but knowledge could not buoy*
> *The will to act ere hope slipped by;*
> *I plucked too soon the flowers of joy*
> *And left the parent tree to die.*

The "secret fear" I mention in the first verse comes close to the heart of my mystery: I wasn't so much afraid of failure as of success. To understand why that was so, you would have to understand our family history.

The Stanihursts had been prominent in Dublin life from the early days of the English colony. One of my ancestors was Mayor of Dublin in the fifteenth century and my great-great-grandfather, Nicholas, was Mayor in the sixteenth century. My great-grandfather, James, was speaker in the Irish House of Commons and my grand-uncle Richard was the famous scholar and historian who translated Virgil's *Aeneid*, contributed the Irish section to Holinshed's *Chronicles* and wrote *De rebus in Hibernia gestis*, the great work on Ireland past and present.

It was during Richard's time – he himself became a Jesuit priest – that our family divided on religious grounds, my grandfather, Henry, and his sister Margaret cleaving to the Established Church and his brother Walter following Richard's example by giving his allegiance to the Church of Rome. Great-Aunt Margaret's son, James Ussher (who was Vice-Chancellor of Trinity while I was a student there), became Archbishop of Armagh and declared at a convention of bishops that toleration of the religion of the Papists was a grievous sin. My father, Nicholas, while no Puritan, was a sincere believer in church reform, though this did not prevent him from falling in love with my mother, Norah O'Flynn, whom he met on a business trip to Roscommon County in the year Seventeen. We never spoke much about my mother's people, and it was understood that my father had married beneath him, something that estranged him further from his Catholic cousins. When I showed some aptitude for learning, my father decided that I would be the one to re-establish the family name by becoming a lawyer: it was as a merchant and lawyer that my great-grandfather had consolidated the Stanihurst position and I would follow in his footsteps.

So it was that my parents scrimped and saved in order that I could go to grammar school and then to Trinity College. Once I had graduated from Trinity, I would have had to seek admittance to one of the Inns of Court in London, where, after spending five or six years perusing legal tomes, I might eventually be called to the bar. The only trouble was that my opinion of lawyers was no higher than Hamlet's ("Where be his quiddits now, his quillets, his cases, his tenures, and his tricks?") but by the time that I realized this, so much had already been invested in my education that I had not the courage to shatter my father's dream. Yet, the more I tried to study, the more I found myself indulging in the secret vice – for so I regarded it – of writing verse. And then to forget my predicament, I would sneak away to Winetavern Street with money I had borrowed from my friends or won from them at cards and spend it on claret, ale and tobacco or stand among the groundlings to watch plays being performed at the new theatre in Werburgh Street. All in all, I was like a boatman drifting towards the edge of a waterfall, trying to deaden his mind to the impending horror.

The clip-clop of hoofbeats roused me from thoughts of student life. Looking up, I descried riders approaching from the north. Suppose they were woodkernes? On the principle that a living dog is better than a dead lion, I jumped a grass-grown drain by the roadside and was soon squelching through waterlogged peat to a small clump of willows. Peeping out through the branches, I could just distinguish in the reduced light two gentlemen mounted on strong horses followed by two other riders, whom I took from their dress to be servants. The little group was preceded by a brace of spaniels so it was certain that my hiding-place would soon be discovered. To avoid the humiliation of being flushed out like a hare, I picked my way back to the road and stood by Nell's side, acutely conscious of my dripping breeches.

The dogs were soon abreast of me, sniffing warily but keeping their distance till their masters should judge me friend or foe. Now I could see that these gentlemen had been out hawking for each carried a hooded falcon on his left arm. The taller of the two, a powerful, sombrely dressed man in his early forties, took in my situation at a glance.

"You've had some trouble, friend," he observed. "Where were you bound for?"

"Kilmore." I named the first place that came into my head.

"And why are you travelling to Kilmore at this late hour?"

I recalled my conversations with Hugh O'Rourke, who had often regaled me with stories about his countrymen, and decided to turn them to account. "Are you familiar with the work of Bishop Bedell?" I asked. Both men nodded. "Well, I intend to study under him so that I can turn the Wild Irish to the paths of righteousness."

The tall man threw back his head and laughed. "Ah, you Palesmen amuse me," he scoffed. "It'll take more than a Gaelic Bible to win the Wild Irish from their Popish superstitions; you might as well try to keep a dog from his vomit."

"Now, Sir Chidley," his companion, a man in his late forties, who was richly dressed in a green velvet suit with lace cuffs and collar, remonstrated, "you must not discourage the young man."

By this time Sir Chidley had dismounted and transferring the falcon to my arm, he ran his hand expertly over Nell's fetlock, whistling quietly to himself as he fingered and probed. The falcon's talons bit into my flesh but I refused to cry out. "Ah!" cried my rescuer, removing something with his knifepoint from the frog of the hoof, "A thorn! No wonder she refused to budge."

Feeling foolish, I thanked him profusely.

"Why, lad, it was nothing." His blue eyes watched me intently. "Would it be presumptuous to ask your name?"

"Charles Scott, sir," I used the name that had served me on my flight from Dublin.

"Ah, Charles." His voice was mocking again. "Not the most popular name at present, though my own brother bears it. This is His Excellency Lord Ranelagh, President of Connacht, and I am Sir Chidley Coote."

I bowed to both in what I hoped was the correct manner.

"It will be dark within the hour," Lord Ranelagh remarked. "Why don't you return with us to Athlone and set out on your journey tomorrow?"

"An excellent suggestion," Sir Chidley concurred. "You are obviously in need of dry clothes and warm food."

One part of me wanted to yield to this invitation but another warned me that to do so would be to take the chance of the fly when he entered the spider's web. This impression was strengthened when I noticed half a dozen or so moorcocks hanging by their necks from one of the servants' saddles.

"I'm sorry gentlemen," I cried, "but I must be on my way for I intend to cover half the journey to Roscommon town before nightfall."

"But where will you lodge tonight?" asked Lord Ranelagh.

"In a native hovel," I replied. "What better way to learn their language and customs?"

"If you lie down with dogs you'll rise with fleas," cautioned Sir Chidley.

"Nevertheless, I intend to press on." I handed the falcon to a servant, who set it on a perch mounted on the pommel of his saddle. The bird fluttered briefly before settling down.

"Have you a letter of introduction to Dr Bedell?" Sir Chidley returned to his original line of questioning.

"No," I confessed; and told how I had encountered ruffians outside Maynooth, who had taken my money and credentials.

"And what do you intend to do if Dr Bedell won't have you?" Sir Chidley obviously smelled a rat.

"'The Lord is my shepherd; I shall not want'; Psalm Twenty-Six, verse two." My quoting of number and verse was the wildest guess.

"A pretty answer." Sir Chidley's tone was dry. "If you really are concerned with furthering the cause of true religion in this province, we could, perhaps, make use of your services."

"What do you mean, sir?" I swung my leg over Nell's saddle.

"I think," Lord Ranelagh interposed, "Sir Chidley is afraid that in this present conflict between His Majesty and Parliament, the Papists may see an opportunity to ... well, to assert themselves; since that would lead to an overthrow of the established religion, any man who could gain their confidence would be of immense ... er ... assistance in furthering God's work and –"

"And would be well rewarded for his trouble," Sir Chidley finished for him.

Anger rose in me. So they wanted to recruit me as a spy! I was about to give them an indignant answer when Lord Ranelagh shouted, "Look out! Over there!" We all turned our heads and saw three fellows skulking in the bog. "Pursuers!" Sir Chidley growled and drawing a large wheel-lock pistol from his saddle holster, he fired deliberately at the strangers. There was a puff of smoke followed by an answering report from the heathery knoll where the men were now concealed and then they broke from cover and went bounding away like hares as the two servants and Lord Ranelagh discharged their pistols.

"Well, do you still intend to travel alone to Roscommon?" Sir Chidley asked, holding his bloody left arm where the ball fired by the Pursuers had grazed it.

"I will not be deterred by a few cowardly woodkernes." My words were surprising even to my own ears. "The Lord said to me, 'Son of Man, I am sending you to the Israelites, to the rebels that have turned against me.' Ezekiel, chapter two, verse three."

"Zounds, there are all kinds of courage," cried Lord Ranelagh admiringly. "God protect you, young man."

Quickly, before my courage could evaporate, I bade goodbye to Sir Chidley and Lord Ranelagh and continued on into the deepening dusk.

In a little time the hunting party was out of sight and the only sounds were the thlott-thlott of Nell's hooves on the rough military road and the plaintive cries of plovers circling their roosting grounds. Since leaving Athlone I reckoned that I had barely travelled four English miles. The bog now gave way to good ground, raising my spirits. Here and there I could glimpse cabins huddled in the shelter of trees. An old man with broken yellow teeth, driving a cow, called out a friendly greeting in Gaelic. Then as I came round a clump of hazels the woodkernes were standing before me and one had an arquebus pointed directly at my heart.

Chapter 3

MY MIND was working like a whirlwind as I surveyed the three men facing me. If I spoke in English they would probably show no mercy and I had not enough Gaelic to plead for my life. There was only one alternative. Raising my right hand I called out, "*Dominus vobiscum,*" as if I were one of their priests. The effect was extraordinary. They immediately approached me with smiling faces, jabbering in Gaelic. Their leader, a stocky, well-built fellow with black hair and dark blue eyes, shook my hand, exclaiming, "*Céad míle fáilte romhat, a athair*" (A hundred thousand welcomes, Father). I answered with another Latin blessing, something that obviously puzzled him. "Speak you English?" he asked. "English no." I shook my head. "*No entiendo. ¿Hablan ustedes castellano?*" I was relieved when he looked puzzled for I had exhausted my knowledge of Spanish. He took Nell's reins and made signs to me to dismount, whereupon he ordered one of his fellows to lead her away. I started to protest but, from a mixture of sign language and Gaelic, he gave me to understand that the mare was being taken to a nearby cabin where she would be fed. We were going to another place further back.

Since defiance would only have aroused suspicion, I allowed myself to be guided by the Pursuers, as Sir Chidley had called them, in the direction of Athlone. When we came to the bog, the leader made signs to me to follow him and led me across the sodden peat at a brisk pace, his two companions holding my arms, either to assist me or to prevent me from bolting.

The first stars were now showing, providing a faint light. We squelched on for what seemed hours, skirting quaking moss lawns and sedge-fringed pools till we eventually arrived at drier ground near a cutaway. In the bright starlight a low rectangular mound was visible; this on closer inspection turned out to be a cabin made of sods, thatched with heather. There was a smaller mound nearby with a dunghill before it, which, from the gaggling inside, I concluded to be a goose house. A dog barked menacingly, then recognizing the Pursuers' voices, he padded towards us, his tail wagging.

Carefully avoiding puddles, an upturned creel and a broken wooden pail, we made our way to the cabin. The wattle door was pulled open from the inside, allowing smoke mingled with the stench of animals and humans to billow out. I was so demoralized by the wilderness of moss and heather we had just traversed that the interior with its glowing peat fire, unkempt human occupants and three or four goats seemed to be a haven of comfort.

The family, which consisted of the father and mother, their seven children and an old *cailleach*, or crone, greeted us most hospitably and seated me on a stool made of bog oak near the fireplace, a small stone circle in the middle of the earthen floor. Since there was no chimney, smoke accumulated in a dense cloud under the low, soot-blackened roof.

After whispering to her husband, the mother produced and lit a rush candle. This was placed on a turf creel while she kneaded some dough in a small wooden dish. I smiled at the children, who gazed at me with wide, wondering eyes. They ranged in age from an infant of about eighteen months to a boy of about twelve years, and, despite their dirty rags, looked uncommonly attractive. One thing I noticed was that the younger boys all wore a kind of gown, intended, as I afterwards learned, to protect them from the fairies, who are reputed to steal male children. The mother must have been pretty once but hard work had left her careworn and pallid, though her teeth were remarkably white and even. Her hair was pale yellow, a colour not uncommon in Connacht, but whether owing to Norman or Gaelic blood I cannot tell. The husband looked a proper rogue, with twinkling blue eyes and red, curling hair and beard. It wasn't long till he lived up to his image, pressing a four-handled wooden vessel, called a *meadar*, filled with usquebagh on my escort and me. When the fiery liquid burned my throat, making me splutter, he laughed and winked. Dualtach – in English, Dudley – the leader of the Pursuers, had no such trouble, swallowing a mouthful at a single gulp before passing the meadar to the next person.

Meanwhile the mother had placed the dough before the fire on a wooden tripod, where the crone tended it; then she took a small wooden pail into which she milked one of the goats. Her husband did not lend a hand in any of these chores but, instead, acted the host, refilling our meadar and entering into animated discussion with Dudley. Before long all the men, including myself, were in a jovial mood so that when the mother offered us a repast of hard, freshly baked oaten bread and strong-smelling goat's milk, I managed to swallow both without any show of aversion.

Dudley now gave me to understand that the family expected me to baptize the two youngest children. I was dumbfounded. It would be no use pleading that I had lost my vestments and breviary because nobody would have understood Latin and I dared not use English. Furthermore, the mother had already prepared a wooden dish of water and a clean hand towel and was looking from me to the children with soft, trusting eyes. Privately asking God to forgive me, I rose and with my head enveloped in smoke, intoned a *Pater Noster*, poured water on the infant's head as his mother held him in her arms and said, "*Baptizmo te in nomine Patris et Filiis et Spiritus Sanctus.*" The infant cried but, otherwise, everything went well; then I repeated the ceremony with the second child, a little girl with fair, curling hair and angelic eyes, who was given the name Orla – the infant had been called Teigue.

Moved by a genuine desire to make the occasion impressive, I now proceeded to add a few lines from Virgil which begin: "*Talibus orabat dictis arasque tenebat*" – those lines where the Sibyl reminds Aeneas that it is easy to take the path that leads down to hell but to climb back to the upper regions: "*hoc opus, hic labor est*" – this is a work, this is a problem. Immediately I had finished I felt Dudley's keen gaze on my face. Had he noticed the change from Christian prayer to pagan poetry? The smoke made my eyes smart and, looking round at the circle of staring, dimly lit faces, the impression that I was really in hell seized hold of my imagination. The husband was a begrimed Charon, his wife was the Sibyl, the others were shades of the dead crowding round us and a large goat was Cerberus, the monstrous, three-headed dog. I could hear the Sibyl declare, "*Praeterea iacet exanimum tibi corpus amici*" (Furthermore, the body of your friend is lying dead), and cold sweat broke out on my forehead. Then the hallucination passed; I was back in the cabin and the parents, with tears of joy in their eyes, were thanking me for having performed the ceremony. Weakly I repeated the only Gaelic blessing I knew, *"Beannacht Phádraig agus Bhríde ort,"* before collapsing on the stool. When the mother tried to give me a shilling, probably the family's entire wealth, I felt like crying.

It was now close to midnight so we all lay down on rushes at one side of the cabin, first the father, mother, infant and children, then the Pursuers, with myself and Dudley last. The old woman slept by herself near the opposite wall. My clothes had only partly dried out so that I felt extremely uncomfortable. The barbaric surroundings, proximity of strangers and stench of goats kept me awake at first. Perhaps it was just as well for I might have babbled English in my sleep.

Gazing upwards into the darkness, I reviewed the major events of my life, culminating in the horror of the last few days. The girls that I had kissed in dark corners, allowing myself to become inflamed with lust, passed before me. Among them, Marion, whose father owned the Black Raven, walked forlornly, wondering why I had abandoned her. Then my family drew near, their eyes filled with unasked questions: Why do you waste your time on shameful self-indulgence? Why have you repaid our sacrifices with dishonour? Why do you not tell us what happened to you? It was no use denying my guilt. Like the Prodigal Son, I was reduced to living among swine, or at least goats. To hold the furies at bay, I composed a verse:

> *This is the gloomy treasure house*
> *Where lie in wait the first fruits of my years:*
> *Close hidden they in Stygian darkness there,*
> *With doors held fast by frenzied fears*
> *Of wickedness at bay –*
> *Oh, truest guardians they*
> *Should Truth, a dreaded guest,*
> *Return their watchful way.*

Before I could enumerate my various sins, sleep overcame me, a sleep without dreams.

In the middle of the night, I was awakened by some disturbance. Listening uneasily, I heard the crunch of bare feet on rushes, then the unmistakable hiss of urine: a man was relieving himself into the ashes of the fire. Despite my revulsion, the sound aroused in me an overpowering desire to emulate the action, so waiting until my host – for it was he – had settled back to sleep, I tiptoed to the door and removed the wooden bar. No sooner had I taken my first step into the icy starlight than the dog approached, growling so fiercely that my captors awoke. Immediately a rough command sent the brute lunging at my throat. With the promptness of a startled cat, I retreated inside, muttering, "*Pax vobiscum.*" Dudley shouted some question to which I replied, "*Requiescat in pace,*" this being my genuine wish for the barking mongrel. Then I paused by the fire but was too overcome by embarrassment to yield to nature's demand.

Taking my place once more beside Dudley, I waited in exquisite agony till the menfolk had resumed their snoring, then I rose, felt my way cautiously past a goat, located the ashes with my bare toes and shamelessly acted the rustic. "The art of our necessities is strange," I reflected, "that can make vile things precious." After that I had little trouble in falling asleep.

The gaggling of geese interspersed with the bleating of goats aroused me. It was day. My bones ached and fever made my head burn. Everybody had risen already, including the crone, who was gathering rushes into a pile at one corner of the room. The older children were playing outside and the mother was nursing the infant beside the fire. There was no sign of the husband or the Pursuers. Somebody had thrown a shaggy mantle over me but, nevertheless, I shivered. The mother, on hearing me stir, called out a gentle greeting, entirely oblivious of her nakedness. Averting my eyes, I recalled the painting of the Virgin and Child I had once seen when my mother brought us to Mass in a friend's house near St Mary's Abbey. In Dublin only beggar women would openly nurse their children yet, in spite of myself, my eye crept back to the robust infant contentedly sucking the white breast. Sensing my gaze, the mother smiled. For a moment it was as if the Virgin in the painting had come to life. Mumbling my one Gaelic blessing, I attempted to rise. When I got to my knees, however, my head swam and I was obliged to lie down again.

For a succession of days and nights the fever raged in me, during which time the woman of the house cared for me like an infant, giving me bitter tasting drinks that must have been brewed from herbs. At last the fever abated and I was able to join the family at their meals. These were meagre affairs since it was then Lent, though occasionally we had a few perch or trout, caught by the father and his eldest son, to share among us.

The father's name was Shawn Rua and his wife was called Oona and they were as unalike as Bacchus and Ariadne, for while he was jovial and sanguine, she was gentle and pensive. In her youth, from what I surmised, many gallants had wooed her; now she was obliged to spend her days in drudgery and isolation. One of her expressions was that it was no use *"beith ag iarraidh cnó ar choillte saileach"* (looking for hazel nuts on sally woods), an expression as likely as not to set Shawn recounting the story about the Salmon of Knowledge, which ate nuts that dropped into a pool from the Nine Hazels of Wisdom, or about the widow's son who on cutting Labraidh Loingseach's hair discovered the king's shameful secret, a secret he confided to a willow tree. The children loved these stories and would beg their father to tell how Fionn Mac Cumhaill had gained the Salmon's wisdom or how the harp made from the willow tree had sung out when played: "Labraidh Loingseach has horse's ears!" Shawn Rua would accompany his recitations with exaggerated gestures like an actor, so that I had little difficulty in understanding them and, indeed, his were the first stories that made me aware of the cornucopia of tales and legends the Gaels possess.

I was now learning to express myself partially in Gaelic, words and phrases that I had learned in childhood from my mother springing to my lips. At bedtime I joined the family in reciting the rosary before a cross woven of rushes, though the emphasis on Mary rather than Jesus did strike me as improper. Nevertheless, in my role as priest I soon mastered the Gaelic version of the *Ave Maria*, *Pater Noster* and *Salve Regina*. Before I could become fluent in my mother's tongue, however, the Pursuers returned.

It was Oona who noticed them as she was feeding the geese. She hurried indoors and pouring out a brief explanation, urged me to get myself ready for departure. Then with a troubled countenance, she added: "You've had your share of misfortune, young man, but worse is in store for you. You'll be in terrible danger and you won't always be able to tell friend from foe, but don't lose heart. Face every danger without flinching and in the heel of the hunt you'll win through."

Though, in looking back, her words remind me of the Sibyl's exhortation to Aeneas about not yielding to adversity, at the time I was too distracted by the headlong rush of events to pay them much heed. Why, you may wonder, had I not attempted to escape before this? The truth is that if I had succeeded in evading the surly vigilance of my hosts' dog – who snarled a warning whenever I ventured too far from the cabin – there was still that great waste – which I have since learned is called Monksland Bog – to traverse. No, it was safer to trust to my wits than risk almost certain death by drowning.

As soon as the Pursuers reached the cabin, Dudley curtly signalled to me to follow him outside, where he informed me in broken English that I was to be taken that night to Ballintober Castle. On asking him why, in Gaelic, he replied: "*Chun a fháil amach* you priest or spy."

"*Ní thuigim,*" I pretended not to understand, whereupon, in a lightning movement, his open palm struck the side of my head, leaving me half-dazed.

So the game was up! I must have spoken English while my mind was crazed with fever or else somebody had discovered the King James Bible in my saddlebag. Looking into Dudley's steely, hawklike eyes, I saw I could expect no mercy.

Chapter 4

THOUGH thirty-three years have elapsed since then, I will never forget that journey to Ballintober. The March wind that cut like a knife through my doublet was gentle in comparison with the apprehensions that pierced my mind. Would I be regarded as a government spy and tortured to reveal my plans? Who would believe that I was only a frightened student who had accidentally killed one of His Majesty's officers? The retribution I had sought to escape would be visited on my head a thousand fold, for hadn't I stained my hands with innocent blood? But I must not get ahead of my story.

We set out after sunset, while there was still light. The Pursuers had taken good care of Nell, though, when I attempted to mount, Dudley indicated that he was claiming her for himself. I was to be given the unshod, rough-haired garron which was being led by a man called MacDockwra. This tall, powerfully built fellow refused to surrender the animal. Jutting out his chin and resting his hand on the miodoge, or dagger, in his belt, he confronted Dudley, growling some challenge in Gaelic.

Deciding that a quarrel would only increase my own danger, I stepped between the combatants and turning to MacDockwra, declaimed the first Latin words that came into my head, "*Nos morituri te salutamus*" (We who are about to die salute you), whereupon he doubled up with laughter. Could it be that this uncouth giant understood the language of imperial Rome or did he simply believe I was still trying to play the cleric? Whatever the reason for his mirth, the moment of crisis passed.

While the garron was sure-footed, the hay-filled cushion that served as a saddle chafed continually. Had any of my Dublin friends been there to see it, what a spectacle I must have presented, my hair long and tangled and my formerly shaven face covered in an untrimmed, reddish beard. If I had on one of their shaggy mantles, I have no doubt that I might have passed for a Pursuer or for one of Essex's "rough rug-headed kernes".

After travelling for a short space, we turned off the Roscommon road and followed a dirt track pitted with bullocks' hoofprints. Nobody spoke and I could gather from the way my captors looked about that they were fearful of being detected. Small clumps of bushes and hazel trees dotted the landscape but in their leafless state they offered only meagre shelter to the lean, black cattle grazing beside them.

The ground rose steadily in a succession of low hills and there were places where it was necessary to dismount to cross a dyke or bank. Soon we could see the waters of a reed-mantled lake gleaming in the afterglow. Keeping this lake on our right, we continued briskly in a north-westerly direction, the three unmounted Pursuers matching the horses' pace without difficulty. One of them carried the arquebus on his shoulder so that if I had tried to escape I would have invited almost certain death.

Gradually the twilight gave way to darkness relieved only by starlight. Then the moon rose, a D-shaped, orange moon that flooded the world with eerie light. Trees took on grotesque, sepulchral aspects and the air was rent with plaintive howlings, but whether of wolves or of wild dogs I could not tell. Had I then known that the Gaels call the wolf *mac tíre* (son of the country), believing it to embody the soul of a malefactor, my terror would have been magnified tenfold. To add to my growing unease Dudley dismounted and the Pursuers crowded round him, whispering. In a moment two of them began to tie their miodoges to the ends of their staffs with rawhide thongs. When they all began to creep forward I remained where I was, for it had occurred to me that this might be my last chance of escape. Turning the garron about, I kicked his flanks gently with my heels. We had not gone more than a hundred paces from the track when, to my horror, a large grey wolf trotted in front of us. The garron reared, throwing me to the ground. By the time I regained my breath the wolf and garron were nowhere to be seen and MacDockwra was bearing down on me, his miodoge gleaming in his hand.

"*Nos morituri te salutamus.*" He repeated my words with cruel mockery.

This is your last moment of life, I told myself, then I became aware of a pungent odour: my hand was resting in fresh cowdung. Determined to die fighting, I waited until MacDockwra knelt to strike. At that very instant I threw a handful of cowdung right into his face. Bellowing with rage, he dropped the miodoge in order to wipe his eyes, enabling me to scramble out of reach.

Attracted by the outcry, Dudley and another Pursuer came running up. Grabbing me by the arms, they marched me away before MacDockwra could renew his attack. In no time at all I was again mounted on the garron, with Dudley riding alongside on Nell.

"Are you *i do chló féin?*" From the tone of his voice I sensed that my besting of his rival had not displeased Dudley.

Assuring him that I was indeed my old self, I asked in English, "Who lives in Ballintober?"

At first he made no answer but when I repeated the question in Gaelic, he replied, "*Uí Chonchubhair Donn,*" meaning the Brown O'Conor. By persistent questioning, in a mixture of Gaelic and English, I learned that this O'Conor Don was a direct descendant of Rory O'Conor, the last High King of Ireland. When I expressed surprise that the line of descent had remained unbroken over five centuries, he corrected me and said, "Three times five, O'Conor Don can trace his descent from Conn of the Hundred Battles, aye and from *Míl Espane*" (Milesius of Spain).

Since my mother had often told us how the Sons of Míl had conquered Ireland centuries before Christ was born, I took Dudley's assertion to be an instance of Native Irish exaggeration. Consequently, I brought the conversation round to my own situation but here he grew less informative. I did gather, however, that the Pursuers had gone to Athlone to meet one of their priests, who was travelling back from Louvain, with the intention of escorting him to Ballintober. As I was the only traveller they saw, they had assumed I was the holy man. Now the reason for the riderless garron and the staring glances was clear.

"Ah," I sighed, "if only I had known that at the time."

"Why?" he mocked. "So that you could inform the garrison?"

It was useless trying to convince him of my innocence; I had walked into a quagmire and the more I struggled to escape the deeper I would sink.

As the moon rose higher, clouds began to obscure it at intervals. The Pursuers, however, never slackened their pace. They seemed to know every gap and byway of the country, so that whenever we approached a mansion or hamlet, they took a wide detour before rejoining the path. Occasionally an aroused dog barked but we were not discovered. I had to walk more frequently now for fear of laming the garron. My shoes were soon heelless and I regretted not having asked for brogues before setting out. Nevertheless, I refused to give the Pursuers the satisfaction of seeing how distressed I was.

The way turned downhill, bringing us at some points to the bank of a substantial river, which we did not attempt to cross. Eventually the moon set, forcing – much to my relief – the Pursuers to lessen their pace. I was chilled to the marrow and my heels were sticky with blood. Every footstep I took caused my head to reel and it was only by clinging to the garron's mane that I could drag myself along. Suddenly the garron lurched, pitching me into oblivion.

How long I remained unconscious I cannot tell but when I came to I was once more on the garron's back. It was now approaching daybreak so that I could see my captors looming out of the darkness like great uncouth demons, one of them holding me upright with his hand, another leading the garron. In a little while I felt strong enough to support myself and they handed me the reins.

"*Go raibh maith agaibh.*" I thanked them brusquely, annoyed by my recent loss of dignity. Their teeth gleamed for a moment under their croimbéals, the great down-curving moustaches that warriors affect; then they withdrew.

In the cold light of dawn we picked up speed again. A flock of black crows flew past on creaking wings, heading for their feeding grounds. When I questioned Dudley about them, he remarked that "those hell fowl" were on the increase everywhere, though a generation previously they were hardly ever seen, the native crow being grey, with black head and wings. He reckoned there was a connection between the increase of black crows and the spread of the English – among whom I was clearly included. "They're all of a kind," he observed, "greedy scavengers that will pick Ireland bare."

Catching sight of a round tower projecting from a hilltop, I enquired if the Danes had built it. At this Dudley laughed. "Why do you Palesmen think that every ancient stone building was put up by foreigners?" he scoffed. "That is the Round Tower of Oran, built by Irish monks."

"And how do you know it was built by monks?" I was stung by his contempt.

"Because," he explained, "there are the ruins of a church founded by St Patrick beside it."

I was going to point out that this coincidence proved nothing but concluded that he would not take the same delight in argument as my fellow students at Trinity. Even Hugh O'Rourke was apt to grow short-tempered when outmanoeuvred in logic.

After a further hour's travel we came to the crest of a hill and saw beneath us a small native village beyond which, on the east end of a ridge, stood a castle, more impressive even, from its extent and isolation, than the Castle of Dublin. There were towers at the four corners and an entrance flanked by towers dominated the nearest end wall. A pennant with the scarlet Cross of St George flew over the battlements of the south-east tower and another pennant with a green emblem that I didn't recognize over the north-east tower.

"You're not going to deny that that fortress was built by Normans?" I couldn't help remarking.

"If Cathal Crovderg O'Conor was a Norman, then it was," Dudley agreed mildly. Not wishing to display my ignorance concerning Cathal Crovderg, I said no more.

Before we reached the village Dudley ordered me to exchange the garron for Nell, something that puzzled me. When I attempted to open the saddlebags, however, he shook his head warningly.

"If you are found innocent, you will get all your chattels back," he said. "If not ..."

The way he left the statement unfinished sent a shiver up my spine.

Nobody was astir in the village so we made our way undetected past the windowless hovels with their noisome middens. At the north end, there was a two-storied, timber and mortar alehouse resembling those in Winetavern Street, with glass windows and a sign hanging above its door on which was painted a golden meadar.

"How did that house get here?" I asked in surprise.

"It was built by Sir Hugh O'Conor for his godson, Brian Oge O'Beirne," Dudley explained. "Sir Hugh reckoned that people would be better off drinking his ale rather than their own usquebagh!"

I was eager to learn more about Sir Hugh but at the sound of our voices a dog had begun to bark furiously. Next moment a great hound came bounding towards us. Acting swiftly, Mac-Dockwra raised his staff like a javelin and as the enraged brute drew near, he hurled the staff with such accuracy that he hit it on the chest, whereupon it turned tail and fled, yelping with pain.

Hurrying on, we skirted a small, roofless church with a burial vault set in its front wall. Crude wooden crosses interspersed with a few carved stone crosses marked the sites of graves. There is a well bubbling up among trees on the lower side of the churchyard – though I failed to notice it at the time – and it is from this well that the name "Ballintober" is derived: *Baile Tobar Bhrighde*, the Town of Brigid's Well. Further south in Roscommon County there is an even more famous well associated with St Brigid to which the Native Irish flock in great numbers, believing its waters can cure diseases, much like the waters of Bethesda.

On arriving at the esplanade before the castle, I discovered that the pennant flying above the north-east tower showed a green oak tree on a white field and that the castle was surrounded by a moat, except where the entrance with its round-faced towers intervened. Before I could observe much more, however, half a dozen wolfish-looking horseboys clad in short, loose coats and tight-fitting breeches, their uncombed hair hanging down to their eyes, emerged from a wicket in the massive entrance door and surrounded our group, jabbering excitedly.

The biggest of the newcomers, a fair-haired fellow of about seventeen with a pimply, beardless face and light blue eyes, looked from me to Nell with an insolent grin, then told me to dismount. My stomach contracted as he grabbed the reins from my hands; in my exhaustion, the necessity of ignoring his unspoken challenge made me swallow my anger. Don't presume too far, you vile savage, I warned him in the inner chamber of my mind. When my blood is roused, I'm capable of murder.

On a curt command from Dudley three of the horseboys pulled back one half of the entrance door and we proceeded across the short, roughly paved causeway and through the arched opening, above which the rusty iron teeth of a portcullis hung suspended. At that moment the conviction seized me that I was entering the mouth of hell and that I might never see the outside world again.

Chapter 5

THE SCENE that met my eyes on passing through the entrance was totally unexpected. There were two rows of sturdy thatched cottages occupying the bawn or courtyard, most of them with chimneys and windows.

Pigs rooted in the dirt of the centre street, wolfhounds and mongrels gathered in a yelping pack, hens foraged on dunghills or under empty, solid-wheeled carts and wagons, while ducks and geese plucked the scant grass behind the cottages.

The inhabitants were obviously expecting our arrival for we had not advanced fifty paces before they crowded around us. A few of the older men were enveloped like my captors in shaggy mantles but the majority wore only coarse doublets and breeches, pointed brogues and bonnets that partially covered their heads and ears. The civil women wore fringed mantles over their long, loose-fitting gowns but while the older ones had on turban-like head-dresses of white linen, the younger ones – some of whom were exceedingly pleasing – left their locks uncovered. As for the common women, they were dressed in simple frieze tunics, the older ones having their hair covered with kerchiefs and the younger ones wearing theirs in plaits tied with brightly coloured lists.

A young gentleman in blue taffeta doublet, black velvet breeches and knee-high boots spoke briefly in Gaelic to my escort and then without so much as addressing me, gave orders that I was to be lodged in the kitchen of the south-west tower. This was a great, gloomy building, unlike the north-west tower, which presented a more ornate, inviting appearance.

"Sir," I cried in desperation, "I demand to speak to O'Conor Don."

"Then you will have to wait." His voice was soft and cultivated. "My father is occupied at present."

Following his glance, I saw on the battlement of the north curtain wall a middle-aged gentleman dressed in a cloak and plumed hat accompanied by a woman with long chestnut hair, who hung on his arm. From the disapproving look on the young man's handsome countenance, it was obvious that the woman was not his mother.

Afraid of losing face if I protested further, I allowed myself to be led by Dudley through hounds, geese and barefooted children to the dark tower, whose slitted, first floor windows gave it the appearance of a Norman keep. On our way we passed some giggling chambermaids, one of whom, a black-haired, comely wench, gave me an admiring glance. Despite my fatigue, I smiled in return. This caused Dudley's grim expression to relax. "You're a cock o' the woods," he observed, "though that one is a bit young for a fellow your age!" Ignoring his sally, I continued to smile, then we were squeezing through a doorway and the gloom of the tower engulfed us.

My life over the following weeks was the life of a scullion, compelled to tend the fire, wash floors, scrub pots and be at everyone's beck and call. Most of the servants treated me with suspicion or contempt, partly because, in their eyes, I was a *Sasanach* and partly, no doubt, because of my filthy appearance.

The kitchen was on the ground floor and in it the food for Dudley's Pursuers and for the ordinary servants, including ploughboys, herdsmen, dairymaids and horseboys, was prepared, the northwest tower having its own kitchen for the O'Conor family and their household servants. My meals were taken on a stool by the kitchen fire after I had cleared away the table on the first floor, where my betters ate. If it weren't for Shawn Bacach, an old jack-of-all-trades, and his wife Úna, who befriended me, I would have despaired.

Shawn Bacach (Lame Shawn) was a former gallowglass who had fought for the Mayo and Galway Burkes and, finally, for the MacDermots, in the rebellions that seared Connacht during the reign of Queen Elizabeth. He had received a musket wound at the Battle of the Curlieu Mountains, which left him lame in the right

leg. To all outward appearance a gentle, courteous old man, he delighted in recounting how he had assisted Ulick Burke in the murder of George Bingham, Sheriff of Connacht, or felled a charging
pikeman with his axe at the Second Battle of the Curlieus. "*Cogar
i leith chugam*" (Whisper here to me), he would begin and I would
endeavour, despite his accent, to follow his account of some youthful adventure.

It was Shawn Bacach who told me about the exciting time
when Red Hugh O'Donnell, after defeating the English at the Battle of the Curlieus, laid siege to Ballintober and breached its walls
with a Spanish cannon. Far from disapproving of this affront to his
employer's family, Shawn thought it the most justified treatment,
since Sir Hugh, the father of Calvagh, the present O'Conor Don,
had given up his Gaelic title for an English knighthood. "*Fileann
an feall ar an feallaire*"(Treachery recoils on its practitioner), was
Shawn's judgment on the whole affair.

Using indirections to find directions out, I questioned Shawn
Bacach about Calvagh and learned that while his wife was visiting
her brother, Viscount Burke of Mayo, he was assuaging his loneliness in the arms of Grainne, the chestnut-haired daughter of one
of his tenants. "Ah, the master always had an eye for beauty,"
Shawn whispered, "and sure wasn't his ancestor Rory, the High
King, said to have a like weakness – more interested in his women
than in fighting to save his crown."

"Why won't he see me?" I complained.

"He never does anything in a hurry," Shawn said, "especially
when Lady Mary isn't here to advise him. She's the one who, most
likely, will decide your fate."

"And what about their son Hugh?" I referred to the young man
who had consigned me to the kitchen.

"Hugh is a deep one." Shawn made circles in the ashes with his
hazel walking stick. "For all his soft ways, he has warrior blood in
his veins. If Hugh was given a free hand, the Cootes and their ilk
would tread warily in Connacht."

It was clear from Shawn Bacach's remarks that until the return
of Lady Mary my situation would not change. While I was not
treated as a prisoner, neither was I allowed out of doors. My confinement was made particularly irksome by one person, Brian
Dubh, a miscreant of two score years, whose sallow, black-bearded face and pig's eyes were a true mirror of his nature. Brian Dubh

(Black Brian) was *reachtaire*, or chief steward, and he never let me forget it. If I was washing trenchers, I was invariably using the wrong cloth; if I was laying out pewter drinking vessels beside the wooden dishes and spoons on the table upstairs, they were in the wrong place; if I was dipping rushes in tallow to make candles, I was not keeping them in long enough. Brian Dubh never tired of correcting my Gaelic pronunciations or of reminding me that I was in the house of a Gaelic nobleman. The fact that I had fine manners galled him most of all; he was determined to take me down a peg.

"*Ná bac leis*" (Pay him no heed), Shawn Bacach advised but I fretted and fumed. The Lenten fare of coarse bread, salted fish and weak ale that I was obliged to live on added to my discontent, and at night I had to lie on a pile of rushes through which the cold from the stone floor crept into my bones. Even in the cabin I had never slept so badly, probably because the goats and thatched roof kept the place warm.

Moved by my wan appearance, Úna found me a pallet with moth-eaten woollen blankets but Brian Dubh, on noticing it, flew into a rage and ordered her, on pain of dismissal, to remove it instantly. "Do you think that what is good enough for the horseboys isn't good enough for him?" he hissed.

To add to my suffering, I was racked by anxiety lest my family should be worried on my account and by remorse for having neglected my studies. If only I could have exchanged my ragged clothes for the gown I had left behind me in Trinity, how happy I would have been. But I was like the unprofitable servant who, because he had buried his talent, had been cast into outer darkness, there to weep and gnash his teeth.

In the midst of my despondency Lady Mary returned, but one day passed, then another and still I was not sent for. "What will I do?" I asked Shawn Bacach. He filled and lit his long-stemmed clay pipe before saying between puffs: "You could do what any poor man who was denied justice in my time did; if a great man refused to abide by the judgment given against him by a Brehon, then the person he had injured fasted outside his door till he shamed him into changing his mind."

The more I thought about Shawn Bacach's advice, the more it appealed to me. There was one *sine qua non*, however, if such a stratagem were to work; I would have to be prepared to fast to the death. It was therefore necessary to goad myself into action. As luck would have it, Brian Dubh provided the opportunity.

Every morning two old women servants cleaned the slophouse and brought the noisome pails to the tower entrance, where a horseboy was waiting to cart them outside the castle. Time and again Brian Dubh seemed on the point of giving me this task but, uncertain of my response, he had refrained. Then something happened which tipped the scales, something neither of us foresaw.

Lent was almost over and Shawn Bacach told me that on Easter Sunday there was to be a great dinner upstairs for the servants, to which some of the chambermaids had been invited. "There's a certain dark-haired young woman who has been making enquiries about yourself," he added with a wink but though I questioned him, he would divulge no more.

Determined to make myself presentable, I shaved off my beard, leaving only a croimbéal, got Shawn to trim my hair with a shears and bathed myself in a tub in the kitchen, to the great amusement of the women servants. Úna had already washed my clothes so that when Easter Sunday came I was as much the gallant as I had formerly been the scullion.

The servants left the kitchen in the morning and from the care they had taken with their dress and the beads they carried in their hands, it was obvious that they were going to Mass somewhere, either inside or outside the castle. I should have mentioned that they had always said grace before and after meals and recited the Rosary before bedtime, so that it was no surprise that they should celebrate Easter after the Romish fashion.

"Will you be all right?" Shawn Bacach felt sorry for leaving me on my own with the three old women who had been charged with minding the spit and cooking pots. I nodded. Úna promised to save a choice portion of meat for my dinner, then impulsively called on Saints Patrick, Brigid and Colmcille to bless me.

As I watched them hurry after the others, Shawn holding on to Úna's arm while he hobbled along with his stick, I wished I too were going. Despite their superstitious belief that Christ was really present in the bread and wine, they were at least celebrating His resurrection, while I was the lost sheep, cut off by sin from His flock. I tried to pray but had the bitter experience of Hamlet's uncle: my words flew up; my thoughts remained below. Maybe if I had my Bible, I would have found a psalm or a parable to comfort me but nobody had returned the one John Crofton had given me. In this extremity I composed a poem, which ended with the lines:

> If I could gain the love that strikes
> Life's earthen dykes in tide on tide
> (The while alone I bide,
> A feeling clod),
> Oh, I would have this soul inside
> Disintegrate in God.

When the servants returned, laughing and chattering, preparations for the dinner went feverishly ahead. In no time the clock struck twelve and we started carrying the food up to the first floor. This must once have been the Great Hall, to judge from the torn Flemish tapestry of knights and ladies on the back wall and the O'Conor coat of arms with its lions and oak tree carved in the stone above the large fireplace. A long table occupied most of the room, while a smaller table set crosswise on a raised portion of the flagged floor was reserved for Dudley and his Pursuers.

Soon the tables were surrounded by boisterous men and women, who, while waiting to be served, rapped their skeans on their trenchers or shouted good-humouredly at one another. As I was carrying in a *ciseán*, or shallow oval basket, of boiled potatoes, I noticed the black-haired chambermaid sitting opposite the horseboy who had taken Nell on my arrival. In my excitement I unbalanced the *ciseán*, much to the delight of the watching servants. Observing my embarrassment, the dark-haired girl went on her knees to help gather up the scattered potatoes.

"I'll be here at nightfall," she whispered.

"Hurry, you imbecile," Brian Dubh shouted, "and get a besom to clean up that *praiseach*."

"Yes," I answered, too happy to mind his insult.

Emboldened by my apparent meekness, Brian Dubh decided that the moment to crush me had arrived. Waiting till I had set down the *ciseán* in the middle of the long table, he said in the hearing of all: "Good fellow. And now for your clumsiness you will clean out the slophouse tomorrow."

"Clean it out yourself!" I retorted.

Brian Dubh's face grew purple with anger. "You'll do as you're told," he hissed, "or, upon my soul, you won't eat another scrap while I'm *reachtaire* here."

"No," I cried, and my words had a ringing clarity in the hushed room, "I won't eat another scrap until I'm allowed to speak to O'Conor Don." Before Brian Dubh could recover from his shock, I turned on my heel and marched out.

Back down in the kitchen, I listened to the renewed revelry from upstairs and wondered if I had leaped from the griddle into the fire. Suppose my request were granted and O'Conor Don decided I was a spy? Would he not turn me over to the Sheriff or, more likely, have someone poison my food? Who would miss a student whose presence in Ballintober was known only to the people of the castle? Ah, well, at least I had my tryst to look forward to!

About two o'clock, Úna crept downstairs with a heaped trencher of meat and potatoes and begged me to eat. On the grounds that a man about to fast to the death had better start with a full stomach, I fell to, sharing titbits with Pangur, the kitchen cat. Later, Dudley sent one of his men with a jug of ale and I accepted it gratefully, heartened by this sign of approval. No doubt there were many others who had enjoyed Brian Dubh's loss of face, though caution would keep them from showing it.

Lulled by the warm glow ascending from my stomach into my brain, I felt indifferent to the slings and arrows that the morrow might bring. In a few hours, when the others were sleeping off the effects of the feast, I would be slipping upstairs to meet the dark-haired chambermaid. Taking soot from the chimney, I rubbed it vigorously on my teeth with one finger, rinsing my mouth afterwards with water. Then I sat on a stool near the fire, lifted Pangur onto my lap and dreamed of nightfall.

Chapter 6

HOW can I describe Beibhinn – for that was the chambermaid's name? Firstly, she was a month short of her sixteenth birthday; secondly, she had a pleasing naturalness of speech and manner; thirdly, she was not as beautiful as some of the girls I had sighed after in Dublin but in her soft, passionate innocence she was Nausicaa welcoming Ulysses or Isolde casting a spell on Tristram. Shawn told me later that she had formerly acted as personal maid to the O'Conors' daughter, Mary – who was now living with her uncle in Mayo. He also said that her people, the O'Cairnens, were descended from the Firbolg, the small, dark people who had ruled Ireland before the coming of the Milesians.

Beibhinn was indeed small but her darkness was the darkness of a dusky rose, of a melodious blackbird, of a summer's night. She opened her mouth to me, she opened her bodice to me and if it were not for pity of her youth, I could have prevailed on her to open her chaste treasure to me. Oh God, how I relished the suppleness of her body, the softness of her breast, the honey of her mouth!

In the gloom of the Great Hall that Easter Sunday evening, Beibhinn clung to me like a wanton and though my mind told me that her embraces would drag me down to hell, my heart told me that to be in hell with her would be the only heaven I would ever want. Shawn Bacach had promised to tell anybody looking for me that I was resting in the tiny upstairs room he shared with Úna but there was always the likelihood that his words would be doubted, so every moment we were risking detection as we pressed against

38

the tapestry of the knights and their chaste ladies.

Suddenly we heard Brian Dubh's rasping voice as he emerged from the kitchen below.

"Hurry!" Beibhinn said and led me up the narrow stone stairway to an upper room dominated by a large canopied bed enclosed with curtains. In the dim light from the narrow, diamond-paned window we could just make out that the room had recently been occupied because there were what appeared to be vestments draped over a chair near the bed and sheets of writing paper, a quill and an earthenware ink bottle left on a table in front of the window alcove. Before I could observe anything else, footsteps sounded on the stairs, followed by the clinks of door latches being tried. Quickly Beibhinn and I crawled beneath the bed.

In a few moments Brian Dubh entered the room, carrying a lantern. We held our breaths as he approached the bed. There was a swish of curtains being drawn back then another as they were closed again. Would he check further? I could see his buckled shoes within inches of my perspiring forehead; then they turned and went towards the panelled end wall. A concealed door, probably leading to a closet or garderobe, was opened briefly. Afterwards, the shoes approached the table.

Peeping out, I could see Brian Dubh examining papers by the light of the lantern. Next he took a key from his belt and unlocked a carved oak chest that stood beside the table. After rummaging about he must have found what he was looking for because there was a grunt of satisfaction and I saw him withdraw a bound package of letters. Leaving these on the table, he tiptoed to the door, where he listened for a few moments before returning. When I next peeped out I could see his black-bearded face bent over a sheet of paper, on which he was writing with great rapidity. Since the window looked west over the moat there was little chance of his lantern light being detected.

Inching back further under the bed, I waited for what seemed an eternity till the scratching of the quill ceased. Presently, Brian Dubh returned the packet to the chest, locked it and, judging from the sound of rustling that ensued, folded the sheet on which he had written and placed it inside his doublet. That done, I could see his shoes move across the stone flags to the door, which opened to let them pass. In a moment the door closed gently and Beibhinn and I relaxed.

"So there is a spy in the castle," I observed when Brian Dubh's footsteps had died away.

"Hush!" Beibhinn put her hand over my mouth. "If he hears us ..." Without finishing the sentence, she crawled out and I followed.

"Who stays in this room?" I brushed dust from her clothes with my hand.

"You must not ask that." She brushed my clothes in turn. "We are not supposed to tell."

"It's a priest, isn't it?" I fondled her warm neck.

For answer she kissed me swiftly, then we both tiptoed from the room, knowing that discovery might well cost us our lives.

Next morning Brian Dubh again ordered me to clean out the slophouse but I announced that I was fasting and would do no more work.

"You may fast till you're carrion," he snapped, "for all the good it will do you."

For the remainder of the day I willed myself to ignore the tantalizing smells of cooking that wafted around me while I sipped water or tried to endure the curious stares of the servants as I sat by the fire composing a poem. On the following day hunger was like a ravenous rat gnawing at my stomach. I lay on my bed of rushes in the corner, dreaming of trenchers piled with slices of juicy roast mutton and hot oaten bread soaked in gravy. Brian Dubh was not sympathetic: my fasting obviously irked him and he sent a succession of tempting dishes that were like burning coals heaped on my head.

That night I couldn't sleep but after sunrise I dozed fitfully. By Thursday I was so weak that when I tried to rise, the kitchen spun around me. Shawn Bacach and Úna grew alarmed but instead of trying to shake my resolution, they brought me water from St Brigid's Well, saying it would do me good. To please them I swallowed a few mouthfuls.

Though the hunger pangs had long since abated, my mind grew increasingly confused: at times I was certain that I was lying on my own bed in Oxmantown, at other times that I was in the Black Raven carousing or in the refectory at Trinity, dining on choice meats and rare fruits while a Scholar read some passage from scripture. In moments when my brain cleared, I grew convinced that O'Conor Don either didn't know of my fast or didn't care. Brian Dubh encouraged this belief. "Do you think the master has nothing better to do than concern himself with the fate of a starving cur?" he jeered, but the pitying looks of once-hostile servants showed that they at least were moved by my plight.

On Thursday night I fainted. Shawn Bacach told me afterwards that when Hugh found out, he was furious with Brian Dubh for having concealed my true condition. He himself came personally to the kitchen, ordered a bed to be provided and sent a native physician to revive me.

When I came to, Hugh was among the people standing around my bed. He begged forgiveness for not having come earlier and assured me that I should appear before his father as soon as I had recovered my strength.

"And don't be anxious," he added. "You'll get the fair play of the Fianna in Ballintober."

As I met his clear, direct gaze, I regretted the ill fortune that made us, if not enemies, then wary of each other. We were like Hamlet and Fortinbras, two young men that had they been fellow students at Wittenberg, would, most likely, have been bosom friends.

Within two days of ending my fast I was walking around once more; within three days I was eating full meals and on Wednesday evening, in response to a message sent through Shawn Bacach, I was preparing to meet Beibhinn in the Great Hall.

On the way upstairs I encountered a middle-aged stranger, dressed like a merchant in sober brown cloak and broad-brimmed hat, coming down.

"God's blessing on you." He gave the usual Gaelic greeting before hurrying past. Was he the man whose letters Brian Dubh had copied? It was impossible to be certain. No doubt many people visited the south-west tower without my knowledge. The stairway allowed a person access without being seen from the kitchen, and there were many small chambers – apart from the dormitory on the second floor where the kitchen servants slept – that might be used by visitors. Brian Dubh, being *reachtaire*, would have keys to all those rooms and to judge by what Beibhinn and I had seen, he used them to good effect. That made it all the more foolhardy to hold our tryst right under his nose but I deemed the prize worth the risk.

Beibhinn rushed to meet me as soon as I stepped through the arched opening from the stairway. She had been frantic with worry when told of my refusal to eat but because of the jealousy of Donal Bawn, the fair-haired horseboy, she had been unable to visit me.

"You must be wary of him," she warned. "He carries a skean and he's also one of Brian Dubh's toadies."

"I'm going to be questioned by O'Conor Don in five days' time," I said. "If I'm allowed my freedom after that, I'll come to you in the north-west tower."

"Oh, no," she protested. "There are too many risks. If Lady Mary caught us, I'd be sent home."

"Doesn't she know that you meet Donal Bawn?"

"No, she doesn't because I don't meet him. He tells everybody I'm his true love but I hate him and his yellow teeth and his stinking breath."

"Does Lady Mary mind that her husband has a mistress?"

"Why should she? Doesn't she have her Oxford gallant to console her?"

"Who is this gallant?"

"Theobald Dillon, nephew of Sir Lucas Dillon of Lough Glinn. All my friends behave as if he were Diarmuid of the Love Spot but he's not nearly so handsome as you."

She went on to tell me that Theobald had left Oxford rather than take the Oath of Supremacy. O'Conor Don, impressed by such loyalty to the Roman Church, had taken him into employment as his secretary and he had since won everyone's praise for his skill in riding, dancing, singing and playing the viola. The chambermaids were all trying to win his heart but he pretended to love only Lady Mary, who received his attentions like a blushing maiden.

"You will easily recognize him at the inquest," she added. "He always wears his Oxford gown on such occasions, though it makes him look like a black crow."

She chuckled with mischievous glee and I kissed her. Immediately her entire body started to tremble. Our ardour became a vortex that threatened to pull us past reason and prudence into its quickening centre. Just in time I broke free of her embrace and drew a deep breath to regain my self-control.

"Why do Dudley and his men stay here?" I willed myself to ignore her parted lips.

"You mean MacCostello?" My question surprised her. "He's Hugh O'Conor's common-suckled brother."

"What's a common-suckled brother?" Her turns of speech occasionally perplexed me.

"Well, when Hugh was a child he was sent to Mayo County to be brought up by the MacCostellos," she explained.

"Oh, you mean a foster brother!" I recalled that my mother had told me that noble families sent their children to be reared by other families in order to establish bonds of friendship.

"Yes." She smiled like a teacher encouraging a slow-witted pupil. "My father says that the MacCostellos were once very powerful but that they lost nearly all their lands in the last century. Hugh and Dudley are very attached to each other. Dudley would give his heart's blood for Hugh."

"I still don't see why he's needed here."

"Don't you? Aren't there discharged soldiers running loose all over the country, robbing and stealing?"

"But surely the Sheriff's men would protect you?"

"My father says the Sheriff is a minion of the English and doesn't everyone know that the English are only waiting for the chance to drive us all from Connacht? That evil man who was Lord Deputy – who was he?"

"Thomas Wentworth, Earl of Strafford."

"Well, my father said that he was going to plant Connacht with Foreigners, just as was done in Ulster and in Brefni – but maybe I shouldn't be saying these things to you."

"Surely you too don't believe I'm a spy?"

"No, I'm sure you're not. Still you're a Palesman and you don't … well, you don't …"

"I don't what? Believe in the Virgin Mary and the Pope?"

"Yes." She was pained by my frankness, as if I had shown her an ugly scar.

"Brian Dubh believes in the Virgin Mary and the Pope but I wonder if that prevents him from betraying his and your master?" My voice was bitter.

"Oh, Charles, don't let's quarrel over religion," she pleaded. "I don't understand all these learned arguments. I only know that I'm glad be near you, to feel your arms about me and your mouth on my mouth."

"I'm not angry with you." I touched Beibhinn's cheek. "My mind is all muddied and confused."

"Why?"

"I don't know. Perhaps it's because I'm no longer sure whether I'm Anglo-Irish like my father or a Gael like my mother. Two months ago the question never entered my head; now it seldom leaves it."

After this conversation we spoke only with our hands and our lips, alone in the gloom of the Great Hall; then, love's sweet ardour dampened, we parted as the last gleam of daylight drained from the mullioned windows.

The nearer the day of the inquest approached the more uneasy I grew. Shawn Bacach confided to me that the Friar arrested in Athlone on the day I passed through had been tortured by having his feet thrust into red-hot coals. Would this not make his co-religionists less likely to show mercy to me? Suppose I were unable to prove my innocence? Would O'Conor Don risk turning me over to the Sheriff when I knew that his servants had attended Mass on Easter Sunday? Wouldn't he be more likely, at the very least, to keep me confined to the south-west tower?

The thought of spending further months, perhaps years, in that smothering kitchen appalled me. Apart from Shawn Bacach and Úna there was no friend to converse with. Here was I, who should be sharpening my mind on Plato's *Dialogues* and Aristotle's *Poetics*, imbibing a barbaric language and barbaric ideas from an illiterate old gallowglass and his wife. And what use was my knowledge of mathematics, logic and natural science if all my daily labour entailed was mindless drudgery? I was like Ovid among the Goths, separated from everything that made life meaningful.

The face of Thomas Hall, our old grammar school master, rose before my mind's eye. It was Master Hall who had planted a love of Shakespeare in us, he himself having acted in *Hamlet* while a student at Oxford. Whenever we were not paying attention, a sad expression would come over his face and he would recite the words of Richard II: "I wasted time and now doth time waste me." How little I realized then that these words would one day take on a dreadful significance.

Even my love trysts were a source of mental discord: the ideals of virtue and morality my parents had instilled in me were being eroded by my dalliance with Beibhinn, who, the voice of conscience warned me, was a youthful Jezebel whom I should spurn as Jehu had spurned the Samarian queen. Would my sisters, Margaret and Bridget, not blush at my behaviour? God would note my iniquities in Ballintober as he had noted them in Dublin and sooner or later I would feel his wrath.

My anxieties must have shown on my face because Shawn Bacach finally let curiosity overcome his natural politeness. "In the name of God, what ails you?" he said.

Throwing caution aside, I told him everything, including the attack on the English captain.

"*D'anam don Diabhal!*" (Your soul to the devil!) he cried delightedly. "Why, in your place, I'd have slit his gullet."

This reaction so heartened me that I began to be impatient for Monday's arrival.

Chapter 7

THE INQUEST was held in the north-west tower, to which, on Monday morning, Dudley and one of his men conducted me. We mounted a spiral stone stairway to the first floor and emerged into a magnificent hall with wood panelling, a Turkish carpet, framed pictures and one large tapestry hanging on the end wall. Five people sat at a cloth-covered table in front of the blazing fire. O'Conor Don, whom I recognized by his plumed hat, occupied the middle chair; Lady Mary was on his right and the man dressed like a merchant on his left. Theobald Dillon in his black student's gown and square cap sat at one end beside Lady Mary, and an old man with long white hair and bloodshot eyes sat at the other, beside the merchant.

While Dudley conferred with his master, I glanced again at the pictures, one showing His Majesty King Charles on horseback, and the other a grave-looking gentleman in green satin doublet, stiff Elizabethan ruff and plumed bonnet. Was this the man who had given up his Gaelic title for a knighthood? The tapestry, which was done in red, blue and pale yellow, depicted a mounted chieftain hunting a boar, but a contrast greater than that between the heroic hunter and the descendant of the last High King of Ireland it would be hard to find. O'Conor Don was in his middle fifties, long faced and long nosed, with a gentle, self-effacing manner and a mild, cultivated accent. His wife, on the other hand, was a large, robust woman with the haughtiness and accent of a duchess. Her collar and sleeves were trimmed with fine lace and she wore a gem-studded crucifix suspended from her neck by a chain.

46

Most of the questioning was done by the merchant, who spoke good English but with a Connacht accent. This man had strong, ascetic features and his black beard was streaked with white, so that he reminded me of a badger. Deciding that it was better to conceal nothing, I gave a frank account of everything that had happened since my encounter with the Englishman in the Black Raven.

"Why at first did you conceal the fact that you spoke English?" the merchant wanted to know. I told him that my father had often recounted how during the O'Neill rebellion, his ally, Red Hugh O'Donnell, had killed every male in Connacht between the ages of fifteen and sixty who couldn't speak Gaelic.

"So you were afraid that the same fate awaited you?" O'Conor Don sounded incredulous.

"Yes," I asserted. "After all, your men had just fired on Sir Chidley."

"Is that true?" O'Conor Don assumed a severe expression as he questioned Dudley, who was standing with his companion by the door.

"One of my men pulled the trigger by accident," Dudley said casually in Gaelic.

As Theobald wrote down this reply, I noticed that my Bible and *Aeneid* were lying on the table beside him. Once finished, he whispered something to Lady Mary.

"Was your father ever in Connacht?" Lady Mary enquired.

"Yes," I said and I told how on a trip to Croghan in the year Seventeen to purchase wool, he had met my mother, who was then working in the home of Sir William O'Mulloy.

"And what, pray, was your mother's name?" she demanded.

"Norah," I said. "Norah O'Flynn."

"And her father's name?"

"Fergus O'Flynn."

If I had been a toad who had just assumed the shape of a prince, I couldn't have occasioned more surprise.

"Why, then, Teigue O'Flynn from Ballinlough must be your uncle!" O'Conor Don exclaimed. When I nodded, he rose and with both hands outstretched, proclaimed, "Your mother's son is welcome to Ballintober."

This turn of events did not please Badger Face, who pointed out that a man of mixed birth, raised as a Protestant and attending "that heretic university in Dublin" was such as the government might well employ as a spy. The fact that I had baptized two children showed how far I was prepared to go to mask my true sympathies.

"If I did baptize them, they are no less Christians for that." Indignation gave my words conviction.

"*Talibus orabat dictis* – since when has the Tribe of Luther included Virgil's *Aeneid* in its baptismal ceremony?" Badger Face leaned forward expectantly.

I glanced around at Dudley who had a twinkle in his eye. So he had understood. "Those words were written by the greatest poet of the Roman world," I said. "It did not seem to me sacrilegious to use them."

"Why, I agree with the young man," O'Conor Don interposed. "Didn't Dante, the greatest of Christian poets, take Virgil as his guide on the journey through the Inferno?"

"*Omnia bona bonis.*" Badger Face rebuked his credulity.

"*Cad é do thuairim, a Chormac?*" (What is your opinion, Cormac?) O'Conor Don addressed the white-haired ancient, whose face lit up at this belated recognition of his presence.

Speaking in an excited manner and employing many obscure Gaelic words, Cormac, in so far as I could gather, approved of my actions. He reminded them that Fergal O'Gara, who had so recently assisted the Franciscan scholars in their work of compiling the *Annals of the Kingdom of Ireland* was a Protestant, as indeed was that learned man William Bedell, the Bishop of Kilmore. Furthermore, the fact that I had confessed to killing a man, albeit accidentally, put me at their mercy, since they could now easily hand me over to the authorities to be hanged. Here he digressed to show how much superior the Brehon code of justice was to the new English system, giving as an example how when one of his own ancestors, Gregory O'Mulconry, had been accidentally killed by one William Garbh Burke of Dunamon, the latter's family had paid six score and six cows as *eric*, and this compensation had been accepted. Now, in similar circumstances the English would have hanged William Garbh – was this not simply returning evil for evil? In conclusion, he reminded them that I had refused Sir Chidley and Lord Ranelagh's invitation to become a spy, and while this could be a clever attempt to hoodwink them, he was not prepared to believe that a grandson of Fergus O'Flynn, whose ancestors had been

48

loyal *uirríthe*, or vassals, of the O'Conors and whose *coarb* had always been given O'Conor's steed on his inauguration as King of Connacht, would ever betray his own people.

These words carried great weight with the others. O'Conor Don told me that they would send for my uncle Teigue to confirm my parentage and that in the meantime I would be given the freedom of the castle. I thanked him for his belief in my innocence and to show that it was merited I offered to inform him of a real spy in his household. Motioning to Dudley's companion to leave the hall, O'Conor Don told me to proceed, and they all listened in stunned silence to my account of how Brian Dubh had opened the locked chest.

"May we ask what you were doing in the bedchamber?" Lady Mary's voice was icy. To tell the full story would have meant Beibhinn's dismissal, so I pretended that I had gone to the upper floor to attempt an escape through one of the windows.

"Brian has complained of your insubordination." O'Conor Don's voice was grave. "How do we know that you are not trying to ... well, to make us distrust him?"

"Sir," I replied, "I cannot prove that what I have told you is true but you might ask yourself how the Athlone garrison knew that a priest from Louvain would be passing through the town in early February?"

O'Conor Don held a consultation with his wife, pressing his hands nervously together.

"Who told you about the priest?" Badger Face was like an implacable Rhadamanthus.

"He did." I pointed at Dudley, who nodded in confirmation.

"Well, young man," O'Conor Don looked at me with his mild blue eyes, "it appears you may have rendered us an important service."

"*Timeo Danaos et dona ferentes*" (I fear the Greeks bearing gifts), Badger Face was comparing me to the Greek captive who had deceived the Trojans about the true nature of the Wooden Horse. His sally worked. The faces watching me were now clouded with suspicion. Oh, God, why hadn't I kept quiet about Brian Dubh?

Theobald Dillon, who was a few years older than myself and who, with his reddish hair, even teeth and fresh complexion, might have been quite handsome were it not for the fact that his eyes

were a little too close together, hastily wrote a note which he handed to Lady Mary. She, having read it, passed it to her husband and
Badger Face for their perusal. The upshot was that I was obliged
to swear on my own Bible that if given the freedom of the castle
bawn, I would not attempt to escape. Having no desire to languish
indoors, I readily complied.

"You will continue to eat and sleep in the Old Tower," Lady
Mary directed, "and to render such help to the cooks as may from
time to time be required."

I received this information in silence, whereupon O'Conor
Don, obviously struck by my crestfallen appearance, added kindly,
"These times – what with Strafford in prison and the Calvinists in
the English Parliament turning like ravening dogs on His Majesty
– well, they behove us to be … mindful of our own safety and the
safety of our people. We will be seeing you again as soon as your
uncle arrives. In the meantime you may have your *Aeneid* back."

Summoning up my self-possession, I bowed courteously, then
Dudley was escorting me to the stairway and the inquest was over.

Though it was cold for April, no prisoner ever greeted the open
air with more joy than I did when I walked with Dudley through
the bawn that afternoon. Those weeks in the south-west tower
under the baleful eye of Brian Dubh had taken a greater toll on my
spirits than I had realized. Now I was free, free to watch an eagle
sailing high overhead, to mingle with the people going about their
daily work, to talk to the carpenter or the weaver, to admire the
young women with their clear complexions and bright eyes.

The bawn had been laid out by O'Conor Don's father, Sir
Hugh, in the orderly manner of an Ulster Planter village: on the
south side of the central street there was the buttery, bakery, physician's house, ollamh's house and smithy, while on the north side
there were the houses of the weaver, cobbler, carpenter, butcher
and cowherd. In addition to these there was a byre and pigsty at
the east curtain wall, north of the main entrance, and stables on its
south side, near the smithy. Various storehouses and kennels had
also been built against the north and south curtain walls so that,
despite its great size, the bawn had little unused space.

Dudley told me that the north-west tower had been completely
rebuilt in Twenty-Seven, five years before Sir Hugh died.

"Was it his portrait that was hanging in the hall where the inquest was held?" I asked.

"Yes, that's the knight," Dudley said. "He was shrewder than many of his generation, including my own grandfather. Did you see that perfumed fox, Dillon, whispering to Lady Mary? Well, an ancestor of his, another Theobald, tricked my grandfather's people out of the Barony of Costello. The Dillons could build a nest in your ear and rob it again."

I asked about the old man, Cormac, and learned that he had been ollamh – a profession combining the duties of poet and chronicler – to Sir Hugh, who had been obliged under English law to discharge him when he received his knighthood. He had subsequently been reduced to teaching in a native school but, at the entreaty of young Hugh, O'Conor Don had invited him back to Ballintober. The house he now lived in had once been a priest's house but because of the persecution of the Romish clergy, it had not been occupied for years before Cormac's coming. "You might say that the goshawk has taken over the abandoned nest of the raven," Dudley commented.

"Who was the man with the black and white beard sitting at the end of the table?" I had kept my most important question for last.

"He's a friend of the O'Conors," Dudley's voice was guarded, "a wine merchant from Galway. Sometimes he stays here for a few days before travelling on to Tulsk and Elphin." I was on the point of asking his name but decided that too much curiosity might prove dangerous.

"Would you like to visit the ollamh?" Dudley took my arm to draw me away from the bakery, where there was a tempting aroma of hot bread. "Did you note how he spoke up for you at the inquest? I'll wager that you and he will prove birds of a feather."

"Can we not visit the horses first?" I was eager to see Nell again. Dudley assented and we turned right at the castle entrance, which was now fully open, and approached the thatched stables near the south-east tower, stepping carefully to avoid horse dung and urine. Donal Bawn and another horseboy, seeing me, began to guffaw. Pretending not to notice, I followed Dudley into the dim, pungent-smelling interior, where about two dozen mares, colts and fillies were tied up to a long manger. Nine or ten horseboys were lounging about but immediately some began to comb their charges, while others busied themselves sweeping the stone channel behind the horses.

Nell whinnied a greeting but I had only time to pat her glistening side before a young fellow rushed in shouting, "English riders!" Dudley questioned him, then he ordered some horseboys to take a dozen of the best horses, including Nell, and gallop with them through the west postern gate. Next he sent word to his Pursuers to hide with their muskets on the battlements of the four towers, swung himself up into the hay loft above the remaining horses and pulled me up beside him.

Rummaging about in a corner, he retrieved a sack from which he took a long-bladed miodoge, a horsepistol, a powder horn, rags, lead balls, a tinderbox and a ramrod. Working with feverish speed, he poured some powder down the pistol barrel, then dropped in a ball and rammed it home. Next he thrust a wad of rag into the barrel and rammed that down also.

"God's blood! If only I had one of those new wheel locks," he muttered, as repeatedly striking the flint against the steel he finally succeeded in igniting some tinder, which he used to light the pistol's slow-match. Carefully he primed the pan, then rested the charged pistol in an opening in the end wall, lest, he explained, the odour of the smouldering match waft down to the stalls. After that we waited, Dudley crouching like a panther with the miodoge in his hand.

In no time there was a clatter of hoofs at the main entrance, an outburst of barking from the castle dogs, loud, confident greetings in English, followed by the milder voice of O'Conor Don welcoming the visitors to Ballintober. Presently the voices dwindled, to be replaced by the familiar noises and chatter of the bawn. Donal Bawn slipped into the stable. "It's the Cootes – Sir Chidley and his nephew – and another *Sasanach* lord," he whispered. "Our master is entertaining them in the New Tower. They said they came to buy horses."

"How many of them in all?" Dudley demanded.

"Just six, three gentlemen and three servants. The servants are holding the horses by the forge. They want us to bring them oats."

"Take them one sack, then get word to my men to keep their heads down. They're not to discharge their muskets unless the English begin a search."

After what seemed hours I heard the loud English voices again. Dudley checked his pistol. First through the door was a servant, then Sir Chidley, followed by a powerfully built younger man with a hard, clean-shaven face under his broad-brimmed hat. Behind them came O'Conor Don and a slightly younger, distinguished-looking man in rich clothes and plumed hat. My stomach tightened as Sir Chidley's eyes swept the loft. "Where is your eldest son, Hugh?" he was saying.

"Oh, he went to see his brother and sister," O'Conor Don replied. "They are living with their uncle at present. As you know, we have no school here and Viscount Burke's tutor is undertaking their education."

"Let's hope he makes loyal citizens out of them." Sir Chidley's booming laugh filled the stable.

"I am sure the O'Conors have always revered His Majesty." O'Conor Don's voice trembled with suppressed indignation.

"Come, come," the third nobleman chided. "We are here to purchase horses not to debate loyalties. Calvagh, are these your only saddle horses?"

"We have a few more out in pasture, Sir Robert," O'Conor Don admitted. "If you like I'll send for them."

"No, no," Sir Robert declined courteously. "We have to be back in Castlecoote before nightfall." Then turning to the young man, he asked, "What do you think of these animals, Sir Charles?"

"Nags," said Sir Charles gruffly. "I'll give you twenty pounds, O'Conor, for those three mares and the roan colt."

"Twenty pounds for three English brood mares and a two-year-old colt!" O'Conor Don laughed uneasily.

"Well, then, thirty, and that's a better offer than you'll get from any of your recusant friends."

"I couldn't sell them for less than a hundred." O'Conor Don managed to sound unruffled.

"Lord Ranelagh wouldn't be pleased to hear that." Sir Chidley's voice had an undertone of menace. "He needs horses to defend the province. Ask a more reasonable price."

"One hundred pounds is a reasonable price," O'Conor Don's self-possession was clearly wilting, "but on account of the great esteem in which I hold his Lordship, I'll give them to you for ninety."

As the bargaining continued the two Cootes between them browbeat the proud descendant of the kings of Connacht till he was constrained to accept their final offer of thirty-five pounds. At this point Sir Robert graciously redressed the balance of justice by purchasing another colt for thirty pounds, though it was clearly not worth half that amount.

While the horses were being led outside, Sir Chidley remarked suddenly: "There's another matter, sir, on which you might see fit to help us. We're looking for a young Dublin cleric, Charles Scott, whom, we believe, has been captured by Pursuers. Perhaps they offered his mare for sale, a fine English animal with a red coat and black mane and tail? She had a white stripe on her face and her back feet were also white."

My blood froze. So this was the real reason for the visit: somebody must have informed Coote that I was being held in Ballintober. What O'Conor Don started to say in reply was drowned out by an outburst of shouting from the bawn, followed by a loud pistol shot.

Chapter 8

DUDLEY leaped to the ground with the ease of a cat and ordering me to reach down the pistol, glided to the door with it in one hand and miodoge in the other. Just then O'Conor Don's voice rang out: "Stop! Stop! How dare you threaten our guests?"

His appeal worked because the commotion died down instantly.

"What happened?" I asked, crouching behind Dudley.

"Keep back," he whispered. "That fool, Donal Bawn, must have started a fight. Upon my soul, those horseboys have more courage than sense."

When the visitors departed we learned the full story from the O'Cahan brothers, who worked in the forge. It seemed that Donal Bawn resented the manner in which the English servants had been ordering him about. In retaliation he and the horseboys began to jeer at the English because one of them had been riding a mare, something in their eyes unworthy of a man. The English had responded by attempting to draw their saddle pistols but the horseboys had sprung on them. In the ensuing confusion one of the Englishmen, seeing his companion disarmed, had panicked and fired his pistol. It was at this point that O'Conor Don had intervened, much to the disgust of the O'Cahans, who reckoned that the English should have been taught a lesson.

From the accent of the O'Cahans it was obvious that they were not Connacht men and later they told me that they had fled from Ulster to escape harassment by the Planters. They maintained that the Planters regarded the dispossessed Gaels as no better than wolves and, indeed, sometimes organized hunts to extirpate them. In self-defence the more desperate men had begun to prey on the Planters, who called them *Tóraí*, or Pursuers.

"That's what Sir Chidley calls your men," I reminded Dudley.

"I wouldn't pay much attention to Sir Chidley," Dudley snorted. "Old Coote was a crow and his two sons are bad eggs out of a bad nest. As for young Sir Charles, that arrogant get was lucky that I didn't send a ball through his head when he began abusing the master."

"Which of them lives in Castlecoote?" I enquired.

"The young get." Dudley spat. "We passed within a stone's throw of its walls on the night you came here."

"That was a dangerous path." The elder smith, Rory O'Cahan, wiped sweat from his soot-blackened face with the back of his hand. "It's the strongest castle in the county."

"It wouldn't be a patch on this place if we strengthened the eastern towers," Dudley asserted. "Not that any castle would withstand a bombardment for more than a few days."

"Sir Robert seemed to be a true gentleman." I rested my weight on an upturned wooden plough.

"Do you reckon so?" Dudley smiled grimly. "It was his father, Sir John King, who got all the lands of Boyle Abbey granted to him by royal patent and who cheated our master out of his seat in the Dublin parliament. It was the same man who got his claws on the O'Mulconry lands in Carnebooley – as Cormac will, no doubt, tell you. So don't be fooled by appearance. The Kings and the Cootes are birds of a feather."

"That's the truest word you ever spoke." Rory brought his hammer down fiercely on a white-hot ploughshare his brother was holding with tongs on the anvil. "The New Foreigners won't be content until every last Gael has been driven from his land into the mountains."

Dudley asked the O'Cahans for one of their bone-handled skeans, which he presented to me, saying, "Here, use this at dinner and supper but don't carry it at other times – Lady Mary doesn't want blood spilt."

"That's right." Rory's brother thrust the ploughshare into a hissing tub of black water. "Only the Foreigners can go armed; we Gaels must be kept meek and defenceless like bullocks."

When we left the forge, Dudley, noticing that my toes were protruding from my shoes, suggested that we should visit the cobbler. On the way, Donal Bawn jostled me deliberately. "Why don't you look where you're going, Diarmuid of the Love Spot?" he jeered. I apologized for colliding with him, at which his friends burst out laughing.

"Get back to the stables!" Dudley grabbed Donal Bawn by the arm. "Do you think that because half a dozen of you fell on two unsuspecting gillies, it makes you champions?"

Donal Bawn scowled but he and his friends moved off.

"If I were you, I'd keep my eyes open near that fellow," Dudley observed. "He's a vengeful cur and he saw how O'Cairnen's daughter favoured you at the Easter dinner."

"Who was Diarmuid of the Love Spot?" I was reluctant to discuss Beibhinn.

"The man we're about to meet will be the best person to answer that." Dudley stopped outside a crudely fashioned door and knocked.

"Niall," he said to the pale, unhealthy-looking hunchback in a leather apron who admitted us, "would you believe that this son-of-learning from the great City of Dublin never heard of Diarmuid of the Love Spot?"

"Indeed, I would not." Niall motioned us to a bench near the stone fireplace. "Sure every child knows that Diarmuid was one of the bravest champions of the Fianna and that he had a spot on his forehead so that any woman who saw it fell in love with him."

While Niall was searching in his kish for a suitable piece of untanned leather, he began recounting the story of Diarmuid and Grainne which, to my mind, was not unlike the story of Tristram and Isolde, except that after Diarmuid had been killed by a wild boar, Grainne married Fionn, the counterpart of King Mark. Listening to Niall recite while he sat on his stool, deftly folding the leather over a foot-shaped block of wood held between his knees, I could well imagine that we were back in Homer's Greece, when the adventures of gods and heroes were as familiar to tradesmen as they now are to students.

"And did Diarmuid and Grainne ever come to this part of Connacht when Fionn was pursuing them?" I took another sip from the meadar of fiery usquebagh our host had provided.

"Oh, most certainly," Niall assured me. "Sure didn't Shawn Bacach see one of the enormous stone beds they used to sleep in below at Tinacarra, just beyond Abbeyboyle – and here's another thing Shawn told me," Niall paused dramatically, "if a couple is childless they have only to sleep in that bed and the wife will conceive. Now what do you think of that?"

"It's a pity Shawn and Úna didn't sleep in it then," Dudley remarked humorously.

"Maybe Shawn had enough children already." Niall lowered his voice to a conspiratorial whisper. "Haven't you heard tell that he left a wife and family back in MacWilliam's country?"

I was deeply shocked by this revelation, though Dudley seemed to regard it as of no great importance. Many husbands had remarried under the Brehon Code and often it was the first wife who wanted the marriage ended. What bothered Dudley more was that Shawn Bacach had fought for Richard Burke, Lord Dunkellin, on the Queen's side at the First Battle of the Curlieus. When I pointed out that O'Conor Don's father had also fought for the Queen, Dudley readily conceded the point.

"That's the curse of this country," he declared. "We can always be bought with a title or a promise of favour. In that way, the English turn us like dogs on one another. But if once we were united like the Scots ..." A faraway look came into his hooded eyes and he smiled grimly.

"Ah, we'll never be united." Niall made another hole with his awl. "Didn't the Fianna fight each other at the Battle of Gowra and didn't the Burkes fight each other and the MacDermots and the O'Conors? This country is sword land. Any man who rules it will only do so by the strong hand. If truth were told the Foreigners have only done to us what we did to ourselves."

"That may be so," Dudley drained the meadar, "but when we were united in the last war, we showed that we could beat the English time and again. Now the English are getting ready to fight among themselves and that will be our opportunity."

"Maybe it will and maybe it won't." Niall cut the ends of the waxed threads with his skean. "But one thing is certain, whoever wins, I'll still be slaving over my last. Now, sir, try those on."

I removed my shoes and forced my feet, with their torn stockings, into the brogues.

"Rub some goose grease into them and they'll fit you like your own skin," Niall advised.

"What's the price?" I tried to conceal my dislike for the tight-fitting, heelless footwear.

"Sixpence," he said, "and I'll give you a luck-penny if you leave your old shoes."

I paid him out of my last, small store of coins.

"You're like one of ourselves now," he observed, "for I always maintain you can tell what a man is by the way he's shod."

"'As proper men as ever trod upon neat's leather have gone upon my handiwork',," I quoted in English and his uncomprehending look assured me I was still different from him and his kind.

Next morning we called on the carpenter, Rury, a friendly, forthright man, who was delighted to show off his skill. "Look at that!" he held up a stout stick with a flat, rounded head for my inspection. "That's the hundredth *camán* I've made for this fellow here and still he's not satisfied. If his men would only play like Christians instead of Firbolg, he might do with half that number."

Dudley smiled at this genial abuse, then handed me a camán. "Did you ever wield one of these?" he asked. "We're hurling against Castlerea on May Day and the more champions we can muster the better."

I told him that while I had played football in grammar school and bowls in Trinity I had never before even held a camán but if he thought he could teach me to use one in twelve days, I would certainly join his troop, provided I was allowed outside the castle.

"Don't, for the love of all that's holy," Rury admonished, "not unless you want your shins broken or your skull cracked open. Do you know who is leader of the Castlerea troop? That man's brother, Tomás – better known as Tomás Láidir (Strong Thomas). I'm not exaggerating when I say he could fell an ox with one blow of his hand – am I, Dudley?"

"Well, maybe a little." Dudley grinned. "But we'll send him and his Castlerea warriors home with their tails between their legs."

The two got into a discussion of the merits of various players, which soon tired me, though I did learn that Hugh Oge O'Conor, brother of O'Conor Don, was patron of the Castlerea troop and that he had sent for Tomás Láidir to lead it to victory. Because of the rivalry between the O'Conor brothers, the contest was expected to draw people from all parts of *Magh Aí*, the central plain of Roscommon County. A feast was to be held in Ballintober Castle afterwards and already butter, ale, candles and other provisions were being prepared. The cattle, sheep and pigs would not be killed till the eve of the feast.

On Wednesday Dudley introduced me to Cormac O'Mulconry. The ollamh greeted me with great informality, launching at once into a discussion about books: "I have just been reading a *duan* by your ancestor, Eochaid O'Flynn – he died in the year Nine Hundred and Eighty-Four – or was it Eighty-Five? It's about the Battle of Moytura – the one between the Firbolg and the Tuatha de Dannan for the sovereignty of Ireland. You are familiar with Eochaid's great poem I'm sure?"

When I shook my head, he looked incredulous. "Hasn't your mother ever spoken to you about your ancestors?" he asked.

I explained that she had told me various things when I was young but that I had only a vague recollection of them.

"Well," he conceded, "that isn't to be wondered at. You must have had so many other things to learn ... so many things ... Look at those." He indicated some handwritten books. "It took years to write them and already they're as brittle as autumn leaves ... so much time wasted and so much to be done ... Now if we only had printed books, we would be able to teach people about their history and religion, especially those Irishmen who are studying at the university in Dublin. I see by your smile that you don't consider that a very good idea."

"I don't think that Provost Washington would approve of books written in Gaelic – though in Dr Bedell's day, I'm told, they did have Gaelic lectures and prayers."

"Then you could convince this Provost of his error."

"I'm afraid not; men like him listen only to themselves and God."

"Well, well! At any rate, I have a Protestant translation of the New Testament, which was printed in Dublin. Perhaps if you studied it, you would learn to read Gaelic – you can't read it, I presume?"

"No," I admitted, glancing at one of his handwritten pages with its twin columns of small, almost Grecian script, "but I would be willing to learn, whenever my work in the kitchen was done."

"Perhaps you will ... perhaps you will," Cormac mused. "If the Bishop of Kilmore can translate the Bible into Gaelic, why should a descendant of Eochaid O'Flynn not learn to read his mother's language, especially if it's printed? That's where the Foreigners surpass us ... though my cousin Fearfeasa writes me that, God willing, our friars in Louvain will soon be printing the *Annals of the Kingdom of Ireland* – oh, I have great hopes, in spite of everything, great hopes ..."

He took a pair of spectacles from the cluttered table and placing them on his nose, began to search impatiently through various baskets and niches. I took advantage of this interlude to gaze around the whitewashed room at the satchels filled with sheets of yellowing paper, the straw pallet and the wooden statue of the Virgin, standing on a little shelf by the window. It could have been a cell of a monk in some ancient monastery instead of the home of a scholar living in an age illuminated by the writings of John Donne and Francis Bacon. Over the door there was a cross, made from plaited rushes, and above that a white wand of ash or hazel.

When I asked Cormac what the wand was for, he explained it was a replica of the rod of sovereignty given to the King of Connacht at his inauguration on Carnfree. Before walking to the inauguration stone the king gave his arms and clothes to O'Mulconry and his horse to O'Flynn. It was O'Mulconry who handed O'Conor the white rod, after which MacDermot of Moylurg had the lesser task of putting on the new king's shoe in token of submission. The MacDermots still retained great estates near Abbeyboyle, in the north of the county, while the O'Mulconrys had lost most of theirs to Sir John King. Here Cormac recited a verse in praise of MacDermot's fair fortress, though "for mine own part, it was Greek to me".

"If you would really like to read and write Gaelic, come to me again," Cormac offered. "By then I will have found that Bible. In the meantime, here is a Gaelic catechism which was printed in Louvain; my kinsman Florence, the Archbishop of Tuam – may his soul be on God's right hand – wrote it."

"Perhaps you would ask O'Conor Don for my Bible," I suggested. "A comparison of both versions, the Gaelic and the English, should enable me to master the Gaelic script."

Cormac readily agreed to this request. He then wrote out the Gaelic alphabet, explaining how vowels could be lengthened by the addition of a stroke and certain consonants softened by the addition of a dot. Next he read the Lord's Prayer in the catechism aloud and told me to practise it on my own. Thus it was that the prayer Christ taught his apostles guided my first uncertain steps on the road trodden by generations of bards and ollamhs. My only misgiving was lest the use of the catechism might subtly lure my mind away from true religion into the quagmire of Popish superstition.

"That's a great sign of favour, for O'Mulconry to offer to teach you," Dudley remarked after we had taken our leave. "You're likely to become the next ollamh of –"

His words died on his lips. A Pursuer was riding headlong through the entrance and his garron's flanks were lathered with sweat.

Chapter 9

"WHAT happened?" Dudley yelled at the Pursuer.

"It's Shawn Rua," he gasped, dismounting. "Coote got him."

Dudley didn't try to conceal his dismay. "Where is he being held?" he demanded.

"In Athlone town," the man answered; then noticing me, he whispered something in Dudley's ear. Obviously, I was still regarded with suspicion.

It suddenly dawned on me that Shawn Rua's apprehension made my own position more dangerous; even if he were not tortured, worry for the welfare of his family might well make him confess that Dudley had brought me to his cabin. Then another thought struck me: my shoes! Suppose Coote obtained my old shoes? Could he not use them as proof of my imprisonment?

Immediately I hurried to Niall the Cobbler's house, only to find my worst fears confirmed. Niall had already sold the repaired shoes to a pedlar named Phelim, who had come to the castle that morning. When I informed Dudley, he swore softly to himself, told me that in view of everything that had happened, he could not risk taking me outside the castle to play hurling, then bidding me return to the kitchen, he strode over to Niall's house.

When I entered the kitchen, Brian Dubh asked sarcastically if I could help the cooks prepare dinner – that is if such work wasn't too strenuous for a gentleman. To avoid an argument, I complied. What part, I wondered, had he played in the apprehension of Shawn Rua and the disappearance of my shoes? While I stirred the broth, I watched him out of the corner of my eye as he strutted about, overseeing everything from the cutting up of the cheese to the mixing of buttermilk and sweet milk to make troander. How did he send his messages out of the castle? That would not be difficult since, in addition to the ploughboys and herdsmen who travelled daily to the fields, there was a steady flow of carts and wagons between the castle and the village, not to mention the intermittent coming and going of pipers, tinkers and pedlars. Ballintober was the hub of a great wheel and Brian Dubh might use any of its spokes for his purposes. From the lack of any noticeable change in his behaviour, it was unlikely he knew I had named him as a spy but when he did find out, he would be as dangerous as a wounded boar.

I thought of confiding my worries to Shawn Bacach; then changed my mind. It would be unfair to involve him too much in my misfortunes – or was it that I was no longer certain whom I could trust? If as a result of Shawn Rua breaking, I fell into the hands of the authorities, they would seek to use me as a weapon against O'Conor Don, who would be charged with maintaining armed Pursuers and imprisoning a young cleric – not that I doubted but that Coote and Lord Ranelagh had by now learned my true identity. They would use the threat of sending me back for trial in Dublin to try to force me into compliance with their schemes, and though I knew in my inmost being that I would rather die than betray anyone, the O'Conors would be loath to trust me. Did I not already know that they allowed their servants to attend Mass, that they probably harboured a priest and that Dudley and his men lived openly in the castle? If I were in their shoes would I release a virtual stranger who could so easily harm me? Such being the case, the sooner my uncle Teigue arrived, the sooner he could vouch for my identity – that is if he cared to acknowledge a Dublin Protestant as his nephew?

Though these considerations clouded my mind, they could not eclipse forever the bright sun of youth, which shone all the brighter through rents in the gloom. In retrospect, it is obvious that Beibhinn was mainly responsible for my ascents from despondency into troubled joy: the more I saw her, the more I forgot about Dublin. The danger involved in our trysts made them all the more intoxicating: she was Eve offering me the forbidden fruit and I was too besotted with desire to resist.

Three or four evenings in succession we crept up to the deserted Great Hall, my new brogues giving me the silence of a prowling cat, my ears alert for the faintest sounds of intrusion. On the first evening Beibhinn told me that she had overheard Lady Mary telling Theobald Dillon that my uncle was reluctant to travel; Hugh had, therefore, undertaken to ride up from Castleburke to Ballinlough in order to escort him to Ballintober.

I questioned Beibhinn about Hugh and learned that he had been in love with a girl from the north of the county, but, because of her youth, his parents had disapproved. Now, though outwardly Hugh seemed reconciled to the ending of the liaison, Beibhinn divined a broken heart, otherwise somebody with Hugh's pleasing looks would quickly have found a new lover.

"Do you think I'm too old for you?" I forced myself to ask.

"No, of course not." Beibhinn tossed back her shiny black locks. "Many girls of my age are married – not that I would want that. Do you consider me too young?"

Without waiting for a reply, she kissed me in such an open-mouthed, intoxicating way that my senses reeled. Shuffling backward she led me behind an oak settle and there in near darkness we lay side by side on rushes covering the hard flags, our bodies and mouths pressed together. There is a poem in Gaelic about the King of Moy's son, who came upon a maiden in a summer wood and she gave him fruit from thorn bushes and "an armful of strawberries on rushes". Beibhinn's generosity was as guileless and unstinting as that maiden's.

The following day Theobald Dillon approached as I was crossing the bawn to Cormac's house. Without his student's gown, he was as brilliant as Reynard the Fox in a green taffeta doublet and russet velvet breeches, his red shoulder-length hair covered with a wide-brimmed, plumed hat and his shoes tied with green ribbons. Suddenly I was conscious of how shabby my own clothes must have appeared.

"Here is your Golden Bough," he said in his polished English, handing me my Bible with a smile. "I heard you say that you had almost completed your third year at Trinity. No doubt you've heard that I have been to Christ College in Oxford, so we have much in common."

"I imagine that Trinity is very insignificant compared to Oxford." Self-consciousness made my voice stiff. "After all, it has only one college."

"Quite so. How many students have you in attendance?"

"About one hundred and fifty. Some of us live outside the walls because there aren't enough rooms at present."

We discussed student life for a while then the conversation turned to the subject of religion.

"Do you really believe that there are only two sacraments?" Theobald asked.

"Yes," I said. "Baptism and the Lord's Supper."

"And you don't believe that Christ is really present in the Holy Eucharist?"

"No."

"How then do you explain St Paul's Epistle to the Corinthians: 'For as often as ye eat this bread, and drink this cup, ye do show the Lord's death till he come'?"

"You can show the Lord's death without that death being repeated: Christ died once and once only for mankind."

"But he said, '*Hoc est enim corpus meum.*' Surely that means that the bread is really his body?"

"He also said, 'I am the good shepherd.' Does that mean that he spent his time tending sheep?"

"How do you explain: 'Whosesoever sins ye remit, they are remitted unto them, and whosesoever sins ye retain, they are retained'?"

"If you are asking whether I believe that priests have the power to forgive sins, the answer is no. Why should I ask of another man that which I may ask directly of Christ himself?"

"If the King of England, France, Alba and Eire appoints men to sit in judgment in the courts of law, why should the King of Heaven not do the same?"

"There's a great difference between the King of England and the King of Heaven."

"But the King of England is the head of your Church. If we want to graduate in the universities or hold office in the state are we not required to take an oath acknowledging his supremacy in all things spiritual or ecclesiastical? Look at the Dedicatory Epistle in that Bible where James is addressed as 'Defender of the Faith' and 'Your most Sacred Majesty'."

"The devil can cite scripture for his purpose." Even as the words escaped my lips I was aware of how weak and unjustified they were.

"You argue well." Theobald refused to take offence. "God be with you." And doffing his hat, he bowed slightly and went on his elegant way.

That evening, still angry at my own demeaning rudeness, I crossed the bawn and, on an impulse, climbed the stone stairway to the top of the north curtain wall. Beyond the corner tower, the sun was touching the low, western hills and under its rays the waters of the moat seemed on fire so that I imagined myself surrounded by Phlegethon, the burning river of hell. How long would I remain behind these massive walls, growing every day more resigned to my fate? With my shabby clothes, my greasy brogues, my drooping croimbéal and a moral state to match this physical appearance, it was clear that some hideous transformation had befallen me. I was like the man St Paul describes who looked at his own face in the mirror and then went off and forgot what person he was. At the same time I realized that the traditional pitfall of the Palesman had opened before me: I was slipping into the easy-going Gaelic way of life, becoming in that infamous phrase, *Hibernis hiberniores*, 'Irish of the Irish'.

My trysts with Beibhinn were partly to blame for this fall from grace. What did I care for the wisdom of Greece and Rome when I had the wisdom of the earth itself in one sweet, rounded body? Beibhinn was the goddess of my idolatry, the Circe who made me happy to wallow in shame like a beast.

How differently my father had behaved! He had not let his love for my mother turn him into a mere native. If anything, it had strengthened his resolve to raise his family with Anglo-Irish learning, manners and ideals. He did not forbid my mother to practise her religion but neither did he encourage her. We all knew instinctively that to please him we would have to be God-fearing upholders of the Reformed Church, not priest-controlled, superstitious Papists. The words of Phlegyas occurred to me: *Discite institiam moniti et non temnere divos*, 'Warned by example, learn righteousness and not to scorn the gods'.

An outburst of laughter brought me back to the world of Ballintober. Donal Bawn and a group of horseboys were looking in my direction. Deciding that it was better to retreat to the kitchen, I hastily descended the steps, only to find my way barred by a pack of snarling mongrels.

"Get him, Stracaire!" Donal Bawn called out. "Good dog! Get

him!"

Edging to one side so that my back was against the curtain wall, I faced my adversaries. "Down!" I shouted. "Down!" at which the pack began to snarl louder. This sent the horseboys into a new fit of laughter. Stracaire moved in closer, while another mongrel circled round to attack my flank. I realized that if I slipped or lost my balance the horseboys would do nothing to save me. Suddenly Stracaire gathered himself together, his eyes on my throat. This was the moment of choice. Taking rapid aim, I kicked upward with all my might. My brogue caught the leaping dog under the chin and sent him toppling backwards. At the sound of his yelps the others lost heart, but before they did, a bolt of pain transfixed me. The cur behind me had bitten my hand.

Numb with shock, I strode across the bawn, which was now filling with people who had heard the commotion. Once past the first row of cottages two enormous, rough-haired wolfhounds blocked my advance to the south-west tower. Would they also attack? Catching sight of Cormac's gaunt figure out of the corner of my eye, I turned in his direction. Every moment I expected to feel the crushing weight of a wolfhound on my shoulders and his teeth sinking into my neck. Then I reached the crowd and safety.

An old simpleton – or as the Gaels put it, "one on whom God has laid His hand" – approached and raising my bleeding right hand in the air, cried, "The *Crobhdhearg* has come to Cruachan!" This caused many of his listeners to gasp in astonishment. Immediately, Cormac intervened.

"Silence, Ronan!" he commanded. "Don't you know that the red-handed saviour will be named Hugh? So St Bearchán has written. Now be off with you all!"

Cormac took me to a house beside his where Owen, the *fear leighis* who had revived me when I fainted during the fast, lived. Owen's eldest daughter, a gentle girl of fifteen or sixteen with a large red birthmark on her left cheek, acted as his helper, crushing herbs in a small wooden dish with a knife handle and tearing up linen into strips to make bandages. He himself was a vigorous, open-faced fellow in his thirties who spoke English as well as he spoke Gaelic.

After my wound had been coated with essences of various herbs and bound with moss to staunch the bleeding, Owen entered into a discussion with Cormac.

"Do you know," he said, "that many of the families below in the village are close to starvation? Last year's bad harvest has left them with hardly enough grain to feed a mouse. I'm afraid some of the children may die before this year's crops ripen."

"Oh, they'll survive," Cormac dismissed his worries with an impatient wave of his hand. "You shouldn't waste your time on *Lóipínigh*."

"Father is only doing what the Holy Bishop tells us to do," the girl protested, holding one of her little sisters protectively in her arms. "He said we are all God's children."

"Hush, Brighid." Her father glanced at me; then shook his head warningly.

"Well, whatever anyone says, the children of those *Lóipínigh* are as hardy as wolf whelps." Cormac remained unrepentant.

This was my first indication of the contempt in which he held the poorer people. It was also a reminder of how much better than their neighbours the people of the castle fared, living as they did closer to the table of their master.

I asked Owen how he had become a physician and learned that as the seventh son of a seventh son, his parents believed him to have been born with healing powers. In addition he had acquired an understanding of cures and simples from a renowned *fear leighis*. To perfect his skill, O'Conor Don had sent him as apprentice to Viscount Dillon's physician. Consequently, he had returned to Ballintober well versed in all aspects of medicine.

Thinking to impress him, I mentioned my grand-uncle's belief that true medicine consists in aiding the body's vital natural heat to cure disease, whereupon Cormac demanded to know if my grand-uncle was that Richard Stanihurst who had traduced the Gaels in books written for the amusement of foreigners. Though taken aback by his accusation, I hotly defended my grand-uncle's name, pointing out that while I disagreed with his recusant views, yet I was assured of their sincerity and of his desire to bring about a united commonwealth of all the inhabitants of Ireland, both Anglo-Irish and Gaels. Given my grand-uncle's predisposition, such a commonwealth would, however, be English in language and custom.

"*Raiméis!*" Cormac snorted.

"Have you read my grand-uncle's books?" I asked.

"Indeed I haven't." Cormac's face grew red with choler. "I

wouldn't waste my time on such lies. Your grand-uncle is like all those writers from Cambrensis to Spencer who never notice the flowers in our Irish meadow because they are too busy seeking out the dung."

"But how can you level those accusations against men whose books you haven't read?" I persisted.

"I've read enough to know that what I say is true." He looked at Owen for confirmation. "As for your grand-uncle's books, Theobald Dillon has read them."

"Then you are guilty of the very crime you charge others with," I told him. "You are hearing only what you want to hear and ignoring what is good."

This sally had the desired effect. Cormac admitted that he might have given too much credence to the words of Theobald Dillon, who regarded my grand-uncle's descriptions of Gaelic Ireland as inimical. "If you only knew how galling it is to have to listen to sophists and bodachs mocking what they don't understand," he added, "you wouldn't blame me for being angry. That's why I want you to learn our history and poetry so that you can defend us against slander."

"Can't Theobald Dillon do that?" I demurred, aware of Brighid's clear eyes appraising me.

"He can and he can't." Cormac's voice sounded weary. "Theobald has no interest in poetry and since his years in Oxford he regards the study of Gaelic as a waste of time. The only good things he brought back from England were those spectacles."

When I arrived back in the kitchen after nightfall, Shawn Bacach gave me a hero's welcome, which only added to the shame Brighid's gaze had aroused in me. My readiness to face the pack of mongrels had been elevated by those who saw it into a feat comparable to Setanta's killing of Cullan's hound. "*D'anam don Diabhal* but I always knew you had warrior blood in you," Shawn Bacach crowed delightedly. "Ah, if only you'd been with me that second time in the Curlieus when we faced Dunkellin's pikemen ..."

"Who was Dunkellin?"

"Richard Burke, Earl of Clanricarde, the father of the present Earl. He and Hugh O'Neill were both Catholic noblemen but one fought for the English and the other against them."

"Didn't you fight for the English yourself?"

"Yes, God forgive me. I was one of Richard's pikemen at the First Battle of the Curlieus – that's when I got the musket ball in this leg. Sure I would have died there if Úna hadn't found me lying in my own blood on the side of Sheegora – she's one of the Aghacarra MacDermots, though in my distraction I thought she was a fairy woman. Her hair is as grey now as my own, but back then it was the colour of ripened oats, and that wasn't from washing it in stale urine mixed with ashes as some women do. Anyway, she pleaded for my life and afterwards she nursed me till I could walk and then got her kinsman Conor to take me into his service. It was Conor who defeated us in the First Battle of the Curlieus but, praise be to God, I was able to assist him three years later in the Second Battle. That was the last great victory of the Irish. We sent the Queen's men racing for their lives back down the mountainside to Abbeyboyle. Ah, Charles, you should have been with us that day. We were like wolves ravaging a flock of sheep."

I smiled, reluctant to point out that the Second Battle of the Curlieus had taken place almost two decades before I was born and that even if I had been present I might well, as a consequence of my family's sympathies, have been fighting on Dunkellin's side.

In the following days I commenced my study of the Gaelic Bible. On the title page there were two verses from the Epistle of Paul to Titus, which by comparing with my own Bible I translated: "For the grace of God that bringeth salvation hath appeared to all men, teaching us that, denying ungodliness and worldly lusts, we should live soberly, righteously, and godly, in this present world ..."

These words seemed like a reproach for my conduct with Beibhinn. Was I not being told to deny worldly lusts if I wanted to achieve salvation?

"Yes," my good angel affirmed.

"No," Lucifer whispered. "You are damned already, so salvation is beyond your reach."

Nevertheless, my worries about meeting Beibhinn were removed sooner than I expected when Brian Dubh caught us lying behind the settle in the Great Hall, just beneath the tapestry of the knights and their ladies.

Chapter 10

"So this is what you've been up to!" Brian Dubh's assumed outrage could not conceal his triumph. "It seems that when you're not reading your Bible, you're busy corrupting the innocent. And you, my fine damsel, to the New Tower at once! Lady Mary will deal with you in the morning."

The next day Beibhinn was sent back to her parents' home near Slieve Bawn. Like a pitiless Tisiphone, Lady Mary would not even allow her to say farewell. On hearing this I was about to protest, then thought better of it; Lady Mary was within her rights in what she had done, though I felt certain that Brian Dubh had blackened us in her eyes. To assuage my sense of guilt I composed a sonnet ending:

Ah, Beibhinn, little dark one of Slieve Bawn,
Even the stars grow dim now you are gone.

It was a poor thing and I doubt that even if she had received it, it would have consoled Beibhinn for her misfortune. As it was, I threw it in the fire.

In the midst of the discontent that now seized me, the arrival of my uncle Teigue was a timely distraction. Shawn Bacach told me one afternoon that there was a man waiting for me upstairs and I mounted the stone steps two at a time. Then, as I reached the top, I halted, my heart thumping. Trying to appear composed, I stepped resolutely through the arched opening. As I did so a stranger in a shaggy mantle rose from his seat by the long table.

How can I describe my feelings? Here was my mother's brother, somebody who had been nursed at the same breast, who had shared the same childhood, who had listened to the same stories as she. I expected a warrior, a poet, a nobleman – oh, maybe not all these, but someone at once exalted and familiar, a sort of Gaelic Anchises; instead, I met a small, pock-marked, middle-aged man whose very resemblance to my mother made his disfigurement all the more painful to observe.

"*Fáilte romhat*" (Welcome). I smiled hesitantly, conscious of two mild blue eyes above the pitted cheeks that were partly covered by a grizzled beard and moustache.

At first my uncle was too embarrassed to talk, searching my face pathetically for any sign of rejection. That humble gesture tore at my heart. Impulsively I embraced him and his face lit up. He was delighted that Norah had such a fine man as me for a son. Why, the first moment he looked at me he could see that I had her eyes and smile, though I had my father's dark hair. How was she? Was her hair still golden brown? Did she ever speak of him? How many brothers and sisters had I?

A hundred questions followed one another in rapid succession. The more we spoke the more I forgot his disfigurement. He was a very gentle, kind person with an impish sense of humour. After I told him about the inquest and the charge I had laid against Brian Dubh he confessed that he had delayed coming to Ballintober because he was uncertain how I would receive him. Now that he was here he would persuade O'Conor Don to let me go. Hugh had already told him about the trouble I had in Dublin. Hugh was a good fellow, a true gentleman; he had given him the shaggy mantle to keep out the cold and had also presented him with a garron. You could see that he had noble blood in his veins. There was no substitute for breeding. Now, that Dillon fellow was a different kind of bird, a puffed-up kite masquerading as a falcon. Why, he had assured Hugh he would look after him and had then sent him to this empty, fireless hall without so much as a cup of usquebagh to warm him after his long journey.

On hearing this, I immediately went down to the kitchen and found that Úna had already prepared food and drink for both of us, which I helped her to carry upstairs. She explained to my uncle in her soothing, wheezy voice that Theobald Dillon had left instructions that he was to be treated with all due respect and that he would come over later to see him. Pleased by this evidence of hospitality, my uncle insisted on rewarding Úna for her labours by pressing a shilling into her palm. He then removed his mantle to reveal a faded brown doublet with long skirts and wide breeches tied at the knees with ribbons. These, together with his velvet bonnet, woollen stockings and buckled shoes, gave him the appearance of someone who had once been a man of substance.

As we ate he lamented that he could not invite me to stay with him; he had recently lost his house and was now living in a cabin given to him by Tomultach MacDermot of Dungar. This was another shock.

I questioned him about his reversal of fortune, which he made no attempt to conceal. It turned out that he had been too trusting, had loaned money to people who had neglected to repay it, till, finally, he had been forced to mortgage his land to meet his own debts. The reasons for his indebtedness were many: the big snow of Thirty-Five, which had killed half of his sheep, the fall in cattle exports, a succession of bad harvests and the fact that he had to pay tithes, not only to his own clergy, but also to the Protestant ministers. I suspected that bad management and living beyond his means might also have contributed to his difficulties because he alluded more than once to the need of maintaining the O'Flynn reputation for generosity.

"Have other landowners got into debt?" I asked.

"Indeed they have," he assured me. "I know a dozen families who have had to sell off portions of their land. Why, even MacDermot of Moylurg sold about eight quarters to Sir Charles Coote just after his wife died – that would be two years ago. The trouble is that everybody pays you in kind but rents have to be paid in gold or silver and the only ones with money are the New English and the likes of the Dillons and the O'Conors."

"Are the O'Conors very rich?"

"They're better off than most of us – and do you know why? Half the land they now have shouldn't be theirs by right."

"How can that be?"

"Oh, it all happened when Hugh O'Conor Don got a new grant of Ballintober from the crown – that would be about the time your father came into these parts. By the new patent Sir Hugh acquired the head-rents of several quarters that formerly belonged to the O'Conors, but which were no longer theirs. Now I'm not saying he was wrong to secure possession of his own lands – we ourselves surrendered our lands to Sidney in the Queen's time – but Sir Hugh gained more than he surrendered. Then he divided it among his four sons: Calvagh, the present O'Conor Don – Calvagh moved to here from Knockalaghta Castle when his father died in Thirty-Two – Hugh Oge, Cathal who died in Thirty-Four, and Brian Roe. Hugh Oge is today fattening cattle on land that belonged to my father – your grandfather – but he wouldn't lend me so much as one red penny to pay off my mortgage. What was it he said? 'We're no longer responsible for our old sub-chiefs.' Well, maybe they aren't … they themselves are tenants of the Crown just like the rest of us and, as Wentworth showed, the Crown can take back what it gives. Anyway, it scarcely matters now. Sir Lucas Dillon of Lough Glinn – the man who loaned me money against my land – demanded full repayment and when I was unable to comply, he seized the lot. You know we speak of the greed of the Protestants but it's nothing to the greed of some of our own people. Sir Lucas, the great Catholic nobleman, wouldn't give me even a month's grace, while Tomultach MacDermot, a Protestant, has given me a cabin and a plot of land freehold. But, of course, you're a Protestant yourself – not that that is anything to be ashamed of, seeing your father is a Palesman."

The ale and usquebagh had further loosened my uncle's tongue and he was eager to confide in me. Lowering his voice, he leaned forward: "Never speak ill of the O'Conors; they don't forget a hard word and they haven't lasted this long without their share of cunning. Do you know why O'Conor Don kept you here so long without granting you an interview?" I shook my head. "Well, I'll give you my opinion." My uncle looked around warily before continuing. "You were a hostage to ensure the safety of the priest seized in Athlone. Did that ever occur to you?"

"But if the authorities didn't know I was being held here –" I began to object; then noticed my uncle's smile. "You think Brian Dubh informed them?"

"Isn't it likely? Now you understand why the O'Conors keep him in their service: better the spy you know than the one you don't know – not that I'm saying O'Conor Don isn't a man of honour. The person that isn't strong has to be clever. In his place I'd probably have done no less."

Apart from the subject of Hugh Oge and Sir Lucas, my uncle

showed neither bitterness nor envy. He had his little cabin and, as he expressed it, "*Is leor don dreolín a nead*" (his nest is sufficient for the wren). He told me about our relative Ffeochra's castle at Ballinlough, near Lough O'Flynn, and other members of the clan that were still in possession of their estates at Slieve O'Flynn. A cousin of ours had travelled to Spanish Flanders to join Owen Roe O'Neill's regiment, while another had sought his fortune in the New World. I wasn't to assume that because fate had been unkind to him, the O'Flynns weren't still a great people. If I would help him to regain his land, he would make me his heir.

You can imagine how avidly I listened to this account of my mother's people, most of which was new to me. The thought of claiming my place among them was, however, little to my liking. I was a Dublin man who, by a stroke of bad fortune exceeding even my uncle's, had in one hour lost his home and his birthright. Now I was more eager to escape to Spain or the New World myself than to spend my life as a small Gaelic landowner.

Theobald returned while I was conveying these feelings to my uncle. He had arranged a meeting for us in the New Tower with O'Conor Don, a meeting that went very well. It pleased me to see with what courtesy the descendant of the last High King of Ireland greeted a man who had come down in the world. Surely, I thought to myself, such courtesy is the true mark of nobility?

"Why don't you stay with us till May Day when we will be hurling against Castlerea?" O'Conor Don said.

"I'm grateful for your invitation," my uncle replied, "but I have a cow to milk and my little garden to tend. That gives me more satisfaction than any hurling contest."

"Then you are a fortunate man, Teigue." O'Conor Don laid his hand lightly on his shoulder. "Men like me are fearful, not knowing when their lands and possessions will be confiscated; you are as content as a hermit."

"Yes," my uncle agreed, "but, like a hermit, I sometimes miss my native place. Still, Dungar is pleasant enough ... aye, pleasant enough."

"You may stay in Ballintober for as long as you please, Charles." O'Conor Don turned to me with a gracious smile. "Nevertheless, as Shawn Rua has been taken, it's likely that Sir Chidley or the Sheriff will be visiting us soon, in which case you must judge for yourself what is safest to do. Meanwhile, Cormac needs an assistant to help him in compiling the history of our family, the *Síol Muireadaigh*. If that work is to your liking, we will see that, despite your injured hand, you are engaged."

I assured him my injury wasn't serious and said I would gladly accept his offer.

"Good." He rose to indicate the meeting was over. "Cormac shall be informed of your decision."

Next morning my uncle, enveloped in the great shaggy mantle, trotted off on his garron. Hugh and I rode with him as far as Cloonkearney, then watched in silence till he became a mere speck on the Castlerea road, which in truth was little more than a rutted track.

"Come on," I cried suddenly, wheeling Nell around, "I'll race you back," and before Hugh could answer, I was galloping away. It was a relief to feel the wet wind in my face while my body surged to the mare's powerful rhythm, a relief from the guilt of knowing that I was refusing to take responsibility for my uncle just as Hugh Oge O'Conor had refused. I was a free man, free to leave Ballintober or to remain if I wished, free to tell Brian Dubh he was no longer my taskmaster, free to – to do what? To skulk like a deer till the hounds recovered my scent? No matter. For the time being I was at liberty and the blood was racing in my veins and anything might happen between now and sunset.

Hugh's short-tailed gelding was no match for Nell. On the two miles' stretch to the castle she kept easily ahead, her muscles brimming with energy after eleven weeks of rest and exercise.

"That's a great mare," Hugh acknowledged when I allowed him to catch up as we reached the esplanade. "Still, if I was on Glasan I would have beaten you."

"How much would you wager on that?" I asked recklessly.

"Oh, ho! You're a Milesian sure enough." He was delighted by my challenge. "I'll put twelve sovereigns and a suit of good clothes, with hat, boots and cloak thrown in, against your mare that you can't beat me over three miles."

"Agreed!" I cried – forgetting that Nell belonged to my brother Thomas – whereupon Hugh threw back his head and let out a whoop of sheer exultation such as I had never heard in Dublin.

"Come," he invited, "we'll stable these animals and then repair to O'Beirne's. Felim! Donal Bawn!" When the horseboys arrived he gave them instructions, then, after he had changed from his fine clothes into a frieze doublet and breeches and a leather jerkin – to be in harmony, I suspected, with my shabby dress – we set off on foot for the village.

As I sauntered downhill with Hugh I was in the same giddy state of mind that usually accompanied my visits to the Black Raven. Everything would turn out well – when the race was over I would have new clothes on my back and twelve gold sovereigns in my purse. Was I not entitled to this reprieve after my long weeks of drudgery in the kitchen? "Lay on, MacDuff; and damn'd be him that first cries 'Hold, enough!'"

Halfway down the hill it started to rain so we raced the last furlong past staring villagers and yelping mongrels. Four hard-eyed men playing cards at a corner table looked up in surprise as we burst through the alehouse door. In the light from the rectangular window, I observed that they were dressed like townsmen and yet there was something of the country ruffian in their appearance.

"Ah, Hugh, my heart's delight!" O'Beirne, the portly, moon-faced landlord, exclaimed on seeing us enter. "Here, sit by the fire. You'll be needing a dram of mulled ale to take the chill out of your bones and I expect your friend will too." Then lowering his voice, he leaned over the upturned barrel that did service as a table and added: "Come to the kitchen in a little while – I want to speak to you about those gentlemen. *Fainic!* Don't let them see you looking."

"Have you any French claret?" Hugh spoke in a normal voice.

"Seamus! Boy!" O'Beirne called out. "Two meadars and a jug of our best claret! Hurry."

Presently the boy emerged from an open door partly concealed by two huge ale casks and, to my surprise, he was none other than the eldest son of Shawn Rua. On seeing me, he hesitated, as if uncertain how I would react. My friendly *"Dia duit a Shéamuis"* set him at his ease. While he filled our meadars he told us that his father was still being held in Athlone and that his mother had sent him to Ballintober, fearing the soldiers would come for him also.

"And how is your mother going to manage without the two of you?" I enquired, whereupon tears welled in his eyes and he hurried away.

"Do you reckon if I went to Athlone and spoke to Lord Ranelagh, he would have Shawn Rua released?" My question startled Hugh.

"No," he replied. "The English will hold Shawn Rua while it suits their purposes. If you go to them they may well hold you too. What they really want is evidence against our family – they dare not proceed against us without the trappings of law. My father will see that Shawn Rua's family do not suffer want – who do you think obtained Seamus his apprenticeship? Now drink up your claret while I find out what's troubling O'Beirne."

As soon as Hugh left, one of the strangers, a tall, heavily built man with wind-reddened cheeks above a sandy beard, rose and approached the fire. Turning his backside to the flames, he grinned down at me.

"A wet day for April." He spoke Gaelic with a harsh, northern intonation.

"It is that," I agreed, trying to ignore the fumes of stale beer, sweat and tobacco that wafted towards me.

"You wouldn't be an O'Conor man by any chance?" he remarked.

"Why do you want to know?" I countered.

"We're here to purchase cattle," he said. "If the O'Conors have cattle to sell, we can save them the trouble of bringing them to market."

"I'm a stranger here myself," I confessed, "so I know nothing about cattle or markets. If you want to speak to the O'Conors you have only to walk up the hill to their castle."

"You're a close fellow." The smile had disappeared. "I'd say you were from the castle yourself."

"No." I tried to keep my voice even. "I'm a Dublin man."

"You're lying to me now." His eyes had an angry flash in them. "No Dublin man would speak Gaelic with your *blas*."

"Nevertheless I'm from Dublin," I persisted, knowing that Brian Dubh would already have informed the authorities.

"And I tell you you're not." His hand was resting on the handle of a miodoge jutting out from his belt. "Are you going to call me a liar?"

"It's not my custom to quarrel with strangers in alehouses." I saw a vein start to throb in his forehead but before he attacked, his companions, who addressed him as Manus, shouted at him to leave me alone. Instantly, Hugh and O'Beirne, attracted by the raised voices, came hurrying in.

"Gentlemen," O'Beirne called out, "what's amiss?"

"This gentleman," I pointed to my glowering adversary, "was anxious to speak to the O'Conors."

"Well," Hugh said, "that's easily accomplished; I'm O'Conor's eldest son."

The effect of this declaration on the strangers was extraordinary: they crowded round Hugh as if they were Poins and his fellow robbers greeting Prince Hal. In the hubbub I was completely forgotten. Hugh seated himself at their table and ordered a meadar of usquebagh for every man; then they huddled together, talking in low, excited voices. After a while Hugh came over to the fire.

"Forgive this interruption, Charles." He laid his hand on my arm. "I'll rejoin you within the hour."

When he returned to the strangers the low-voiced, excited conversation was resumed. Now and again, as I morosely sipped my wine, a phrase would reach me: 'regiment in Flanders' ... 'speak to O'More' ... 'recruit them' ... 'a bright day in Ireland' ...

There was no mention of cattle.

Chapter 11

ON THE day of the race the April sky was as overcast and sullen as my mind. I was determined to pay Hugh back for slighting me in the alehouse while he caroused with his new-found friends. That they were in all likelihood disbanded soldiers who were ready for any desperate adventure only added to the insult. Hugh O'Conor might deem himself heir to the Kings of Connacht but the Stanihursts had been leading citizens of Dublin when his ancestors had been butchering each other for an empty title. There he was now, prancing around on his grey, bob-tailed saddle horse, Glasan, to the admiration of his clansmen and lackeys as if he were Alexander the Great bestriding Bucephalus. When he waved in my direction it was as much as I could do to acknowledge his greeting.

We moved to the starting point through small groups of ragged villagers and wild-looking peasants with their barefooted women who, since it was Tuesday, had come into Ballintober for the market. Glasan led the way, snorting and bucking, while Nell followed, stepping lightly but with little show of fire. Theobald Dillon, every inch the courtier from his gleaming spurs to the plume in his velvet bonnet, came trotting up after parting from three mounted ladies who halted too far away for me to observe their countenances, though one sitting astride a roan horse just like a man had her hood thrown back, revealing a wealth of pale yellow hair.

Theobald quickly persuaded Hugh to let him join the race and the way in which his sleek black gelding, Fiach Dubh, pranced and curvetted showed he might prove as dangerous as Glasan. Indeed, this judgment was affirmed by my old nemesis, MacDockwra, the tall, red-faced Pursuer, who, mounting a boulder, began to call out in a town crier's voice: "Come one, come all. Here's a race to mend your fortunes. By St Patrick's tooth I care not if I win or lose for, as the ancient warrior Caoilte said, 'If the brown leaf that the tree sheds were gold or the bright wave silver, Fionn would have given it away.'"

While I cannot further recall MacDockwra's outlandish quips and catchcries, it was clear that Hugh, "the noble Salmon of the Shannon", at three crowns against four was expected to win, and that Theobald, "the lordly Falcon of Lough Glinn", was chief rival. The crowd who had been collecting around an unyoked ale-wagon surmounted by an ivy-bush could only be persuaded to forgo their quaffing to wager on "the boy on the bay mare" – MacDockwra's contemptuous reference to me – by an offer of "three crowns for one, a prize worthy of His Majesty's Milesian father, whose image is stamped on this coin". How so many of the onlookers could afford to hazard their few groats and pennies was a marvel but I can only assume that they had sold their wares in the market and had been beguiled by the voice of the tempter.

Cormac, who was acting as judge, beckoned to us to approach him. "You know the rules of the contest," his voice was stern, as befitted his new-found honour, "straight on till you round the Oak of Knockalaghta, then back by the way you went. The first rider past this spot gets the white rod in token of victory." So Cormac also expected Hugh to win! He would revel in the opportunity of offering the white rod to an O'Conor as his ancestors had done at the inaugurations on Carnfree. Well, he would learn that the race is not always to the swiftest. "*Superanda omnis fortuna ferendo est.*" As he lowered his arm to signal the moment of starting I avoided his eye, nurturing my resentment.

Knockalaghta – which forms part of the O'Conor patrimony – lies quarterway between Ballintober and Tulsk. Since I had never before travelled there, I allowed Hugh and Theobald to take the lead. It was well I did so, for not only did they clear a way through scattered groups of peasants driving cattle and sheep or leading garrons, with panniers in which geese, ducks and even young pigs were being carried, but after following the rough cart track eastward for a mere six furlongs or so, both set out across country. Whether by this stratagem they intended to shorten the distance to the oak tree or to test the mettle of their rivals' mounts I cannot tell but certain it is they tested my horsemanship. The course was most uneven and in places there were banks or grass-grown dykes that sent my heart leaping into my mouth. I was reminded of an occasion in Trinity when moved by overweening confidence I had taken the floor in a public disputation on hereditary versus elective monarchy and faced with row upon row of learned, expectant faces, had found my faculties unequal to the ordeal. Luckily, on this occasion Nell was my Pegasus, carrying me like Bellerophon through daunting perils, and her even, steady strides showed she was capable of greater exertion.

After riding up hill and down dale for one and a half interminable Irish miles – they do not adhere to English measure in Connacht – we came to a turlough, into which Hugh plunged Glasan with reckless courage, sending water cascading on high. Theobald followed on Fiach Dubh and when I reached the shore I decided to emulate them. Nell, however, who was new to such feats, skidded to a halt and I was obliged to make my way around the south edge of the turlough, much to the amusement of a small group of peasants who were watching. Mortified, I proceeded to strike Nell with my heels till she had made up the greater part of the ground lost but by now my rivals had rounded Knockalaghta Oak and passed me on the homeward journey. "*Fág an bealach!*" Hugh yelled lustily as he thundered past and Theobald gave me a mocking wave with his gloved hand.

Clenching my teeth, I urged Nell forward and on reaching the oak – a leafless tree of great age and girth – wheeled around it under the watchful eye of a horseboy, who called after me, "Victory to O'Conor!" That only pricked my resolve and with voice, knee and rein I urged Nell to greater effort. Before long we were once again at the turlough but this time I refused to allow Nell to balk and after some hesitation, she plunged gamely into the water. Soon she was up to her flanks and my breeches were drenched. Halfway across she started to swim; then a few plunges and she was scrambling up the far bank. Much to my surprise, the watchers cheered.

Heartened, I continued west, ignoring brakes and sheughs in my determination to catch up. I saw Hugh swerve aside from a kesh to jump the adjoining dyke, while Theobald kept straight on. Suddenly Fiach Dubh stumbled, throwing his rider. That was warning enough so I followed Hugh's course and Nell cleared the dyke with one great bound. Out of the corner of my eye I glimpsed Dillon struggling to his knees, bonnet gone and face begrimed, while his horse raced ahead with stirrups flapping wildly.

Now there was only Hugh and myself in the race and it was clear that Glasan's fiery pace was lessening. Slowly, relentlessly, Nell drew closer. If only I could keep her from stumbling or falling … My eyes were streaming from the wind and my ears were filled with the noise of my own breathing but I husbanded my dwindling anger to goad myself on: Hugh O'Conor would rue the day he had accepted my challenge. Already he was swinging north to regain the road, hoping to block me in the straits formed here and there by blackthorns and hazels. Like a hound pursuing a stag, I kept on his track, passing small groups of peasants, who cheered on their chieftain's son, though some – probably those who had been seduced by the prospect of tripling their wealth – shouted "*An t-ógánach gallda abú!*" (Victory to the foreign youth!)

As we neared the last quarter mile of the race, I drew alongside Hugh, who was lashing Glasan with his reins in a desperate effort to stay ahead. Neck and neck we raced, then, almost imperceptibly, Nell left the wild-eyed gelding behind. Her sides were drenched with sweat and foam flew from her mouth yet staunchly she pressed on, close on the heels of Fiach Dubh, still galloping furiously home. Now I could see the towers of Ballintober with their bright pennants and the thatched roofs of the village below the castle. A thrill of savage joy coursed through my veins: in a few moments the white rod would be mine!

Suddenly, in a place where the road was hemmed in by hazels, I saw Donal Bawn and another horseboy jump out in front of Fiach Dubh, shouting and waving branches. The gelding slithered to a halt, then reared to avoid the attack. I resolved to dash past but at that very moment the frightened gelding lurched sideways. "*Fainic!*" Hugh's voice rang out behind me. That was the last word I heard as I sailed headlong through the air. Next moment I hit something and darkness engulfed me.

How long I lay unconscious I cannot tell but when I opened my eyes faces were pressing around me and Dudley was endeavouring to pour an eggshell of usquebagh down my throat. "You're as hard to kill as a badger." He grinned when my eyes met his. "If you hadn't landed in those hazels, you'd probably have broken your neck.

Here, Peadar, give me a hand."

Assisted by my benefactors, I rose to my feet. "Bring me to Nell," I begged Dudley. Somebody caught the mare and presently I was again mounted on her back. I urged her forward; she limped badly and my heart sank. Once more fate had wrecked my hopes. Instead of acquiring new clothes and golden sovereigns, I would have to surrender Nell to the victorious Hugh. After that I would have to trust to the generosity of O'Mulconry to earn my living. Blood from a cut in my scalp trickled into my eyes and my right shoulder hurt. Three riders trotted past in the direction of Tulsk but apart from a confused awareness that they were the gentle-women who had earlier been with Dillon, I did not see them clear-ly. My only concern now was to remain upright in the saddle. That Nell might be lamed by my actions did not deter me – I was re-solved, come what might, to avoid the humiliation of finishing the race on foot.

A hush fell on the crowd as I approached. I perceived as in a dream faces staring at me and among them the faces of Hugh and Cormac. Pain seared through my shoulder as I dismounted but I forced myself to ignore it. I would bear defeat like a Roman.

"Here, she's yours." I offered the reins to Hugh.

"Upon my word, she's not," he declared. "Do you think I'd be-smirch my honour by accepting an undeserved victory? O'Mul-conry, give him the rod."

Cormac, with a brave effort to hide his disappointment, hand-ed me the white rod, saying, "I bestow this wand on the victor."

"That's as may be," MacDockwra came striding up, "but I'm not paying out one groat. First past this spot wins; you said so yourself."

There were loud protests from those who had wagered on me. "Wait!" Hugh remonstrated. "Let Cormac decide."

Everybody turned to the ollamh, wondering how he would sever this Gordian knot. Cormac reflected for a while, his red-rimmed eyes shut; then, opening them, he spoke slowly, spittle fly-ing from his lips: "Hugh won in deed but not in truth and Charles won in truth but not in deed. That makes each both winner and loser. So it should be with those who wagered on them: let them be losers by forgoing their rewards and winners by receiving back their wagers. Straight to straight and crooked to crooked – isn't that what the proverb says?"

"And will those of us who wagered on Sir Theobald also get back our wagers?" a small, sharp-featured churl asked.

"No," Cormac replied. "You threw out a trout to catch a salmon and you caught the Salmon of Knowledge, which should teach you that a wise man doesn't wager."

There were murmurs of approval from many in the crowd, though MacDockwra scoffed, "It's easy to be generous at another man's expense."

"Why are you dissatisfied?" Cormac turned to him. "Aren't you the richer for your labours?"

"That's true enough," MacDockwra conceded, "but I'm richer in truth than in deed."

This witty retort produced an outburst of merriment, which galled Cormac. "'*Procul o procul este, profani*,'" he muttered, with a confidential glance at Hugh and me.

"'*Conclamat vates, "totoque absistite luco"*,'" MacDockwra responded, showing that he too could recite Virgil. None of the peasants understood but they sensed that Cormac had been bested by their champion and broke into triumphant cheers. At this point Dudley arrived with Donal Bawn and his accomplice and the cheering instantly subsided.

"Why did you interfere with the race and throw this man?" Hugh accosted the horseboys.

"By the tooth of St Patrick, we were only trying to catch the riderless horse," Donal Bawn declared.

"Is that true?" Hugh turned to me.

"Yes," I said bitterly, "if you catch a horse by shouting and waving a branch in his face."

"I was just trying to slow him so that Fergus could grab the reins." Donal Bawn's voice was full of injured innocence. "Isn't that right, Fergus?"

"Upon my soul it is." Fergus gave a foolish grin.

"We never would have done it if we saw him coming," Donal Bawn assured Hugh.

The oaf's effrontery so robbed me of my faculties that I could only mutter, "Sir, I leave you to judge the truth of that assertion."

"That's easily done." Hugh glared at the horseboys. "If I didn't suspect that misguided loyalty to my family prompted your action, I would send you both packing this instant. Now get out of my sight."

"Wait!" he added. "Tomorrow you will take Glasan back to O'Conor Roe – and tell him to exercise him more; he has grown as soft as a hog."

Though disappointed at this leniency on Hugh's part, I realized it would be impolitic to demur, so I led Nell over to the edge of the crowd, where Shawn Bacach was waiting with a happy smile on his face. "*D'anam don diabhal!*" he exclaimed. "Isn't it you showed them that a bay mare is the equal of a black horse, aye, and of –" he lowered his voice – "a grey one too. But the poor creature looks as if she's hurt herself." He touched Nell's leg and she flinched.

"You'd better let Rory O'Cahan examine her," Hugh said, coming up, "and be sure to get Owen to bathe your own head."

Leaving Hugh to repair to the alehouse, where a carouse was beginning, I made my way on foot back to the castle, Nell and Shawn Bacach limping on either side of me. On the way, I learned from my companion that Hugh had been obliged to loan Glasan to his kinsman, O'Conor Roe of Castleruby, for a year in consequence of some debt he had incurred. It seemed that Hugh was famous for his prodigality and this was confirmed later that evening when he summoned me to his chamber in the north-west tower, where he presented me with a handsome suit of clothes, high leather boots and a broad-brimmed hat, though I assured him that Cormac's judgment relieved him of this obligation.

"Not at all, Charles." He slapped me on the injured shoulder with drunken camaraderie, causing me to wince. "Cormac may be an ollamh but he's not a gaming man; you got the branch of victory so you're entitled to the … to the … Why, a quarrel broke out in the alehouse on this very matter: a man who had wagered on you accused MacDockwra of fleecing him and in the blink of an eye there were staffs clashing and blood flowing. If Dudley's men hadn't imposed *smacht*, there would have been carnage … aye, red carnage." He smiled in the manner of a boy, who is elated at the prospect of danger. "Now remove those rags and dress yourself like a Prince of Connacht – an O'Flynn."

"But the cost …" I resumed my protest.

"Stop talking like a Dublin merchant." He fumbled in his doublet and took out a purse. "I have here the twelve gold sovereigns we agreed on. Take them before they're spent … and may they … … may they …" His eyelids drooped sleepily.

"Who were Dillon's fair companions?" I asked to cover my embarrassment at accepting such largesse.

"Ah, the Three Graces!" He jerked his head, recovering his faculties. "One of them – the wild damsel with the amber hair – is Oona, daughter of MacDermot of Moylurg; one is my sister Mary and the third is Isabel, daughter of Burke – but put them out of your mind, Charles ... Ireland needs swordsmen ... not lovers ... that's what I tell my mother ... There's going to be a new day in Ireland ..."

II

WAITING

Nox ruit, Aeneas; nos flendo ducimus horas.

(Night approaches, Aeneas,
yet we waste the hours in weeping.)

Virgil, *The Aeneid*, Book VI, l. 539

Chapter 12

NOW BEGAN one of my most wonderful and wretched periods at Ballintober, a period that brought sufferings that might aptly be compared to those of Tantalus, who languished within sight of plenty. With my new suit I was to outward appearance a Connacht prince but inside I felt like a jay dressed in the feathers of a peacock; I had won the race and I had not won it; I was Cormac's assistant but I still slept on a pallet in the kitchen and, greatest anguish of all, I was able to see Hugh's sister almost every day but not to woo her. However, let me return to the beginning.

On the morning following the race, I was on my way to Cormac's to return the white rod when I encountered Hugh and Mary, or Maura, as she was called within her family, walking across the bawn. If Maura were one of the *spéirmhná* or fairy women that Irish poets see in visions she could not have wounded my heart more deeply. I have told myself since that it was because she was an O'Conor princess that I was so overcome by love, and it may be so, yet there was such loveliness in her girlish face and clear grey eyes and such comeliness in her bodily aspect that had she been a pedlar's daughter, I would still have regarded her as a goddess in human form. When she spoke, her voice was as musical and unaffected as a skylark's, yet there was a restraint in her manner that made one conscious of her high birth. To add to my uncertainty in the presence of this apparition, Hugh was barely friendly. Probably he regretted the wine-induced intimacy with which he had spoken to me the previous evening. After all, I was merely a retainer in his father's household and, furthermore, one whose loyalty was uncertain.

What did I speak of to Maura? *Mirabile dictu*, I cannot recall. No doubt we discussed the race and Theobald's and my own mishaps and since it was late April, we must have mentioned the loveliness of the countryside with its blossoming wild flowers and bushes and its singing birds. The only thing I can be certain of is that every turn of Maura's head, every inflection of her voice, every glance of her clear grey eyes strengthened the spell with which she bound me; Beibhinn's image was totally erased from my mind by one sweep of her shiny brown locks and I, who prided myself on my learning, showed less wit than a dunce. When she moved away with Hugh it was as if the sun had retreated behind a pall of clouds.

Cormac was working on his history of the O'Conors when I entered his house. He took the white rod without comment; then, having returned it reverently to its place over the door, he told me to copy a worm-eaten manuscript onto new sheets of paper. After attempting to decipher the archaic handwriting while my mind drifted to grey eyes and pale red lips, I made the excuse that my shoulder hurt and begged Cormac's permission to visit Owen, hoping to catch a glimpse of Maura on the way.

"Ask him to rub in some heron oil," Cormac advised. "It can cure any ailment, from spasms to aching joints."

"What is heron oil?" I rose from my stool at the table.

"Heron oil?" Cormac laid down his quill. "You know the dunghill opposite the cowshed? Well, Owen buries a heron in it with only his head sticking out and as the creature rots, oil trickles from his beak into an eggshell, which Owen ties there beforehand. Since herons can stand in water all day without harm it is clear that their oil can keep muscles and joints limber, though Owen adds various simples to it."

Cormac then proceeded to discuss the heron's history, concluding with the story of how Henry II during his victorious progress through Ireland had induced the native chieftains to dine on its flesh, which only went to show how barbarous the English were. It was this same Henry who had come over to reform the Irish Church – after he had first murdered the Archbishop of Canterbury!

While Brighid was rubbing the heron oil into my shoulder, I questioned her about the Three Graces, hoping thereby to bring the conversation round to the fairest of them. To my surprise she divined my thoughts and looking at me with her direct gaze, said: "Though the acorn grows on a high tree, the sweetest fruit is found on the lowest bush."

At the time I thought she was reproving me for forgetting Beibhinn; it was only in after years that I came to recognize that she might have been alluding to the inner life of grace. Brighid was a strange girl, who had wisdom beyond her years, but in my ignorance I only regarded her as a kind creature with a disfigured cheek. She told me that my shoulder would be better in a fortnight and whether it was the oil or the passage of time that did it, the pain had completely vanished by then.

Nell's leg took longer to mend. Rory O'Cahan's brother, Finbar, who was as skilled at healing horses as he was at shoeing them, had put a splint on her cannon and tied her in the stable. "You shouldn't have ridden her," he accused in his blunt, Northern fashion. "Even a child would have recognized that she had a bone broken." Poor Nell, I had made her suffer by my thoughtlessness as I had made so many others who were near to me. The foolish animal whinnied softly when I approached her, unaware of my perfidy. Thirty-three years later the memory of that moment still remains with me.

In the following days I saw Maura at intervals, sometimes with Hugh, sometimes with Theobald Dillon, sometimes with her fair companions. Oona, because of her amber hair and tall, limber form, was the most striking of the three, while Isabel, a smiling, black-haired maiden, was the most amiable, but Maura took the palm for grace of feature and form. If the other two were aware of how much I wished them to leave me alone with my grey-eyed goddess, they did not show it. Time and again I suffered their banter, while secretly praying that Theobald would arrive and escort them elsewhere. It may well be that they found my Dublin speech and manners entertaining, though I suspect they wished to shield their companion from my attentions. She, for her part, did not give the slightest sign that she was aware of my adoration. I could only gaze covertly at her serene face, tormented by its beauty, yet knowing I would never touch it. So the damned must look on God's countenance before they are led away to the everlasting fires.

To keep myself from brooding on my unhappy state I resolved to acquire a better knowledge of my beloved's language. Already by comparing the Gaelic translation of the New Testament with my own King James Bible I had learned to read passably well; now with Cormac's assistance I ventured further afield, perusing stories, chronicles, lives of saints, fables and, inevitably, poems. To claim that I could fully comprehend what I read would be untrue; the strangeness of the words and density of the thought often baffled enquiry and since I no longer had any English version at hand, I could only surmise what the long-dead poet or ollamh had intended. Added to this were the further difficulties that all the material, even that in O'Conor Don's *Duanaire* or poem book, was handwritten and that there was little order in its presentation. I was like a man who, exploring a dark cavern by the wavering light of a deal torch, finds a hoard of treasure in which fine jewels and base ornaments are heaped together so that to distinguish the merits of any object requires the eyes of Argos coupled with the wisdom of Athena. If it hadn't been for my mentor I would certainly have abandoned the enterprise.

Cormac, who had once taught in the Bardic school which the O'Duigenans maintained at Castlefore in West Brefni, delighted in expounding arcane points of learning, whether it was explaining that each letter of the Gaelic alphabet is also the name of a tree or that *bóthar*, the word for a road, means "cow track" or that the ancient Irish had their own form of writing called *Ogham*, after the De Danann god Ogma.

It would be tedious to enumerate the diverse ideas with which he entranced me but there is one idea which winds its way through this learning as a gold thread winds through a multi-hued tapestry, and that is the importance of the number three. All the ancient stories were divided into three groups: *An Finscéalaíocht*, dealing with gods and immortals; *An Rúraíocht*, dealing with Cuchulainn and the Red Branch Knights, and *An Fhiannaíocht*, dealing with Fionn Mac Cumhaill and the Fianna. There were also three principal sorrowful tales and a collection of proverbs in the form of triads. Music was of three types: *Suantraí* or sleeping music, *Goltraí* or weeping music and *Geantraí* or laughing music. When the Milesians, as the Gaels call themselves, first came to Ireland they encountered three queens of the De Danann, who were to give their names to the country: *Éire*, *Banba* and *Fódhla*.

This last conceit had inspired Cormac to write a poem soon after James succeeded Elizabeth on the throne of England. Believing that the Milesian son of Mary Queen of Scots would favour the Irish, he saw a new age dawning, not an age of poetic splendour – that would be the Age of *Fódhla* – nor a return to the worn-out Age of *Éire*, but the Age of *Banba*, in which there would be peace between Norman, Gael and Saxon and in which prosperity would replace the lean years of war and rapine. Needless to say, James proved to be more Protestant than Milesian, so that Cormac declared to me, "What more should we have expected from a man who surrendered O'Conor Don's grandfather, Brian O'Rourke, to Elizabeth and stood idly by while that same heretic queen beheaded his own mother?"

Yet, despite his disillusionment with English monarchs, Cormac was a firm believer in the mixture of bloods. "Do you know," he said to me one day, "that Niall, one of the greatest High Kings of Ireland – he brought back St Patrick after a raid on Britain – was the son of an Irish king, Eochaid Muigh-Medon, and an English princess, Caireann, who had been carried off on a previous raid? This Niall was the ancestor of the O'Neills, who were High Kings for six and a half centuries, until the coming of the Danes."

"But weren't the O'Conors the High Kings of Ireland?" I interjected.

"No! No!" Cormac spoke as if explaining some simple lesson to a dull pupil. "The first O'Conor to become High King was Turloch Mór. He made himself *Ard-rí* by the strong hand and the same was true of his son, Rory, the last High King – it was during his reign that Henry II and the Normans came. Anyway, to return to the point I was making about the intermingling of races, Richard De Burgh, the Norman conqueror of Connacht, married Hodierna, grand-daughter of Cathal Crovderg O'Conor, so all the great Burkes since then have Gaelic blood, and Red Hugh O'Donnell, who was O'Neill's chief ally in the last war, was the son of an Irish father and a Scots mother – Finola, daughter of MacDonnell. All the chief Gaelic families of Connacht, the O'Conors, the MacDermots, the O'Rourkes, have intermarried with the Normans, in particular the Burkes – Lady Mary is a MacWilliam Burke; her father, Sir Theobald, is the son of Richard 'the Iron' Burke and the Sea Queen Grania O'Malley – and, signs on it, they have produced generations of warriors. You can see the same result when you cross an English mare with an Irish stallion."

Here Cormac digressed to tell the story of how nine of Fionn

Mac Cumhaill's warriors had brought back a dark-grey stallion and a bay mare from a foray into England and how these two became the ancestors of the Fianna's horses. "Truth indeed," he added, "you are lucky that your father is Old English and your mother a Gael for you have a double richness in your blood that many of us lack."

At first I was somewhat taken aback by this association of my parents' marriage with horse breeding but, on reflection, I saw that Cormac had meant it as a compliment. Nevertheless, whatever the excellence of my bloodlines, it served little to win me the love of Maura. I tried to compose a poem to her in Gaelic that began:

> Blood-kindled flame of brightness;
> Waxen brow, grey shining eye!
> What joy that radiance which
> Distracts the world brims my sight!

Despite Cormac's teaching, however, the intricacies of Bardic verse, with its nine different forms of metre, had eluded me and concluding that the result would no more have impressed my beloved than a street ballad, I did not show it to her. I had one great success with my poetry, nevertheless, and it came about in this way.

One evening as I was discussing predestination with Theobald Dillon and MacDockwra outside the buttery, the Three Graces joined us. It was an opportunity to display the subtlety of my reasoning and I held forth with as much vigour as if I were taking part in a disputation in Trinity. "Take the story of Deirdre," I exclaimed. "Just before she was born, didn't Cathbad the Druid foretell that she would bring evil and calamity on Ulster? Now, how could he foretell something would happen if its future occurrence were not already ordained in the present? That shows that the ancient Irish believed in predestination."

"They also believed in the transmigration of souls, as we can see from the story of Tuan MacCarell," Theobald countered. "Does that mean that we should believe in it too?"

"Indeed," MacDockwra removed his pipe from his mouth, "some of us still do. The other day I spoke to a man below in Oran who maintained that a wife of his that he had waked and buried returned as a cat. He swore he could recognize her by her squint."

The Graces laughed at this sally and begged MacDockwra to tell them more.

"I hardly think that such pishogues are relevant," Theobald protested. "The point is that Charles is trying to give the Calvinist heresy an ancient foundation."

"I'm no Calvinist." Consciousness of Maura's gaze made my voice heated. "Surely a man can propound a doctrine without embracing it? Isn't that how Socrates sifted truth from error?"

"I didn't mean to imply that you are a Calvinist," Theobald replied, "only that the abominable creed which would assign a soul to heaven or hell at the moment of birth is the cornerstone of Calvinist doctrine. Why, many of your Protestant ministers consider themselves as the elect and us as the damned."

"Maybe the Puritan ones do," I conceded, "but they do not control the Reformed Church in Ireland."

"They soon will if the situation in England is anything to judge by," Theobald asserted. "Haven't they already got Archbishop Laud of Canterbury thrown into prison? How long will it be till the same happens to your own kinsman, Archbishop Ussher of Armagh?"

No doubt as he had intended, Theobald's display of knowledge in regard to my family connections undermined my confidence. Luckily, MacDockwra seized this opportunity to re-enter the lists.

"There's one Protestant at least who doesn't believe that all Catholics are destined to be damned," he informed his fair admirers. "I was talking to Teigue O'Reilly of Kilmore about a fortnight ago and he told me that he heard the Protestant Bishop in his area – Beadle I think he called him –"

"Bedell," I corrected. "Dr William Bedell."

"Well," MacDockwra released a puff of smoke out of the corner of his mouth, "he heard Bishop Bedell publicly rebuking a minister who referred to the Pope as the Antichrist. He also heard him speaking out against the tithes and other exactions poor Catholics are forced to pay. According to Teigue, if Bedell didn't dig with the left foot, he'd be the most popular man in Kilmore."

"One swallow doesn't make a summer," Theobald observed, "neither does one worthy bishop make a refutation of my argument. Isn't it true that in Twenty-Seven Archbishop Ussher along with twelve other bishops declared it a grievous sin to tolerate the religion of the Papists?"

"I don't know," I protested. "I was only seven years old then."

"A lame answer." Theobald was relentless.

"Well, Charles, what do you say to that?" Oona prompted.

"Yes, Charles," Isabel smiled, "are you leaving the field to Theobald?"

"We are straying from the point," I answered, meeting Maura's serene gaze. "If a person believes in predestination, it does not follow, *ipso facto*, that he believes that he himself is among the elect. Maybe we're all among the damned, even Theobald."

Before Theobald could respond, Brian Dubh approached from the entrance of the south-west tower, where he had been listening.

"Ladies," he said, "your supper is waiting." Then when the Three Graces had taken their leave he turned and remarked, "I see that Stanihurst is as usual full of windy talk but it will take more than Protestant rhetoric to win the Lady Maura."

To Dillon's credit, he seemed embarrassed by this crude insult and MacDockwra said, "The woman who cannot be won with words, be she Protestant or Catholic, isn't worth winning."

"That may be so," Brian Dubh retorted, "but there is a great difference between the baying of a wolfhound and the barking of a mongrel."

I refused to be drawn and, making an excuse, walked away but that night I decided to resort to the fiercest weapon of the Gaelic poets and wrote a satire in which I compared Brian Dubh to the Wild Boar of Ben Gulban, who had killed Diarmuid of the Love Spot. MacDockwra was greatly amused by my composition and read it aloud next evening in the Great Hall. If Brian Dubh had been thrown in a bed of nettles he could not have been stung more deeply. I understood then the wounding power of words, which could make the O'Haras cut out the tongue of Tadhg Dall O'Huiginn after he had written a satire about them. Brian Dubh did not cut out my tongue but he stormed from the Great Hall, vowing to pay me back for my presumption.

"Let him go," MacDockwra called out, "and when we massacre Castlerea in the great contest on Wednesday, we'll ask Charles here to write a poem in praise of our victory. By thunder, he has the makings of another Tadhg Dall!"

Chapter 13

BRIAN DUBH kept his word. The very next day Maura and Isabel left the castle early, accompanied by four armed Pursuers. I have no doubt that Brian Dubh had informed Lady Mary of my passion for her daughter and that she had decided to avoid any chance of its being returned. When I questioned Hugh he told me that Maura was returning to Castleburke in Mayo to resume her education.

"Charles," he looked at me with his frank eyes, "I know you admired her but she is promised to another man, a son of the Great O'Mulloy of Croghan. Don't be downcast. I have a girl in mind for you who will make you forget any girl you've ever seen."

I smiled wanly, trying to conceal the desolation in my soul. No girl would ever make me forget Maura's alabaster brow and clear grey eyes.

"Isabel must have been reluctant to part with you." I kept my voice light.

"Yes." A boyish grin spread over Hugh's face. "Between her and Oona I'm like a stag between two hinds. Maybe I should follow my ancestor Rory's example and marry them both."

For the rest of the day I tried to help Cormac with his history of the *Síol Muireadaigh* but my heart was not in the work. If Maura had been sent away, did it not indicate that she might have thought more highly of me than she had revealed? Should I follow her to Mayo and declare my love? No, I was deluding myself. Had she felt any tenderness towards me she would have sent some message. In her eyes I was no more than a poor, lovesick scholar and a Protestant one to boot. The shrieks of pigs being slaughtered for

99

the feast the next day was an echo of that thought screaming in my head.

"Why don't you help the others bring back green bushes?" Cormac noticed my wretchedness.

"What are they for?" I forced myself to respond.

"Pishogues!" Cormac snorted. "The people believe that if they carry them home on May Eve they ward off evil from their homes and ensure that the cows yield plenty of milk. To my mind it's just a pagan custom, an opportunity for the lads and girls to go awooing. Nevertheless, I did it myself when I was young, though more for the devilment than out of any belief in such matters. Maybe I'll wander round the bawn this evening to watch them setting up the bushes."

"Why is May Day celebrated so early here?" I asked.

"Oh, don't you know that we follow the Calendar of Pope Gregory?" Cormac sounded surprised. "I'm told it's more in harmony with the movements of the sun. Of course in the towns they still use the old calendar, just as you do in Dublin. If you were at home now, it would be – let me think ... Yes. Almost the middle of April."

If I were at home ... How far away Dublin with its teeming, cobbled streets, close-pressed houses and overhanging taverns seemed! *Tempus edax rerum* ... Somewhere in Mayo there was a castle which would soon shelter my beloved and here was I, cut off for ever from her presence, condemned to earn my living as a scribe ... If only I had continued to study law, as my father wanted ...

When I went out into the bawn the first things I noticed were the children and dogs crowded around the butcher's house to watch the carcasses of pigs, sheep and heifers being cut up. The nauseating smell of blood, intestines and scalded hides filled the air. Donal Bawn and Fergus emerged from the stable, leading two brood mares. When they saw me in my finery they sniggered. "*Procul o procul este, profani.*" Liquid twittering fell from the sky; I looked up and saw a lone swallow, slender winged and forktailed, gliding here and there. Summer's harbinger had arrived but what was that to me?

Not wishing to remain in the vicinity of the butcher's house, I walked to the western end of the bawn, where a group of barefooted urchins were engaged in mock fighting with blackthorn and ash sticks. They held the sticks about a quarter way from the end and wielded them like swords, cutting and parrying with great skill. "What are they practising for?" I asked Rury the Carpenter, who was calling out advice and encouragement.

"For the hurling contest with Castlerea tomorrow," he shouted. "You may be sure that whichever side wins, blood will flow afterwards. The last time we clashed with Castlerea there was a fight that lasted till sunset. Oh, there'll be great feats done!"

"But these boys are too young to fight," I objected.

"They're too young to join in the hurling but not to fight other boys," Rury assured me. "Look at that gosoon there! In a few years he'll be a true warrior. It's a great pity your own hand was bitten by the dog for you could be out practising now with Dudley's men."

Sensing a reproach in his voice, I drifted away to the kitchen, where the servants were busy with preparations for the feast. "Where is Shawn?" I asked Úna, who was moping by the fire.

"Oh, he went out to the North Field to watch the hurlers." She spoke without her usual cheerfulness.

"What's the matter, Úna?" I touched her arm.

"Nothing," she replied.

"I know that's not true," I persisted.

"Then you may as well know," she looked at me directly, "I heard the banshee last night."

"The banshee?"

"Shawn told me that it must have been a cat but no cat made the sounds I heard. There's going to be a death in this place, you mark my words. I always dread May Eve, for it's a time when the Good People from the raths are abroad and there's no telling what mischief they can get up to, but the banshee is the worst of all."

"I thought she only cried for certain families?"

"That's true. She cries for the great ones of the land. But my people are related by blood to the MacDermots of Corrslieve and Shawn's mother was a MacWilliam. Oh, Charles, there's a weight of dread on my heart – will you promise me not to let Shawn out of your sight tomorrow? Promise."

I assured her that I would not leave Shawn's side and tried to convince her that there was no truth in pishogues, yet as I left the kitchen some of her fear followed me like a dark shadow.

The hurling contest was held on the level stretch where we had finished the race. People thronged both sides of the playing area, the *Lóipínigh*, as Cormac called them, in their coarse homespuns mingling freely with the brightly dressed ladies and gentlemen. Hawkers sold wizened apples, dried *duileasc* and griddle cakes; pipers played sheepskin pipes; tinkers called on passers-by to find the shell with the pea under it or to put a wooden pin in a looped belt and barefooted girls hopped and skipped, while small boys followed by barking mongrels chased each other with excited screams.

Behind the west gap, there was an ale-wagon surrounded by men and women; riders raced each other on shaggy garrons and horseboys carrying blackthorns or ashplants swaggered about with insolent looks. Many of the wilder-looking men also carried sticks but despite this martial display, the air was filled with an excited, cheerful babble.

I strolled around with Shawn Bacach and Cormac, enjoying the strangeness and colour of the gathering and occasionally risking a halfpenny on the Trick-o'-the-Loop or Find-the-Pea. Suddenly Shawn gripped my arm. "Look over there!" he whispered.

I followed his gaze and, to my amazement, saw a number of armed English horsemen; Sir Charles Coote the Younger trotted at their head, while sitting sideways behind him, her arm about his waist, was none other than Beibhinn.

"Isn't she the shameless damsel?" Cormac snorted. "To think that she could associate with that devil! Don't so much as nod to her, Charles."

I was in a quandary. Beibhinn had given me love yet to become the mistress of a Coote, as her behaviour proclaimed, was in the eyes of her own people a most heinous betrayal. Nevertheless, Sir Charles was a nobleman and, despite his dour appearance, handsome. It was easy to see how the attentions of such a man would have turned the head of a chambermaid. Taking into account that it was my dalliance with her that had brought her to this pass, was I now justified in slighting her?

But why had she and Sir Charles come to Ballintober? Did she wish to flaunt her lover before the O'Conors or did he expect her to point out wanted men? I watched her pass in front of me dressed in rich apparel, her girlish face half proud, half defiant. For a moment I felt an almost uncontrollable urge to hail her; then the riders were gone and with them the moment for action. It was likely she hadn't seen me or, if she had, had not recognized me in my new clothes.

"Hasn't Coote great courage to come here?" I observed, removing my wide-brimmed hat to wipe my brow.

"Oh, he knows that as long as he doesn't interfere with our people he won't be attacked." Shawn Bacach spat.

"Though to give the New Foreigners their due they never lacked courage," Cormac added. "There they go now, down past the village. I doubt that they'll be back."

By this time the contest was in full career. Two dry stone gaps, each not more than three feet wide by four feet high, had been built facing each other about fifty perches apart and these were defended by the hurlers, the Castlerea troop taking the east gap and the Ballintober troop the gap nearest the village. There were at least one hundred young men on the field, many of them wearing only breeches and brogues because of the warm afternoon sun. The *sliotar* was made of horsehair mixed with beeswax and this hard ball the players struck with their camáns, sending it whizzing towards the opposite gap.

Never have I seen anything to match the speed and dexterity with which the men sent the *sliotar* back and forth between them, picking it up with their camáns before hitting it or simply driving it along the ground as is done in hockey. Frequently two camáns would strike together with a resounding clash, which might shatter one or both. At other times the *sliotar* would come dropping down from the sky to be met with a dozen upraised camáns. Before long there were curses and scuffles as opponents in the heat of combat struck each other, either accidentally or deliberately.

Shawn Bacach kept drawing my attention to outstanding feats of skill performed by our men and dastardly actions resorted to by their attackers, in particular by Dudley's brother, Tomás Láidir, a black-haired man of small stature but of amazing strength and speed. At the same time Cormac might be recounting how Setanta had single-handedly bested the boy-corps of Emain Macha in hurling or how a battle fought between the Firbolg and the Tuatha De Danann on the Plain of Magh Nia, south of Abbeyboyle, had begun with a hurling match, something which didn't seem implausible in the light of what was happening before us. It even occurred to me that the hurlers could well be the metal from which O'Conor

Don and his brother, Hugh Oge, would quickly forge a company of foot soldiers, should the need ever arise. That might explain Dudley's real purpose in coming to Ballintober.

During a lull in the play I asked Cormac how victory was determined.

"It depends on what the leaders have agreed to," he said. "Today the first troop to get nine *cúl* will be given the cask of ale."

"Upon my word," Shawn Bacach declared, "if our men don't rally soon, it won't be they who will drink it. Castlerea have scored eight *cúl* already and Dudley's heroes have only repaid them seven times. Wake up, men, or the day will be lost!" he bawled suddenly.

Though Úna's story about the banshee and Beibhinn's return with Coote had filled my mind with foreboding, I tried to give my full attention to the contest. As far as I could judge, the outstanding champions in the Ballintober troop were Dudley, MacDockwra and Rory O'Cahan, while, next to Tomás Láidir, the greatest champions in the Castlerea troop were Daniel O'Conor, Hugh Oge's son, and Fiachra O'Flynn, who, Cormac declared, was a cousin of mine.

After one skirmish, MacDockwra lifted the *sliotar* on his camán and sent it soaring up the field, where Dudley caught it in his left hand. Turning smoothly he found himself beset by a dozen Castlerea men, one of whom struck him a treacherous blow with his camán on the knee but not before he had sent the *sliotar* low and hard through the eastern gap. While Dudley was being carried off, moaning with pain, his men renewed the attack and in its wake the Castlerea hurler who had injured him was left writhing on the ground. Across the field I could recognize Oona by her amber hair among the group of women bending over Dudley and for an instant my heart missed a beat, thinking that Maura might be with her.

Meanwhile, Tomás Láidir was exhorting his troop to launch a counter-attack. With his mane of glossy black hair falling about his eyes, he played with the energy of a demon, circling, closing, cleaving, meeting every charge of the Ballintober men head on, springing into the centre of every scrimmage, pursuing his opponents with relentless ferocity. If he was not as graceful a hurler as his brother, he was more dangerous, a wolf fighting greyhounds with all a wolf's savagery. Shawn Bacach cursed him for his dangerous use of the camán when he felled MacDockwra, who had robbed him of the *sliotar*, but Tomás did not hear. He was in a world of his own, smelling victory, determined to gain it.

Hugh O'Conor caught the *sliotar* in his left hand and deftly tapped it to O'Cahan. Instantly Tomás swooped, knocked Rory's camán from his hand with a savage blow; then, balancing the *sliotar* at the end of his own camán, he cut and wove through our men like a hawk through sparrows. Hugh tried to stop him but he easily shouldered him aside, steadied himself then drove the *sliotar* humming through the west gap.

With a deafening cheer the Castlerea people came flooding across the field. They hoisted Tomás on their shoulders and carried him around in a great circle of victory. This was too much for the Ballintober horseboys, who regarded Tomás as their mortal enemy. Soon blackthorns and ashplants were being wielded on every side and the air was filled with barbaric war cries, the clashing of stick against stick and the terrified screaming of women.

For those who have never experienced the blind malignity of a fighting mass of people it will be difficult to comprehend the panic which now possessed me. Here I was, trapped in a maelstrom of threshing, charging bodies and while my mind urged me to break free, my conscience told me I could not desert my aged companions. To add to my predicament, Shawn Bacach, instead of cowering, started to challenge the enemy. Fortunately, most of his hearers ignored him but a group of long-haired savages dressed in goatskin doublets and greasy frieze breeches took offence at his taunts and in an instant we were surrounded.

"Come on if ye're fit to fight, ye cowardly bodachs!" Ignoring my pleas, Shawn waved his stick in the air.

"Shut your gob, old cripple, or we'll brain you!" they shouted.

"Aye, the way you tried to brain our leader, you shleeveens. If it weren't for your treachery we'd have gained the victory!"

"Not likely, Shawn Bacach," one of them replied. "Wasn't it yourself left your wife beyond in Carra and took another in Moylurg? Don't talk to us of treachery."

"The curse of Bingham on ye for a pack of wild Mayo gets!" Shawn rushed at them in fury. I can still hear the horrible sound of sticks against bone and the choking cry that escaped from the old gallowglass's lips as he sank to the ground. Immediately his attackers withdrew and Cormac and I rushed to our fallen companion. Oh God, what a sight awaited us! The skin of his crown was like one great open wound, while his eyes had rolled back in his head.

What happened next I cannot say because the world swam around me. Cormac told me later that I held Shawn's hand, pleading with him over and over to speak to me. Eventually O'Conor Don and Badger Face rode up and their presence put an end to the fighting. Shawn, now moaning feebly, was carried home on a horse-drawn cart, his head cradled on my lap. Owen the Fear Leighis succeeded in restoring him to full consciousness and within an hour he was able, with Owen and Úna's help, to make his way back to his room in the south-west tower.

As for me, my new clothes were crusted with blood and I was expected to attend the banquet that evening. Added to this worry was the awareness that I had failed Shawn Bacach in his hour of need. Was I fated to betray every person that trusted in me? It was Brighid who soothed my conscience, pointing out that, unlike Shawn's attackers, I had been unarmed, without even the short skean that most men carried in their belts.

"There's no shame in being a man of peace," she assured me, "for, despite what others may think, that's the most difficult path to follow."

I wanted with all my heart to believe her.

Chapter 14

THE GREAT HALL, lighted not only by its wheel-like chandelier but also by candles set in tall wooden standards, was transformed into a magic cavern filled with talk and laughter. Bright banners distracted the eye from the torn Flemish tapestry, logs blazed in the large open fireplace and glass goblets and silver dishes sparkled on the cloth-covered, raised table at which the O'Conors and their kin sat. The long table had been moved closer to the hearth and between it and the back wall had been placed a line of trestle tables covered with large boards to form a continuous surface. All the tables were laden with food: heaps of freshly baked cakes, trays of meat and bowls of troander.

Most of those present were unknown to me so as we waited for Brian Dubh to conduct us to our seats, Cormac pointed out the chief guests: Hugh Oge O'Conor and his wife Jane, daughter of Lord Dillon; Brian Roe O'Conor and his wife Mary, daughter of O'Conor Roe; Anne, the widow of O'Conor Don's dead brother, Cathal; her sister Eleanor with her husband Cathal Roe MacDermot of Moylurg; O'Conor Roe of Castleruby and many others whom I now forget. A harper sat on a stool near the fire, plucking the brass strings with his long, curved fingernails; servants hurried here and there carrying heaped trays or leather wine jugs and two wolfhounds wandered about eating whatever morsels fell to the floor.

"Ah, Cormac!" Ignoring me, Brian Dubh led the ollamh to a place near the head of the long table where Theobald Dillon presided. I saw Lady Mary pointing me out to Hugh Oge's wife, who was Theobald Dillon's cousin, and thought what an absurd figure I must have seemed standing there in the blue taffeta doublet and black velvet breeches Hugh had loaned me till my own suit should be washed. Indeed, I regretted having come at all, despite Hugh's vow to show me a girl who would make me forget his sister. How could any girl surpass Maura in comeliness and grace? Her clear grey eyes and noble countenance would always be a lamp searing my soul.

At that moment Hugh caught sight of me. "Charles!" he cried, approaching. "You're the very person I was waiting for!" Taking my arm, he guided me to a place near the centre of the trestle tables, between MacDockwra and a girl dressed in red velvet. She was about fifteen, with large grey-brown eyes, soft, dark brown hair and full red lips. Her skin, though freckled, was creamy white suffused with pink and her nose turned up ever so slightly.

"Meet Frances, daughter of Patrick French-Fitzstephens, steward to the Earl of Clanricarde." Hugh laid his hand lightly on her neck, above the white lace collar. "Frances, this is my friend Charles Stanihurst, grand-nephew of Richard, the Jesuit scholar, and cousin of James Ussher, the Archbishop of Armagh. He's helping O'Mulconry to write our history."

"I'm only his scribe," I protested, secretly pleased by Hugh's graciousness. With a bashful smile Frances made a space for me on the long bench.

"Now, Charles, you must act with decorum," Hugh bantered. "Her father and mother are seated over there opposite my cousin Daniel." He nodded towards Theobald's table. Even at a brief glance I couldn't help noticing how much younger than her husband Frances's mother seemed. She was a sweet-faced, shapely woman of about thirty-three, while he was a tall, aloof-looking greybeard in a plumed hat.

"Why aren't you sitting with your parents?" I asked when Hugh had withdrawn to the head of the table.

"Oh, I'm old enough to sit by myself," Frances pouted. Her voice was low and soft, not unlike Maura's but without its coolness. At that moment I lost my heart, lost it completely. "To judge from your accent, you're not Irish." She held a piece of bread daintily in her fingers.

"What!" I feigned indignation. "Surely you don't regard Dublin people as foreigners?"

"Oh, I meant no offence." Her confusion was bewitching. "I like the way you speak Gaelic and, anyway, I'm half-foreign myself."

"How is that?" I did not conceal my surprise.

"Well, my mother is from England. She came to Ireland with the Earl of Clanricarde's household – she was chambermaid to Anne, Sir Ulick's wife, before he succeeded his father as Earl and when the family visited Portumna my mother accompanied them. Now we live in Ballytrasna, beside Abbeyboyle."

"My mother was a chambermaid too," I confessed. "She worked for the O'Mulloys of Croghan."

"I know the O'Mulloy family; Croghan is only a two hours' ride from Ballytrasna. Eleanor, daughter of O'Mulloy – that fair-haired woman above Hugh patting her brow with a handkerchief – is sister-in-law to my friend Oona, daughter of MacDermot." She indicated Oona, who was now seated at the raised table beside O'Conor Roe, dressed in a green open-fronted gown and buff skirt, which greatly became her.

"Why does Oona wear men's clothes?" I asked.

"So you know her then," she observed.

I told her how I had encountered the Three Graces, though I did not reveal my infatuation for Maura.

"Oona finds it easier to ride and hunt in doublet and breeches," she said. "Anyway, nobody in Moylurg minds how she dresses, least of all her brother Turlough."

"Does your mother miss England?" Sensing a rebuke, I changed the subject.

"Yes, she often talks about Barnet, where she grew up – that's a village north of London. Perhaps you've heard of the Fair of Barnet?"

I confessed that I hadn't, then brought the conversation back to her parents. She told me that her father had been raised in Galway city but had come to Roscommon at the desire of the Earl of Clanricarde, who had many quarters of land scattered throughout the county.

"You must be careful that he doesn't see you talking too much to me," she cautioned. "He would kill you."

"In that case I would gladly risk death." I cut another slice of roast pork from the bone on my platter. She smiled, a slow smile that made her brownish-grey eyes sparkle and parted her lips over even, white teeth.

"You are the most beautiful girl here tonight," I heard myself say.

"I'm not beautiful," she blushed, "at least not half so beautiful as Oona."

I glanced again at Oona, whose long amber tresses were set off by the green gown, yet for all her magnificence, I would not put her ahead of my companion.

"You are both beautiful in different ways," I declared. "She is a bright flame but you are a still pool glimmering in the moonlight."

"Oh, so you're a poet," she teased. "That's amusing because Oona's admirer is a poet too – Tomás MacCostello. Do you know him?"

"No, but I saw him playing today." I held my pewter goblet poised near my lips. "I'm surprised that a demon like that should be a poet or think himself worthy of such a lady."

"Hush!" she warned. "He's sitting just below you, on the other side of that man."

Turning, I could hear Tomás berating MacDockwra: "What use is your knowledge of Virgil? It won't stop the wolves howling or put a halter on the wind."

"If we don't learn these things," MacDockwra protested, "we'll be no better than wolves ourselves."

Frances and I smiled, enjoying the apt retort; then we turned our attention once more to the platters before us, only pausing now and then to peruse each other's faces. The delicious roast pork, the fresh oaten bread, the claret and the proximity of my sweet, young companion so worked on my mind that I felt like a person transported to a world where there was only beauty and delight, the music of the harp mingling with the contented babble of Gaelic. If somebody were to tell me that within a twelvemonth that world would be shattered beyond repair, I would have dismissed him as a dawcock. While the troander, a delicious whey made with buttermilk and sweet milk, was being spooned out into smaller wooden bowls, I feasted my eyes on my companion, noting how her brown hair wreathed itself about her smooth, white neck and how her little shell-like ear peeped from beneath it. Everything about her, from her swelling bosom to her soft, rounded chin, was at once girlish and enticing.

It was a disappointment when the meal came to an end and we had to give our attention to the music of O'Connellan, who played interminable airs I had never heard before – at one point MacDockwra, challenging Tomás Láidir to another hurling contest in Castleruby, had to be hushed into silence before the offended harpist would continue. Shawn Rua's son, Seamus, while refilling our goblets, whispered, "I have something for you," then hurried away. Under cover of the applause, I hastened to the wine barrel at the back of the hall, where Seamus handed me a folded sheet of paper tied with ribbon. On opening it, I discovered a letter written in misspelt Gaelic:

> Charles, you will understand the risk I take in communicating with you. Sir Charles Coote the Younger has been good to me and offered me protection when my own people turned against me. He is not a man to cross but for the sake of the love you gave me I must.
>
> You are in great danger. The President, Lord Ranelagh, and his counsellors know that you killed a man in Dublin. How they came by this information I cannot ascertain but suspect Brian Dubh. Yet, on their first meeting with you, Lord Ranelagh and Sir Chidley were alerted, for you told them you were travelling to Kilmore to see Bishop Bedell and Kilmore is in East Brefni, not in Connacht. Needless to say, they have questioned me about you but I have not allowed myself to be drawn. Shawn Rua is still held in Athlone Castle. Beyond that I know nothing of his fate, except that he has been offered his freedom if he will give evidence against O'Conor Don – I overheard Lord Ranelagh say as much to Charles. Father Bernardine, the young priest they tortured, died last week of the malignant fever.
>
> Footsteps approach! Farewell. Remember me with kindness. From my chamber in Castlecoote, this twentieth day of April. Beibhinn.

The following message was scribbled at the end of the page:

> I am in O'Beirne's alehouse, where the men are looking for Seamus, son of Shawn Rua. If they capture him they will use him to break his father. They are also enquiring after

you, having failed to espy you at the hurling. Fly, Charles,
before it is too late. I am entrusting this letter to O'Beirne.
In haste, God protect you always, B.

You may imagine the flurry of emotions that assailed me on receiving this warning. A gust of cold air pierced the warm glow enveloping my mind. What if Frances learned that I was a murderer? Surely fate could not be so cruel as to kill my happiness at the very moment of its birth? I turned to question Seamus but he was now pouring wine for O'Conor Don and Lady Mary. Observing Frances gazing in my direction, I concealed the letter in my doublet and returned to her side.

"What were you reading? A love note?" She gave me her slow, beguiling smile.

"Indeed it wasn't!" I protested. "It was from a person who had news for me about the young priest who was tortured," and I told her how I had seen Father Bernardine arrested on the day I had passed through Athlone and how he had since died.

"May his soul be on God's right hand." She blessed herself; then, perceiving that I did not follow suit, a puzzled look crossed her face.

"Amen," I murmured, reluctant to confirm that I was a Protestant. As if sensing my unease, she smiled and laid her hand trustingly on mine. I turned my palm upward and when her soft fingers rested on it, my senses swooned.

After that, the night was dreamlike with enchantment. MacDermot's daughter, known as Oona Bawn because of her pale yellow hair, sang "Deirdre's Farewell to Alba", accompanying herself on the lute, and at the insistence of the gathering, she followed it with "Eileen Aroon", a love song in which the singer urges Eileen to flee with him from her father's castle and she complies. No sooner had Oona finished than Tomás Láidir was on his feet, warbling an invitation to a young woman to lay aside her weapons, these weapons being her curling tresses, her bright glance and her white bosom. There was no doubt that the song was intended for Oona, who smiled with pleasure at every verse, much to the annoyance of her brother, Cathal Roe, a powerful, red-bearded man of about thirty-five, whose flushed face showed that he had drunk too freely. He whispered something to his wife and soon afterwards she and Oona left the hall. That Tomás Láidir took their departure as a snub could be inferred from the loud way he called out to Brian Dubh to bring usquebagh instead of "that cursed claret".

To divert attention, Hugh called on me to sing and though somewhat befuddled, I launched into Marlowe's "Come Live with Me and Be my Love". O'Connellan, quickly mastering the air, helped me along on his harp and Frances smiled with delight whenever I met her eye. Most of those present understood English so there were cries of "*Goirm thú!*" when I finished but I would not risk a second performance. MacDockwra now caused great merriment with a song in which he gave advice to a couple on their wedding night and another in which he made fun of an old man with a young wife. Frances joined freely in the laughter, either because she regarded such bawdiness as natural or, as seemed more likely, because she was too innocent to understand MacDockwra's allusions.

Other singers followed with as much diversity as a dawn chorus: lusty drinking songs, mournful elegies, fierce satires and gentle songs of praise. Hugh sang "Róisín Dubh", a song in which Ireland is addressed as a beautiful, dark-haired woman, and there was such emotion in his voice that he brought tears to many eyes. "Tomás Láidir's father composed that," Frances whispered. I resolved then that Tomás and I would become friends.

Now the gathering pressed Cormac to recite and accompanied by O'Connellan on the harp, he began a long address in verse to the O'Conor family, praising their bravery, generosity and loyalty to the Milesian race; there was not the equal of Calvagh for nobility nor of Lady Mary for graciousness but it was Hugh who would outshine them both for he would restore the glories gained by his illustrious ancestors, Cathal Crovderg, Rory and Turloch Mór. Everybody applauded, though more out of tribute to their hosts than out of admiration for Cormac's long-windedness.

About midnight the ladies rose to retire to their chambers, Lady Mary alone remaining seated. Determined to accompany Frances, I rose too. Frances's mother seemed pleased that there was a man to escort her and her daughter to the New Tower, French-Fitzstephens having no inclination to bestir himself. She smiled when I took Frances's arm and I could see that she had a soft, gracious disposition, which must have won many a heart.

"Theobald Dillon informs me you're a Palesman," she remarked as we made our way past the frowning Brian Dubh.

"My mother is from Ballinlough." I wondered what else Theobald had said. "Frances told me that you come from London."

"Yes." Her expression grew pensive. "I left in the same year that Her Majesty Queen Henrietta Maria arrived from France."

"What persuaded you to leave Shakespeare's 'sceptr'd isle' for this barbaric land?" I asked in English.

"The recusancy fines." She spoke English with a musical London accent. "I lived in dread of being exposed as a Papist."

"But isn't Queen Henrietta Maria a Catholic?" I said.

"Yes," she agreed, "but she's not well loved in England. When Lady Anne and Sir Ulick de Burgh asked me to accompany them to Portumna, I –"

She left the sentence unfinished. We were descending the torch-lit stairs and had encountered Badger Face coming up. He stared at me disapprovingly, bowed to my companions; then, squeezing past us, he continued on his way.

"Who is that?" Frances's mother reverted to Irish.

"A wine merchant," I replied in the same language, "or so at least I'm told."

"I'm certain it's His Lordship the Bishop of Elphin," she said in her frank English manner. "They say he wears a Franciscan habit under his clothes. He's a very saintly man."

Her words did not come as a shock because I already suspected that Badger Face was a priest; that he was, in addition, a bishop would explain his power over the rabble that afternoon. No wonder he disliked me, a Dublin Protestant who had masqueraded as a priest! Well, he himself was masquerading as a merchant, so I would continue to regard him as such.

As we stepped out into the chill night air, the sights and sounds that assailed our senses were such as one might expect in hell. A large bonfire had been lit in the middle of the street, around whose crimson flames men, women and children danced and sang like demons to the music of a piper, while others staggered about in extreme stages of intoxication. Now and again some lout would emit a hoarse, barbaric yell that would be answered by his fellow revellers. Dogs slunk here and there avoiding thrashing feet and in the shadows of the branch-decorated houses standing couples swayed in lustful embraces.

Placing my arm around Frances's shoulder, I tried to shield her from the shameless spectacle. "If that man is a bishop, surely he wouldn't tolerate this bacchanalia?" I observed to her mother.

"It's May Day," she replied. "Don't you think, Charles, that the Bishop is wise enough to realize that old customs must be tolerated? People can't always be on their knees praying, though the Puritans in our towns and cities would like them to be."

"Forgive me Mistress French-Fitzstephens." I was glad the night hid my crimson face. "It was the Protestant in me that spoke."

"Queen Henrietta Maria's father was a Protestant," she replied, "and yet he decided that Paris was well worth a Mass. Maybe one day, Charles, you will find something that is worth a Mass."

I realized that she was alluding to Frances and my pulse raced. Yet, when she learned that I was a murderer, would she still consider me a proper suitor? In a fit of desperation, I decided to recount everything that had befallen me in Dublin.

"Mistress French-Fitzstephens –" I began.

"Oh, Charles," she laid her hand on my arm, "why don't you address me simply as Emily? That's what Hugh and Theobald do, and I prefer the Irish way."

Emboldened by this proof of favour, I was about to begin again when I felt Frances start. Next moment somebody was blocking our path. In the lurid light from the bonfire, I recognized Donal Bawn.

Chapter 15

"SO IT'S Diarmuid of the Love Spot!" Donal Bawn's voice was slurred with ale. "I see you've got yourself two women this time. It didn't take you long to forget Beibhinn."

"Out of my way!" Emboldened by Frances's presence I made to brush past him and his two comrades, the grinning Fergus and another horseboy whose name I didn't know.

"Not so fast, Palesman," Donal Bawn swung his fist at my head. I sidestepped to avoid the blow but in doing so almost knocked Frances over.

"Run!" I yelled at her and her mother. "Run to the New Tower!"

Donal Bawn charged. I ducked and hit him under the ribs with my fist. He grunted, pretended to double up; then he lashed out with his brogue. Fortunately he was too drunk to take proper aim. Grasping his raised leg, I heaved and sent him toppling. When he rose there was a skean gleaming in his right hand. Horror seized me. Death was only a few feet away, yet people continued to carouse, unaware of my plight.

"So you're too cowardly to fight like a man!" I mocked, hoping to shame him into dropping the skean.

"How dare you call me a coward, you Protestant whoreson," he snarled.

In that instant my mind became as clear as a crystal spring. "Now you must pay for the Englishman you killed," my conscience reminded me. "An eye for an eye ..." Surprisingly, I was more afraid for Frances than for myself; she had halted her flight and was screaming for help. Alarmed by her outcry, Fergus and the other horseboy took to their heels. Gradually a hush descended on the crowd. As the bolder revellers approached, Donal Bawn sprang. Instinctively, I raised my arm to shield my face.

"*Fág an bealach!*" With a bloodcurdling yell somebody hurled himself on my attacker. I staggered back. Donal Bawn let out a startled curse. The skean clattered on the stones and two inter-locked bodies crashed to the ground, where they rolled over and over. There was a sickening crunch as of bones breaking and Tomás Láidir rose from his moaning adversary.

"Are you all right?" His voice as he addressed me was quite un-ruffled.

"Yes," I said. "How did you happen to be nearby?"

"Hugh told me to keep an eye on you and Frances." He picked up Donal Bawn's skean.

I thanked him for saving my life; then, pushing through the cir-cle of onlookers and taking Frances by the arm, I hastened to the New Tower, where her mother was anxiously waiting.

"Oh that ruffian!" Emily cried. "You were so brave to tackle him."

"Your sleeve is wet," Frances exclaimed. "Oh, Charles, it's blood!"

On touching my left arm I discovered a shallow wound near the elbow where the skean must have opened the flesh.

"It's just a scratch." I was pleased with her concern.

"Nevertheless, you had better come with us." Emily led me up to a richly furnished bedroom on the second floor, which her fam-ily was sharing with the MacDermots. Oona and her brother's wife, Lady Eleanor, were playing cards by the fire with Mary, the wife of Brian Roe O'Conor, and they helped Emily clean and ban-dage my arm. While the women fussed over me, I noticed that the room had two pallets, in addition to the large curtained bedstead, and that there was also an oak settle long enough to sleep a man. Where, I wondered, did Frances sleep? Then I pushed the thought out of my mind. She was busy now, washing my torn doublet sleeve, her delicate hands immersed in the bloodstained water.

"And you're certain Donal Bawn isn't dead?" Oona said to me.

"No," I assured her, "though he deserves no pity."

"I wasn't anxious on his account." Oona's gaze dropped.

"She's thinking of the wrestler that Tomás Láidir killed in

Sligo," her sister-in-law, a buxom, fresh-faced woman, explained. "That sort of deed wins little honour."

"Yes." Oona's blue eyes flashed. "It's honourable to kill a man with a sword but not with your bare hands."

An image of the Englishman's head striking the wall flashed into my mind and I grimaced. Luckily Frances was drying my doublet sleeve before the fire and did not look up. Suffering from the effect of the wine, I requested permission to visit the garderobe. When I eventually returned there was a chill silence as if the women had been arguing.

"Did you know my mother, Norah, daughter of O'Flynn?" I asked Lady Eleanor in order to relieve the tension. "She was working in your house when she met my father."

"To tell the truth, I was just a child then," Lady Eleanor looked at me keenly, "though I have heard my parents speaking of the brown-haired chambermaid who won the heart of the Dublin merchant. Your father, it seems, created great excitement with his line of packhorses and his gillies. You must have inherited his bold spirit."

"Hush, you'll make him conceited," Emily chided. She was sewing my doublet sleeve, the needle and thread passing through the cloth with great rapidity. "Have you many brothers and sisters, Charles?"

I told her about my family, silently praying that she would not ask why I had left them. She must have sensed my unease because she turned the conversation to what the young women of Dublin were wearing and how they arranged their hair. I assured her that they dressed much as she and her friends did, though some of the more religious women favoured plain dark frocks with white linen collars and white bonnets.

"That's how they dress in Abbeyboyle." Emily bit through the thread with her even, white teeth.

"They always remind me of crows," Lady Eleanor chuckled, "so dull and sober."

"Here, Charles, the sleeve is a little damp but you can put it on." Emily helped me into the doublet, taking care not to hurt my arm. "At least nobody will mistake you for a crow in this plumage."

"What does it matter what a person wears?" Oona demanded. "I find the Puritan dress most becoming." Nobody made any rejoinder to this.

Promising her mother to hurry back, Frances accompanied me down the stairs. Now that we were alone in the dimly lit entrance I was so overcome by the loveliness of the girl beside me that I grew tongue-tied. "Would you like to meet me tomorrow?" I blurted out at last.

"Yes." She laid her head against my shoulder and as if she were a newly opened rose, I inhaled the sweet scent of her hair. My senses swam. Blindly I lowered my face to hers. When our lips touched a joy that was almost pain coursed through me. Filled with wonder, I kissed her soft cheeks, her rounded chin, her closed eyes and little ears. Then she was gone, and I was walking out into the bawn, lighthearted with ecstasy.

"A word with you, sir!" The authoritative tone more than the words themselves halted me in my tracks. Badger Face approached from the direction of the weaver's house, which was close to the New Tower.

"Yes?" I tried to keep my voice even.

"I feel I must speak to you about your conduct." His form was black against the red glow of the bonfire. "You have already been responsible for two young ladies being sent away from here and this moment I have just left the bedside of that unfortunate nephew of Phelim the Weaver, who had his ribs cracked because of you – no, hear me out. I'm not implying that you are personally to blame but your pursuit of another young lady obviously rekindled his jealousy."

"That wasn't my fault," the unfairness of his attack filled me with indignation, "though I'm sure Donal Bawn has convinced you it was."

"Be that as it may," he replied, "I am more concerned with the reputation of the young lady in question. Don't you think she's a little young for a man of the world like yourself?"

"If her mother didn't object to my being with Frances, why should you?"

"Perhaps her mother knows less about you than I do."

"If you're referring to what happened in Dublin; that was an accident."

"An accident incurred by your neglect of your studies while you frequented taverns. Do you wish to be known as a corrupter of young women?"

"If you're concerned for the virtue of young women, why don't you tell those damsels over there to stop what they're doing and go home? Or is my real offence the fact that I don't believe in the teachings of Rome?"

"I don't question your beliefs, only your readiness to lead others into error. Because of you O'Cairnen's daughter is now the mistress of that arch-heretic Coote. Even should your intentions towards this other young lady be honourable, would you consent to adopt her faith? No, you would do as your father did, lead her into the fold of Luther. But I suspect you're less interested in marriage than in satisfying your own lust."

"You are being unjust, sir. My father never asked my mother to renounce her faith or to attend services in the Reformed Church. Surely you of all men should not judge a man you have never met – or have you never read the words of Our Saviour: 'Judge not, that ye be not judged'?"

"Well spoken!" Tomás Láidir stepped from the shadow of the buttery, where he had obviously been listening. "Good night, my Lord Bishop. Cool for this time of year, isn't it?"

Badger Face glared at him; then, without uttering a word, he raised his left hand in admonition and strode away.

"Is he really a bishop?" I asked.

"Of course!" Tomás spoke in the loud tones of the inebriated. "That reverend gentleman is Doctor Boetius Egan, Lord Bishop of Elphin ... forced to go in disguise because of you Lutheran heretics. You ought to be hung, drawn and quartered for ... for bandying words with him – but I forgive you. I too have drawn the ire of His Lordship. He accused me of trying to kill the horseboy – as if I would do such ... such an unchristian act. Wait a minute –" and he turned his back and began to urinate on the street, oblivious of the people dancing round the bonfire.

"Why did you stay out here?" I kept my eyes fixed on the orange half-moon gazing in wonder down on us.

"That's easily answered." Tomás turned around. "I was waiting for a glimpse of the fair Oona. Did you by chance lay eyes on her during your visit to the New Tower?"

I gave him a brief account of what had happened in the bedchamber, emphasising Oona's concern for his reputation, which pleased him greatly.

"And yet she won't stand with me against her family." His

voice was sombre – leading me to suspect that he might be less drunk than he pretended. "No matter! No matter! Come on, my bold lover, let's return to the feast!"

"No." I feigned a yawn. "I just want to sleep."

"Sleep! You can sleep enough when you're in the grave. Tonight let us keep the meadar dancing," and he gave me a slap on the back that left me breathless.

Before returning to the Great Hall we visited Shawn Bacach in his small dark room. He was asleep on a bed of straw, a coarse blanket wrapped around him, his head wounds covered with a poultice held in place by bloodstained bandages. The light from our candle woke him. At first he did not recognize me, then his eyes grew steady.

"Charles," his voice was a hoarse whisper, "you'll be burying me soon in the abbey beyond. It's little I thought I'd ever be returning to Mayo but it's where I was born and it's where I want my bones to lie."

I tried to persuade him that he would soon be well again but he only squeezed my hand then closed his eyes. Presently he opened them and murmured, "We should have greeted Beibhinn; it wasn't right to turn our backs on her."

With a start, I recalled the letter but on searching my doublet I found it was gone. It must have fallen out during the fight with Donal Bawn or else when Frances removed my doublet. If Brian Dubh got his hands on it, Beibhinn's life would be in danger.

"Did you find a letter down in the bawn?" I asked Tomás.

"No," he replied. "Can we go now? Your friend is asleep."

Feeling like a person who is dreaming, I tiptoed out after Tomás. "What did he mean by saying he'll be buried in the abbey beyond?" I asked as we made our way cautiously along the narrow passage.

"Oh, he must be referring to Ballintober Abbey, not far from Castleburke."

"Is that the Castleburke where Hugh's uncle, Viscount Burke, lives?"

"Yes. Hugh's sister, Maura, is over there since May Eve. Dudley told me she had to be sent away because of some besotted gallant."

"How is Dudley now?" I decided it was better to change the subject.

"Ah, there's nothing wrong with him that a few day's rest won't cure. It would take more than the blow of a camán to cripple that playboy." Despite his mocking tone, I sensed that he admired his younger brother.

When we stepped into the Great Hall it was filled with lusty babble and acrid tobacco smoke. Lady Mary had left and the only woman present was Úna, who was standing by a window alcove with a wooden dish on which a few long-stemmed clay pipes were laid. O'Conor Don was on his feet, his goblet raised.

"To the health of His Gracious Majesty, Charles, King of England, Scotland and Ireland," he called out.

"With the exception of Connacht!" Tomás Láidir added in a loud voice. "The King's writ never ran west of the Shannon."

There was a moment of consternation; then some guests drank, while others sat in uneasy silence.

"If the King's writ never ran west of the Shannon," Theobald Dillon rose to his feet, "how does our friend from Mayo explain the Treaty of Windsor and the Composition of Connacht?"

"The Treaty of Windsor!" Tomás scoffed. "What does it matter what was agreed at some treaty five centuries ago? And as for the Composition of Connacht, if the English want your lands they'll find some flaw in your titles no matter how much you declare yourselves loyal subjects. Isn't that what Wentworth was doing when he was here in Thirty-Five? Isn't that what your grand-uncle did fifty years earlier when he robbed our family of the Barony of Costello?"

"*Fubún!* Shame!" Dillon's supporters cried.

"When will you realize," Tomás shouted, "that your only protection lies in your strong right hands? Ask Con O'Rourke there how much land the good King's father took from his family?"

"Enough!" O'Conor Don remonstrated. "I will not tolerate such talk under my roof."

Theobald Dillon rose again. "If as the gentleman avers," he directed his words to those seated about the raised table, "my grand-uncle, Sir Theobald, robbed his ancestors of the Barony of Costello – a charge which I utterly reject – perhaps he will inform us how the MacCostellos got that land in the first place. Were they given a gift of it by its former owners, the O'Garas?"

"No," Tomás cried. "They won it by the sword, not by lawyers' tricks."

There was a confused outburst, in which calls of '*Goirm thú!*' and '*Fubún!*' strove for dominance. I glanced at O'Conor Don, who was toying nervously with his goblet. Would he have Tomás ejected before the dispute flared into a brawl?

A handsome young man with a strong, sun-reddened face now got unsteadily to his feet. "Could somebody answer me one question?" he demanded in a slurred voice. "If the Scots can fight for their religion, why can't we fight for ours?"

"Con!" Hugh reproved.

"Well, I just want to say that my uncle's son told me when he returned from Dublin at Easter that the new Lord Justices, Parsons and Borlase, are black Protestants, and he said they won't rest until we're all –" Hugh pulled him down before he could finish.

"Who is he?" I whispered to Tomás, who was sitting beside me, enjoying the results of his mischief.

"Con O'Rourke from Leitrim." He drained his meadar of usquebagh. So this was a cousin of my old fellow student, Hugh!

"The fool!" I muttered to Tomás. "Doesn't he realize that every word he says will be reported back to the authorities?"

"By whom?" Tomás looked at me closely.

"Ask your brother," I countered, noting how Brian Dubh pretended to be totally engrossed in directing servants as they refilled meadars and goblets.

In the lull that followed O'Rourke's outburst Úna came to our table with pipes and tobacco.

"Úna, are you still up?" Hugh reproved her.

"Brian Dubh told me not to leave," she explained.

"I'll speak to him," Hugh promised. "Now be off. Shawn Bacach may need you."

She thanked him and shuffled away, looking old and tired.

"Well," Hugh whispered to me, "was Frances as beautiful as I promised?"

"Yes." I smiled my gratitude, hoping he wouldn't notice the mended sleeve. "Can I have a word in your ear?"

When Hugh sat in the empty place that Frances had occupied I told him about losing Beibhinn's letter and recounted what it had said about Seamus and his father, Shawn Rua.

"You did right to tell me." Hugh laid his hand on my sore arm. "I'll pass the word to my father and I'll speak to Frances myself. Those Cootes are proper scaldcrows!"

As soon as Hugh had returned to the head of the table Tomás decided that the time was ripe for more mischief. "Gentlemen," he cried, taking the floor, "is this a feast or a meeting of Puritans? Let us have some merriment. I myself will offer for your pleasure a few verses."

Whereupon, throwing out his right hand like an actor, he began to declaim a poem in which the submission of various Irish clans to the Foreigners was decried. Finally he came to the Uí Briúin, or descendants of Brian, which included the O'Conors, O'Rourkes and MacDermots, and, indeed, most of those present:

> *The race of Brian Mac Eochaid,*
> *A crowd famous in battle,*
> *They are all down on their knees,*
> *Those hosts of Connacht Province.*

While reciting these lines, Tomás knelt in a representation of such abject servility that many guests were offended. O'Conor Don and his brother Brian Roe left the hall and Hugh whispered to his uncle Hugh Oge who thereupon commanded Tomás to resume his seat. Since Hugh Oge was his patron, Tomás reluctantly complied.

MacDockwra now rekindled the discord with an extemporaneous satire dealing with a foray in which MacDermot of Moylurg had taken three score cows from MacCostello. Tomás retaliated in kind, comparing MacDockwra's verse-making to his hurling and asserting that his own ancestors, the Shan Gall, or Normans, were better fighters than the Gael. Immediately there was an acrimonious outburst from the gathering. Con O'Rourke demanded to know what part the MacCostellos had played in O'Neill's war and reminded him that his own kinsman, Brian-of-the-Battle-Axe, had been one of the foremost participants in the Battle of Corrslieve. Theobald Dillon, forgetting his own Norman ancestry, pointed out that it was Red Hugh O'Donnell who had destroyed the Mac-Costello's stronghold, Castlemore, near Ballaghaderreen, to which Tomás retorted that for a Dillon to praise Red Hugh was the equivalent of a wolf praising a wolfhound. He then reminded his listeners that few of them had much to boast of when it came to the last war for Hugh O'Conor Don had fought on the English side at Corrslieve and Conor MacDermot had only become O'Donnell's ally in exchange for his own freedom. As for MacDermot of the

Rock, he hadn't played any part whatsoever in the war.

"My father was just sixteen years old in Ninety-Nine," Cathal Roe banged his fist on the table, "and I won't have his memory traduced by a penniless upstart."

"It's easy to throw disrespect on an empty estate when you have a quantity of worldly goods," Tomás conceded, "but my father, Jordan Boy, was a poet and I count that no mean inheritance."

In the midst of these exchanges, Hugh's calls for peace were ignored and Cormac raised his head from his folded arms, blinking like an owl. I cursed myself for having allowed Tomás to persuade me to return to the feast. As the only Protestant in a hall full of Papists what would be my chances should words give way to deeds? On the other hand, I now had an opportunity to repay Hugh for his many favours. Impulsively, I rose to my feet. Silence fell, as through the smoke-filled candlelight bearded faces turned to stare at me.

"Gentlemen," I heard myself say, "tonight I was reminded of what Cormac told me about the 'Contention of the Poets', that it broke out not long after the Irish had been defeated at Kinsale and their great leaders, O'Neill and O'Donnell, were dead. Now what were the poets contending about? Nothing less than the question: who was entitled to the High Kingship, the Eremonians of the North or the Eberians of the South? As Cormac's cousin, Florence, put it, the poets were like hounds fighting over an empty dish."

"What gives you the right to preach to us?" Con O'Rourke growled, turning his bloodshot eyes on me. "You're not even from Connacht."

"That's true," I conceded, "but my mother is; and like her, I prefer the music of the harp to the snarling of hounds."

There was a burst of applause at this retort.

"And," I continued, "inasmuch as Cormac has also told me that whenever there was dissension among the Fianna, Cnu Deireoil had only to touch his strings to restore harmony, I will call on your harpist to play one of the lovely airs I heard tonight, 'Eileen Aroon'."

My speech won warm approval, not least from Cormac, who was gratified by my mention of his name. O'Connellan took up his harp and soon the rich, throbbing notes were reminding us of Oona Bawn's singing. Tomás glanced at me and there were tears in his eyes. Marry, I thought, what passionate creatures these Gaels are! Then the image of Frances filled my mind, the pouting red lips revealing even white teeth, the eyes bashful, as if denying their own beauty ... Despite what Badger Face had said, I would meet her in the morning – but what if she had already learned that I was a murderer?

Chapter 16

SUNLIGHT filtering through the oiled parchment covering a narrow, recessed window woke me. My mouth tasted of ashes and my nostrils were assailed by the stench of ale-soured breath and urine. A moment's reflection told me I was in the south-east tower, where Hugh had conducted me only a few hours previously. I was lying on a *súgán* pallet in shirt and breeches with a blanket drawn over me. Similar pallets were arranged along opposite walls of the low-ceilinged room, three of four of them occupied by snoring men. Shaggy mantles hung on pegs or were thrown carelessly on benches, pikes jutted up like hedgehog spines from a barrel and in one corner three ancient arquebuses and half a dozen muskets with their iron forks rested against a wooden frame.

While martlets twittered contentedly outside I watched the thin vertical rectangle of sunlight in the smoke-darkened mortar wall, thinking of Frances. My reverie was interrupted by the sound of footsteps ascending the stairs. When I sat up my head ached.

"Ah, Lazarus has arisen!" Hugh called out cheerfully as he stepped through the arched entrance.

"Good morrow, Hugh. Where are the other men?" I nodded towards the empty pallets.

"Gone!" Hugh shook his head in resignation. "Dudley stayed with Rury the Carpenter last night to avoid climbing the stairs, so they took off with their wenches. Wait till he hears about it – especially since he left MacDockwra in charge!"

"Are you up long?" I set my toes hesitantly on the icy flags.

"Long enough to have visited the New Tower. Ah! Now you're

alert! Do you know what game is afoot?"

"Not another feast, I hope." I pulled on my high boots.

"No, but I spoke to Oona Bawn and Frances. They're eager to visit Cruachan, where our ancestors lived centuries ago. Do you feel capable of sitting on a horse?"

"Hugh!" I exclaimed. "You're the equal of Merlin! One day I'll repay you for everything."

"Repay me?" he seemed puzzled. "You owe me nothing."

"Don't I? You loaned me your good clothes and presented me to the loveliest girl in Ireland and in return I've got your doublet sleeve cut. At least let me return the sovereigns you gave me."

"No, Charles," Hugh was adamant. "What's fairly won is fairly won."

"Then take Nell," I cried impulsively. "Rory the Smith believes she may always have a limp but she'll prove a good brood mare."

"And your brother ..." Hugh looked like a boy who has been given permission to raid an orchard.

"I'll pay him back." I spoke emphatically to assuage my sense of guilt. "Thomas has other horses."

"Charles!" Hugh grasped my shoulder, his eyes shining. "I'll breed one foal from her then I'll return her. In the meantime you can ride one of our saddle horses."

We shook hands to seal the bargain.

"Oh, by the way," Hugh drew Beibhinn's letter out of his doublet, "Frances found this."

"You may read it," I offered, wondering if Frances had already done so.

As he scanned the uneven Gaelic script, Hugh's face clouded. "So she suspects Brian Dubh," he muttered. "And Father Bernardine dead ... Father will want to see this. May I show it to him?"

"Yes," I agreed, "if you promise to burn it afterwards."

"I give you my word," he said.

"Why did your father not order Tomás Láidir to leave the feast, instead of walking out himself?" I asked in a low voice after I had returned from the foul-smelling jakes.

"Tomás is my foster brother," Hugh explained. "For all his wild ways, he's as devoted to our family as Dudley. Is your arm sore?"

I had removed my shirt before approaching the crude washstand placed in a window alcove.

"It doesn't hurt." I touched the dark bloodstain in the middle of the bandage.

"Nevertheless, go to Owen," he advised. "A knife wound always needs care. There's warm water in that skillet," he added. "I had it sent over from the kitchen. Till the visitors depart, we'll both be sleeping here with Dudley's men."

While I was shaving, I questioned him about Frances. He told me that her mother, Emily, was the daughter of William Johnson, a master builder from Barnet who had fallen under suspicion in the aftermath of Guy Fawkes's attempt to blow up the Parliament and King James. Emily had come to Ireland to avoid being harried by government spies. Her husband, Patrick French-Fitzstephens, was chief steward for Clanricarde in the Barony of Abbeyboyle.

"Clanricarde is richer than the king himself," Hugh continued, "so his steward is a man of consequence. He has two mansions, one in Dungar and one in Ballytrasna, beside Abbeyboyle, where Frances and her mother live."

"Do they not live with French-Fitzstephens then?" I asked.

"Only when he visits them," Hugh explained, "though, of late, he has made Frances spend the winter in Dungar. Emily likes to be near the town; it reminds her of London. Her husband cannot abide the inhabitants of Abbeyboyle. Like most Galway men, he's proud and stiff-necked."

"Would he approve of a suitor who belonged to the Reformed Church?" I carefully wiped my razor on the towel.

"No," Hugh shook his head, "but surely you could consent to attend Mass for such a prize?"

I remained silent, reluctant to enter that quagmire till it couldn't be avoided. Maybe it would be possible to find a way around it as my father had done?

"Don't look so glum," Hugh chided. "If you weren't a man of honour you would have given a glib answer. I won't meddle with your conscience. Are you ready?"

I accompanied him across the deserted bawn, past the ashes of the bonfire, to the house of the *fear leighis*, where he left me. Owen's wife and family were astir.

"Where's your father?" I asked Brighid as she tended my wound.

"Beyond with Shawn Bacach." She ripped a strip from an old linen shirt, watching me with solemn eyes.

"Is he better?" With a feeling of nausea I waved away the ale and griddlecake her mother proffered.

"You'll have to ask father that." She bent her head so that her long black hair covered the disfigured side of her face. "You haven't asked about Donal Bawn."

"How is he?" I noticed the unseeing way she was staring at my arm.

"He's going to be on his feet in a week or two –" she looked up, her eyes troubled – "then you must pray."

"Why must I pray?"

"You will know great sorrow."

"What's going to happen?"

"I only know you will suffer. In a little while you will go on a journey and at its end you will meet someone who will show you the road you must follow; before that you will suffer."

"Can't you tell me more?"

"Only that you will lose someone dear to you." She closed her eyes as if exhausted.

"Leave her now," her mother said.

As I stepped outside a party of devil birds came swooping and screeching over the bawn, their sickle wings dark against the grey sky. I watched them disappear beyond the New Tower, my mind filled with misgivings.

It was nine o'clock when we eventually set out for Cruachan, Hugh on a fine bay gelding, with Frances seated behind him, Oona Bawn and Tomás on sturdy grey hackneys bred from a garron mare and an English stallion and I trotting along in the rear on Breac, a white-faced, spotted, brown mare which Hugh had provided. Any stranger watching would have thought there was only one girl, since Oona Bawn was again dressed in doublet and breeches, her amber hair partly hidden under a broad-brimmed hat. The countryside we traversed was very pleasant, with open champaigns, leafy groves, patches of cultivated ground and a few native hamlets, though I was too concerned with glimpsing Frances's soft brown hair and rose-tinged cheek to take much note of anything else. Tomás rode silently ahead of me, obviously suffering the effects of the night's carouse.

We passed the strong house of Lislaghna, which, Hugh told us, had formerly belonged to their *urragh*, or vassal, O'Finnegan, but was now owned by the Plunketts, and after an hour's steady riding

– for the road was little better than a cart track – reached the southern outskirts of Tulsk. About half a mile further south Carnfree rose into view and the sight of this venerable mound prompted Tomás to remark that it was the spot where Oona's ancestor had put the sandal on Felim O'Conor's foot to show that he was the new king's humble subject. Oona told him, somewhat tartly, that he was only being jealous because none of his ancestors had hand, act or part in the inauguration, after which retort, Tomás relapsed into moody silence.

At Tulsk itself we saw, on the banks of the Ogulla River, an abbey and a castle built by an earlier O'Conor Roe – though the castle was at that later date the residence of Sir Richard Lane and the abbey had an English garrison, being one of the strong points on the road to Sligo. Turning north-west, we travelled at a brisk trot, which brought us within the hour to Cruachan.

If I say that my first reaction on seeing this ancient capital of the Kings of Connacht was a feeling of profound disappointment that is hardly to be wondered at since I was expecting ruins such as travellers tell us exist at Carthage in North Africa, Stonehenge in Wiltshire or even Dun Aonghus in Aran. Instead we found a rounded plateau with cattle grazing its lush grass. The only suggestion of the rath's former glory was a certain massiveness, together with its prominent, commanding location. Hugh pointed out, away to the south-east, the solitary eminence of Slieve Bawn, where Beibhinn's people lived, and in the north the inky blue mountains of Sligo and Leitrim.

"Look!" Oona cried. "There's Slieve Anierin, near O'Rourke's Country and there's Corrslieve, the northern part of Moylurg."

I followed her pointing finger with my eyes and, whether it was the effect of distance or the realization that this was the country where she and Frances lived, it seemed to me that I was catching my first glimpse of Elysium, such was the mingling of greens and blues and purples that the vista presented.

"Where is Ballytrasna?" I turned to Frances.

"On this side of Corrslieve," she replied in her soft voice. "But I don't think you can see it." Then, conscious of my admiring gaze, she smiled and the sun danced in her hair and eyes. O, King of Glory, why did I not die at that instant?

Hugh told us that long ago Ailill and Maeve had a splendid house of pine with bronze ornamented pillars and a shingled roof in the middle of the rath. There were seven compartments between the centre fire and the outer wall and sixteen windows, as well as a roof opening. This royal house was so large that it could hold hundreds at one time.

"Who were Ailill and Maeve?" Frances asked.

"Ailill was the king of Cruachan and Maeve was his warrior queen," Hugh explained. "They lived here about the time of Christ."

Seizing an opportunity to display some of the knowledge I had acquired from Cormac, I told her about the Brown Bull of Cuailnge and how Maeve had led a great army from Cruachan to wrest this bull from Conor, the King of Ulster. Frances's eyes grew troubled when I spoke about Findabair, the fair-haired daughter of Ailill and Maeve, whom they had offered to Ferdia to induce him to fight his old comrade-in-arms, Cuchulainn, the Ulster champion.

"I think Findabair was a fool to accept such treatment," Oona sniffed. "Nobody would give me to any man against my wishes." As she said this, I could see Tomás Láidir's brooding gaze linger on her face.

We visited the cave next. Its opening was so small that I wondered how it could have gained its fearsome reputation as the "Hell-gate of Ireland". According to Hugh, goblins, demons and monstrous cats issued from this opening at *Samhain*, the Gaelic Hallowe'en. Oona was amused by the earnestness with which he spoke.

"Don't smirk, Oona," Hugh warned. "Would you be brave enough to come here on *Samhain* night?"

"Only if you were with me." She removed her hat so that the sun blazed in her hair.

Hugh smiled then, his easy, boyish smile. "If you were with me," he said, "I might mistake you for the Morrigan."

"I am the Morrigan," she cried, "and I shall sleep with you on the eve of battle." Her sauciness brought a frown to Tomás Láidir's face.

Dark rain clouds were now drifting across the sky and a breeze stirred the nearby hawthorn.

"Maybe we'd better be heading for Ballintober," Oona suggested.

"Wait," Hugh begged, "I have one last thing to show you."

With that, he led us to another rath, Relignaree, the Cemetery of the Kings, beyond which there was a large pillar stone. Hugh told us that many great kings, including Conn of the Hundred Battles, had been buried in the cemetery and that Daithi, the last pagan king of Ireland, had been buried under the pillar stone. At last, here was something that excited everyone's interest, including Oona's, and I felt pleased for Hugh's sake. With great enthusiasm, he recounted how Daithi – who was nephew to the O'Conor's great ancestor, Brian – had been killed by lightning at the foot of the Alps while pursuing Roman legions retreating from Britain. To convince us that this was indeed the tomb of the warrior king, he recited an ancient poem:

"*There lies under thee the King of the men of Innisfail,*
Daithi, the son of Fiachra, the triumphant."

Before he could tell us more, rain began to spatter down. Losing no time, we galloped back to a hazel grove we had passed earlier. After dismounting, I led Frances to the opposite side, where an ivied hawthorn with newly opened clusters of milk-white blossom provided good shelter. Without speaking, I took Frances's wet face in my two hands.

"No, Charles!" she protested. "Not in daylight."

"Why not?" I stroked her hair. "Nobody can see us here."

"Well, just one kiss," she conceded.

How my senses swooned at her honeyed breath, her soft rounded body and the moist fullness of her red lips. She pressed her mouth to mine till our teeth met, then she pulled her face away and I had to breathe deeply to recover self-control.

"Charles," she whispered, "do you … do you think that one day you might love me?"

"I've loved you from the moment I set eyes on you." My answer was so ardent that she smiled bashfully.

"Then there is something I must tell you." She lowered her gaze. "Perhaps you won't want me when you hear it."

Swearing that nothing she told me could lessen my love I at last prevailed on her to confide in me.

"Charles," her eyes remained downcast and she played nervously with a ring – which I hadn't noticed before – on the third finger of her right hand, "Patrick French-Fitzstephens is not my true father."

"How is that?" I kept my voice even.

"Mother told me that I am the daughter of the man who gave her this ring."

She removed the little hoop of gold with its oval garnet and I read on the inside the inscription, *Ó Dhia gach aon cabhair* (from God every help).

"That's the motto of O'Conor Don," I said, returning the ring.

"Yes." Her eyes met mine, troubled, searching. "Mother told me that I am the daughter of Calvagh, Hugh's father. She fell in love with him before she got married."

"Does French-Fitzstephens know?"

"I don't think he does. Now do you still love me?"

"Oh, Frances," I touched her cheek with my hand, "of course I do. If anything I love you more – you are the daughter of O'Conor Don, descendant of the Kings of Connacht. But what is that to me when you yourself are the loveliest girl in Ireland?"

"And you won't forsake me as you did Beibhinn?" If she had driven a knife through my ribs she couldn't have wounded me more.

"That's not fair," I protested. "I never told Beibhinn I loved her. We were good friends. Did you read her letter?"

"Forgive me, Charles." She laid her hand on my left arm. "I didn't mean to hurt you. It's just that ... that I'm afraid you will grow tired of me too."

"You little fool!" I cried. "How can you imagine such a thing?" and I kissed her half-parted lips so fiercely that she flinched. "Oh, Frances," I whispered, as she rested her yielding body against me, "I will never love anybody but you ... never ... never ..."

Just then Hugh called out that the rain had stopped. I kissed Frances once more and taking her hand in mine, led her slowly back to the others. My wounded arm ached but I didn't mind.

One look at Oona and Tomás showed that things had not gone well in our absence; both were staring straight ahead as if intent on some distant vista. Hugh seemed relieved at finding somebody to talk to.

"So there you are!" He smiled at our flushed faces. "I thought you had wandered away into the world of the Sidhe – you know, Cruachan is one of their underground citadels!"

As he spoke I studied his features, looking for any resemblance to Frances. They both had brown hair, grey-brown eyes and fair complexions, but there the similarity ended; Frances's face was oval and her nose slightly upturned, while Hugh had the long face and long, slightly aquiline nose of his father. Yet, there was as much difference between Hugh and Maura as there was between him and Frances. I recalled what Beibhinn had told me about a young girl Hugh had given up to please his parents. Now I knew why they had disapproved; the girl had been his half-sister.

When we prepared to leave, Frances sat behind me on Breac. Tomás wanted to borrow Hugh's horse so that he and Oona could ride him but Oona refused.

"Why should I sit behind you when I have a horse of my own?" she demanded. "Especially when you finished up last night by in-sulting our friends."

"If they found the truth insulting, that's hardly my fault," Tomás retorted.

"Isn't it?" Oona's voice was icy. "You're always right and everybody else is wrong."

"What do you want me to do?" Tomás fumed. "Become a Teigue-of-Both-Sides like Cathal Roe?"

"Oh, it's no use talking to you." She struck her mount's rump with her reins and galloped away.

If it weren't for the tension between Tomás and Oona, and one incident that I shall presently recount, that ride back to Ballinto-ber would have been heavenly. Frances's arms were about my waist, her lovely cheek resting on my shoulder. People we encoun-tered driving sheep or sitting on their low, solid-wheeled carts smiled at us and called out blessings. Some ploughmen recognized Hugh and doffing their close-fitting, blue bonnets, shouted, "Long live O'Conor!" It wasn't all friendliness, however.

As we approached Tulsk a troop of soldiers armed with swords and pistols came trotting towards us. Deciding that prudence was preferable to valour, we moved to the side of the dirt track – all, that is, except Tomás, who held doggedly to his course.

"Out of the way, Teigue!" the captain yelled, slowing his men to a walk.

"I don't yield to dogs," Tomás replied in Gaelic, whereupon the captain drew his sword. Before he could use it, Oona charged up and led Tomás's horse to one side.

"Who are you and where are you bound for?" the captain de-manded.

"I'm Hugh, son of O'Conor Don, and these are my father's guests," Hugh explained. "We've been to Cruachan and are now on our way home."

"Did you see any Pursuers on your journey?" The captain's tone was less peremptory.

"No," Hugh said. "Have any been reported?"

The captain nodded, sheathing his sword. "Cattle have been stolen from the land of Sir Richard Lane. That's why we must accost those we meet, even gentlefolk such as yourselves. God be with you," he added pleasantly and bowing to Frances, rode off with his men. I drew a breath of relief. Had the captain questioned us more closely, I might have been seized as a fugitive.

The rest of the journey was uneventful. Oona and Tomás rode side by side, while Hugh fell back to join Frances and me. Soon the five of us were singing at the tops of our voices, "Colleen Oge Asthore", "Eileen Aroon" and "An Coolun", a song in which a youth addresses a girl whose parents disapprove of him because he has no wealth. I have attempted to render the last verse of "An Coolun" – which has a most felicitous air – into English:

Do you remember the time that you and I were
Under the quicken tree and the night turning drear?
We'd no shelter from wind or refuge from shower
But my cloak spread beneath and your gown for a cover.

Oh, how happy I was on that afternoon! Even Badger Face's certain disapproval did not bother me – at least not till we came in sight of the castle and could see the red cross banner of St George and the green oak banner of O'Conor Don flying from its eastern towers. Then for some reason that I couldn't fathom a sense of foreboding swept over me. Maybe it arose from the realization that French-Fitzstephens would never approve of a penniless Protestant as his son-in-law or from the memory that was always at the back of my mind of an afternoon in Dublin when I had smashed a man's head against a wall till he had fallen down lifeless. "*Carpe diem*," I told myself, "for as sure as winter follows summer, your day of bliss will come to an end."

We had no sooner ridden through the castle entrance than my foreboding proved accurate. There was a strained look on the faces of the people running towards us and where Cormac's house had stood there was only a smouldering ruin.

Chapter 17

"WHAT happened?" Hugh demanded.

"That black whoreson, Coote –" Rory O'Cahan began, then a score of voices drowned him out.

"Silence!" Hugh shouted, dismounting. "Let Rory speak."

Rory told us that soon after we had departed a small band of men dressed like villagers had appeared. Anybody who saw them took them to be people from Castlerea who had not yet returned home. The raiders had boldly entered the south-west tower to apprehend the Lord Bishop. Fortunately, at the time His Lordship had been saying Mass in the New Tower. Shawn Bacach had raised the alarm, whereupon the strangers had beaten a hasty retreat but not before one of them had wounded Shawn Bacach with a pistol shot. On their way out, the raiders had grabbed Cormac and had set fire to his house. When Rory had tried to intervene he had been threatened at gunpoint.

"And where is His Lordship now?" Hugh's face was grim.

"MacDockwra and six of Dudley's men are taking him to Glinsk," Rory replied. "Dudley and the rest of his men have gone after the raiders, though they'll hardly catch them, not with Dudley's bad knee and the start the raiders had."

"Weren't they on foot?" Tomás Láidir broke in.

"They had horses hidden below at the churchyard," Rory said. "It was a well-planned raid. There's no doubt but that Coote was behind it. I'll wager my weight in gold that they were watching you ride off this morning."

Leaving Rory to take care of the horses and Tomás to escort the girls to their room, Hugh and I raced to the south-west tower, where we found Shawn Bacach being tended by Owen. The ball had entered Shawn's chest not far above the heart and he was now as still as a corpse. Úna told us that he had heard the raiders whispering in English and had rushed out into the passage, shouting his old warcry, "MacDonnell Aboo!" The raiders had fired point blank at him before fleeing. Though bleeding profusely he was still conscious when Úna reached him.

Since there was nothing we could do to help, Hugh and I set off for the New Tower. We found O'Conor Don in the hall of the inquest, holding council with Lady Mary, his brothers, Hugh Oge and Brian Roe, his nephew Charles and Theobald Dillon. He rose at our entrance.

"Hugh, they've taken Cormac!" His voice quavered with indignation. "We didn't know till it was too late. Upon my word, Coote will answer for this outrage."

"Let me ride to Castlecoote with Con O'Rourke and as many men as we can muster," Hugh pleaded. "We can join forces with Dudley."

"I'll go with you!" Charles and I cried together.

"No." O'Conor Don shook his head. "We mustn't rush blindly into trouble. It's clear that Coote's raid was prepared in advance – they knew when to strike and where to look. We must be as well prepared. And, remember, for all their foresight, His Lordship got away."

"How were they so well informed?" Lady Mary looked at me accusingly. "What Brian Dubh says about this man may well be true."

"Nonsense!" O'Conor Don spoke with a decisiveness that was unusual for him. "Hugh gave me a letter today that O'Cairnen's daughter wrote to Charles. Here, I intended to show it to you but so many things were happening. You see that she suspects Brian Dubh of betraying us."

Lady Mary read the letter in silence then handed it to Theobald.

"From what she writes, it appears as if they may also have come to arrest ... Charles." She reluctantly pronounced my name.

"Begging your pardon, madam," I blurted out, "I don't wish that letter to be passed around. I should have burned it last night."

"Just a minute." Theobald held the letter behind his back. "Who was the last to ride out of the bawn this morning?"

"I was," I said.

"And did you ensure that the door was closed after you?"

His question took me by surprise. It was customary to leave the massive entrance door open during daytime unless there was some particular reason to do otherwise and, furthermore, it was the duty of the Pursuer on guard to push across the beam on the inside.

"I didn't think it was necessary," I explained, "and, anyway, the raiders may have been hiding in the stable or cowshed."

"And they may not." Theobald was relentless. "You know it was you they came for." In confirmation he held up the letter.

The directness of this accusation left me speechless. Fortunately, Hugh intervened. "The responsibility is mine," he said. "It was I who proposed the visit to Cruachan. The fact that Charles was last through the entrance is a mere trifle."

Theobald accepted the rebuke in silence but the look he gave me showed that he no longer regarded me with benevolence.

"Give me the letter," O'Conor Don said. "We mustn't let our anxieties set us at one another's throats."

"Nevertheless, Charles can hardly expect us to shelter him any longer," Lady Mary observed. "We must think of our own safety."

"Our own safety!" Hugh snorted. "It's not by turning our backs on our friends that we'll ensure our safety."

"No, Hugh," his father agreed. "But we must be prudent. Coote cannot proceed against us without the trappings of the law – this letter shows as much. We must give him no reason to charge us with any disaffection. So far he has failed to break Shawn Rua and, God willing, neither will he succeed with Cormac. If, on the other hand, he or the Sheriff were to capture the Lord Bishop, or you, Charles, here in Ballintober, it would be a different matter."

"What are we to do then?" Hugh said hotly. "Crouch like frightened hares till the hounds nose us out?"

"No." His father assumed a grim expression. "I still have friends who wield power in this kingdom. Coote will find that the name of O'Conor Don can call down lightning on his head. In the meantime, Charles must not leave the castle. We'll act as if the raid never took place."

"Sir," desperation made me bold, "I must insist that you burn that letter. If Brian Dubh were to learn of it, Beibhinn's life would be forfeit." I told them then how Beibhinn had been with me that evening when Brian Dubh copied another letter in the Bishop's chamber. O'Conor Don and his wife exchanged glances.

"You acted honourably in keeping this hidden at the inquest," O'Conor Don said. "We may have erred in sending the girl away. Nevertheless, what's done is done."

Lady Mary took the letter from her husband and threw it on the fire. "She's a brave girl," she murmured, watching the paper shrivel. "But I was obliged to think of her good ..."

"And what about your *reachtaire*?" Hugh Oge asked. "Is he to be given the freedom to work more mischief?"

"Don't worry about Brian Dubh," O'Conor Don told his brother. "I'll deal with him in good time. For the present I don't want Coote to know that we have uncovered his spy – it might lead him to suspect Beibhinn."

I glanced at Theobald but his expression showed that he wasn't appeased. Was it because I had outshone him at the feast or because I was a Protestant and Protestants had taken Cormac – or was there some other reason? As Hugh and I left the hall, I saw Theobald whisper to Lady Mary – no doubt, something to my discredit – but with Hugh as my comrade, I felt safe from intrigue.

Now there occurred another of those escapades that bedevilled my youth. While approaching the south-east tower we ran into Con O'Rourke. On hearing that Hugh had previously intended following Dudley and his men, nothing would content him but that we should set out for Castlecoote on the instant. Hugh gave in, arguing that if we disguised ourselves as Pursuers, his father's safety would not be compromised and I, anxious to appear worthy of Frances, rashly concurred. So it was that the three of us, attired in nondescript doublets and breeches, torn bonnets on our heads and brogues on our feet, slipped out through the wicket gate and drifted down to The Golden Meadar, where O'Beirne provided us with garrons, miodoges, a quarterstaff, a rusty musket and a matchlock pistol.

As we mounted in the alehouse yard, the simpleton who had once hailed me as the *Crobhdhearg*, or red-handed saviour, called out, "Don't despair, men: you'll get help from France and Spain," to which Con replied, "We're only going to hunt some wolves, Ronan."

"Aye," Ronan cried, "but where is King Charles now?"

By the time we rode out from the village the sun hung above the western horizon and my head was aching with tiredness. Few of the features of the countryside we traversed remain in my memory, though I recall passing the broken tower on Oran Hill and soon afterwards glimpsing the battlements of Dunamon, home of the McDavid Burkes. At this point a disagreement arose between Hugh and Con as to whether or not we should cross the River Suck by the castle bridge, Hugh arguing that since Sir Hubert Burke's deceased sister had been the wife of Turlough MacDermot, eldest brother of Oona Bawn, it would be safe to do so and Con insisting that he would no more trust a McDavid Burke than he would a badger. In the end, Con's arguments prevailed and we turned east, forded a small tributary of the Suck and followed its course till we were able to cross the river itself further south, the water swirling about our garrons' flanks.

By now the sun had disappeared and as we trotted through the deepening gloom I could not help recalling the ditty about the three blind mice. The miodoge stuck in my belt offered little reassurance. Eventually, after it seemed I could not stay upright on my garron's cushion a moment longer, we came in sight of a dark fortress, its massive corner towers looming up against the pale sky. To say that my heart sank into my bowels would not be an exaggeration; this was a place as forbidding as the abode of Hades himself.

"If Dudley's men are mounting an assault, why is everything so quiet?" Hugh's voice was almost a whisper.

"They must have planned to overtake Coote's wolf pack before they reached the castle," Con decided. "Only a fool would risk his men in a direct assault."

"They might have feigned an attack in order to draw Coote's soldiers into the open," I conjectured.

"What would a Palesman know about such tactics?" The ride had not improved Con's temper.

"I know that our only chance of finding out what happened to Cormac is for me to go in there alone." My answer robbed him of speech. "If I pretend to have escaped from Ballintober, the Cootes may believe me."

"You'll do no such thing," Hugh declared. "Do you want to

end up in Newgate? No, Charles, you wait here while Con and I spy out the castle's defences."

Ignoring my protest, Hugh loaded and primed the musket, while Con lit a piece of tinder with his flint and steel, which he then applied to the slow match.

"Take this," Hugh handed me the smouldering musket, "and at the first sign of danger, fire it."

With that they trotted away, Hugh armed with the pistol and Con with the quarterstaff, leaving me on my own in the eerie starlight.

After my companions disappeared below the crest of the low hill on which the castle stood, I removed the garron's cushion and, placing it near a bank, sat down with the musket across my knees. Despite the coolness of the night air, I soon began to doze, jerking awake whenever the cry of a bird or the rustle of some unseen creature disturbed me. Nevertheless, though I realized that my own life and the lives of my companions might thereby be put in jeopardy, I could not keep my head from again dropping on my chest.

Suddenly the clatter of hooves mingled with loud voices roused me. Overcome with confusion, I discharged the musket. Immediately I was surrounded. Harsh English voices screamed at me to lay down my weapon. A musket butt hit my back so that I writhed in torment. With kicks and curses I was pulled to my feet and hurried to the castle, stumbling and moaning. The massive entrance door swung open and I was marched through.

Once the door closed behind me I expected to be set upon again; instead, I was propelled across the torch-lit bawn, up a stone stairway and into a large, oak-pannelled room gleaming with candlelight, where two mastiffs rose to their feet growling. The man in a broad-brimmed hat and sombre clothes writing at a desk near the fire was the same one I had glimpsed from the stable loft in Ballintober, Sir Charles Coote the Younger.

Chapter 18

"WHAT have we here?" Sir Charles laid his quill carefully alongside the inkhorn. "Down, Gryphon! Down, Grim!" he commanded the bristling mastiffs.

"A bloody-minded Pursuer who tried to murder one of my men," the captain of the guard responded.

"Ah, another of O'Conor's bogtrotters." Sir Charles drummed on the desk with his fingers. "Put him in leg-irons and throw him in the dungeon with the old rhymer. I'll deal with them tomorrow."

"Wait!" I cried, knowing that once I was fettered my chances of escape would be those of a mouse in a trap. "I'm on my way to His Lordship the Bishop of Kilmore."

The effect produced by my clear English was almost comical, the captain and his men staring open-mouthed.

"And who are you that the Bishop of Kilmore should receive you?" Sir Charles retained his composure.

"Charles Scott," I replied, using the name I had given to his uncle, Sir Chidley, and to Lord Ranelagh.

"Ah, the divinity student who wishes to convert the Wild Irish – though I see that you've laid aside your student's gown for the native raiment." A faint smile played about Sir Charles's lips. "And why did you, Master Scott, a self-proclaimed man of God, discharge your musket at my soldiers?"

"I thought they were Pursuers, sir." The captain made to strike me but Sir Charles waved him back. "I escaped from Ballintober this evening," I continued. "There was a raid on the castle and in the confusion nobody noticed my departure."

Sir Charles nodded, whereupon I briefly recounted what had happened since meeting his uncle, omitting any detail that might tend to my own harm or that of the O'Conors.

Sir Charles heard me out then instructed the captain and his men to withdraw.

"It seems you and I have found favour with the same lass." He watched me with the benign gaze of a cat playing with a mouse. "You didn't know that she is O'Conor Don's daughter, Master Scott?"

My look of amazement pleased him. And yet what he said would account for Beibhinn having been brought from Slieve Bawn by the O'Conors and for Lady Mary's hostility to her.

"For a nation of paupers the Irish have the pride of Satan." Sir Charles rang a small handbell. "They fawn on the unworthy and fail to –" He broke off as a servant boy dressed in sober livery entered. "Bring supper for two," he instructed, "and tell your mistress to come here. There's a guest I wish her to meet." So the cat had decided to pounce!

Without asking for permission I sat on a chair to ease the pain in my back. Sir Charles seemed not to notice this impudence. "You have studied at Trinity College," he remarked. "I too have studied at Trinity College, though in Cambridge, not Dublin. Have you decided to return there?"

I repeated what I had said about Bishop Bedell, adding that under Cormac's guidance I was now able to read the New Testament in Gaelic.

"When you speak of O'Mulconry you forget to mention the seditious poem he recited at the May Day feast." Sir Charles's voice had suddenly acquired the chill of ice. "It's rhymers like that who keep men like O'Conor puffed up with pride. King of Connacht indeed! My father is Vice-President of Connacht and I am a Member of Parliament for Leitrim but I don't pay rhymers to flatter me. The sooner we teach all men, including our own King Charles, to respect the will of Parliament the better. And why should you waste your time learning a barbaric tongue when you speak the language of Spenser and Bacon?"

"The Irish consider English a barbaric tongue," I couldn't help pointing out. "They call it *Béarla*, 'mouth-talk', 'babble'. Anyway, how can we win the Irish over to true religion if we don't preach the gospel to them in words they will comprehend?"

"Ah, that is just what Bedell propounds." Sir Charles smiled. "He even believes that the Church of Rome is a true Church, though under the tyranny of the Pope. What nonsense! The Irish are superstitious heathens who will always believe their priests before they believe God's word. It's a waste of time ministering to them but men like Bedell won't be advised. That's why we must rid the Church of prelates, from Archbishops Laud and Ussher right down to the Bishop of Kilmore. Clear them out root and branch so that the work of reform can proceed: 'Every tree which bringeth not forth good fruit is hewn down, and cast into the fire.' Isn't that what the gospel says?"

I was gathering my wits to reply when the servant boy entered with bread, cheese, a bottle of sack and two pewter goblets on a wooden tray.

"Is your mistress coming?" Sir Charles barked.

"She's getting dressed," the boy answered meekly.

"Well, tell her to make haste." Sir Charles began filling the goblets with sack.

As the boy departed my eye strayed to a large portrait of my host in what I took to be some parliamentary robe gazing down at us. At that very moment Sir Charles began to say the grace-before-meals and, having mumbled a response, I fell to ravenously, gulping the sack to moisten the mouthfuls of bread and cheese, while Sir Charles shared his supper with the mastiffs. In the midst of my gorging Beibhinn entered, dressed in a brocaded gown of green satin, so that, conscious of my own outlandish appearance, I almost choked. This may have been to our advantage because it gave Beibhinn a pretext for her own look of astonishment. Lurching to my feet, I bowed, while she, adopting an air of polite reserve that reminded me of Maura's, welcomed me to Castlecoote in hesitant English.

"So, Beibhinn, this is the Dublin scholar who wooed you at Ballintober?" Sir Charles remained seated.

"Yes." Beibhinn nodded. "Why have you brought him here?"

"He ran away from the O'Conors." Sir Charles regarded her shrewdly. "Maybe he wanted to meet his true love one last time."

"I've told Sir Charles I was setting out for Bishop Bedell's," I interjected.

"Let Beibhinn speak," Sir Charles commanded.

"How can I know why he came?" Beibhinn replied. "What passed in Ballintober no longer touches me; I was a child there with a child's giddy ways. Now, Charles, may I return to bed?"

"But what am I to do with him?" Sir Charles persisted. "Will I send him under guard to Dublin – he is, you'll admit, Charles Stanihurst, not, as he claims, Charles Scott – or will I keep him in the dungeon here till my father returns from Roscommon?"

On hearing my correct name spoken, my blood ran cold, though I should have realized that, if not Beibhinn, then Brian Dubh would already have informed the Cootes of my true identity. I had lied to no purpose. "Woe unto him who does evil and is poor after it." The words of a Dublin street preacher resounded in my head, almost drowning out Beibhinn's reply: "It's not for me to decide such matters."

"Granted," Sir Charles conceded, "but if it were, what would you do?"

"I'd let him go to Bishop Bedell in Kilmore." Beibhinn's voice remained aloof, almost indifferent.

"But he doesn't even know where Kilmore is," Sir Charles objected. "And, furthermore, the man is a murderer."

"Charles is no murderer but a true Christian who reads his Bible and can recite parables and psalms by heart." Beibhinn gazed at him steadily.

"I'm sure he can," Sir Charles mused, "but then a person may recite psalms and be a hypocrite. What am I to do with you, Master Stanihurst? If I imprison you, people will say I acted out of jealousy and if I let you go, they'll say I am assisting a malefactor to evade justice. I know what: I'll send you back to the O'Conors *pro tempore*. Let them decide your fate. Guard!" he shouted.

"Are you sending me back tonight?" A conviction that he intended some treachery had seized hold of me.

"Yes," he said. "You came in darkness and in darkness you'll depart."

"But what if there are Pursuers lurking about?" I pretended to be terrified.

"There won't be." Sir Charles stroked the mastiffs. "My soldiers sent them racing back to Ballintober. Now, Beibhinn, bid farewell to your erstwhile admirer."

"God be with you." Beibhinn spoke in a low voice then walked abruptly from the room.

After that everything happened so quickly that in a few moments I found myself out in the bawn being helped onto my garron's back by the same boy who had brought in supper. As he checked the rawhide girth holding a new cushion in place, he slipped something under my leg. It was a *sliotar*, the hard ball used in hurling. Cormac had explained that girls wound them from plaited horsehair set with beeswax, giving them as a gift to the youth they admired. Surely this was Beibhinn's way of telling me that her aloofness in Sir Charles's chamber had been feigned? With a pang of mingled gratitude and guilt I concealed the *sliotar* in my doublet, intending to cherish it always. Then, with a mounted guard on either side of me and another leading the way, I trotted out the entrance gate, past two musket-armed sentries, my body aching, my mind full of apprehensions.

Following the outer wall of the castle round to the opposite side, we descended to a wooden bridge that echoed hollowly beneath the horses' hooves. Once across the river, we headed in what I judged from the position of Polaris to be a north-easterly direction.

"I thought Ballintober lay to the north-west," I remarked but my guards pretended not to hear.

"Where are you taking me?" I demanded. For answer the guard on my right drew his sword and prodded me in the arm.

"You're going to be lodged in Roscommon Castle," he informed me. "Lord Ranelagh will decide where you go from there."

Like a mouse under a cat's paw, I quaked with fear: Roscommon, an O'Conor fortress in Queen Elizabeth's time, had been strengthened by successive governors so that it was now one of Lord Ranelagh's chief strongholds in Connacht. Not only would I be a prisoner there; I would never set eyes on Frances again. It did not occur to me then that my guards, prompted by Sir Charles, might well have been hoping that I would attempt to flee so that they could slay me without compunction.

We rode on in silence, the moonlight proving sufficient to reveal the wheel-rutted track. With every furlong exhaustion and despair pressed more heavily on me so that when a voice shouted, "Halt!" as we passed through a thicket I did not feel any elation. Instead, like somebody in a dream, I saw the guard on my right reaching for his sword and the one ahead levelling his pistol. Without thinking I threw the *sliotar*, hitting the leading horse on the flank. He plunged forward, causing the guard to fire harmlessly into the air. At the same moment another shot rang out from the thicket, almost deafening me. By this time the night was filled with cries of "*Fág an bealach!*" mingled with the curses of the guards, the whacks of quarterstaff on sword, the snorting of horses and thumping of hooves. Glimpsing a clear way ahead, I kicked my garron's flanks, sending him charging past the shadowy combatants.

In a little while I heard hoofbeats behind me and at the risk of being thrown headlong, urged my garron to greater speed. Imagine my joy when familiar voices yelled at me in Gaelic to slow down. The attackers were none other than Hugh and Con, who had been on the point of abandoning their vigil outside Castlecoote when the thudding of horses' hooves on the bridge reached them. Losing no time, they had forded the river and set out in pursuit.

"Have you killed any of the guards?" I asked, my voice full of misgiving.

"No," Con growled, "but, by the grace of God, we may have left the whoresons with some broken ribs."

"I think I wounded one with my pistol," Hugh confessed. "Anyway, he was able to gallop off so he won't die."

I told them about the *sliotar* I had thrown at the horse, begging them to help me search for it.

"No!" Hugh was adamant. "They may be waiting for us back there and, anyway, we must be home before daybreak."

On the ride back to Ballintober I recounted all that had happened in Castlecoote, with the exception of Sir Charles's claim that Beibhinn was the daughter of O'Conor Don.

"For a Palesman you didn't do badly," Con's voice was almost jovial, "though you might have found out a little more about Cormac."

"Don't pay any heed to Con," Hugh advised. "He's still recovering from last night's carouse."

"I have more than that to trouble me." Con's voice was suddenly grave. "My thigh is covered in blood."

We ministered to Con's sword wound – for such it was – as best we could, binding it with strips torn from our shirts. Then we continued on our way, making such good time that we were back in the south-east tower by dawn, where Owen, the *fear leighis*, tended to Con's thigh and my bruised back. The three blind mice had, with the exception of Con, escaped the carving knife, though ours had been a foolhardy enterprise which had achieved nothing, for it would make the Cootes more determined to hunt me down and keep Cormac a prisoner.

Chapter 19

As soon as Owen – who had been sworn to secrecy by Hugh – left, Dudley came limping up from his pallet. He told us that he and his men had overtaken the raiders just as they were about to enter Castlecoote but dared not discharge their muskets for fear of hitting Cormac. When they were withdrawing, a band of soldiers had issued from the castle and given chase, harrying them as far as Oran.

"You have saved our honour." Dudley lowered his voice lest the men lying on nearby pallets might overhear. "Coote must be livid to find that you have snatched Charles from his clutches."

What Hugh and Con said in reply I didn't grasp: exhaustion overcame me and, collapsing on my pallet, I fell instantly into a dreamless sleep.

It was late afternoon when I awoke. Even though my back hurt and every muscle in my body ached, my mind was clear. The room was empty except for Con's pallet, from which a loud snoring issued. Shaving with cold water, I dressed in the clothes I had worn at the feast and went in search of Hugh. He assured me that our foray to Castlecoote had not been noised abroad. If anybody questioned us about our absence during the night we would claim to have been carousing in The Golden Meadar.

Frances slipped out to join me before bedtime and, concealed by the gathering dusk, we walked to a shed built against the north curtain wall. Once inside we embraced. Intoxicated by her soft, perfumed warmth, I feared I was in danger of yielding to temptation, so in order to distract myself I told her about the meeting in the New Tower the previous evening.

"Cathal," she addressed me by the Gaelic form of my name, "you mustn't pay heed to Theobald. He has often given me fond glances but I don't care for him," and saying this she turned up her fragrant mouth to be kissed. Holding hands, I walked with her back to the New Tower, vowing I would meet her in the morning before she and her family departed for Ballytrasna.

That night, lying on our pallets in the south-east tower among the snoring Pursuers (Con, despite his wound, had set out earlier for Castleruby with O'Conor Roe's son), Tomás, Hugh and I discussed Cormac's imprisonment. To my amazement, I learned that Cormac's real name was Muiris – he, on returning to Ballintober, having assumed the name Cormac O'Connellan in order to confuse the English. In time he had abandoned his deception but the name Cormac had clung. I also learned that seven years previously, Muiris – or Cormac – had for a month assisted Brother Michael O'Clery and his fellow scholars in compiling *The Annals of the Kingdom of Ireland*, a work that was regarded by Tomás – who had seen a manuscript copy in the possession of Fergal O'Gara, patron of the enterprise – as surpassing the histories of Livy or Thucydides.

"Can the Cootes hold Cormac without the sanction of law?" I asked.

"Yes," Hugh said. "Theobald told us that we must not bring a suit because in the eyes of the law Cormac doesn't exist. Furthermore, the Cootes will deny having raided Ballintober."

"And do you think Cormac will survive?" Anxiety gnawed at my mind.

"Cormac has accustomed himself to frugal living," Hugh tried to reassure me. "He'll use his time in Castlecoote to compose an epic. I'm sure he's told you how, in the Bardic schools, poets lie in cubicles in the dark, fashioning their ranns."

"Have you heard the lament he composed for Brian Oge Mac-Dermot, Oona's father?" Tomás asked, and he recited a quatrain that for restraint and pathos equalled the best elegies of Catullus.

"When did Brian Oge die?" I realized that I was ignorant of most things that were known to my companions.

"Five years ago," Tomás said. "Wentworth made him go to Athlone to have the titles to his estates investigated – that was Wentworth's method of acquiring the lands of the Irish. While

Brian Oge was there he seems to have contracted dysentery – though I wouldn't be surprised if Coote had him poisoned."

In this manner we spent the greater part of the night, our words shielding us from the dread that lurked beyond the walls of the tower. That dread was to increase as the days went by and there was no word about Cormac. Shawn Bacach continued to hover between life and death. Sometimes he would imagine he was driving cattle to the summer booley in the mountains, at other times that he was carousing with friends or fighting old battles. I visited him daily but he did not recognize me. Brighid was often there with Úna, changing poultices or coaxing the invalid to drink some broth from a spoon.

During those days my back ached constantly so that Brighid's father reckoned a bone-knob had been chipped. Nobody spoke of the raid and at times I myself doubted that it had ever happened.

By this time Frances, Tomás and Oona had long departed and while Cormac's house was being rebuilt, I moved into the house of Niall the Cobbler, a dim, smoky place, cluttered with pieces of rank rawhide and half-finished brogues. Niall cleared a table by the back window, where I tried to work, using a quire of discoloured folio paper and some quills and ink that Hugh had provided. Since my new finery would have sorted ill with such crude surroundings, I began to wear my old clothes and brogues and to forgo shaving. My appearance mirrored my inner desolation for I missed my family and Cormac but, in particular, I missed Frances.

Not that I was entirely displeased with my new habitation. Niall had a quick mind, which belied his deformed body. Unlike his neighbours he did not regard all Englishmen as oppressors, for, said he, "Our own nobles were harsher to us than the Foreigners ever were. They called us the slave clan and the *Lóipínigh* and condemned us to a life of drudgery. We were no better than the dirt under their feet."

One evening when Niall and I were sharing a meadar of usquebagh by the fire I brought the conversation round to Brian Dubh – who had begun to demand that, since I was no longer helping Cormac, I should return to the kitchen. Niall told me that Brian Dubh's mother's grandfather had been Dudley O'Conor, a rival of Hugh's grandfather, Dermot. Dudley had even been given Ballintober Castle by the English but Dermot had quickly recovered it. Knowing the propensity of the Gaels to nurse old grievances, I began to understand why Brian Dubh was willing to destroy the present O'Conor Don.

"Answer me one thing," I handed the meadar to Niall, "why are the Cootes so set against the O'Conors?"

"That should be no cause for wonder." He gave me a shrewd look before drinking. "Greed."

"But it seems to go deeper than that," I objected.

"Ah, you have keen eyes." He nodded approvingly then lowered his voice to a confidential whisper. "They say Old Coote asked for the hand of Maura for his son Charles."

"Hugh's sister?" I gasped.

"Yes." My surprise pleased him. "She was just about thirteen at the time and as lovely as the morning star. Well, the notion of a foreign upstart marrying a girl with the blood of High Kings in her veins was unthinkable and the master must have said so. Anyway, the Cootes took offence and they have it in for the O'Conors ever since. They thought they had their chance when Wentworth came here to plant Connacht with Foreigners but, praise be to God, that plan –"

"But how could Wentworth take land from the O'Conors?" I broke in. "Weren't their estates regranted to them by King James? Surely the law would uphold their title?"

"Is it the law?" Niall gave me a pitying look, then handed me the meadar.

"Where be his quiddits now?" Hamlet's words came back to me as I sipped the fiery liquid. In Ireland, I should have realized, the law of the brehons, administered in hilltop assemblies, had given way to an alien code that few comprehended or trusted.

"Let me tell you what Phelim the Pedlar told me." Niall leaned forward on his stool. "While he was in Portumna, Wentworth summoned a jury to examine people's titles to their lands and where do you think the inquisition was held? Right in the castle of the Earl of Clanricarde, the biggest Catholic landowner in Connacht! And listen to this: when the Galwaymen refused to bring in the verdict Black Tom wanted, he had every last man jack of them thrown into prison till they changed their minds. That's how the law will protect the O'Conors if the Cootes ever get sufficient grounds to arraign them. You mark my words."

In due course Cormac's house was rebuilt and I did my best to furnish it as he had done, even paying Rury to carve another statue of the Virgin and to provide a whitened wand, which I fixed over the door. Unfortunately, I couldn't recreate the burnt manuscripts but I began to copy such poems and fragments of old tales as the O'Conors possessed or they or their retainers could recall. I also wrote poems to Frances in which I poured out the love welling up in my heart:

> *Frances aroon, dwell in the summer shower,*
> *Bright in thy beauty, light in thy being;*
> *Frances aroon, dear as the blissful hour,*
> *Glimpsed like a hidden flower, wistful thy mien ...*

These madrigals I did not send to her, as Hugh had gone to visit his brother Charles and sister Maura in Castleburke and I would not trust another messenger. Despite my efforts to be cheerful, my soul filled with despondency. I fretted at the confinement of the castle with its noise and jealousies. Even the weather seemed against me, being unseasonably wet.

My gloomy mien did not escape the sharp eyes of Niall. "You remind me of Oengus Oge," he observed one afternoon as I sat by his fire, gazing into the flames.

"How is that?" I asked listlessly.

"Didn't Cormac ever tell you how Oengus started to pine away after he saw a beautiful maiden in a dream?" He regarded me shrewdly. "His mother, Boand, and his father, the Dagda, couldn't get him to divulge the reason for his sickness and if a physician they sent for hadn't divined the truth, Oengus would certainly have died."

"And what happened then?" The prospect of a tale was raising my spirits.

"Ah, so Cormac didn't teach you everything!" He paused with his awl thrust into the headstall of a bridle he was making, a triumphant grin lighting up his pallid face. "If I tell you, will you put me into your history of the O'Conors?"

Assuring him that I would, I listened entranced to the tale he unfolded. It turned out that the maiden was Caer, daughter of Ethal Anbuail, who ruled over the Sidhe, or fairy mound, of Cruachan, the place we had visited with Hugh. Caer spent every second year in the form of a swan, one of a troop of swan maidens who frequented a secret lough. Her father, however, wouldn't yield her to Oengus, who had to ask Ailill and Maeve, the mortal king and queen of Cruachan, for help. After a succession of obstacles had been overcome, the story ended with Oenugus and Caer flying away to his home, Brugh na Boinne, in the form of swans.

"Now, who is the maiden you're pining after?" Niall's eyes held mine. "O'Conor Don's daughter?"

My heart skipped a beat. Was Niall alluding to Maura or Frances or even – taking into account what I had learned in Castlecoote – to Beibhinn?

"I don't think that Maura would have much time for a penniless scholar," I said lightly.

"No," Niall conceded, "but a certain swan maiden from Ballytrasna might – ah, you're reddening now! If you don't want to talk about it, I won't press you – I'll just say this and I'll say no more, you have your fairy princess there. If I were in you shoes, it isn't moping in Ballintober I'd be this hour.

I smiled but kept my counsel. To discuss Frances with Niall would be to dispel the blissful yearning with which her image filled me. At the same time, thinking on her reminded me that, no less than Ethal Anbuail in regard to Caer, her stepfather, French-Fitzstephens, would do everything in his power to shield her from me. In his eyes I would be a fugitive and a heretic and should I ride to Ballytrasna – a doubtful enterprise until my back mended – he would either set the dogs on me or remove Frances to a distant quarter. No wonder that as soon as I took leave of Niall my former mood returned.

Not that I was the only one in low spirits. The raid had cast a gloom over Ballintober, leaving most of its inhabitants tense and quarrelsome, and it wasn't till now that I realized how important Cormac's presence had been to the felicity of the community: he was the font of wisdom and the memory of the people and without him they felt confused. I won't deny that Badger Face's departure may have affected them too; they had been robbed at one fell swoop of their Bishop and ollamh and, apart from Brighid, there was nobody to supply the loss.

In the midst of these woes I turned more and more to the Holy Scripture for consolation. The Gaelic Bible Cormac had given me had been consumed in the fire but I still had my own. The words of the Psalms, in particular, were balm to my spirit: "O Lord, rebuke me not in thine anger, neither chasten me in thy hot displeasure ..." It was while reading them one morning that a thought struck me: if Dr Bedell was translating the Old Testament into Gaelic, wouldn't the help of a native scholar such as Cormac be invaluable to him? I put this proposition to Hugh when he returned from Mayo and the upshot was that MacDockwra was dispatched to Kilmore with a letter from O'Conor Don offering Cormac's services and bemoaning his imprisonment. MacDockwra was graciously received but whether or not his journey would bear fruit only time would tell.

It was soon after this that I myself was summoned to O'Conor Don's presence. Hugh was with him and the sandy-bearded man who had accosted me in O'Beirne's alehouse. O'Conor introduced the fellow as Manus O'Donnell and told me that he was one of the soldiers that Strafford had recruited to fight for King Charles and that had been disbanded the previous summer. Manus could take me to a colonel who was seeking recruits for the Spanish army in Flanders. If I wished to enlist, O'Conor Don would not stand in my way.

"Do the English approve of this colonel's activities?" I asked.

"To be sure," O'Conor Don replied. "They are only too glad to get rid of Strafford's unruly veterans. What do you say, Charles?"

I eyed Manus askance. Did O'Conor Don expect me to trust my fate to this ruffian?

"You'll be well paid and, being a scholar, you'll be certain of preferment." Manus misread my glance. "The Irish have a great reputation abroad as fighters – you may have heard of Col. Owen Roe O'Neill's defence of Arras last year?"

The thought of escape to Flanders was tempting but if I enlisted I might never set eyes on Frances again. I shook my head. "I cannot leave till Cormac is free," I demurred.

"Well spoken." O'Conor Don smiled. "But if the Cootes refuse to release him – what then?"

I remained silent.

"Haven't you heard the prophecy that is being whispered everywhere?" Manus asked.

"*In the year Forty gorse will be without seed or bloom,*
And in the year following Saxons will lie stretched on the ground."

"No more of that!" O'Conor Don frowned. "I won't have treason spoken in my presence. Hugh, see that this gentleman is conducted on his way."

"You may dismiss me now, O'Conor," a vein was rising in Manus's forehead, "but you will need me sooner than you think. The King hasn't abandoned his intention to plant Connacht," and saying this he turned on his heel and stalked out.

"Wait, Manus!" Hugh ran after him. "I'll walk with you to the alehouse."

That interview convinced me that my days in Ballintober were numbered. I had no doubt but that O'Conor Don was playing a subtle game, for why, otherwise, had he still not dismissed Brian Dubh? It occurred to me that he might have entertained the idea of exchanging me for Cormac and then thought better of it – I knew too much about what went on in Ballintober and I was a Protestant. Nevertheless, I had no dislike for this man; in his eyes I must have been a Jonah who imperilled the safety of his household.

For my own part I longed so much to see Frances that there were times when I was on the point of stealing a horse and setting out for Ballytrasna. Calmer reflection, however, convinced me that, even if my back didn't prevent it, such a course would be disastrous, for not only would I risk capture by the Cootes, I would also incur the enmity of the O'Conors. No, I had to stay where I was and endure uncertainty and separation and the dwindling of my hopes. To add to my predicament, Donal Bawn was on his feet again and staring at me with undisguised hatred. Between him and Brian Dubh I was in a constant state of anxiety, though the friendship of Hugh saved me from open attack.

Early in June Shawn Bacach died, the wound in his chest having, despite Owen's ministrations, turned gangrenous. His straw bed was set alight at the doorway of the south-west tower, while he himself was laid out on a table in the Great Hall with a linen sheet covering him and candles at his head. When Hugh and I entered, a group of Pursuers, servants and villagers were sitting near the fireplace drinking ale and smoking pipes just as if they were at a feast. Eight or nine crones were gathered like banshees around the corpse, rending the air with shrieks of lamentation, though occasionally they would pause to swallow a mouthful of usquebagh.

Hugh and I knelt by the side of the table. I tried to pray but the fetid, smoke-filled air and hellish shrieking muddied my thoughts. I gazed at my old companion, noting the pennies covering his eyes, the joined, bony fingers with a rosary twined about them, the compressed, bloodless lips and craggy features, peaceful in the glow of the candles. A feeling of remorse swept over me then; I should have defended this man with my life's blood for he had been as a father to me. "May your soul be on God's right hand, last of the gallowglasses," I prayed silently.

Just as I rose, there was a sudden hush and Úna entered, accompanied by Owen and Brighid.

"I gave her a sleeping draught this morning," Owen whispered to Hugh. "She was likely, otherwise, to have done herself harm."

On reaching the table, Úna broke into a loud ullagone. Gradually the fury of her grief abated and she started to speak. At first she uttered only broken phrases, then this simple, unlettered woman began talking in verse:

> Pulse of my heart, many a hard fight you fought
> And now you are lying on these boards,
> Robbed of your strength and your breath:
> My grief and my grief and my grief!

The crones now joined in with "Oh, oh, ochone," as if they were taking part in a familiar ritual. When they had finished, Úna continued, pausing after each rann for the chorus:

> I remember the first day I saw you
> Under Sheegora's dark heather;
> Blood crimsoned your manly, white body:
> Your eyes called to me and I answered.

And so on the keen went, telling of Shawn's life and deeds. If I had been listening to the performance of a Greek tragedy, I could not have been more enthralled. It was all the more exceptional in the light of what would happen later.

Chapter 20

THE GLOOM which Shawn Bacach's death cast over me was lifted by the unexpected arrival of Tomás Láidir. I had just entered the kitchen for my evening meal when he strode through the door, hair dishevelled and doublet open.

"Wait till you hear the news I have for you, Palesman." He grinned, slapping me on the back so that I winced a little. "Is there some place where we can talk?" he added, eyeing Brian Dubh, who was staring at his perspiring face and bare chest.

I grabbed a cake of oaten bread and Tomás a jug of buttermilk and we retired to Cormac's house.

"Why haven't you visited Frances?" Tomás took a deep draught of the buttermilk before breaking off a handful of bread. "Does your cold Dublin heart not recognize her worth?"

I explained my reasons for staying in Ballintober, none of which satisfied Tomás.

"You don't deserve such a prize," he scoffed, "you and your cautious Dublin ways. God's blood, man, don't weigh every action like a miller weighting corn!"

"Tell me your news." I drank from the jug and handed it to him.

He swallowed half the remaining buttermilk, wiped his mouth with the back of his hand and belched. "Palesman," he said, "fortune has smiled on you. You're to come to Moylurg!"

Between enormous mouthfuls of bread he told me how Oona had persuaded her brother Cathal Roe to employ me as tutor to his children. Since the MacDermots were friendly with Sir Robert

King – who lived scarcely three miles away in Abbeyboyle – they did not fear Coote's displeasure.

"And hearken to this," he added. "Sir Robert told them that Wentworth – the Earl of Strafford – was beheaded in London not two weeks ago. Isn't that a good omen?"

"Is it?" The image of Black Tom in his robes of state crossing the quadrangle of Trinity flashed into my mind. "For all his ruthlessness, Strafford was the king's right-hand man. The Puritans have now tasted blood."

"Oh, don't be a prophet of doom!" Tomás drained the jug. "Let's go to the wake before all the ale is finished."

Munching the last piece of bread, I followed him to the Great Hall. Smoke dimmed the candles so that they gave off only an amber glow and the reek of perspiring bodies mingled with the odours of ale, tobacco and melting wax. Scullogues and their families from the outlying farms – among them, Grainne, O'Conor Don's former paramour – had swelled the gathering in my absence. A piper was playing dance music and young fellows and their wenches were wheeling around in a circle, their bare feet slapping the flags. In the centre Donal Bawn with a woman's kerchief bound about his head sat on the shoulders of his grinning friend, Fergus, urging on the dancers. Now and again he would emit a wild whoop, which was echoed by his compeers. Grainne, her long, chestnut hair flying, beckoned to me to join her but I declined. Tomás had no such scruples. He threw off his brogues and was soon part of the revels.

The table with Shawn Bacach's corpse had been moved to a window alcove, near which Úna and the older men and women sat, puffing on pipes and drinking ale. I made my way to Úna, wondering how she could endure this insult to the dead.

"Charles," she cried, clasping my hand, "I'm glad you're here."

I told her of my regret at Shawn's death and she nodded, wiping her tear-reddened eyes with a corner of her linen kerchief.

"He always enjoyed talking to you." She raised her voice to make herself audible above the din. "Here, Brighid, fetch Charles some ale."

"No." I shook my head.

"Oh, go on," she coaxed, as Brighid dipped a meadar in a wooden pail. "Shawn would want you to enjoy his wake. Wasn't he always one for wakes himself?"

Not wishing to give offence, I accepted the dripping meadar, though I still hesitated.

"Drink up, *a ghrá*." Úna touched my arm. "Shawn died a warrior's death and he'd not want the young to mourn."

I raised the meadar to my lips and drank. "That was a fine lament you made for Shawn," I told her. "Even Cormac could hardly have bettered it."

Úna smiled, a faraway smile. "I can't remember a word of it," she said. "It came to me and now it's gone."

Cormac's motto, "What's written endures", resounded in my mind. Vowing that I would make Úna's words endure, I left her to her grief and moved over to Brighid.

"What do you think of this?" In the amber light I could hardly perceive her disfigurement.

"The dancing? It shows how much everyone loved Shawn." She refilled my meadar. "Have you heard about Beibhinn?"

"Heard what?" I asked.

"Old Sir Charles Coote made his son cast her out," she said. "He found her with the key of Cormac's cell."

"Who told you?" I did not conceal my dismay.

"Phelim the Pedlar." She fixed me with her calm, direct gaze. "Phelim arrived today from Roscommon – and, Charles," she lowered her voice, "Beibhinn is working in a tavern."

"Where is Phelim now?" My trysts with Marion in the Black Raven came crowding into my mind.

"Somewhere over there." She pointed to the dancers.

"Has O'Conor Don been told?" I asked.

"Not yet," Brighid admitted. "I had to help Úna."

"Shouldn't Úna be in bed now?" I didn't allude to the shameful conduct taking place before us but Brighid divined my thoughts.

"Yes," she agreed. "If she doesn't rest, she'll be too tired for the funeral tomorrow."

Brighid and one of the kitchen maids escorted Úna from the hall. It was just as well, for the revels were reaching new extremes of depravity. Egged on by Donal Bawn, the young men had hoisted the lassies on their shoulders and these were attempting to throw one another to the floor, much to the amusement of the onlookers. MacDockwra, carrying Grainne, was face to face with Dudley, who was carrying a red-haired damsel; the two riders had caught each other by the arms and were locked in combat, legs and bosoms bared.

"Over here, Palesman!" Tomás shouted. "I've got a jug of bulcaan."

I picked my way through the revellers to the raised table, where Tomás was sitting in O'Conor Don's place.

"Here, drink to Shawn Bacach's memory." Tomás extended his meadar.

"Do you know Phelim the Pedlar?" I took a sip of the fiery liquid, which almost burned my throat. "I must speak to him."

"Phelim!" Tomás bellowed. "Phelim the Pedlar!" A pockmarked fellow with shrewd brown eyes broke away from the dancers and lurched towards us.

"What do you want to buy?" he enquired. "Pipe or purse, skean or spur, ring or razor? My packs are below in the kitchen."

"Nothing," Tomás informed him. "My Dublin friend, Charles here, wishes to converse with you. Charles, you may address this Midas of the highways and byways."

Once Phelim heard my name he said he had a message for me, which he would impart for a crown. I promised him a shilling and he told me that Beibhinn wished me to know that Cormac was in good health, though much dispirited by his imprisonment. Beibhinn also warned that the Cootes were more determined than ever to capture me and were pestering Lord Ranelagh to that end. Finally, she implored me to plead with the O'Conors on her behalf so that she might again be taken into their employment.

I paid Phelim for his information and assured him that, when the first opportunity arose, I would speak to O'Conor Don.

"I'll wager that's the third time he's been paid," Tomás said in Phelim's hearing, "once by Beibhinn, once by the O'Conors and now by you!"

Phelim grinned and hurried away.

"So long as he hasn't been paid by Brian Dubh, what does it matter?" I said; then, disturbed by the lewd behaviour around me, I informed Tomás that I was retiring to Cormac's house and he could either accompany me or stay. Despite his recent journey, he chose to remain and it was long after midnight when he blundered in the door.

The next morning food and drink in abundance were provided for the mourners and after Tomás and I had tasted a little, we begged Hugh to take us to his father. O'Conor Don gladly assented to my joining the household of Cathal Roe, only warning me to tread warily if I visited Abbeyboyle. He evinced no surprise when I recounted Beibhinn's misfortune, giving me to understand that he had already spoken to Phelim and that he would send for Beibhinn once the funeral was over.

"That reminds me," he turned to Hugh, "I want Shawn Bacach buried in the precinct of the church."

"But his grave —" Hugh began to demur; then, perceiving his father's grim expression, he fell silent.

"You may go." O'Conor Don dismissed Tomás and me. As we walked out the door he and Hugh began conversing in low voices.

At noon a priest read Mass in the Great Hall – a service I avoided by telling Tomás I had manuscripts to complete before my departure.

"I see how it is," Tomás observed slyly, "the sandpiper cannot attend both strands."

After Mass the coffin was carried downhill to the churchyard, the priest in his vestments and a boy with a tall crucifix leading the way and the Pursuers walking in a double line behind the bier. I won't recount the details of the funeral: the cries and clapping of hands, the baring of heads and beating of brows, the ear-piercing howls of the keening women, the barbaric display of grief that would remind one more of a concourse of demons than a procession of Christians.

At the ruined church there was an unexpected disturbance when Brian Dubh insisted that the grave be moved as it adjoined the family vault of the O'Conors. I saw Úna – who was supported by Brighid and her mother – flinch, then O'Conor Don stepped forward.

"Who gave you authority to interfere with this burial?" he demanded.

"I was only defending your family's prerogatives." Brian Dubh was taken aback.

"In that case," O'Conor Don spoke quietly but distinctly, "go to your masters in Castlecoote and tell them to release my ollamh."

"I don't know what you're talking about." Brian Dubh showed the courage of a cornered rat.

"Don't you?" O'Conor Don was livid. "I've had you watched

since April. Now be off before I forget that this is sacred ground."

"I've served you –" Brian Dubh began then Hugh grabbed his arm.

"Be off!" he commanded. "And take your hirelings with you!" He pointed to Donal Bawn and Fergus.

The crowd began to mutter and the three slunk off, flanked by Dudley and MacDockwra.

"This is your doing, Palesman," Brian Dubh looked back at me from the gate of the churchyard, "and one day soon you'll rue it."

You may imagine how dismayed I felt that evening taking leave of my friends. Yet, with Brian Dubh's dismissal, I was too aware of the need for a hasty departure to remain in Ballintober another day. O'Conor Don had asked Tomás to accompany me and he made no protest. Dressed in my old clothes and a shaggy mantle and mounted on a garron, I trotted at Tomás's side out through the hollow-sounding entrance just as rain began to fall. On looking back I could see Hugh standing before Cormac's house, his arm upraised.

"Take good care of Nell," I shouted, too moved to say what was in my heart. He had been a true Prince of Connacht to me, though I was neither a kinsman nor a Catholic.

The light began to pale as we skirted Tulsk and took the road to Cruachan. Tomás had not said a word since setting out, either because he resented having to escort me or because of the bulcaan and lack of sleep. His silence suited me, however, for my mind was like a tree tossed this way and that by contrary winds. I recalled Brighid's prophecy about going on a journey and suffering because I would lose somebody dear to me. In the evening of that fatal day I convinced myself that she had been referring to the journey to Cruachan and to Cormac's capture. Now I knew that this was the journey because I had yet to meet the person who would show me the road I must follow. Who, then, was the person dear to me that I would lose? Was it Frances? Surely fate would not raise my hopes only to dash them down once again? And yet when I rode this way just over a month previously I had been dressed in a nobleman's finery, not in shaggy mantle and greasy brogues … The knowledge that I was only dressed as a bodach to avoid notice and that Hugh had promised to send my good clothes after me could not set my mind at ease, so much did my change of apparel seem an omen.

Yet, though plunged in a slough of despair, two thoughts consoled me: MacDermot's village, known as *Baile na Carraige*, the Town of the Rock, lay within an hour's ride of Ballytrasna and it was also within a good day's ride of the sea. If Cathal Roe proved a hard taskmaster, I would persuade Frances to flee with me to Sligo where, fortune favouring us, we would obtain passage on a ship bound for Spain or Flanders. Once we were in Flanders, I could join an Irish regiment and with my Gaelic learning I would soon become a captain and, in time, a colonel. My grand-uncle Richard had been the Great O'Neill's agent in Brussels and there was every chance that O'Neill's nephew, Owen Roe, the defender of Arras, would remember such service.

What a life of adventure Frances and I would lead, meeting strange people, exploring ancient streets, visiting Ghent and Louvain! And every night alone in our room, locked in each other's arms, inhaling the honied fragrance of her neck and –

"*D'anam don diabhal!*" I was startled out of my reverie by a muttered curse from Tomás.

"What's wrong?" I spurred my garron till I was riding abreast of him.

"A hare!" he cried. "That's an ill omen on a journey."

"Why?" I asked.

He mumbled something about "a witch's beast"; then asked if I had a rosary.

"No," I said, "just a Bible."

"We'd better take the Military Road." He turned his garron to the right and in a short time we came to a broad, paved road leading north.

"Aren't we more likely to encounter soldiers here?" I remarked.

"It's not soldiers I fear," Tomás admitted. "That other way would have taken us past the Cave of Cruachan. It's not a place to be near after dark."

"How did you come to Ballintober yesterday?" I changed the subject lest my voice should betray amusement at his superstition.

"Through Castlerea," he said. "Do you know that in Ninety-Nine Clifford's army marched along this road from Athlone to Abbeyboyle?"

"Judging from what happened at Corrslieve's Pass, they should have stayed in Athlone," I commented.

"Not bad, Palesman!" He gave a short laugh, his teeth gleaming in the dusk. "They taught you well in Trinity."

"It was Cormac who taught me," I said, "Cormac and Shawn Bacach. Where did you go to school yourself?"

"In the city of French-Fitzstephens," he replied. "I spent a few years at the Free School in Galway, then my father – God's blessing on his soul – learned from Master Lynch that I was more interested in taverns and merchants' daughters than in Caesar's *Commentaries*."

"Is the Free School a grammar school?" I asked.

"It's as much a college as your Trinity." There was an edge to his voice. "We had over a thousand students from all parts of Ireland, even from the Pale."

Hoping to smooth his ruffled feathers, I confessed my own lack of success at Trinity and the pain this had caused my parents.

"Don't trouble yourself about such things," he advised. "If you hadn't failed, you wouldn't have escaped the crow's nest."

"What's 'the crow's nest'?" I asked.

"A Protestant house." He was still resentful.

"My mother is of the old faith," I said. "Wouldn't that make me a lapwing, half white, half black?"

Tomás laughed and the tension between us was broken.

"Your father was a poet, wasn't he?" I leaned to avoid a projecting branch.

"Yes," he replied, "a poet of the people but because he didn't compose by the rules or master the seven grades, the men of the Bardic schools dismissed him as a rhymer. Did you hear that eulogy O'Mulconry recited at the feast – 'the noble defender of the Gaels of *Magh Aí* '? The only thing that Catholic noblemen like O'Conor Don defend is their own interests."

Tomás then launched into a diatribe against his countrymen who had adopted English ways or the Protestant faith in order to preserve their worldly wealth. "We were the first Norman family in Connacht to throw in our lot with the Gaels," he continued, "and now we're not even good enough to marry one of them. I tell you, Charles, it matters little having noble blood in your veins if you have no money in your purse."

To lift him out of his despondency, I said, "Suppose you were a magician and could shape the world to your desire, what sort of Ireland would you fashion?"

"The Ireland that Oisín described to St Patrick," he replied. "An Ireland of hunting, fighting and feasting, where every day would be the beginning of some new adventure."

"I mean as regards its laws and form of government," I explained.

"Oh, now I see the hare you're starting." He paused for a moment. "That's easily answered. An Ireland where we would have justice, where our estates would be restored and where we could practise our religion without fear of persecution."

"But would your Ireland be a kingdom in which princes, earls and lesser nobles held sway or would it be a republic?" I gripped tightly with my knees as my garron lurched through a puddle.

"I've never considered such questions before," he confessed. "Do you mean a republic such as the Romans had?"

"Yes," I said, "except that it would be an Anglo-Irish republic, where Gaels, Normans, Old English and New English would live side by side in harmony."

"And who would be the patricians and who the plebeians?" Tomás's voice was mocking. "No, such an Ireland can never exist while the New English have their hands on our throats."

"My grand-uncle, Richard, believed that something like it could," I asserted, recalling what my father had told me.

"Then your grand-uncle was a fool," Tomás scoffed. "I prefer to put my trust in the sword."

"'All those that take the sword shall perish with the sword,'" I reminded him.

"In that case, the Protestants will surely perish." Tomás spoke with grim satisfaction.

By this time the rain had ceased and a crescent moon shed fitful light on the empty, undulating landscape.

"Where are we now?" I asked.

"We're coming to Shankill," he said. "After that we'll be in Elphin. In the last century three territories met hereabouts: Tir-Briuin, O'Beirne's Country; Clann Cathail, O'Flanagan's Country and Moylurg, MacDermot's Country. Now the English have most of the good land and the Cathedral of Elphin to boot."

"Who is Bishop there?"

"Henry Tilson – though by rights it should be Dr Egan, the man you bearded on the night of the feast."

"He seemed to regard me with some aversion."

"Well, that's hardly to be wondered at. Henry Tilson was, I'm told, until two years ago Dean of Christ Church in your heathen city; now he's ensconced in the episcopal palace in Elphin while the rightful incumbent, Dr Egan, has to sneak around in disguise. Everywhere you look in this diocese you'll find churches, convents and abbeys abandoned or destroyed or, worse still, turned into dwelling houses for Protestants. Only a few priests and friars remain, most of them living in hovels or hiding in the woods. Can't you understand then why the good Bishop looks on your tribe with a certain jaundice?"

"Yes, but that does not justify him in standing between me and Frances."

"Doesn't it? When the wolf threatens the lamb, does the good shepherd not – Cross of Christ!" his voice filled with horror.

Immediately we both reined in our garrons. The sky was so overlaid with scudding clouds that there was barely enough moonlight to reveal, between it and the darker earth, the ghastly spectacle looming up before us.

Chapter 21

My father had often told us of the afternoon in the year Twelve when he had seen Bishop Conor O'Devany hanged for his part in O'Neill's rebellion. My father was a young man then, ready for any adventure. Encountering a large crowd of common Dublin people – tradesmen, apprentices, housewives, beggars, children – following the hurdle on which the aged Bishop was being hauled from the Castle to the gallows, he had joined it, partly out of curiosity, partly out of sympathy. He had stood watching while the condemned man fixed the rope around his own neck and pulled the hood down over his face. Just then a strange thing happened: the sky, which had been dark with clouds, turned crimson. My father said that the actual execution had filled him with horror. For weeks afterwards he had been unable to sleep. He kept seeing the suspended body writhing in mid-air, the hands bound behind the back, the neck twisted sideways by the knot. Now I understood his horror.

At a fork in the road a crude gibbet had been erected. From its crossbeam a man's body hung, dark, motionless, grotesque. There was a sickly sweet odour in the air. When the moon broke through its pall of clouds, I could see the swollen face only a few feet above my own, the untrimmed beard almost hiding the staring eyes. It was Manus!

"I know this fellow," I cried and told Tomás about my encounter with Manus in O'Beirne's alehouse and his recent offer to enlist me in a Spanish regiment.

"He recited a prophecy about Saxons lying stretched on the

ground," I recalled. "Maybe he recited it later in an alehouse and somebody reported him."

"Maybe." Tomás was only half listening.

"Or he might have been shot while stealing cattle." I pointed to a dark stain on the doublet. "That looks like dried blood. Do you remember the soldiers who questioned us on the journey back from Cruachan? They were looking for Pursuers."

"It's likely he was one of Rory O'More's men, God have mercy on his soul." Tomás blessed himself.

"Amen," I murmured, unable to take my eyes off the distorted features. "Who is Rory O'More?"

"I'd swear this is Old Coote's doing." Tomás ignored my question. "He's showing us what's in store for us if we fight back. Well, Bloody Sir Charles, you'll get your answer."

Sliding from his garron, he began rocking the gibbet backward and forward till its hold in the soil loosened. Then he wrapped his arms about the pole, shouting to me at the same time, "Catch him as he falls!"

It was useless to demur. Grunting and heaving, he lifted the entire gibbet out of the ground. Instantly, it toppled so that the body with its hempen noose fell onto my garron. I attempted to hold it but the garron shied, causing me to tumble off with the body in my arms.

Even now I break out in cold perspiration as I recall that moment, the heavy, rigid bulk of the dead man, the sweet odour, mingled with the stench of excrement, the bearded face next to mine! My father told us that when the hangman began to cut Bishop O'Devany open so that he could be drawn and quartered he, my father, had rushed away and vomited. I didn't vomit but I must have grown faint because Tomás was obliged to raise me to my feet. Without saying a word, he helped me to remount; then he dragged the body to the side of the road, where he laid it on the grassy verge. That done, he wrenched the crossbeam from the gibbet and tossed the pole into a ditch. We rode off, Tomás carrying the crossbeam before him.

Presently it dawned on me that we weren't skirting Elphin. "Aren't there soldiers in the town?" I asked.

"Don't worry about soldiers," Tomás laughed mirthlessly. "If any whoreson challenges us, we're just two itinerant poets bound for Moylurg."

This answer hardly set my mind at ease, yet, being unacquainted with the region, I had no choice but to follow. Soon we were trotting down the narrow, cobbled street between silent, shuttered houses, the hoofbeats of our unshod garrons loud in the gloom. The dogs must have been used to strangers for they did not announce us. Passing the looming bulk of the cathedral, we came to the Bishop's residence, which, to my mind, seemed to have been constructed as a fortress rather than a palace. As we drew near the locked entrance, Tomás tossed the crossbeam over the high wall enclosing the outer courtyard. It fell with a great clatter. On the instant a dog started to bark furiously, which caused others to give tongue. We lingered till somebody opened an upstairs window and shouted in the accent of my native city, "Stop thief!"

"We're not thieves," Tomás yelled in English. "We're honest men who wish to return your gibbet. You will need it to hang Sir Charles Coote for malfeasance and murder."

"In God's name be quiet," I implored, "or you'll bring the whole town about our ears."

By this time candles were flickering in nearby windows and other voices had taken up the cry of "Stop thief", while the chorus of dogs added to the growing clamour. Without further ado Tomás and I dug our heels into our garrons' sides and with Tomás crying "*Fág an bealach!*" we galloped off northward.

When it became clear that we weren't being pursued, we slowed to a walk.

"Do you know who owns this land?" Tomás panted.

"No!" I spoke curtly, annoyed at him for having exposed us to danger.

"Well, I'll tell you." He pretended not to be aware of my mood. "Bishop Tilson, the gentleman whose sleep we disturbed. He doesn't believe in selling all his goods and giving the money to the poor."

"If you consider me a defender of bishops you're mistaken." I removed my mantle, as I had grown exceedingly hot.

"Oh, ho! A Presbyterian!" he scoffed.

"Neither a Presbyterian nor a Papist," I retorted, "just a man who believes in the *aurea mediocritas*. It seems to me that before the dissolution of the monasteries, your bishops, abbots and monks weren't renowned for poverty either, at least to judge from their large houses and estates."

"True," he admitted, "but at least they gave alms to the poor and welcomed travellers and took care of the sick. Could you see Henry Tilson doing that, though his palace was built with the stones of the Franciscan abbey?"

"I know nothing of Bishop Tilson," I pointed out, "but I do know that Catholics are just as fond of wealth as Protestants. Why, the Earl of Clanricarde – with whom your Bishop Egan is living – has more wealth than the king himself."

"He's living with the Burkes of Glinsk," Tomás corrected me. "Nevertheless, it galls me to think of that hireling, Tilson, sitting in his place, a place founded by St Patrick himself. You know, don't you, that St Patrick founded three churches in this region: Kilmore, Elphin and Shankill?"

"Isn't Kilmore in East Brefni?" I said, recalling MacDockwra's mission to Bishop Bedell.

"Oh, that's the diocese of Kilmore, you bodhrawn," Tomás chided. "I'm speaking of the parish of Kilmore over there to the east of us, where the O'Mulconrys – Cormac's people – live."

Once again I was conscious of my ignorance of his world, which was also the world of Frances. Would I always be a foreigner here as Bishop Tilson was a foreigner?

"Have you and Dudley any hopes of recovering your family's estate?" I asked, more to keep my mind off the dead man who had been lying on top of me than to gain information.

"How?" he snorted. "The only way we could do that would be to side with the English. If I became a Protestant like you, Charles, and spoke the King's English and went to your heathen university, I might end up being as rich as the Cootes, Joneses, Lanes, Kings and all the other men of the Bible. They're the ones that control the lawcourts and the towns. Do you know that since I was born three of the towns about Moylurg have been granted charters: Abbeyboyle, Carrickdrumrusky and Jamestown? And why?"

"Their populations have grown?"

"No. It's because those charters enable them to elect two Protestant members to the Parliament in Dublin. I tell you, Charles, the New Foreigners are growing fatter and fatter while we grow leaner and leaner."

Tomás's about-turn from attacking his own people to attacking the English might have amused me if I did not perceive that I was just as inconsistent myself. What was I? I certainly wasn't one of the New English, men like Sir Charles Coote who had come to Ireland to make their fortunes by any means they could. My father's people, it is true, had always been loyal to the crown but then Strafford, the king's deputy, had suppressed the woollen trade because its success threatened England's wool merchants and my father had seen how little his loyalty mattered. Maybe I was what my grand-uncle, Richard, had designated as "Anglo-Irish" – though my mother's blood made me something else again. And, yet, I was still a member of the Reformed Church, whose head was the King, notwithstanding that I had not attended Divine Service in four months. And what about Frances with her soft red lips and bashful smile? Wasn't she worth a Mass?

The faint drumming of horses' hooves behind us interrupted my thoughts.

"Who could that be at this hour?" I tried to keep the alarm out of my voice.

"Soldiers!" Tomás cried. "Tilson must have roused them."

He urged his garron into a canter and I followed his lead. Glancing back I could see lights bobbing in the distance, as if our pursuers were carrying lanterns. We rode like demons, though the uncertain moonlight and rutted track made disaster imminent. After a quarter of an hour or so we slowed down. The hoofbeats of our pursuers had grown louder, a dull insistent rumble.

"They must be able to hear us," I panted.

"Aye," Tomás concurred. "We'll have to take to the bog. There's one about five furlongs ahead."

We cantered past ghostly farmsteads, with shadowy clumps of trees and darkened cottages, while all the time the pursuit drew closer. Never in my life did I so long for the safety of my parents' home. With Tomás Láidir as a companion I would either die from a musket shot or end up drowning in a boghole. I was tempted for a moment to draw rein and face the soldiers; then I realized the folly of such an action. If I weren't shot on the spot as a woodkerne, I would be sent to Castlecoote as a prisoner.

"Follow me!" Tomás Láidir shouted as we came to a flat, empty waste. Our garrons struggled through the marshy, grass-covered ground, sinking and plunging. Before long we were obliged to dismount. Leading the garrons, we picked our way forward while the soldiers came on like a band of centaurs, their lanterns glowing yellow in the moonlight.

Presently we came to a ditch, beyond which moss and heather stretched into the distance.

"Halt!" a harsh voice shouted in English. "Halt in the King's name!"

"Keep going!" Tomás urged. "We'll soon be beyond reach of their pistols."

Frantically we jumped the ditch alongside our garrons. My mantle slipped from the garron's back, where I had draped it over the rawhide bag containing my Bible and razor. As I bent to retrieve it there was a salvo and pistol balls thudded into the earth around us.

With my heart in my mouth, I jumped from one heathery hummock to the next, dragging the garron behind me. Missing my footing, I landed in a patch of quaking moss but managed to struggle out. Behind us I could hear the soldiers squelching through the marshy ground. Seconds later the same harsh voice shouted: "In the king's name come out! We have you within musket range."

"Keep going!" Tomás hissed. "Even if they have muskets, they still have to prime and light them."

As he spoke clouds hid the moon. Blindly we struggled on, deeper and deeper into the heart of the bog, our garrons sinking to their hocks, yet somehow managing to free themselves. On glancing back, I could see, low down, a cluster of yellow lights. Next moment I stepped into a quagmire. Floundering around, I grabbed a tussock and hauled myself, spluttering and gasping, onto firm ground. Just then the moon re-emerged. Instantly, a shot rang out. With a frightened squeal my garron lurched to one side and collapsed. When I reached him he was kicking spasmodically, while low groans issued from his throat.

Tomás hurried crouching towards me. Quickly he felt the wound then drew a miodoge from a sheath attached to his belt and thrust it into the stricken animal's heart. With a horrible choking sound the poor beast expired, whereupon Tomás cut the belt holding the rawhide bag and handed the bag to me.

"Keep low!" he commanded as I rose to retrieve my mantle, which lay further off in the heather. "They may be able to detect movement."

"What if they come closer?" I asked, on returning with the mantle wrapped around me.

"They won't," he declared. "Townsmen dread bogs."

His prediction proved correct. After waiting fruitlessly by the ditch for us to show ourselves, the soldiers retreated to the road. Once there, white lights flared among the yellow lantern lights and presently our ears were saluted with dull discharges followed by a louder discharge, and the hiss and thud of a musket ball. Soon afterwards the lantern lights receded towards Elphin.

"The curse of Bingham on ye!" Tomás shouted. "Ye'll pay for this one day."

"Will we go back to the road?" I tried to keep my teeth from chattering with the cold.

"No," Tomás said. "They may have sent a few men to waylay us at Croghan. We'll have to keep to the rough tracks."

Having found his garron standing unharmed by a willow, we swung north, Tomás leading the garron and I floundering after him. The bog was not extensive so we were soon on firm ground. From there on we followed cow tracks and boreens, riding by turns whenever possible but more often trudging up hills and across callows with the aid of two sturdy hazel staffs. How I managed to keep up with Tomás I cannot tell for I was drenched and exhausted. Gradually the eastern sky lightened and on breasting a low ridge we saw below us the faint gleam of water.

"Lough Clogher!" Tomás called out. "Moylurg Castle used to stand on its far side. We'll be at Ardcarn in no time at all."

Leaving the lake on our left, we forded a small river then struck across country, passing a roofless church and a few scattered hovels. The eastern sky was now flushed with dawn. An owl passed overhead on soundless wings, while larks rose singing into the grey sky. When the sun edged above the horizon we could see all around us fertile green hillsides on which cattle and sheep were beginning to graze and further to the north-east and north, mountains rising one above the other in blue and amethyst ranks. Truly it was a noble prospect and if I had not been so wet and weary it would have gladdened my heart. As it was, my thoughts remained fixed on a soft bed in a dark room where I might sleep till Gabriel's trumpet sounded.

Near Ardcarn we stopped to rest. Suddenly Tomás espied in the distance a band of horsemen riding directly towards us.

"Hurry!" he cried. "Up behind me and we'll race for the village!"

"No," I said. "The garron is almost too tired to walk. Remove his bridle and turn him loose." When I explained my intended ruse, Tomás quickly complied.

By the time the horsemen reached us we were leaning on our staffs, minding a flock of sheep. The two leading horsemen drew apart from their companions and beckoned to us to approach. Both were accoutred like English travellers with saddle rolls, leather bags, swords and horsepistols.

"Hey you, Teigue, which is the road to Abbeyboyle?" the taller of the two, a man of about fifty-five, with sombre clothes, hard, piercing eyes and thin, cruel lips under a neatly trimmed moustache, demanded in English, looking from Tomás to me.

Fearing that his contempt might provoke Tomás into defiance, I quickly replied, "*Ní thuigim*," whereupon he asked his companion to repeat the question in Gaelic.

Tomás pointed to the north. The tall stranger nodded, then turning to his companion, who was a handsome, clean-shaven man of my own age, he said: "Didn't I tell you, John, that these fellows were all rogues and liars? Look at their clothes and faces. Did you ever see such jackanapes? I'll wager they have just come from stealing their neighbour's sheep or relieving some honest man of his purse."

"My father believes that with Gaelic-speaking ministers to explain the Word of God to them and wean them away from Popish idolatry, they can be made into honest, industrious subjects," John replied in an accent that was partly of Dublin, partly of England.

"The only way to deal with these woodkernes," the older man declared, "is with the sword in one hand and the Bible in the other. First teach them to know their masters, then reform them. In God's name, let's be on our way." He stared at us once more with cold, amused eyes then he and his companion trotted off westward, followed by the other horsemen.

"They're going the wrong way," I remarked, wondering why the older man's aspect seemed so familiar.

"No, they're not." Tomás spat. "I pointed out the road to Knockvicar. That whoreson knew the right direction all along. I never met any of the clan at close quarters but from what Dudley told me, that's Old Coote himself."

Immediately, I recalled the young Sir Charles and Sir Chidley and knew he was right, for this man mingled the mocking self-confidence of his brother with the truculent arrogance of his own son.

Now I had met the third person of the unholy trinity. Sir Charles Coote Senior was somebody who, in native Irish eyes, had taken as his motto Cicero's "*Oderint dum metuant*" (Let them hate provided that they fear). But why was he travelling to Abbeyboyle?

"Do you think he's on his way to Sir Robert King?" I asked.

"You may be sure of it," Tomás said. "Though I never set eyes on him before, I'd swear that his companion, John, is Sir Robert's eldest son. Oona tells me he lives in their Dublin castle, where Sir Robert spends the greater part of the year."

"And where would they be coming from now?" I asked.

"Either from Coote's castle in Jamestown or his iron works in Arigna." He retrieved his miodoge from under a nearby bush.

"Then Sir Charles mightn't have been responsible for Manus being hung on the gibbet," I pointed out.

"If he wasn't there in person," Tomás attached the sheath to his belt, "you may be sure it was done on his orders or the orders of one of his family. The scaldcrows are never far from the corpse."

"Where does Frances live?" I asked as we resumed our journey, Tomás walking and I sitting on the garron.

"Over there!" Tomás pointed to the direction that the horsemen had taken. "Her father owns an estate of rich grazing land just south of Abbeyboyle. He also collects the tithes of Ardcarn parish for the Earl of Clanricarde."

I wanted to question him further but my thoughts drifted into a waking dream in which Frances raced to meet me.

Presently we came to the mound of Knockmelliagh, which, Tomás assured me, is a dwelling place of the Sidhe or fairy folk.

"We'll take Oona and Frances there," he grinned, "and nobody will venture near us."

"Maybe we'll all get lost in the fairy world and never find our way back!" I warned.

After journeying on for what seemed a league but was probably not more than half that distance, we came to a broad, rolling upland with flocks and herds, from the summit of which rose Mac-Dermot's two-storied house, Carrick Mansion. If I had not been so utterly exhausted, I would probably have stood gazing at it in admiration, for though not imposing like Ballintober, its thatched roof, lime-white walls and circular palisade of leafy hazels was infinitely more pleasing to the eye. Corncrakes filled the meadows with their lusty chanting, blackbirds and thrushes sang on treetops and a cuckoo's double note floated down from a distant wood. Truly it was, as the poet Eochaidh O'Hussey had described it, a "round fair-pathed fort of sap-rich hazels".

Was it here, I wondered, that I would meet the person Brighid had told me of, the one who would show me the road I must follow? Eagerly I urged the garron forward.

III

REAPING

Devenere locos laetos et amoena virecta
fortunatorum nemorum sedesque beatas.

(They came to the regions of joy, delightful green places
and blessed abodes in the happy woods.)

Virgil, *The Aeneid*, Book VI, ll. 638, 639

Chapter 22

NOW BEGAN what I can only describe as my sojourn in Elysium. Carrick Mansion was situated on a low hill facing the Plains of Abbeyboyle to the south and, on its north side, overlooking Lough Cé, beyond whose wooded islands and azure waters, hills and mountains formed an undulating rampart of damasked green and blue. Some of the islands contained monasteries, while an island close to the south shore was completely occupied by a square fortress about thirty cubits high, from whose battlements flew the red cross banner of St George and the banner of the MacDermots, with its three azure boars on a white field. Between the lake and Carrick Mansion there was a village of mud-walled cabins, haphazardly grouped in the Irish fashion.

Cathal Roe had five children; the eldest, Brian, just eight and the youngest, Hugh, a babe in arms. In between, there were Turlough or Terence, Cathal Oge and Anne. My job was to teach Brian and Terence English, Latin and the rudiments of geometry, something that made no great demands on my talents for they were bright boys, if a little unruly. All the children had inherited their parents' good looks and three-year-old Anne, with her blue eyes and amber hair, was a delight to behold.

My master, a tall, powerfully built man, whose trimmed, red hair and beard framed a long, bright-complexioned face, was pleasant and agreeable, though in my presence he rarely revealed his deeper thoughts and few people would dare to cross him. His wife, Eleanor, to whom I had already spoken in Ballintober, was a plump, fair-haired young woman, nearly always warm and cheerful, except when the squabbling of the children frayed her patience. I should mention that both husband and wife dressed just as well-to-do Dublin citizens did in those times, though Lady Eleanor usually wore a folded linen headdress in the Irish fashion and the master on returning home from inspecting his herds and flocks or settling a dispute in the village replaced his high boots with deerskin brogues.

Cathal Roe's father, Brian Oge, had, as I have related elsewhere, died in Athlone five years prior to my arrival but his mother, Lady Margaret, was still very much alive and her alert eye missed nothing. Fortunately, she decided that since I had attended the same university as her dead husband, I was an interesting young scholar and delighted in questioning me about life in Dublin while we played backgammon or cards. She herself was a Burke – or, rather, De Burgo – and would frequently remind me that her mother's father was the second Earl of Clanricarde.

Oona, the children's aunt, was like an older sister to me. If her treatment of Tomás at Ballintober had led me to consider her a trifle haughty, it soon became clear that this was only one side of her nature. She was far better educated than most young women I had met, even my own sisters, and could discuss poetry and philosophy with great acuity.

There were two other people in the household whom I must mention, Bridgeen and Niall. Bridgeen had been a nursemaid to Oona and her brothers and still fussed over them as if they were children. Niall was *reachtaire* but a person less like Brian Dubh it would be hard to find. He belonged to Shawn Bacach's generation and he and I became good friends. About half a dozen girls worked in the kitchen in the east end of the house but since I had seldom any reason to go there, I did not get to know them nearly so well as those in Ballintober.

On the morning that I arrived Niall conducted me to my sleeping quarters, a small cabin with one glass window, nestling at the east side of the mansion. Neither as Stygian as Shawn Rua's house nor as monastic as Cormac's, it looked comfortable enough, though furnished only with a roughly made table, two stools, a pallet and a crude washstand placed near the back wall. There was a stone fireplace at one end of the room and an open loft for storing goods at the other.

Niall brought me oaten bread and ale and as soon as I had

eaten and drunk, I threw myself fully clothed on the pallet and fell asleep. The first thing I heard on awaking was the singing of black-birds, thrushes and linnets, their voices so loud and cheerful that, lying in that small room with the sun flooding through the win-dow, I could imagine myself in an enchanted forest. Quickly I pulled on my brogues and stepped out into the bawn. The place was deserted except for a brown, curly haired spaniel that came up and let me pat him. Going behind the cabin I urinated, vowing that I would ask Niall for a chamber pot at our next meeting.

Observing my surroundings more closely than on the previous day, I noticed that here and there hazel poles had taken root in the earthen bank in which they had been fixed and were now leafy trees. There were also a number of whitethorns, some of which were still in bloom. The mansion was thatched with reeds and had diamond-paned windows on the ground floor and under the eaves. Its walls were whitened with lime and its oak door was golden brown. The only indication of the inhabitants' nobility was a stone coat of arms inset above the doorway on which could be discerned the three wild boars of the MacDermots.

When I ventured behind the mansion, Niall emerged from the nearer of two cabins.

"God's blessing on you," he said in his rapid, guttural Gaelic, "but it's you had the long sleep. And just as well too for we had visitors yesterday afternoon."

"Who?" I asked.

"Coote and his steward, Richard Lawrence." He spat. "Lucki-ly the master got wind of their coming, so he and the mistress and Oona rode off to Cloonybrien. You should have seen the scowl on Coote's face when I told him they weren't home."

"Sir Charles Coote Senior?" I found it hard to follow Niall's discourse.

"Yes," he almost shouted, "the very same man that two years ago talked Turlough into selling him some of the best land he had – but how did you know it was the father?"

I told him about the narrow escape Tomás and I had at Ard-carn.

"So the Old Crow was with Sir Robert's son." He scratched his grizzled beard. "Well, bad cess to him! I wonder what he's plotting now … He pretended he was only calling on the master out of friendship."

"Has the master returned yet?" I wanted to put Coote's visit out of my mind.

"No," he said. "It's likely they went from Cloonybrien to Croghan – you know, don't you, that the mistress is the daughter of O'Mulloy of Croghan?"

I assured him I did, adding that my mother had worked there until my father took her to Dublin. On hearing this, he began with great animation to tell me that it was no wonder my father had travelled all the way from Dublin to buy wool, for it was well known that Moylurg was one of the best places in Ireland for sheep and in olden days the principal wool market in Connacht was held in Ardcarn, where the O'Mulloys now owned many quarters of land.

Having shown me round the bawn, with its lean-to sheds, buttery, pigeon cotes, and bee skeps, Niall took me outside. Smoke was beginning to rise from the cabins below in the village and a pookawn with its two black sails raised was heading out across the rippling waters of the lough. On the pasture south of us a lone shepherd leaning on his crook was watching sheep graze, while unseen larks carolled overhead. How tranquil the world seemed after our nightmare flight through the bog! The words of the psalm came to me: "They drop upon the pastures of the wilderness: and the little hills rejoice on every side."

Niall led me to another ringfort nearby containing some cabins, a forge, a mews and a carpenter's shed, as well as a byre and stable, with their pungent dunghills. He told me that there was a third ringfort further back in Derreendarragh Wood, where the sheep were penned and sheared. When I commended this arrangement, Niall told me it was the plan of Brian Oge, the master's father. "You see," he explained, "when the MacDermots lost their lands after the last war, King James made Sir Theobald Dillon Brian Oge's guardian and Sir Theobald sent him to the Protestant university in Dublin, so he always admired the Foreigners' sense of order – not that his father, Brian, wasn't just as clever. Look at the Mansion back there. Well, Brian was the first chieftain to build a two-storied house in the English fashion – he started that in Seventy-Eight, two years after I was born. But he had the roof thatched instead of covering it with quarried slabs – and do you know why? It's warmer in winter and cooler in summer."

"How many acres have the MacDermots?" I asked.

"How many acres?" Niall scratched his beard. "Well, apart from what they own in other parishes, I'd say hardly three hundred – I'm talking now about what the master and Turlough have left here in Kilbryan parish. But when I was a boy the MacDermot lands stretched further than you can see, from Loch Eidin over there to Loch Clogher over there to Loch Techet over there." He swept out a great half circle with his arm. "Then the O'Neill War came and the English saw their chance. They made Brian Oge, as I told you, a ward of court, intending to turn him into a good loyal Protestant, and when he came of age, they gave him this demesne but Brian Oge stuck by the Old Faith and for that they never forgave him. Everybody says that he died of a bleeding of the bowels but, if you ask me, he was poisoned in Athlone. Oh, I tell you, there's nothing the Protestants won't do to get their hands on our lands – but sure I'm forgetting you're a Protestant yourself. You'll have to forgive me."

"Don't be uneasy," I said. "I'm not one to betray those who worship as my mother does."

Reassured, he told me it was no more then he expected since the O'Flynns had always been renowned as pillars of the Church and had given their name to the Monastery of Assylin, O'Flynn's Waterfall, which was just a mile beyond Abbeyboyle.

When I had finished the simple meal Niall provided in his cabin, I walked down to the village, past barking dogs, wallowing pigs, pairs of goats yoked together with twisted withes and a flock of geese led by a hissing gander. Wild-looking women peered from doorways and a group of barefooted urchins playing football with a pig's bladder stopped their game to stare.

"*Go mbeannaí Dia daoibh*," I called out but, probably deducing from my accent that I was not the bodach my dress proclaimed, they did not answer. "*Sasanach!*" one of the older boys muttered.

Ignoring their stares, I picked my way between piles of firewood, broken creels and evil-smelling middens, around which hens foraged. At the lakeshore, dressed only in goatskin doublet and grey frieze breeches, a brawny young savage was about to push out a currach made of hide-covered laths. A crone holding an otter by a leash sat in the stern, puffing on a pipe.

On questioning the man I learned – with some difficulty because of his accent – that the villagers were allowed to fish the whole lough, except for a portion in the south-west, which belonged to Sir Robert King. The otter had been trained to bring back fish and if I would come out in the currach, I could observe this for myself. The crone, who had a coarse, dirty blanket wrapped about her, smiled as he spoke, beckoning to me to enter. An inner voice warned me that once out on the lough, I would be totally at the mercy of this villainous-looking pair, yet I was eager to see the castle and the islands close at hand.

As I began to wade out into the water, a startled expression spread across the crone's face and turning around, I saw two wolfhounds loping up, followed by a rider on a bay horse. Drawing rein, the rider, a tall, lithe man with shoulder-length, tawny hair, short beard, downcurving moustache and twinkling blue eyes, slid from the horse and bade me leave the water. From his resemblance to Cathal Roe and Oona, I knew he must be Turlough. He was simply clad in leather jerkin, saffron doublet, blue breeches and knee-high boots and though his apparel was somewhat frayed, it was of good quality. A sheathed skean rested on his hip but otherwise he was unarmed.

"I'm MacDermot," he informed me. "You mustn't trust those two." He nodded towards the currach, which was hurrying out into deep water. "They'd slit your throat for the brogues you've on."

I thanked him for having kept me from harm and, while trying to ward off the overfriendly wolfhounds, told him who I was. By this time a crowd of excited villagers had gathered round us, and a buxom wench of sixteen or seventeen offered Turlough usquebagh in an eggshell. Tossing back the drink, Turlough yielded to her entreaties to visit her family, meanwhile instructing me to return to Carrick Mansion.

That was my first encounter with The MacDermot, a man who fulfilled all my expectations of what an Irish chieftain must have been like before the English subdued Connacht. Oona told me later that he had formerly lived in Carrick Mansion with his wife, Margaret, daughter of MacDavid Burke, Cathal Roe being then resident at Meera, not far from Carrick Drumrusky. When Margaret died after falling from her horse, Turlough had moved to Cloonybrien in the parish of Ardcarn, while Cathal Roe and Lady Eleanor had come to live in the Mansion. (It might be pertinent to mention here Tomás Láidir's conviction that Turlough had got himself so deeply in debt he had sold all his property, including Carrick Mansion, to Cathal Roe.) Whatever the truth of the matter, Turlough now divided his time between Carraig-Mhic-Dhiarmada, as the castle on the island was known, and his house in Cloonybrien.

Next day Cathal Roe, Lady Eleanor and Oona returned, Oona sitting astride a grey hackney in her usual fashion. At the first opportunity I made enquiries about Cormac and learned that he was still a prisoner.

"The best we can hope for now," Cathal Roe commented, "is that somebody such as Sir Robert King will intercede for him, though after what befell Bishop Tilson I'm not sanguine."

He then asked if I had been with the miscreant who had hurled a beam into his lordship's garden, smashing his rose bush and calling out insults when he had appeared at the window. Divining from my silence that I had, he added grimly: "Don't say a word! What more could anyone expect from that wild Mayo reprobate? Oona, think well before you again associate with a disturber of the peace."

"Pray, brother," Oona replied tartly, "was it not the Bishop's own people who first disturbed the peace when they raided Ballintober and took O'Mulconry prisoner? And who defiled the body of Manus O'Donnell by hanging it on a gibbet?"

Cathal Roe did not answer. Instead he turned to me and said, "Your good clothes are over there – we met the messenger from Ballintober just as we were leaving Croghan. When you have changed you may begin to tutor the boys in their room upstairs. And till the present furore subsides, it's best that you avoid the village – we don't know whom the Cootes may have bribed to watch us."

You may imagine with what impatience I waited to get Oona on her own so that I could speak to her about Frances but before I could do so, Turlough rode up with the family ollamh, Daithi Ó Duigenan. Though scarcely twenty-five, Daithi had grey locks and a grey beard, something of which he was proud since, as he later informed me, Fionn Mac Cumhaill had been turned grey through enchantment while still a young man. Cathal Roe seemed perturbed at his arrival and reminded Turlough that in view of what had happened to Cormac, it was madness to have Daithi at Carrick Mansion.

"Don't fret, Brother," Turlough replied. "We are further from the Cootes here than they are in Ballintober. Oh, I realize that Old Coote paid you a visit but that was probably to see if Charles was here."

"He couldn't have known that," I protested and told him about my hasty departure from Ballintober and how we had outwitted Sir Charles at Ardcarn.

"Nevertheless," Turlough declared, "if Brian and Terence are to be tutored in English, they ought to be tutored in Gaelic as well, especially if one day Brian is to become chieftain. That would be our father's wish – God rest his soul – and it's mine too."

I could see that Cathal Roe was not pleased with this but he held his peace and, turning to me, said, "Daithi will be tutoring the boys in Gaelic and history. You can both share the same cabin – Niall will put in another pallet."

"Now, Daithi, don't keep him awake with your stories of the Fianna and the Sidhe." Turlough's eyes twinkled. "Palesmen have little time for the Good People. Isn't that so, Charles?"

"Oh, we have our Pucks and Queen Mabs too," I pointed out. "And Cormac O'Mulconry told me about the Sidhe."

"So O'Mulconry was your teacher." Daithi's eyes lit up. "He was a master when I was training in Castlefore. I can still see him reciting the rules to be observed by all true poets: 'Purity of hand and of wedlock, purity of lips and of learning ...' My comrades and I thought him very severe but, despite that, we grew to love him."

"Well, he's in prison now," Cathal Roe reminded us, "and it will go hard with a man of his age."

"If only like Muiredach O'Daly he could soften Coote's heart by writing poems in his honour." Daithi spoke without conviction.

"A musket ball would be the best way to soften that gentleman's heart." Turlough laughed mirthlessly. "Come, Oona," he shouted. "We must be off if we're to reach Cloonybrien before evening."

With a heavy heart I watched them canter downhill, Oona dressed like Turlough in doublet, breeches and plumed hat. Would she, I wondered, send a message to Frances?

The lesson with Brian and Terence kept me occupied for the rest of the afternoon. On finding a copy of *England's Helicon* that had belonged to Brian Oge, I set my scholars to learning "The Passionate Shepherd to His Love", and since they could already converse in simple English, they soon learned to sing, if not to read, the opening verses. Perceiving that they were untutored in written English, I decided to do as Cormac had done when teaching me to write Gaelic and begin with the alphabet. This I made them copy with their quills onto sheets of paper, having first shown them how to form each letter. It was not an easy exercise, for they found my script marvellously strange.

Daithi and I ate dinner with the family in the Great Hall, which occupied most of the ground floor. This was a broad, high-ceilinged room, well lighted by windows on each side and dominated by a massive stone fireplace set in the mortared end wall. The lower half of the three remaining walls had been covered in dark oak panelling, between which and the dark beams of the ceiling the mortar of the upper walls gleamed whitely.

Portraits of Cathal Roe's grandparents dressed in the clothes of Queen Elizabeth's time flanked the fireplace: on the left, Brian, Lord of Moylurg, and on the right, Maeve, daughter of O'Conor Sligo, his last wife. Other portraits hung on the back wall near the wooden stairway leading to the upper floor and on the north wall the skull with enormous antlers of some ancient deer was mounted between tapestries of the chase.

Since it was Friday, our meal consisted of fresh trout, grilled and flavoured with honey; watercress; bowls of troander and sorrel tarts – which, Lady Eleanor informed us, had been specially baked by Bridgeen in honour of my own and Daithi's arrival. For drink we had mugs of buttermilk and, to finish, oaten cakes, cheese and mulled ale.

While we ate, the conversation turned to life in Trinity and, despite some unease, I was able to give straightforward answers to my hosts' questions; they were particularly pleased to learn that I had been a friend of Hugh O'Rourke, who, I gathered, was a cousin of the man who was married to Cathal Roe and Oona's sister Margaret.

Cathal Roe then asked if I was acquainted with Baggotrath Castle, where Sir Robert King's family lived – though Sir Robert himself spent much of the year in Abbeyboyle. I told him that I had only seen it on a few occasions as it was on the side of the city opposite to Oxmantown, but my father had once mentioned visiting Baggotrath to discuss the duties on woollen exports.

"His mother, Catherine, is buried in St Michan's Church in Oxmantown," Lady Margaret interjected, and went on to speak of Sir Robert's younger brother, Edward, who had drowned in the year after her husband, Brian Oge, had died. It appeared that Edward had become a fellow of Christ's College in Cambridge at the age of eighteen and that he was a poet and cleric who was greatly loved by everybody, not least his brother.

"Sir Robert sent his eldest son, John, to be educated in the same college," Lady Eleanor told me. "That's the young man you saw at Ardcarn. I shouldn't be surprised if he paid us a visit, now that he has joined his father."

"Wasn't Old Sir John King secretary to Bingham?" Daithi swallowed a mouthful of ale. At once there was an awkward silence, broken by my pupil Brian, who wanted to know who Bingham was.

"He was a President of Connacht who terrorized the people in your great-grandfather's time," Cathal Roe said, "but by the grace of God those bad days are over forever."

When we returned to our cabin, Daithi told me that he was collecting various accounts of "The Pursuit of Diarmuid and Grainne", which, he maintained, was the equal of any love story in the world. On my recounting Niall the Cobbler's ending, in which Grainne married Fionn after Diarmuid was killed by the boar, Daithi acknowledged that it was one of the many endings he had heard.

"Will you reshape the story then to make it more pleasing?" I asked.

For answer he chanted Grainne's lament over Diarmuid and demanded, "Would you change that?"

Not wishing to displease him, I shook my head.

A week passed before Oona returned, a week made bearable only by the distraction of my new station and the companionship of Daithi. As soon as Oona had dismounted, I hurried up and she, divining my purpose, drew me aside and whispered that she had been speaking to Tomás Láidir, who had arranged to bring Frances to Knockmelliagh on St John's Eve. She and I would travel there together on the pretext of visiting Cloonybrien.

Chapter 23

DAY by day as the weather grew warmer, the countryside arrayed itself in lusher greenness. Elders and wild roses bloomed and the pastures turned yellow with buttercups. Young rabbits ventured out from the thickets, butterflies flitted about the meadows and the air was loud with birdsong. Yet, despite the beauty unfolding about me, I was in a fever of impatience. Would St John's Eve never come? Would Frances have cooled towards me? Oona had hinted that Theobald Dillon was openly her suitor, visiting her with the approval of French-Fitzstephens. Should I too venture to Ballytrasna? Should I first attend Mass to show that I was a proper suitor?

I had no doubt but that the MacDermots and their servants went to Mass, for early on Sundays they would slip out and not return until almost noon. Daithi told me that the church of Kilbryan was only a short walk beyond Derreendarragh Wood, and though roofless, it might still be used for worship. Later in the day, Cathal Roe, with Lady Eleanor sitting sideways behind him, would ride off to Abbeyboyle to be present at Divine Service in a chapel of the Cistercian abbey, which was then used by Protestant townspeople as their parish church. On one of these occasions they returned accompanied by the young man I had seen at Ardcarn.

John King displayed no sign of recognition when I was introduced to him as the children's tutor but greeted me with courteous reserve. On learning that my family lived in Oxmantown and that I had attended Trinity, his manner warmed and soon he, Oona and I were discussing university life as we strolled about the demesne.

It was clear that Oona's beauty, high spirits and mode of dress intrigued him for he gazed at her with open pleasure, delighting in everything she showed him, whether it was an eagle circling high above the woods or a bumblebee alighting on a flower.

"This reminds me of the world described by Milton in '*L'Allegro*'," he exclaimed, gazing at the bright lake and the sheep-dotted pastures:

> "*Straight mine eye hath caught new pleasures,*
> *Whilst the landskip round it measures:*
> *Russet lawns and fallows gray,*
> *Where the nibbling flocks do stray –*

"Have you heard of John Milton? Dr William Chappell, who later became Provost of your Trinity College, was, I'm told, his tutor in Cambridge. Oh, I must bring you copies of his poems," he added, on noting that we both shook our heads. "He has written a most inspiring sonnet on his own twenty-fourth birthday and an elegy on my Uncle Edward, '*Lycidas*', that brings tears to my eyes."

John stayed for dinner and was greatly impressed with the abundance of roast veal, custard pies and cheese provided.

"Had I known that the people of this barony eat so well, I would have come to Abbeyboyle years ago," he declared, smiling at Oona. He did not consent, however, to taste the claret that Cathal Roe pressed on him, explaining that as it was the Sabbath, he would rather drink buttermilk.

As was to be expected from a Bachelor of Arts and a student at Lincoln's Inn, John was a fluent, if earnest, speaker and everyone – with the exception of Daithi – listened entranced to his account of the changes taking place in England.

"People are demanding an end to the King's arbitrary rule and freedom to worship as their consciences dictate," he informed us.

I could see Daithi smile as our guest extolled the virtues of unknown members of the House of Commons such as Hampden and Pym and then he asked in Gaelic if Master King could tell him if there was any truth in the rumour that the Scots intended to use force to crush Ireland's Catholics. Oona repeated the question in English, whereupon John answered with great forthrightness that he could not be expected to know what the Scots intended, that the

Presbyterian religion was not to everyone's liking and as for the Catholics, they did not believe in freedom of conscience, as their behaviour in Italy, Spain and Germany testified.

Daithi was about to respond but Lady Eleanor interposed with a question about the kinds of clothes English women wore and conflict was averted.

As soon as Daithi and I were back in the cabin, Daithi gave vent to his indignation.

"Did you hear that fellow with his talk of freedom of conscience?" he snorted. "It's pride and covetousness that fills the heads of such scaldcrows, not concern for freedom. Do you know that his family owns not only the monastery and lands of Boyle Abbey, but Innis Mac Nerin and Trinity Island here in Lough Cé, places that the MacDermots endowed and gave abbots to and where many of their ancestors are buried? Why do you think that Turlough lives in Cloonybrien? I'll tell you. Up to the time of his grandfather, Lough Cé was the centre of Gaelic hospitality and learning in Connacht; now it's the fishing grounds of the Foreigners."

I gave it as my opinion that John had been sincere in his pronouncements but Daithi would not be convinced.

"You yourself told me that he spoke Irish at Ardcarn," he pointed out, "so why did he pretend not to understand my question?"

"He spoke a few simple words," I conceded. "You, however, refused to speak English; maybe he likewise refused to speak Irish."

"Why should I twist my tongue into knots, pronouncing barbaric jargon?" Daithi huffed.

I was going to retort that the language of Marlowe and Shakespeare could hardly be considered jargon but thought better of it. Instead, I asked him about Turlough's home in Cloonybrien.

"It's a long, thatched, one-storied house," he told me, "the kind that our chieftains built beside their castles in former times. Turlough has no time for panelled walls and pewter mugs. He prefers to eat in the open when the weather is warm and to sleep on a *súgán* pallet, not in an oaken bed. However, he lives on the Rock whenever the mood takes him."

"Is that the castle on the island?" I asked.

"Yes," he replied. "Carrick MacDermot, 'The Rock of the

smooth-flowing Lough Cé'."

"Can we go there some evening?" I suggested.

"No," he said, "not unless Turlough invites us."

Next day a messenger arrived with Milton's poems and John King's apologies that he could not deliver them in person. As soon as Oona had given me the sheaf of papers covered in small, neat handwriting, I read them through with growing excitement. Here was a new, learned kind of poetry that made even the common-place world seem magical. Afterwards, when Daithi asked me to listen to a poem in which Grainne lulls Diarmuid to sleep, I could hardly pay attention, so much was my mind drawn to "fresh woods and pastures new".

That year St John's Eve fell on a Sunday. In the early afternoon, Oona and I set out for Knockmelliagh, Oona on Glas, her sturdy grey hackney, and I on Donn, a bay mare Cathal Roe had lent me.

"You are the only man in Moylurg who would ride her." Oona had a twinkle in her eye.

"She reminds me of Nell," I said.

"Nevertheless," she observed, "most men consider a mare to be fit only for breeding."

"You're riding a mare yourself," I pointed out.

"Yes," she agreed. "But then I'm not a man."

"You wear men's clothes," I reminded her.

"And pray, Charles, how would I ride in a gown?" she asked.

"You could ride side-saddle as English ladies do," I replied. "Don't your friends, Maura and Isabel, have such saddles?"

"Oh, a side-saddle is too refined for the likes of me and, any-way, my family aren't rich like the Burkes and O'Conors." The proud way that she tilted her chin gave the lie to this assertion.

"And my family aren't rich like the French-Fitzstephens," I re-marked. "We're both children of misfortune!"

Instantly Oona threw back her head and laughed and in this happy mood we continued our journey.

When we reached the mound the other two had not yet arrived so we dismounted and climbed up to the summit, from where we could discern Lough Cé gleaming in the distance and beyond it, to the west, the low, blue-green Curlieu mountains. At the foot of the hill on which the mound stood there was a grove of oak trees, well

194

hidden from the road behind us. Sheep and cattle grazed the flower-dappled pastures and larks sang in the blue sky.

"Do you think that some of the dead from the Battle of Moytura might be buried here?" I was enjoying the fresh breeze on my glowing face.

"Oh, you'll have to ask Daithi that." She turned around to gaze in the direction of Ardcarn. "I hate all that talk about ancient times and all those wars. One day I'll go to Dublin or even to London, where they're not always dwelling on the past."

"Is it meeting John King that has put such notions into your head?" I smiled.

"Maybe it is," she confessed. "He seems to believe so strongly that God is on his people's side – and who's to say He's not?"

"And what will Tomás do when you're gone?" I decided to humour her mood.

"Oh, he'll find some other damsel to write poems to." She tossed her mane of amber hair impatiently.

"But he's in love with you," I pointed out.

"He's in love with a golden-haired *spéirbhean* that he thinks is me," she replied. "Has Daithi told you about Oisín and Niamh of the Golden Hair? Well, Tomás likes to imagine that I will take him up on my white steed and carry him off to Tír na nÓg. Poets' dreams! It's not that easy to escape from our misfortunes."

"I can't believe that anyone would wish to escape from here." I gazed around at the green landscape smiling under the afternoon sun.

"That's because you're waiting for Frances," she said. "But one day you'll go back to Dublin and forget us and our wild ways."

"Never!" I cried. "You forget that this is my mother's world."

"You have more of your father than your mother in you." Her mocking eyes met mine.

"So you consider me a Palesman?" Disappointment filled my voice.

"You're a man who thinks much." She spoke gently. "Our people feel more than they think; that's why they're no match for the Foreigners."

While we conversed, a few country people, some on foot, some on garrons or low, solid-wheeled carts passed by on their way to and from Ardcarn, then a group of horsemen approached from the direction of Abbeyboyle. Their leader, a well-dressed, middle-aged

"Foreigner", rode over to the mound. It was one of the gentlemen I had seen in the stable in Ballintober, Sir Robert King.

"Good afternoon, fair Oona." He swept off his plumed hat, bowing his head, on which the hair was beginning to turn silver.

"Good afternoon, Sir Robert." She too spoke in English.

"Why are you waiting at this deserted spot?" His glance encompassed me as well as the mound.

"Why, Sir Robert," she exclaimed, "Charles and I are hoping to see the fairies."

"Oh!" he smiled pleasantly, "So you're the young gentleman from Dublin John told me about?"

Since there was no point in trying to deceive him, I nodded.

"And pray, Oona, what do you think fairies are?" Sir Robert kept his expression grave.

"Why," Oona feigned surprise, "everybody knows they're angels that were thrown out of heaven and that landed on earth – or so Bridgeen maintains. They always emerge at Midsummer's Eve to dance and work mischief."

"But it won't be midsummer for ten days yet," Sir Robert looked puzzled; then his face brightened. "Oh, I forgot; you have a different calendar."

"If the fairies appear, won't that show it's the correct calendar, Sir Robert?" Oona asked mischievously.

"Ha, Oona, your wit is too nimble for me." Sir Robert smiled. "You must both come to Abbeyboyle at the end of the month – I shall have returned from Dublin by then."

"We will, Sir Robert," Oona promised.

"And bring your brother Turlough," he added in the tones of a man accustomed to being obeyed. "I must show him the artificial flies I've made to entice trout from the lough."

"And your apricot tree, Sir Robert!" Oona's eyes twinkled. "Did it bloom this year?"

"Why, Oona, we shall see when you come." He smiled; then, replacing his hat, he called out, "God be with you," and trotted off.

"Sir Robert seems to have been struck by Cupid's arrow," I observed.

"Yes." Oona frowned. "Like other men he desires what he cannot have."

"Is he married then?"

"No, his wife, Frances, died four years ago. But he's a staunch Lutheran."

"Like me?"

"Oh, Charles, I didn't mean to offend you."

"I'm not offended," I assured her. "What troubles me is that Sir Robert may be of a mind to hook me like one of his fish."

"Then when we visit him, we must both contrive to swim past his lures." Oona's blue-green eyes were twinkling again.

Despite her confidence, Sir Robert's invitation made me uneasy. Had John told him about seeing Tomás and me at Ardcarn? Did he know that Nicholas Stanihurst of Oxmantown was my father? Had Coote informed him about the murder and my flight from Dublin?

I questioned Oona about Sir Robert and learned that not only was he a Member of Parliament but he was also Clerk of the Cheque for Ireland. Such a man would be well acquainted with the Lord Lieutenant and with Lords Justice Parsons and Borlase. Before I could glean more information, there was a loud cheer and we saw Tomás riding towards us from the direction of Abbeyboyle. Soon I could discern Frances sitting behind him and my heart beat with a joy that was almost pain.

"What delayed you?" Oona called out as they drew to a halt.

"Theobald Dillon." Tomás threw his leg over the garron's neck and slid to the ground. "He came to pay his respects to Frances, so her father was reluctant to let her accompany me. If it weren't for her mother's intercession, we would still be playing cards in Bally-trasna."

Frances blushed. Her blue mantle was thrown back, revealing a pale green tunic with an open collar of white lace above her swelling bosom.

"His father and mine are friends," she said in her low, soft voice as I placed my hands on the *crios* encircling her waist to help her down. "I sometimes met him when we visited Sir Lucas at Lough Glinn."

Looking into her guileless, grey-brown eyes I saw that whatever her involvement with Theobald might be, her heart was mine.

"Come," I said, restraining an urge to kiss her full lips. "Let's walk to the grove down there."

Tomás and Oona led the way and Frances and I followed. We tethered our horses at the edge of the grove and entered among the trees.

"Did your stepfather know you were meeting me?" I asked Frances when we stopped beneath an enormous oak with ferns growing on its mossy branches.

"Indeed, he did not," she said. "If he ever finds out I wasn't visiting Cloonybrien he'll take my life."

"But he didn't mind Theobald calling," I could not help pointing out.

"That's not the same." She pouted. "Theobald would not be alone with me as you are now."

I gazed at her, noting the smooth, white skin of her neck, the feathery, brown curls by her little ears, the eyes that were speckled with green and hazel lights, the red lips parting over the white teeth. "Frances," I whispered, "my beautiful Frances."

"I'm not beautiful," she protested, "and I hate the name Frances."

"You are the most beautiful girl I've ever seen," I assured her, "and Frances is a lovely name."

"Did you say that to Beibhinn too?"

"No. Since I met you every other girl has faded from my mind."

"Then why did you not send me a message in over seven weeks?"

I explained the adverse circumstances that had beset me; and touching her smooth, glowing cheek with my fingers, swore that she was dearer to me than my life's blood. Then we kissed while sunlight dappled the ground and insects murmured in the leaves around us. Conscious of the fire mounting in my blood, I raised my head.

"Oh, Charles!" she sighed and, leaning back against the bole, closed her eyes. Never was so much beauty offered so temptingly, yet fear of sullying her innocence constrained me. I kissed her eyelids and her parted lips; then, hastily drawing back, I started to recite one of the poems I had composed in Ballintober.

"Do you know to whom that is addressed?" I asked.

She looked at me with yearning eyes.

"You," I said. "I wrote it for you."

"It's lovely." She smiled her bashful smile.

"I would have written it in Gaelic," I went on, "but I'm more accustomed to English."

"I like poems and songs in English," she assured me. "My

mother's favourite song is 'Greensleeves'." She laid her head against my shoulder.

I embraced her, feeling her soft bosom pressed against my chest, determined to be as honourable as a knight with his lady.

"Cuckoo! Cuckoo!" The mocking notes rang through the grove. Quickly I looked round and saw Tomás's face grinning at us from behind a tree.

"How long have you been watching?" I cried.

"Long enough." Tomás stepped into the open with Oona. "We saw everything, didn't we, Flower of the Amber Tresses?"

"Pay no heed to this fool!" Oona hit him playfully across the arm. "We just came up a moment ago."

"Listen, Palesman," Tomás put his arm about Oona's neck. "Oona and I are going for a swim in Lough Fionn. Will you two lovers join us?"

I looked at Frances but she shook her head.

"Oh, come on," Tomás coaxed. "You know that bathing on Midsummer's Eve ensures good health and Charles, there, looks like a sheep in need of a washing."

"Do come," Oona pleaded. "Nobody will see us." At which Frances yielded.

We rode to the edge of the small lake, which was scarcely a mile away, Frances sitting behind me on Donn. Tall reeds grew along the shore and a pair of swans with their cygnets floated on the calm surface. Dismounting, we retreated behind two separate alders, where we stripped off our clothes. Tomás and I, naked as newborn babes, ventured first across the marshy edge into the reeds and Oona and Frances followed, dressed only in their shifts.

For half an hour or so we gambolled like otters, chasing and evading one another. How lovely Frances looked, her white shoulders and limbs pale amber in the dark water! We were as happy as poets say the inhabitants of Moy Mell or Tír na nÓg are, without shame or consciousness of sin, the green reeds and the green trees encircling us, and the sun gleaming on our wet heads.

At last the declining sun hurried us from the water, Tomás and I leading the way. When I looked back from the cover of the trees, I could see Oona and Frances wading ashore like two swan maidens, their upraised arms linked to keep their balance, their wet shifts clinging to their bodies. Never have I beheld anything to match that scene, not even in representations of Diana and Callisto, for what is the loveliness of oil and pigment to that of human flesh and blood?

Since we could not put on our clothes till the air had dried our bodies, it was past sunset when Oona and I rode up to Carrick Mansion. Two great bonfires had already been lit near the fort and under Niall's direction, shouting men and boys were driving terrified cattle between the flames.

"Why are they doing that?" I asked Oona.

"It's to ward off sickness and disease," she informed me. "The men will also throw some of the burning sticks into the crops to ensure a good harvest."

"And do you believe it will?" I dismounted from Donn.

"Yes," she replied, dismounting also. "Fire can heal dog bites, so why shouldn't it prevent other evils?"

The willingness of Oona to believe such arrant superstition did not surprise me for, truth to tell, after what I had experienced that afternoon, I was ready to believe it too.

As we rounded the palisade to reach the fort entrance, we could see that another bonfire had been lit in the village. Pipe music and raucous laughter wafted up from the flame-reddened cabins to mingle with the shouting and lowing behind us. My body was too tired and hungry and my heart too full of happiness, however, for me to desire anything other than food and rest, so I gratefully joined the family at their evening meal.

Cathal Roe was annoyed when he learned that Sir Robert had invited me to Abbeyboyle.

"Why didn't you say that you would have to obtain my permission before accepting?" he fumed.

Oona explained that it was she who had accepted for both of us, at which point Lady Margaret intervened.

"What have we to hide that we should keep Charles here?" she demanded. "And, furthermore, won't Turlough and Oona be with him?"

"You're right, mother." Cathal Roe stroked his beard. "After all, we only took Charles into our service as a tutor – and Charles, if they question you about Daithi, say that he's here at Carrick as your helper, not my ollamh."

Chapter 24

JUNE came to an end and we did not go to Abbeyboyle, mainly because Turlough found various reasons to postpone the visit. I sensed that it was not just aversion to the Foreigners that made him hesitate. The plying of coracles and pookawns between Cloontykilla on the eastern shore of Lough Cé and Carrick Castle on the island made me suspect that the Rock was being used as more than an occasional resting place for its owner. If I asked to go there, I was always met with a flat refusal. Not that I minded the restriction; I had other matters to occupy me.

Since John King's gift of Milton's poems, there was a subtle change in Daithi's attitude towards me. He was less forgiving if he came upstairs to give the boys their Gaelic lessons and found them still conning some poem from *England's Helicon* or practising their writing. My coolness towards his work on "The Pursuit of Diarmuid and Grainne" irked him too. Not that I found the occasional lyrics with which the story was interspersed lacking in beauty; it was the interminable ballads he chanted that tried my patience.

One evening he mocked a sonnet by Shakespeare that he had heard me read to Brian and Terence so I challenged him to name an Irish poet who could match my beloved bard in diversity or excellence. He admitted that he had not understood the poem he had dismissed but added that Donnchadh Mor O'Daly, Eochaidh O'Hussey and Tadhg Dall O'Huiginn were three poets associated with Moylurg who were unsurpassable both in their mastery of form and felicity of diction. To prove his contention, he recited

O'Daly's poem "On a Wren", O'Hussey's "Ode to Maguire" and O'Huiginn's "First Vision", all of which were very pleasing, especially O'Huiginn's, for the idea of the blind poet pining for a mysterious, rosy-cheeked maiden who had visited him in a dream could not but ensnare the imagination. The poet's refusal to go away with the maiden and her instant disappearance had a pathos such as I had never found in English poetry and I can only account for this by assuming that the maiden was an embodiment of the old Gaelic world which had vanished.

On perceiving that I liked the "First Vision" best, Daithi recited another poem in which Tadhg Dall incited Brian O'Rourke – the chieftain who had been hanged at Tyburn in Elizabeth's time – to make war on the Foreigners and warned him about accepting an invitation to their court, using as a parable the story of the lion who invited the other animals to his den. Had Daithi, I wondered, recited this poem for Turlough?

In the beginning of July, John King came to enquire why we hadn't visited his father and during dinner, when he had drunk freely, made some dismissive remarks about "Gaelic rhymers". Immediately, I sprang to the defence of the bards and, with Daithi's assistance, translated O'Daly's poem on the wren. When John learned that O'Daly had been interred in Boyle Abbey, he was greatly surprised that the existence of such a "sweet poet" should be unknown to the townspeople.

"But, then, they have nobody like Charles to translate his works into English," he observed. "And that reminds me! My father has received a letter from Bishop Bedell, who is translating the Bible into Gaelic."

"Did he speak of Cormac O'Mulconry?" I tried to suppress my eagerness.

"I don't know," John confessed. "But father will be able to inform you when you visit us."

"Is the Archbishop of Canterbury still in prison?" Cathal Roe refilled John's goblet with claret.

"Yes," John said. "Some people believe he is a secret Papist – otherwise, why did he confer so many government offices on bishops? Indeed, not a few Members of Parliament would like to eradicate prelacy root and branch. Even John Milton has written pamphlets against the bishops. You can see in 'Lycidas' – one of the poems I sent you – where he alludes to those who 'for their bellies' sake / Creep and intrude and climb into the fold'."

"Do you believe we should get rid of bishops?" I asked.

"Yes." John swallowed a mouthful of claret. "We should try to return to the simplicity of the early Church. There were no bishops in Christ's time."

"Didn't Christ make Peter head of the Church?" Oona took a pinch of snuff.

"That is what the Papists maintain," John replied. "But you have only to look at the men who claim to be Peter's successors to see how false the premise is."

"An instance, pray." Oona offered him the snuffbox but he waved it aside.

"Didn't Leo X authorize the selling of indulgences and Paul IV state that he would gather the wood to burn his own father if he were a heretic?" John spoke hotly. "And the present Pope has used Church money to enrich his family and has made several of them cardinals. Furthermore, at the behest of the Jesuits, he has forbidden Galileo to teach or discuss the Copernican system and sentenced him to house arrest. So much for those Antichrists, the Bishops of Rome!"

"You said we should get rid of bishops." Oona's expression was guileless. "Should we then drive Henry Tilson from his palace in Elphin?"

For a moment John's brow furrowed, then he spread his hands, palms upward. "You have laid a trap for me, Oona," he charged. "I acknowledge myself bereft of words."

"We have a saying in Gaelic," Oona grinned, "'*Is binn béal in a thost*', sweet is a mouth in its silence."

"I must remember that," John promised ruefully.

After John had departed, Cathal Roe told me that there was an entry in his grandfather's Annals concerning O'Daly's death. The Annals were kept in the library, at the west end of the house, and with unwonted ceremony he ushered Daithi and myself into this favourite room of his father's, who had furnished its shelves with many leather-bound volumes purchased in Dublin. On the wall opposite the fireplace the Latin charter of King James, granting Brian Oge "the manor-castle and town of Carrick-MacDermot, i.e. Dermot's Rock with certain parts of his ancient patrimony", was hung in a gilt frame and on the north wall there was a tapestry showing the wild boar killing Adonis.

Cathal Roe laid the handwritten Gaelic Annals reverently on the table and under the year 1244 the death of Donnchadh Mor – who was described as "an eminent man who was never surpassed in poetry" – was indeed recorded.

"Your father's grand-uncle, Ballach, copied that entry for my grandfather," Cathal Roe told Daithi.

"I didn't realize that O'Daly lived so long ago," I observed.

"That's because you're a Palesman," Daithi said. "For us four hundred years is as a day."

Ignoring Daithi's jibe, I asked Cathal Roe's permission to read through the annals, which he willingly gave. In this way I came in time to know the history of Moylurg, a history of wars and cattle raids, of treachery and courage, of brother fighting brother for the chieftainship, of great feasts at which lavish gifts were distributed to poets and ollamhs, of burnings and destructions that did not spare even the Abbey of Boyle. But most of all, I came to know Brian, Cathal Roe's grandfather, who not only had caused the Annals to be written, but had completed them himself in his castle on the Rock.

This Brian was both warrior and scholar, a man who, to secure his rightful succession, had fought his way to the Lordship of Moylurg then, like Hugh O'Conor Don of Ballintober, surrendered his Irish title to the Queen's Lord Deputy in return for recognition of his position under English law. I came to understand the grim necessity that made these proud men abandon their ancient prerogatives, thus dividing their hearts in two, as my own heart was divided. And like them, I must now venture into the lion's den, for in a few weeks I would go to Abbeyboyle, the seat of English law in Moylurg, and nobody could predict what would befall me.

Although this Sword of Damocles hung over my head, I was nevertheless happy, for every Saturday Oona and I met Frances and Tomás at Knockmelliagh and under the shielding oak, Frances and I kissed and embraced. Since neither of us allowed the canker of lust to mar love, it bloomed like a rose in a secret garden. At last I had met my *spéirbhean*, somebody who could reconcile the cravings of flesh and spirit as neither Beibhinn nor Maura could. If it ever occurred to me that such love is like a summer's dawn, a dawn that must, sooner or later, yield to daylight, I kept the thought from the forefront of my mind; I was lost in a blissful dream with no awareness of the waking world.

Despite or, more likely, because of a quarrel that had occurred between him and Sir Charles Coote's steward, Turlough finally named Crom Dubh's Friday, the last Friday in July, as the day on which we would visit Abbeyboyle. He had decided to go stag hunting on Crom Dubh's Sunday and wanted to obtain Sir Robert's permission to pass through his lands on the way to Corrslieve. It was about midday when he, Oona and I reached the east edge of the town and began to walk our horses into the shallow waters of the Boyle. There was no need to ford the river, the townspeople having recently constructed a wooden bridge further west, at Ath da Laarg, but Turlough balked at the notion of paying a toll to Protestant burghers.

Women washing clothes on flat stones by the water's edge called out blessings in Gaelic as our horses lunged up onto dry land. We paused to talk to them, whereupon they invited us into their thatched cabins but Turlough explained that we were expected at the castle. To our right I could see an enclosed orchard with apple and pear trees rising above its walls. On our left, the great Cistercian abbey, its tower and church roofless, stood grey and forlorn, except for a wreath of smoke drifting up from some hidden chimney.

"It grieves my heart to think that the parson has his home inside these walls," Turlough muttered, little realizing that I knew his grandfather, Brian, had twice attacked the abbey and, on the first occasion, taken the abbot prisoner. Niall had even confided to me that, because of Brian's depredations, the monks had cursed the MacDermots.

Leaving the abbey behind, we rode uphill towards the castle, which was situated between the road and the river. This was a dark, oblong structure ending in circular towers. The massive walls had musket slots and lancet windows but no entrance on the sides facing us. The banner of St George flew above the battlements of the east tower and, to my surprise, the red saltire on a white field of Ireland above the west. At the rear, to the south, the base of another tower was visible and according to Turlough, the intention had been to build the castle in the form of a square with corner towers representing the four provinces.

"Old Sir John brought workers from England to build it," Turlough smiled grimly, "but they only finished Munster and Leinster; the other two will never be completed – you can tell Sir Robert that!"

"I intend to tell him nothing he doesn't already know," I answered stiffly.

"That's my darling! You're a true O'Flynn!" Turlough cried and immediately I felt like a prince. Turlough made you want to serve him.

As we rode along, we passed a few old men and boys leading garrons with panniers of vegetables, women carrying baskets of washing on their heads and a band of warders armed with muskets and led by a kettledrummer. Fear gripped my heart. Was I venturing with eyes open into the lion's den? The warders marched by, two by two, without turning their heads and I breathed more freely.

"Sir Robert wishes to show us how vigilant his people are," Turlough remarked. "But then, as Tadhg Dall put it, 'Towards the warlike man peace is observed.'"

"Sir Robert isn't warlike." Oona pulled on the reins as a mongrel started yapping at her horse's heels.

"He was Muster-Master General," Turlough replied. "Don't be deceived by his sheep's clothing."

In a few moments we had rounded the rear of the castle and there on our left was the arched entrance guarded by two sentries with half pikes, breastplates and helmets. Wishing to delay my meeting with Sir Robert, I expressed a desire to see the town, so we turned right into a straight, cobbled street that was cleaner and less crowded than those in Dublin. Timber-framed houses with tiled roofs stood close together on either side, the black beams forming a stark contrast with the white mortar of the walls. Sombre-looking people, the men for the most part dressed in black doublets, breeches and high-crowned hats, the women in dark gowns with white linen collars and cuffs, their hair concealed under white linen kerchiefs, glanced at us with cold eyes. Only the children – many of whom were as sombrely dressed as their elders – stared with open curiosity and, indeed, with our stirrupless saddle cushions and Oona's attire, we must have presented an unusual sight.

"Isn't it like being surrounded by a flock of crows?" Turlough's blithe question echoed my thoughts.

"Turlough!" Oona admonished. "Those people are our neighbours and, as you well know, many of them understand Gaelic."

"*Go mbeannaí Dia duit.*" Turlough doffed his hat to a comely young woman emerging from a baker's shop. For a moment a smile hovered at the corners of her mouth, then she frowned and looked away.

"Look! There's somebody in the stocks." Oona gazed past carts and tethered horses to the end of the street, where a number of urchins were gathered. On drawing nearer I thought there was something familiar in the appearance of the ragged fellow with dirty glibs and tangled beard whose feet were clamped between the heavy boards; then he looked up and I recognized Fergus.

"That's one of the horseboys O'Conor Don banished," I whispered to Turlough, conscious of Fergus's eyes on my face.

"Why are you in the stocks?" Turlough asked the dejected Fergus, who was sitting in the dust with the sun scorching his head.

"They caught me stealing a pie." Fergus brightened up at the kindly question spoken in Gaelic. "For the love of Patrick, Brigid and Colmcille give me some food and drink."

Bidding me wait, Turlough and Oona rode back to the baker's shop. While they were gone I tried to avoid Fergus's gaze by noting that at this point the street joined a road leading south to the bridge and north past the fair green to a low hill. There were more thatched cabins near the fair green, so I concluded that the town had a mixed population of English, Anglo-Irish and Gaels, though in what proportions I could not be certain.

Presently, Turlough and Oona returned carrying a loaf and a mug of buttermilk, which Fergus received with pathetic gratitude. The urchins tittered as he wolfed down the bread and gulped the buttermilk, spilling some in his eagerness.

A crowd was now beginning to gather, one or two of the rougher youths muttering about "Wild Irish" and "the Papist witch", so we deemed it expedient to withdraw. While we trotted back up the street, the thought that it should be me, and not Fergus, sitting in the stocks gnawed at my conscience. It also occurred to me that since Fergus was in Abbeyboyle, Donal Bawn and Brian Dubh would not be far away.

The sentries stood to attention as we rode through the hollow-sounding entrance into the courtyard. On this side, the completed part of the castle had large, mullioned windows in the centre of the first and second stories. The unfinished remainder of the castle had been built in such a way that the outer wall formed a low parapet facing east, south and west, the rooms beneath being used as stables, carthouses and granaries.

After grooms had led our horses away, we followed the porter's boy through a doorway in the west tower, up a winding stone stairway, and down a corridor with framed portraits of solemn-looking noblemen. In contrast to the heat and bustle of the town the castle interior was cool and tomb-like. At a closed door the boy paused, knocked lightly then made a sign for us to enter. Sir Robert was sitting at a large table strewn with books and papers.

"*Fáilte roimh!*" he called out, rising with a gracious smile and extending both hands. "Forgive the lack of ceremony but I'm a plain man and these letters must be answered. Have you shown our young Trinity scholar Abbeyboyle?"

"Yes, Sir Robert," Turlough replied. "We rode down to the stocks. There's a half-starved fellow in them who was caught stealing a pie."

"That's not my doing," Sir Robert said firmly. "The borough court deals with thefts and other such offences. Sometimes their judgments may appear harsh but with disbanded soldiers waylaying our merchants, and rogues and woodkernes slipping in by night from the Curlieus, we must protect ourselves."

"Surely justice should be salted with mercy, Sir Robert?" Turlough's tone was affable.

"True! True!" Sir Robert rang a handbell. "I'll speak to the judge about the matter. Richard," he addressed a servant who had just entered, "a jug of sherry-sack for our visitors and tell the cook to prepare some cold capon and bread with our best cheese and whatever sweetmeats she can muster – and, of course, some bonnyclabber."

"You must forgive the frugal fare," he added, "but most of my servants are in Baggotrath with the younger children. Which reminds me that when the Earl of Strafford, may the Lord have mercy on his soul, was here in Thirty-Five, he said that the only thing which made Abbeyboyle endurable was the bonnyclabber – it was, I'm told, mixed with beer!"

While Sir Robert chatted in his urbane manner, I noted the shelves of leather-bound books lining the walls and the portrait of a knight, who from the similarity of features, I took to be Sir Robert's father, hanging over a high-backed, cushioned bench near the elaborately carved stone fireplace. Through an open section of the window I could glimpse the River Boyle gleaming in the afternoon sun, which also fell in golden shafts on the polished wood of the table and the open pages of a Bible.

"Ah, Oona, how well that doublet becomes you." Sir Robert's voice flowed on. "You will make our women abandon their gowns out of envy."

"Fie, Sir Robert!" Oona pretended to be horrified. "God forbid they should do anything so sinful."

"Now, Oona, you mustn't mock our attempts to live by God's injunctions." Sir Robert fingered his neatly trimmed moustache. "I'm sure this young man will tell you that virtue lies in simplicity and moderation." He surveyed me with a glint in his eye. "Sir Charles Coote informs me that you're a cleric."

"I once told his brother, Sir Chidley, that I was travelling to Kilmore to see Bishop Bedell –" Confusion made me uncertain how to continue: did he know about my Castlecoote escapade – or had young Sir Charles kept that repulse a secret?

"And at that time you were, I believe, travelling to Roscommon Town?" Sir Robert had the knowing expression of a master questioning a devious schoolboy.

"No doubt Sir Chidley misconstrued what Charles said." Turlough came to my rescue.

"No doubt," Sir Robert conceded. "Now let us refresh ourselves."

He led the way to another room with an arched wooden ceiling and a large tapestry of St George slaying the dragon, where a repast had been prepared for us, the simplicity of the food contrasting with the richness of the engraved silver plates. Richard brought in a leather jug of wine and a tray of Venetian glass goblets and after our host had said Grace, we fell to eating and drinking.

"Where is John today?" Oona enquired.

"I'm afraid he's gone fishing with his brothers, Henry and Robert." Sir Robert sipped from his goblet. "We didn't expect you'd arrive so early but I'm sure they'll be back before you depart."

"I've read the poems by John Milton which John sent to Oona," I forced myself to remark. "The one on your brother was very moving."

"Yes." Sir Robert's voice grew sombre. "Everyone loved Edward but, as the saying goes, 'He whom the gods love ...'"

"*Quem di diligunt adolescens moritur*," Oona murmured.

"You haven't forgotten your father's lessons, I see." Sir Robert's face brightened. "He often told me you were his favourite, Oona. Isn't it strange that he should be buried in Clonmacnoise and my own father in the abbey here?"

"There are over twenty MacDermots buried alongside him in the abbey, thirteen of them Kings of Moylurg." Turlough drained his goblet. "We're all united in death, Sir Robert."

"True! True!" Sir Robert agreed. "But we mustn't think only of the past. Have you hunted any stags this summer?"

"No," Turlough shook his head. "The only herd left is on Corrslieve. I thought I might go there on Sunday."

"You're welcome to pass this way." Sir Robert divined his intention. "If it weren't the Sabbath I would join you myself."

Soon Turlough and Sir Robert, their tongues loosened by the sherry, were discussing the best places to catch trout and whether fishing or hunting offered the more pleasant recreation. While I was mentally comparing them – Sir Robert neatly dressed, pink-skinned and, for all his affable manner, intense as a leopard, Turlough carelessly attired, ruddy-complexioned and with the indolent haughtiness of a wolfhound – Henry and Robert came in, supposedly to inform their father that John would be up presently, in reality to ogle Oona, who with her amber tresses and man's clothes shone like a candle against the dark panelling.

"Gentlemen, have I not told you always to change before meeting guests?" Sir Robert chided.

"We beg your pardon, sir." Suppressing grins, the youths prepared to withdraw.

"Wait!" Sir Robert called out. "Since you're here you may as well show our guests my apricot tree. I and this young man will join you by and by – and ask John to accompany you to the orchard."

The move separating me from Turlough and Oona was executed so adroitly that I awaited with misgiving whatever Sir Robert had in store for me.

Chapter 25

"THOSE sons of mine!" Sir Robert sighed when the door closed. "Since their mother, Lord have mercy on her, died, their lives have grown undisciplined. Henry will be off to Christ's College this autumn – and none too soon! You will be returning to Trinity yourself?"

"That will be as God decrees." I forced myself to withstand his gaze.

"Why, so it will." He nodded gravely. "Are you still desirous of meeting Doctor Bedell?"

"Yes." My mouth felt dry. "I can now read the New Testament in Gaelic. It would give me great pleasure to read Genesis, Psalms and The Song of Solomon in the same language."

"Why, your choice shows you are more the poet than the divine – but no matter." He stroked his pointed beard. "It may be that I can help you – but you must help me in return. Is it true you murdered an Englishman in Dublin?"

The question, despite what young Sir Charles had revealed in Castlecoote, was so direct that for a moment I was rendered speechless. On recovering my voice I made a truthful confession of all that had happened on that fateful afternoon when I had met the stranger in the Black Raven. Sir Robert listened without interruption, then he asked me to describe the man's features and mode of dress, meanwhile writing occasionally on a sheet of paper.

"It's just as I expected," he said. "The gentleman you assaulted was Edmund Devereux, a naval lieutenant who was visiting Sir John Borlase. Fortunately, he did not die. Now don't get overjoyed," he admonished, on seeing the delight leaping in my face. "It's true the man's body has returned to health but, as for his mind, he has no memory of where he was that day or of his life in England. Our Vice-President, Sir Charles Coote, urges that you be brought to Dublin to answer for the grievous harm you inflicted on one of His Majesty's officers. If the court finds you guilty, you could be sentenced to twenty years in Newgate. Now don't be downcast; I believe there are certain quiddities, such as your youth and the nature of the quarrel, that may work to your benefit."

"Is Edmund Devereux still in Dublin?" I felt like someone in a nightmare.

"No." Sir Robert placed his quill in the inkpot. "He has returned to his family's estate in Leicestershire. I spoke earlier of you helping me – if you do, I can ensure that you are absolved of the charges against you. Furthermore, Richard Washington, the new Provost of Trinity, is well known to me and should I speak on your behalf, why, he would doubtless turn a blind eye to your absence."

"How do you want me to help you?" I asked.

"Well, to come directly to the point," Sir Robert stroked his moustache, "you have clearly won the trust of the O'Conors and the MacDermots. Now, I'm not asking that you betray that trust but the times compel us to be watchful. Already there's a prophecy being noised about among the natives that in this year 'Saxons will lie stretched on the ground' – I believe those are the words. You may also have heard that the House of Commons has forbidden colonels from the Spanish army to recruit any more disbanded soldiers – that's because of fears that in a future conflict these same troops might well be used against us. Now, I know your father, Nicholas, is a loyal citizen – he came to Baggotrath two years ago to seek my help in obtaining a reduction in the wool tariffs – and I'm confident his son will not leave treason unreported."

"You're asking me to spy on my friends!" I charged.

"God forbid I should do that!" Sir Robert cried. "For how could enemies of the state be your friends? No, I'm not concerned with failure to attend Sunday services or even with the harbouring of priests and bishops – if our neighbours are lukewarm in their allegiance to the Reformed Church, the blame is mainly ours – what concerns me are these rumours of rebellion."

"I have heard no such rumours," I replied.

"Think well," Sir Robert regarded me with great intensity.

"Have you heard anyone recite the prophecy I alluded to or any mention of a Rory O'More from Longford who now lives in Armagh County or, indeed, anything that smacked of treason?"

I was in a dilemma. If I persisted in a flat denial, Sir Robert might conclude that there was something to hide; if, on the other hand, I told only what Brian Dubh would already have reported, it might convince him of my good faith.

"I once met a man in Ballintober who offered to bring me to one of the Spanish colonels," I said and recounted how O'Conor Don had introduced me to Manus but had then ordered him to quit the castle when he had the impudence to recite the prophecy.

"Good." Sir Robert looked pleased. "And have you seen or heard anything untoward at Lough Cé: pike heads or swords being forged in the smithy, strangers arriving, clandestine meetings, anything that aroused your suspicion?"

I shook my head.

"Well, have you ever visited the castle?" Sir Robert tapped his fingertips together.

"No," I said. "Why?"

"Oh, I was just curious." Sir Robert looked uncomfortable. "It distresses me to have to make such enquiries but with the breach between His Majesty and Parliament widening daily, it may embolden certain discontented men to have resort to arms. Not that I regard the MacDermots as disloyal – yet, they lost most of their estates after O'Neill's Rebellion and Turlough is proud and obdurate. If I tell you these things, it's because I trust you not to report our conversation."

"They will guess what we've been discussing," I pointed out.

"No matter." Sir Robert spread his hands. "A nod is as good as a wink to a blind horse. If they turn you out of doors, I shall employ you as my secretary until such time as you're permitted to return to Trinity – John tells me you write Gaelic as well as Latin and that will prove most useful here in Abbeyboyle."

"You said you would help me to meet Dr Bedell," I reminded him.

"Yes," he replied. "Dr Bedell is soon to visit Fergal O'Gara at Cuppanagh Castle. O'Gara, though a Gael, is a loyal member of the Reformed Church and a graduate of Trinity, where, as I'm sure you know, Dr Bedell was Provost in the late Twenties. I could invite the learned Doctor to stay for a week in Abbeyboyle before proceeding to Cuppanagh."

"That would please me greatly," I assured him, adding that I hoped Cormac would be released from Castlecoote to help with the translation of the Bible.

"I'm afraid O'Mulconry has refused to lend his assistance," Sir Robert said. "That's why Dr Bedell is visiting O'Gara, who is highly respected by his countrymen as a patron of learning."

"And will Sir Charles Coote continue to keep Cormac imprisoned?" I did not hide my dismay.

"You will have to ask Sir Charles that," Sir Robert replied, "though he is not easily swayed by pleas for mercy. That is why I advise you to prove your loyalty in the way we've discussed; become my eyes and ears and I will ensure you're not arraigned."

"Unless Gaelic scholars such as Cormac take a hand in Dr Bedell's translation, few of his countrymen will consent to read it." I was anxious to guide the conversation onto safer ground.

"Yes," Sir Robert agreed. "I sometimes think that religious reform is like my apricot tree; it doesn't flourish in our Irish climate. My brother Edward, had God spared him, might have accomplished great things for the Church – but not among our stubborn neighbours. Perhaps you, Charles, with your knowledge of their ways, will one day succeed where others have failed."

"'The stone which the builders rejected is become the head of the corner.'" The words rose unbidden to my lips, laden with self-mockery.

"You are troubled now," Sir Robert pressed his thumbs together, "but so is every man of conscience: are we to support the King or Parliament, the bishops or the Puritans? Sometimes in acting righteously, we may appear to betray those who are close to us but doesn't Christ say: 'I came not to send peace but a sword,' and, 'A man's foes shall be they of his own household'? He also said that his followers would be hated by all men."

We continued to talk in this manner for half an hour or so, Sir Robert trying to draw me on to further revelations, I trying to resist him, while appearing to comply. At last the porter's boy entered to tell Sir Robert that the MacDermots and his sons had returned. As I followed Sir Robert down to the courtyard, I realized that everything had been altered by our conversation for I was now obliged to make a choice between Gael and Foreigner and neither side would ever trust me fully.

When we stepped out of the narrow entrance Sir Robert's three sons were gathered about Oona, laughing at her saucy wit, while Turlough examined a cannon resting in the nearby carthouse. On seeing us, Turlough strolled over, pausing to toss a gooseberry in the air and catch it in his mouth.

"We were expecting you in the orchard, Sir Robert." He glanced at me. "Do you think your apricots will ripen this year?"

"God willing," Sir Robert replied. "The April frost burnt some of the blossoms but if the weather continues sultry, I hope to see a crop that will make Lord Ranelagh envious – you know he maintains they can only be grown in the south of England, that our Irish weather is too cold and wet?"

"Perhaps it is," Turlough said. "For my own part, apples will do well enough. Still, if anybody can make them thrive, it's you, Sir Robert. You have performed miracles with Abbeyboyle."

"The apple flowers late." Sir Robert tried to hide his pleasure. "That's why it escapes the frost. Nevertheless, if I have apricots even once every decade it will be worth my pains."

"What were you and Sir Robert discussing?" Turlough asked as we rode back towards the river.

"You." I decided to be blunt. "He was anxious to know what you kept in the castle."

"Was he?" Turlough laughed his hearty laugh. "Bold Sir Robert! He even served us meat on Friday."

"I'm sure it wasn't done on purpose," Oona said.

"Wasn't it?" Turlough snorted. "You know the saying: 'Hoof of a horse, horn of a bull, smile of a Saxon!'"

"'And vengefulness of a Gael!'" Oona added.

Despite Turlough's unconcern, once the family learned that Sir Robert wished me to report on them, a subtle frost chilled our evening meal. Cathal Roe and Lady Eleanor were delighted that I was innocent of murder and grateful that I had told them everything that had passed between me and Sir Robert but I could discern in their eyes the unasked question, "How much of what we're saying now will you report?"

After we had eaten, Oona, noting my dejected look, invited me up to her room, which, though neat and tidy, was furnished only with a bed, washstand, chair and table. Sitting on the bed she played soft airs on her lute, while I sat on the chair gazing out at

Lough Cé and thinking how Tomás, if he did not know the darkness of my mind, would have regarded my situation with envy.

By and by Oona put the lute aside and asked me what was troubling me. Overcome with emotion, I poured out the thoughts gnawing at my mind: how I was regarded by her family as a Jonah; how my own family must be grieving at my absence; how I didn't know if I could forsake the faith I had been raised in; how I feared Frances would not have me if I could neither support her nor become a Catholic.

Oona heard me out in silence; then, instead of counselling me, she laid bare her own heart. She was in a quagmire: her family wanted her to marry someone like Hugh O'Conor, but Tomás loved her and Hugh did not; and then her sister, Margaret, had married Con O'Rourke and Con had since gone mad, oppressed by the misfortunes that had befallen his family – his father, Brian Oge of the Battle Axe, had died when Con was still a boy and his cousin, Brian, Chief of the clan, was now a prisoner in the Tower of London. She herself would marry no one but would devote her life to ensuring that Hugh O'Conor was inaugurated King of Connacht at Carnfree. This, she felt certain, was her destiny. St Bearchán of Clonsast had prophesied that a man named Hugh would liberate Ireland – and who could that Hugh be if not the descendant of the last High King? Furthermore, the Virgin had told her that she had been chosen to assist him. That was why she wore men's clothes, as her heroine Joan of Arc had done, and why she hadn't agreed to marry Tomás – though I must never tell him this lest he be driven to desperation. As for myself, she knew that Frances loved me but I must do something to prove I would not leave her as I had left Beibhinn.

"What can I do?" I asked. "Shall I swear on the Bible?"

"You yourself will have to decide that," she replied. "But perhaps I can help you to see the way more clearly. Tonight we'll visit the Rock."

Refusing to enlighten me further, she asked me to meet her after sunset behind the western fort. If anybody asked why I was standing there, I could say that I was waiting to see an owl fly from the nearby wood.

At the appointed time she arrived carrying a hooded cloak, which she asked me to put on. We then made our way by twilight down to a small inlet where three or four upturned coracles were beached. Oona selected an oval coracle made from a single cowhide, which we carried down to the water. She directed me to take the seat while she herself knelt in the front and paddled us past reeds and hidden rocks well out into the lough so that we couldn't be recognized by anyone watching from the village. The frail craft danced so lightly on the surface that every moment I expected it to capsize but Oona's skill preserved us and soon we were alongside the gloomy castle.

At first I didn't see where we could land, as the castle's outer wall was built right at the island's edge. On the east side, however, there was a recess with stone steps leading up to a narrow entrance closed by an iron gate. Oona pulled on a bell rope and after a short delay, a halberd-armed porter appeared. On recognizing Oona, he unlocked the gate and straining to glimpse my face, which was concealed by the hood, led us down a passageway into the shadowy bawn. From there we walked round to the castle door and were admitted by a tall, grey-haired monk dressed in a white habit with a black chasuble. Oona addressed him as Father Bernard.

"You've come to pray at the shrine?" Father Bernard spoke with the strong, though kindly, accent of a ploughman. When Oona nodded, he continued, "And who may your friend be?"

Throwing back my hood, I told him I was Charles Stanihurst from Dublin, at which he exclaimed: "Stanihurst! Not a kinsman of the great Jesuit scholar, Richard?"

On learning that I was, he confided that Richard's book on the Blessed Virgin, *Hebdomada Mariana*, was among his favourite devotional works. It was a pity that Protestants saw fit to impugn the virginity of Mary, for by her intercession she could obtain great favours for us. Hadn't Red Hugh O'Donnell invoked her aid before his army did battle with Clifford on the Feast of the Assumption and look what an outstanding victory he had won? If I visited Trinity Island I could see the grave in which – God between us and all harm – Oona's kinsman Conor had buried Clifford's headless body after the battle. Had Oona told me that the shrine of the Blessed Virgin we were about to see had formerly been fixed in the inside wall of the church on Trinity Island, from where the White Canons had removed it for safe keeping after that drivelling pedant King James confiscated the abbey?

I said, "No," and was about to add that I was not a Catholic, as he obviously supposed, when Frances's image rose before my mind and stayed my tongue.

By this time we were standing in a sparsely furnished room whose only light came from the glow of a turf fire. Father Bernard lit a candle and telling me to leave my cloak on a chair, led us down a musty passage, with pikes resting on brackets and swords hanging from pegs, up a winding stair, through the Great Hall, where dust covered the table and benches, and into a small chapel. At the far end a beeswax lamp burned feebly on a stone altar, revealing a crucifix and some veiled object that I took to be a chalice.

Father Bernard lit the two altar candles from his own and I was able to see behind them painted wooden panels flanking an oblong stone. The panel on the left showed the Annunciation and the one on the right a Premonstratensian canon in his white habit gazing upwards towards the stone, upon which was carved, in high relief, the Virgin with the child Jesus sitting on her lap. The Virgin was crowned and carried a sceptre and she looked directly at us as if she were a queen surveying her subjects.

"On Trinity Island the shrine was set in an arch to the left of the altar," Father Bernard whispered to me, "but we decided it looked best in the centre. If you desire to be shriven, I can hear your confession outside in the Great Hall."

I assured him I didn't and, having conducted me to a prie-dieu, he departed, his sandals scuffling on the bare flags.

Following Oona's example, I knelt at the prie-dieu, traced the sign of the cross on myself and gazed at the crowned Virgin. I could understand why this shrine would have offended my fellow religionists, for not only was it a graven image but it made Mary appear more majestic than her Divine Son. In the glow of the candles her eyes held mine, gazing into my soul, seeing all, understanding all, waiting for me to turn to her for help.

I glanced across at Oona. Her face had a soft expression as if she were seeing a vision. Was it the influence of our surroundings, the tomb-like chapel, the heavy air and the uncertain light? The words of Genesis came back to me: "Thou shalt not bow down thyself to them, nor serve them: for I the Lord Thy God am a jealous God ..." But another part of my mind said, "'Behold thy mother!'" and I looked again at the stone image and it seemed that the Virgin's eyes were smiling as my mother's used to smile, tender, compassionate, loving.

"Mary, mother of Jesus, intercede with your Divine Son so that He will show me the right road to follow," I prayed, then rose hurriedly. Soon afterwards Oona rose too and, taking a candle each from the altar, we made our way in silence back to Father Bernard.

"Are you a Cistercian?" I asked, anxious to forestall any questions about my experience in the chapel.

"Indeed I am," Father Bernard laughed, "though I'm like Oisín after the Fianna. The Protestants have taken over our beautiful abbey in Boyle and now hold their services in one of the chapels. Sir Robert is a lenient man, however, and doesn't persecute us. Can I offer you supper?" he added. "The people, God reward them, bring fresh bread every day and I caught some trout this morning."

"Oh no, Father!" Oona pressed a silver coin into his hand. "We have to hurry back."

"Don't forget this." Father Bernard handed me the cloak. "Now God go with you both and protect you, for there are evil days ahead."

"Why do you say that, Father?" I felt a chill enter my heart.

"Haven't you noticed that the quicken berries have turned crimson already?" Father Bernard lowered his voice to a dramatic whisper. "That's a thing I haven't seen since the year Eight, when your people, Oona, lost Moylurg. And last week while I was out fishing, I saw an eagle attacked by scaldcrows. He alighted on Doon Rock and two scaldcrows began pecking him – but you mustn't pay heed to an old man's ramblings. Now God keep you both free from harm."

When we left the island the moon was rising, red and enormous, spilling its beams down on the water as if lighting our way to disaster.

"This is a sign from heaven," one part of my mind said but another part told me I was becoming as superstitious as Father Bernard.

"Are you pleased that we went?" Oona asked when we had carried the coracle up onto land.

"Yes," I said. "The shrine was very beautiful."

"You must never tell Sir Robert about it," Oona warned. "We're not supposed to keep such things."

"But doesn't Father Bernard fish openly on the lough?" I followed her up the steep path.

"He doesn't wear his habit when fishing," Oona said. "And by the way, we won't be meeting Tomás and Frances tomorrow; they'll join us at the hunt on Sunday."

"Why is it called Crom Dubh's Sunday?" I gave her back her cloak.

"I don't know," Oona confessed. "You'll have to ask Daithi."

"Where were you?" Daithi asked as I crept into the cabin.

"Over at Derreendarragh, watching an owl," I said.

"Ah!" Daithi exclaimed. "The Screecher of the Graveyard, the messenger of death! And was any *girseach* watching with you?"

"Who was Crom Dubh?" I ignored his question.

"He was a pagan god who was also known as *Crom Cruaich*, the Bent One of the Mound," Daithi answered sleepily. "It's said our ancestors sacrificed one third of their offspring to him to ensure an abundance of milk and corn." He then began to recite an ancient poem but dozed off after the second verse.

I myself slept badly, twisting and turning to escape the nightmarish voices besetting me. My father and Sir Robert were pleading with me to return to Trinity College and Oona and Father Bernard were telling me not to go or I would be thrown into Newgate gaol.

"Edmund Devereux isn't dead," I pointed out.

"He has lost his memory," Father Bernard cried. "That too is a kind of death."

"If you go back you will lose Frances forever," Oona warned.

"But my mother went to Dublin with my father," I protested. "Frances could do the same."

"You would lead her into the fold of Luther," Father Bernard accused. "Pray to the Virgin, Charles. She will show you the right path. Pray to –"

"Don't!" Sir Robert interrupted. "He is a disciple of Satan who wants to lead you into idolatry. Doesn't the Bible tell us that false prophets shall arise and show signs and wonders to seduce even the elect?"

"Luther and Calvin are the false prophets!" Father Bernard retorted.

And so it went, on and on, till I woke up in the dark, gasping. It was a relief to hear Daithi snoring on his pallet at the upper end of the room.

Chapter 26

I LAY on my back staring into the darkness. How strange that the knowledge that I wasn't a murderer had brought me so little happiness! Instead, I was poised on a knife's edge, determined to keep the love of Frances without denying the religion in which I had been raised. And, yet, was it possible to do so? The afternoon, just over a fortnight previously, when Frances had visited Lough Cé with her stepfather rose before my mind.

It was Tuesday, the first day of the *Aonach* or annual three-day fair, which was being held on the level ground south-east of the village. Since their father was in bed with an ague, I had taken my pupils, Brian and Terence, and their little brother, Cathal Oge, to view this gathering of the people of Moylurg, for such to my untutored eyes it appeared: villagers, scullogues and *Lóipínigh*, with their bare-footed wives and children, freely intermingling; drovers shouting and cursing as they belaboured sharp-horned black cattle with ashplants; shepherds with long crooks guarding nervous flocks of hoggets; dogs barking; beggars imploring; pedlars bawling their wares; a *geocach* singing a mournful ballad; four men tossing a fifth in a blanket; horseboys cantering half-wild garrons up and down to show off their form, and just beyond the fringe of low, solid-wheeled carts and tethered horses, two bodachs turning sheep carcasses on spits over a banked fire of glowing woodcoals.

Near the fire a long table had been set on trestles, and further back a maypole, gaudy with flowers and ribbons, jutted up into view. On catching sight of their uncle among the behatted gentlemen seated at the table, my pupils, ignoring my injunctions, raced ahead through muck and cow-dung to meet him, while I followed, leading Cathal Oge by the hand. Malachy, Turlough's *reachtaire*, escorted us the last few perches.

"How goes it?" I asked.

"Not as well as we hoped," he confided. "In Brian Oge's time you'd see creaghts streaming in from all sides but last year's bad harvest forced the scullogues to slaughter half their bullocks. Still, it's only Gathering Day."

Turlough invited us to partake of his hospitality, so we took our seats, Cathal Oge climbing onto his uncle's lap. Malachy whispered that our companions were, for the most part, big landowners or their agents who had come not only from the vicinity of Abbeyboyle but from distant parts of Moylurg. Sir Charles Coote's steward, Richard Lawrence, was there, a florid bull of a man, dressed in black, as well as Thomas Hewett, Sir Robert King's agent.

"And what do you teach these young gentlemen?" Richard demanded in his harsh, booming voice.

"English," I replied. "Shakespeare, Marlowe, Milton ..."

"Who is Milton?" Richard set down his meadar of ale. "Not some Jesuit rhymer, I hope."

"He's a poet who's highly thought of by the Puritans," Thomas Hewett informed him. "He was in Cambridge with Sir Robert's brother, Edward."

"Was he, by God?" Richard wiped his moustache with the back of his hand. "Then he must be a worthy scholar. I'm glad those nephews of yours, MacDermot, are being raised with the truth."

"Indeed," Turlough agreed drily, surveying me with hooded eyes, "though the Fianna of old valued truth too:

"*Le fírinne is le neart ár lámh*
Do thigimís slán as gach gleo:
With truth and the strength of our hands
We'd come safe out of every conflict.

"Now gentlemen," he added as two bodachs approached carrying a steaming carcass of mutton, followed by another with a wicker sciathan heaped with freshly baked griddle cakes, "let's see if your appetites are worthy of the Fianna."

It was pleasant sitting there in the warm sunshine, eating and drinking our fill and watching the activity of the fair, while a blind harper crouched on a stool played lively melodies. Now and again gillies would emerge from a cowhide tent with leather jugs of ale to replenish our meadars or servants might arrive from the mansion with bowls of cheese and troander. I asked Malachy how Turlough could afford such lavish hospitality and he told me that the MacDermots collected a toll for every beast sold – though this was usually paid in kind rather than money. If I looked carefully I would see long-haired fellows armed with quarterstaffs among the crowd; these were Turlough's and Cathal Roe's men, who were keeping an eye on haggling groups, not only to prevent fights but also to ensure that the MacDermots received their share.

"And whisper here to me," he continued, "why do you think that Presbyterian bodach over there is visiting us?" He nodded towards Coote's steward.

I shook my head.

"He's keeping an eye on our takings." He smiled grimly; then, before I could question him further, one of his drovers hurried up to report that Richard Lawrence's manservant was being overbearing and would Malachy come to prevent a brawl.

No sooner had Malachy left than, on glancing behind me, my heart almost stopped beating: Frances and Patrick French-Fitzstephens were walking towards us from the direction of the maypole! Turlough welcomed them with great warmth and put Frances sitting in the place of honour at his right hand. While her stepfather was talking to Turlough, Frances's eyes met mine and a smile of pleasure curled her full lips. At once her stepfather stared at me and I dropped my gaze.

Turlough and his guests resumed their discourse on the prices of cattle and the difficulty of shipping them to England because of the conflict between His Majesty and the Parliament. All the time I kept stealing glances at my *spéirbhean*, noting the soft glow of her cheek and how the sun gleamed on her brown hair. It was torment to be so close to her without the opportunity to talk or touch her hand and I felt like a knight who is condemned to worship his lady love from afar. The sight of MacDermot's fortress out on the lough, beyond the heads of men and cattle, with the wild boar banner hanging above its battlements only strengthened this illusion.

"In Armagh we reckon that four sheep will eat as much grass as a cow and two cows as much as a horse." Richard Lawrence's voice broke in on my thoughts.

"We reckon one cow to one horse here," Turlough replied.

"That's because those garrons of yours are little better than nags." Richard guffawed. "I'm talking of English horses."

"What do you know of farming in the North?" Turlough retained his good humour. "You had to come to Moylurg to see the sweetest grazing in Ireland and the best land for growing corn."

"Aye," Richard boomed, "but when ploughing we don't tie our horses by the tail or burn our corn to save ourselves the bother of threshing."

"That griddle cake you're eating was made from burnt oats," Turlough declared mildly, "and I'll wager you won't find better bread in Armagh. And as for ploughing by the tail, we do that to save our ploughshares, for the horses won't continue to pull once the *soc* hits a stone or root."

"And is a ploughshare of more consequence than the pain inflicted on a poor dumb beast?" Richard snorted.

"I'm told that in England they reckon bull-baiting and bear-baiting among their chief diversions," Turlough rejoined. "Aren't you then like the pot that calls the kettle black?"

"I'm a Scotsman, not an Englishman," Richard bellowed, "and I'll thank you to remember it."

There was no saying what might have happened next had some of the young men and women who had begun to dance about the maypole not called out to us to come and join them. This was my opportunity, I decided, but before I could catch Frances's eye, Turlough had led her away from the table. They were followed by French-Fitzstephens and the other guests, with the exception of Thomas Hewett – who decided to accompany the harper on a visit to Cathal Roe – and Richard, who sat resolutely by himself.

Intrigued by this gruff fellow who did not hesitate to upbraid The MacDermot on his own ground, I engaged Richard in conversation and found him to be a man of great independence of mind, a trait that was overshadowed by his blunt manner.

"Look at those bogtrotters!" He included scullogues, drovers, villagers and shepherds in the scornful sweep of his arm. "Doesn't it stand to reason that they'd be better off as tenants of ours than as dependants of the MacDermots? Why, you can smell them before you can see them and as for that gibbering they call Gaelic, how a man of learning such as yourself can abide it is beyond comprehension."

I tried to defend the common people against these imputations and, to my surprise, he conceded readily enough that as a newcomer to Moylurg, he might have been too quick to judge by appearances. "But," he continued; "if the Composition of Connacht hadn't freed these people from bondage to their so-called lords and chiefs, mark my words, they'd still be living like woodkernes. You have only to compare the good people of Abbeyboyle to the Papists in yon village to ken that."

Again I protested and he acknowledged that where the Irish had adopted civil ways, they were as God-fearing and industrious as any people in the Three Kingdoms. It was their allegiance to Popish superstition and to the backward ways of their vainglorious chiefs that kept the others as they were. For his part he would abolish all titles and privileges, whether religious or worldly, and make all people equal under the law.

"What do we need with lords and bishops?" he snorted. "Didn't Christ tell us that we are all 'children of the Highest' and that 'whosoever exalteth himself shall be abased'?"

I pointed out that Turlough, who was now dancing barefooted with Frances and the others about the maypole, was certainly not exalting himself but Richard was appalled that I should seem to approve of such heathenish antics, for the maypole was naught but a stinking idol and the dancers no better than Satan's disciples. No sober Christian would turn his back on a fair to leap and jig like a devil incarnate, but then it was well known that the self-styled Lord of Moylurg was as lustful as a barnyard cock and that there were few women in the barony who had not enjoyed his attentions.

"And you can tell him that," he declared, "for I've seen him making eyes at my own daughter. Aye, there's wild boar blood in yon MacDermot!"

While I did not doubt that Richard's personal aversion to Turlough had provoked this outburst, I was, nevertheless, alarmed enough to betake myself to the vicinity of the maypole, where a crowd of onlookers had collected. A piper was playing a *rince fada* and the dancers with linked hands approached the pole – to which a griddle cake decorated with daisies and thyme had been attached at a height of about nine feet – and retreated or spun round it like froth round a whirlpool.

Turlough's nimbleness surprised me. For a man in his late thirties he moved with the grace of a deer, his bare feet keeping perfect time to the music. It was Frances, however, that held my gaze. How lightly her white feet tripped over the grass! How tantalizingly her breasts quivered as she skipped and whirled! How pearl-like her teeth flashed between her parted lips! If only I were in Turlough's place, clasping her hand, smiling into her eyes ...

On and on the dancers swirled, whipped by the quickening music, then one after another the couples dropped out or fell to the ground panting, till only Turlough and Frances were left. At once a cheer went up from the onlookers: "MacDermot! MacDermot! MacDermot!" A pang of jealousy seared through me as Turlough placed his arm around Frances's waist and swung her off her feet before depositing her lightly beside her stepfather, who was holding her shoes. Then he leaped up and tapped the cake from the pole, catching it like a football before it could fall to earth. Another outburst greeted this display of agility. Two young scullogues hoisted him on their shoulders and bore him in triumph round the fair, accompanied by a dozen or more of their fellows. Everywhere they went the people hailed Turlough as if he were a victorious Roman general leading a triumph.

Taking advantage of this diversion, I approached Frances but before I could say two words, Patrick French-Fitzstephens conducted her back to the table.

"A fine victory," Richard Lawrence observed when Turlough, his face glowing, finally returned. "But then who would be so bold as to better his chief? Eh, MacDermot?"

"I'm not your chief." Turlough smiled as he drew on his stockings. "Maybe you would like to try me?"

Richard was momentarily taken aback. "I didn't come here to issue or accept challenges," he protested.

"No," Turlough agreed. "You came to dun me for the Composition rent. Well, you can tell your master that when he pays me the full price of the land I sold him, I'll pay the rent."

"That's not a wise course of action." Richard placed his hand warningly on his sword hilt. "Sir Charles is not a man to be trifled with."

"Very well." Turlough thrust his feet into his high boots. "Send me the Receiver-General of the Composition money and I'll pay him. But I'll have no truck with his lackeys."

"My master is not only Receiver-General, he's also Vice President of Connacht and a member of the Privy Council." Richard rose deliberately. "If you chose to malign him then on your head be it."

"Here." Turlough held out the cake he had won. "Take this back to your master. We wouldn't have him impugn our hospitality."

Ignoring the cake, Richard scowled and strode away.

"You took a risk in sending him off like that with a flea in is ear," Patrick French-Fitzstephens observed.

"Did I?" Turlough sniffed. "Well, he took a risk insulting me before my own guests and telling me how my nephews should be raised. 'Eh, MacDermot?'" he mimicked Richard's booming voice and we all laughed, including Brian and Terence and Cathal Oge, who was again seated on his uncle's lap.

"Nevertheless," French-Fitzstephens resumed his grave expression, "from now on I'd keep my eyes open: the Cootes will likely bide their time and then they or their minions will strike. Look what happened in Ballintober."

"Moylurg is a long way from Castlecoote." Turlough airily dismissed the warning. "Now, Patrick, it's time you and I cast an eye over those bullocks of mine. Frances can help Charles to look after this young warrior."

Bidding his stepdaughter not to venture into muck and darting a suspicious glance at me, French-Fitzstephens moved off with Turlough, and though Frances smiled, I wondered if she found me a poor substitute for the chieftain of Moylurg. Burying my doubts, I led her round the outskirts of the fair, each of us holding one of Cathal Oge's hands.

Word of Turlough's clash with Coote's steward had spread rapidly, causing a stir such as affects a hive when bees are about to swarm. I wondered if Turlough might not have sown the wind, especially when the *geocach* raised his voice defiantly in the last verse of "Róisín Dubh", the song that Hugh had sung at the feast in Ballintober:

> *The Erne shall gather in torrents*
> *and hills shall be rent;*
> *The waves of the sea shall redden*
> *and blood shall be spilt;*

Every mountain glen and bog
in Ireland shall quake
One day ere my Little Black Rose shall die.

If this stir made me uneasy, Frances did not seem to notice it. I asked her why Tomás hadn't come, and over Cathal Oge's head she pointed towards Kilbryan Wood, giving me to understand that he and Oona were meeting there. How I wished we were with them, not the target of all eyes. I was acutely aware that for these scullogues and villagers I was less Frances's gallant than Cathal Roe's Protestant tutor. Once I heard some horseboys calling out "*Sasanach!*" but I forced myself to ignore them. Every step we took people turned to greet my companions, the men doffing their blue bonnets, the women clucking over Cathal Oge or openly admiring Frances.

"She's the girl MacDermot danced with," they told one another. "No wonder they bore the cake away."

When Richard Lawrence and his manservant came trotting past, the crowd surged forward menacingly but the young men with quarterstaffs pushed them back.

"Won't Turlough be arraigned for refusing to pay the Composition rent?" I asked Frances as the black-cloaked pair disappeared round a bend.

"How should I know?" she pouted. Next moment she stepped into cow-dung and let out a cry of annoyance.

"If we go to the lough shore, I can wash your shoes," I said.

"It doesn't matter," she frowned. "They'll only get dirty again."

"Then I'll wash them again," I assured her.

"No," she decided. "I'll clean them later with moss."

As she stopped to examine a pedlar's wares I stole glances at her little ear and the soft, brown curls resting on her white neck above the lace collar and my heart ached with longing. In her red velvet gown she looked like a rose dropped in the mire.

"A necklace for your bright love." The pedlar held up an enamelled mermaid on a silver chain.

"How much?" I asked.

"Only two sovereigns, noble sir." The pedlar gave me an ingratiating smile.

Extracting from my purse one of the remaining sovereigns that Hugh O'Conor had given me, I said, "This is all I can offer."

228

"Don't buy it, Charles," Frances admonished. "It's too costly."

"Costly?" The pedlar rolled his eyes. "A mermaid of rainbow-bright enamel on solid silver! Why, I paid an English sailor twice that for it Monday week in the town of Galway. But since you're both in love, I'll accept this trifle." And hastily taking the sovereign, he handed me the necklace.

"I can't wear it now." Frances stepped back when I attempted to place it round her neck.

"Me wear it," Cathal Oge lisped. "Give it me, Charles."

"Why can't you wear it?" I tried to conceal my hurt.

"You know why," she pouted.

I was going to ask whether it was her stepfather or Turlough that she didn't wish to offend but managed to hold my tongue.

"Why do you want to give me a mermaid anyway?" She smiled reluctantly. "Do you regard me as somebody who lures men to their doom?"

"No." I put the necklace into my purse. "I think of you as my good angel."

"I'm not an angel," she protested. "I'm just like any girl. Anyway, it pleases me that you bought me such a costly gift. You can give it to me next Saturday at Knockmelliagh."

At these words the gloom lifted from my mind. Swinging Cathal Oge across ruts and cowdung, we made our way to the small harbour beside the village, where, watched by a group of half-naked children, herders were endeavouring to lead and drive a young bull up a gangplank into one of the moored pookawns. Whirling suddenly, the frightened animal caught the nearest man with his horns, knocking him into the water. The man floundered ashore, his thigh streaming blood. In the midst of the commotion, Turlough arrived with French-Fitzstephens and a hard-eyed man that I recognized as one of those who were with Manus in O'Beirne's alehouse.

"We'll have to skull that fellow before he gores another man," Turlough observed. Immediately, a boy was dispatched to the carpenter's for a saw and the half-crazed beast was roped and thrown to the ground. Telling French-Fitzstephens to lead Frances and Cathal Oge back to the mansion and sending the injured man to the nearest cabin so that his wounds could be tended, Turlough quickly restored calm. I asked a herder if he knew who owned the bull and he told me that Turlough was sending him as a gift to his cousin, MacDermot of Drumdoe, who lived on the far side of the lough.

When the boy returned, one man sat on the bull's back and another on his neck, then the hard-eyed stranger grasped the horn with his left hand and began sawing it close to the skull. I could see the poor beast's eye rolling in horror as the jagged blade moved back and forth. Finally, the man removed the saw and broke off the horn, allowing a crimson jet to shoot out. Nausea engulfed me. Turlough took a handful of mud and clapped it on the stump to staunch the bleeding. "Now the other one," he said.

Feeling unmanned, I slunk away. The whole day had gone badly from the moment Turlough had asked Frances to dance.

On the following Saturday, however, she accepted the necklace.

"I will have to keep it hidden from my stepfather," she reminded me as we embraced under the oak.

"And where will you hide it?" I asked. "'In a valley between two soft hills'?"

"You mustn't say such things." Her eyes were troubled.

"Why not?" I demanded. "Doesn't the Bible say: 'Thy two breasts are like two young roes that are twins, which feed among the lilies'?"

"You know that we don't read the Bible." She looked at me bashfully. "Is that really in it?"

"Yes," I assured her. "In The Song of Solomon. I'll show you the words if you wish."

"No, don't," she demurred. "I believe you."

Gently, I kissed her eyes and her lips and her neck, conscious of the soul trembling within her. "Frances, my beautiful Frances," I murmured …

Now I lay in the dark, listening to Daithi snore and inhaling the sour smell of unwashed stockings. "'Vanity of vanities; all is vanity,'" I reminded myself. Why did I think that I would so easily escape the punishment my sins merited? And yet, if I became a Catholic, I could ask Father Bernard to shrive me and then I would be able to marry Frances … The image of the bound bull returned, however, his eyes rolling as the blood jetted out.

Chapter 27

"COME ON, Charles! I'll race you to the top." Oona, her fair hair streaming, urged her garron through heather, sedge and squelchy peat up Sheegora, the eastern peak of Corrslieve. With my heart in my mouth, I followed as best I could on Donn, praying the mare would not break a leg. Tomás and Frances were already standing on the crest with Theobald Dillon, who had brought Frances from Ballytrasna on his black gelding, Fiach Dubh. Near the top I was forced by the steepness of the incline to dismount but Oona persevered and seated like Camilla on her half-wild garron triumphantly awaited my arrival.

"Ah, Charles," she mocked, "it's a good thing we didn't wager on the outcome."

I smiled ruefully at Tomás and Frances, who were grinning at my discomfiture.

"Your own mare would have done better," Theobald remarked unctuously. "I saw Beibhinn riding her last week and her limp was hardly noticeable."

Suppressing my annoyance, I turned to survey the valley, through which the road to Sligo known as the Bealach Buidhe or, in former times, the Red Earl's Route wound. From our vantage point I could discern Turlough and his men moving like beetles along the flank of the wooded northernmost peak, their wolfhounds straining on the leashes. It was clear why Turlough had sought Sir Robert's permission to cross his lands, for the two dozen or so long-haired fellows armed with miodoges and hunting poles that accompanied him must have aroused disquiet among any Englishmen they encountered. So far the hunt had not gone well, only hares and one or two badgers having been taken. I knew that Turlough blamed the scarcity of deer on the Foreigners but the disbanded soldiers and woodkernes infesting the mountain must have done their share of harm.

While these thoughts were passing through my mind, I was acutely aware of Frances standing vivid as a quicken tree beside Oona. Never had she appeared more desirable, her stillness and grace drawing my very soul as her companion's restless beauty never could. And yet, I sensed an invisible wall between us. Was she fonder of Theobald than she pretended? I must lose no time in telling her of my decision to become a Catholic – a decision I had finally arrived at in the early hours of the morning. That would put an end once and for all to Theobald's hopes.

"Where is Garoo?" I spoke casually to mask my deeper thoughts.

"Over there." Oona pointed to a peak beyond the partially wooded valley we had just crossed. "And down there is the spot where our kinsman Conor defeated Clifford in Ninety-Nine."

"With the help of O'Rourke and O'Donnell," Tomás added.

"Maybe we would have succeeded without their help." Oona tossed her head. "The MacDermots were never defeated in the Curlieus."

"And what is Conor's son, Owen, doing now?" Tomás demanded. "Writing poems to honour the King of the Saxons?"

"You can find that out for yourself." Oona retained her good humour. "I'm going to visit Drumdoe. You may accompany us if you wish."

I met Frances's eye, silently pleading with her to remain behind but instead of comprehending, she seemed eager to be off.

"I think I'll join the hunt." I decided that a show of independence might bring Frances to her senses but far from evincing disappointment, she looked relieved.

"What will you do, Frances?" Tomás enquired. "Will you go with Charles?"

"It grieves me to see poor dumb beasts being killed." Frances looked appealingly at Theobald, who was mounting Fiach Dubh, then at the ground.

"Come, then." Theobald reached down his arm. "Tomás, lift her up."

"We could stay here for a time," I tried not to sound abject; "then if you wished, we could catch up with Oona."

"Oh, do, Frances!" Tomás vaulted onto his garron's back. "You can't leave poor dumb Charles abandoned in this wilderness: he might get carried off by the Pooka!"

"All right." Frances raised her eyes.

My heart was thumping with a mixture of hope and uncertainty as the others trotted away northward, leaving me alone for the first time in over a week with my *spéirbhean*.

"If we walk over there, we should get a good view of Lough Cé," I remarked and tying Donn to a gorse bush, I led the way eastward, Frances stumbling and sinking. When I offered her my hand, she refused to take it, annoyed that her buckled shoes were soaking wet. I regretted not having mounted her on Donn but we had by now gone too far to turn back.

At last we came to the brow of Corrslieve and there below us was the lough, dotted with wooded islands, and beyond it the blue-green sweep of Moylurg. No wonder the MacDermots had fought Gael, Norman and Saxon to retain possession of this enchanted world, for such it seemed at that moment under the bright afternoon sun.

"Isn't it like Elysium?" I said.

Frances didn't answer, staring ahead without enthusiasm.

"Look!" I pretended not to notice her mood. "That must be Trinity Island where Sir Conyers Clifford was buried and isn't that brown spot among the trees the roof of Carrick Mansion?"

"I suppose so," Frances pouted. "Can we go now?"

"Only if you give me a kiss." I touched her soft, brown locks.

"Up here where everybody can see us?" Frances moved her head away; then, seeing my crestfallen air, she pressed her lips briefly to mine.

"What's the matter?" I forced myself to ask.

"Nothing's the matter." Her eyes were fixed on the distant hills.

"Frances ..." I began.

"Yes?" She turned to me reluctantly.

I was about to blurt out that I had made up my mind to become a Catholic but decided that this wasn't the moment to reveal it. "You want to be with the others, don't you?" I observed.

When she didn't answer, my heart sank. "All right, I'll take you," I said.

"Charles," she laid her hand on my arm, "I have something to tell you."

Her tone filled me with unease. "I have something to tell you too," I began then decided to let her continue.

"Turlough, Oona's brother, has asked for my hand in marriage and my mother and stepfather have given their consent." She searched my face as she spoke.

If a thunderbolt had smitten me, I couldn't have been more dumbfounded. Turlough! The man with the carefree ways and hearty laugh ... the man I had admired above all others in Moylurg ...

"But he's almost three times your age," I murmured in disbelief.

"He's The MacDermot," she pointed out with unexpected pride. "Any woman would give her right hand to be his wife."

"But you love me." My words echoed hollowly in my own ears.

"You're a Palesman, Charles." Frances dropped her eyes. "Even if I returned your love, sooner or later you'd leave."

"But I'm going to become a Catholic," I protested.

She remained silent and I knew she regarded my declaration as a desperate ploy to win her back.

"Don't you believe me?" I demanded.

"Why did you wait so long to make up your mind?" Frances smiled wistfully.

Her question was like a knife in my heart. "Come." I was surprised at my own calmness. "We'd better hurry if we want to catch up with your friends."

Neither of us spoke as I galloped Donn recklessly through sedge and heather towards the pale blue waters of Lough Arvach, near whose southern shore Drumdoe lay. After half an hour of furious riding I spied Oona and the others and hallooed to them.

"Come with us." Frances's voice was almost a whisper.

"No," I answered stiffly, helping her to dismount.

"Charles, don't go near the hunt." Frances's eyes were troubled. "There could be danger."

"Why should you care?" I smiled bleakly. "I'm a Palesman," and climbing onto Donn's back, I hurried away before the others could reach us. I heard Tomás calling after me but I did not turn my head. For some unknown reason Oona's boast about the Mac-Dermots never having been defeated in the Curlieus kept ringing in my ears. If I challenged Turlough would I suffer the fate of Clifford, whose corpse, according to Daithi, had been beheaded on the orders of Brian Oge O'Rourke? The dripping trophy rose before my mind's eye like a ghastly warning; nevertheless, I was determined to have it out with Turlough for he had treacherously robbed me of my heart's pulse.

A distant outburst of baying and hallooing told me that the hunters had flushed some quarry and I headed in their direction down the sparsely wooded slope. The breeze tore at my face and blood pounded in my ears. Donn's flanks were lathered with sweat but I urged her on relentlessly. Through a gap in the nearby birches I saw dark figures slipping from cover to cover, then tears blurred my vision. The trees closed round me again but I did not slow down, forcing Donn over mossy logs and clumps of briars. Suddenly the mare tripped, sending me flying across her shoulders. There was a blinding flash as my head struck the ground, then blackness.

On opening my eyes the first things I saw were damp brown leaves. An oppressive silence, broken only by the croaking of a raven, hung in the air. Pain seared through my forehead and on touching it, my hand came away bloody. Fighting wave after wave of nausea, I rose to my feet. Donn was nowhere in sight. As my strength returned, I ventured carefully down an overgrown deer-path, following the mare's hoofprints. I had gone no more than fifty paces when I became aware of footsteps. With a feeling of relief I turned, then fear gripped my heart. Donal Bawn, armed with a miodoge, was slinking towards me.

Wheeling around, I was about to flee when Fergus and Brian Dubh stepped from cover into the path ahead. Brian Dubh was carrying a long musket with a wooden-shafted iron fork on which the barrel rested. A powder horn and small purses hung from a rawhide strap looped across his chest and left shoulder. Fergus was brandishing a heavy stick. Instinctively, I thought of plunging among the trees on my left but realized that I was too dazed to escape that way. I would have shouted for help but the shame of allowing Brian Dubh to observe my panic kept me silent. Like a cornered stag I stood my ground, knowing I was doomed.

At a command from their master, Donal Bawn and Fergus seized me and tied me hand and foot to a young oak with rawhide thongs.

"What do you want with me?" I croaked, my throat dry with

fear.

"I warned you, Palesman, that you'd rue the day O'Conor Don dismissed me," Brian Dubh hissed. "You thought you were a great man with your fine clothes and your satires but what use are they to you now?"

"If I shout for help, MacDermot's gillies will tear you to pieces," I blustered.

"Will they?" Brian Dubh smirked, steadying the fork with his left hand and lowering his head alongside the butt to take aim at my heart. In my state of acute alertness I could see and smell the burning match poised above the pan.

"Why don't you shoot, boarface?" I taunted. Now that Frances had rejected me, death would be a blessing.

"No, Palesman." Brian Dubh raised his head. "You're going to suffer the daily hell I suffer. You made me a laughing-stock and an outcast and I intend to repay you. 'An eye for an eye and a tooth for a tooth' – isn't that what your Protestant Bible says? Donal, this is the fellow that robbed you of your mistress and earned you three cracked ribs."

What were they going to do to me? A cold sweat broke out on my forehead yet at the same time my mind seemed to hover outside my body, calmly watching my predicament. Donal Bawn advanced, a grin curling his lips. I decided that my only chance lay in goading my adversary into discharging the musket, so I began to declaim:

"Brian Dubh, your like's that Stygian boar
Which terrorized Con's land of yore:
No wonder Charles was put to rout
By one shrill squeal from your black snout –"

"Why are you standing there?" Brian Dubh yelled at his henchman. "Skull him!"

"He wants to hear the satire," I cried and continued:

"Indeed your wit is sharper than
Athairne's tooth or Bricriu's tongue;
And yet –"

I got no further; Donal Bawn's fist slammed into my jaw, almost stunning me. Before I recovered, a dirty kerchief was forced between my teeth and tied at the back of my head.

"Now, Diarmuid of the Love Spot," Donal Bawn sneered, "we'll see how many women will fall in love with you when I'm finished."

Swinging his arms in wide arcs, he hit me repeatedly in the face, first with his left fist, then with his right. Blood from my nose and mouth flowed over my lips and down my chin. The world reeled about me. Just when I imagined that he was tiring, he grabbed my hair and brought the gleaming point of his miodoge up to my eye.

"Wait!" Brian Dubh handed the fork and musket to Fergus and approached the oak. I could see his flushed face and small vicious teeth as he snatched the miodoge out of Donal Bawn's hand.

"You know how the O'Haras repaid Tadhg Dall for his satire?" Brian Dubh's eyes were blazing into mine. "Well, I'm not going to cut out your tongue, Palesman, but I'm going to cut off something else."

I mumbled with terror, while sweat trickling from my forehead half blinded me. Brian Dubh grasped my ear and raised the miodoge: next moment exquisite agony seared through my numbed brain. There was a deafening explosion and Brian Dubh's head floated like a crimson pall towards mine. I felt myself sinking down, down, down beyond thought and sense into a void of blackness.

When I regained consciousness, I found myself lying on a crude litter made of branches, which was being carried by four long-haired hunters. On my right side a brace of wolfhounds with bloody muzzles were trotting after a garron, across whose back the gutted carcass of a stag was tied. The stag's felt-covered antlers hung down so that their tips brushed the heather. My throat was parched with thirst and every jolt of the litter sent waves of pain coursing through my head. Raising my hand, I felt for my ear but my fingers encountered only a lump of moss held in place by a rag that was sticky.

On seeing my crimson fingers I groaned aloud. Immediately the hunters lowered the litter to the ground and Turlough approached to ask what I wanted.

"Water," I mumbled through my bruised mouth.

"There's no spring on the mountain," he replied.

Turlough's face drifted out of view and when it reappeared I begged again for water. I could see him at what seemed a great distance shaking his head and in my fevered state I imagined that he was thinking of Frances and me together.

"Water!" I croaked. "Water!" But he seemed not to hear.

The third time I called him he relented and cradling my head in his arm, dribbled usquebagh from a goatskin bottle into my mouth. The fiery liquid scalded my bruised gums and throat without relieving my thirst and I twisted my head away. After that I sank back into a state bordering on delirium. At times I was aware of the hunters moving against the bright sky, at other times I was alone in a dark wood where wild boars and wolves lurked behind the trees or I was drowning in a lake while Frances and Oona watched indifferent from the shore. I tried to pray but it was clear that even God had abandoned me and I would never again be part of the happy world of living people.

For what seemed an eternity the journey went on and on, across marshy hollows, down rushy slopes, past meadows of scented hay, through a treacherous waist-deep river, around farmhouses guarded by barking dogs, up twisting sheep paths infested with flies, into cool woods of dappled sunlight, by reeking dunghills, but eventually we reached Carrick Mansion and I was laid on a pallet in the Great Hall.

The next few days are a blur. Oona told me later that I hovered between life and death and if it were not for the ministrations of Bridgeen – who knew more about cures than any *fear leighis* – I would not have recovered. Not that I wanted to live once I knew the sum of my hurts: four teeth loose, the light of both eyes dimmed, my nose broken, my right ear gone. I remember begging Oona not to tell Frances about my condition and my dread that she would ignore my pleas.

At last I was considered strong enough to be moved out to the cabin, where I sat day after day by the empty hearth, brooding over Frances and wishing death would release me from my hopeless plight. Oona, accompanied by her spaniel, Daithleen, would come to read my Bible to me, in particular the Psalms and the book of Job.

"Why won't you let me send for Frances?" she would plead but I would only shake my head. Finally, I blurted out the accusation that was festering in my mind, that she had concealed from me her brother's betrothal to Frances. Her astounded look convinced me that she was entirely ignorant of this occurrence but she allowed that Turlough might have said nothing for fear of their mother's disapproval. Next evening she confirmed that this was indeed the case, both Lady Margaret and Cathal Roe having set their minds against a family connection they deemed unworthy of The Mac-Dermot.

"Turlough will follow his own course no matter what anyone says." Oona laid her hand on my arm. "If I could persuade him to withdraw his suit, Charles, I would."

I felt tears welling in my eyes and, not trusting myself to speak, nodded. She then told me that she believed Frances was acting out of duty rather than passion, Patrick French-Fitzstephens being a man who would not allow his daughter to refuse so advantageous a marriage.

"We must accept that we cannot always have the person our heart is set on," she added pensively. "That is why Frances is doing this – I know in my heart it is."

Her words dissolved some of the bitterness gnawing at my mind, for I truly believed that were I a Catholic and had the means to support her, Frances would have chosen me rather than Turlough. As things stood, however, I had nothing to throw on the scales that would outweigh the honour of being mistress of Moylurg, and since my encounter with Brian Dubh I had not even the advantage of pleasing features – for what girl could look on me now without aversion? Yes, Brian Dubh had gained his revenge but gained it – as Oona Bawn informed me – at the cost of his own life.

It seems that he and his companions had, at the instigation of Sir Charles Coote, been lying in wait for Turlough, hoping to kill him with a musket shot. My arrival on Donn had upset their ambush and they had turned on me their thwarted malice. Fergus, however, had been an unwilling accomplice, Turlough's kindness to him while he was in the stocks having touched him deeply. When Brian Dubh cut off my ear, Fergus had discharged the musket in a fit of revulsion, killing his master. Donal Bawn had immediately taken to his heels but Fergus had attempted to staunch the flow of blood from my wound. Notwithstanding his efforts, by the time Turlough's hunters arrived I was close to death. Fergus was now staying with Turlough at Cloonybrien and Donal Bawn was a fugitive from the vengeance of the MacDermots.

"And what happened to Donn?" I asked.

"She came limping down towards Ballaghboy just as the hounds were making the kill," Oona replied, "so Turlough knew something was amiss. He sent a few of his men back along her tracks; then, when the musket shot rang out, they went racing up into the wood. If it weren't for Donn you might have bled to death. She's resting now in the stable, waiting for the day when you'll be strong enough to take her out for a canter."

I said nothing, too heavy hearted to respond to her blandishments. It was generous of her not to chide me for abusing the mare, but I felt certain that I would never ride again.

Chapter 28

As MY face cleared up and the wound where my ear had been healed, Cathal Roe insisted that I resume my duties as tutor. At first I was in dread that Brian and Terence would recoil from my features but after some passing curiosity, they showed no signs of aversion and I found that, though I was sand-blind in one eye, the effort of teaching allowed me a respite from the deadness within me. Once I returned to the cabin, however, gloom settled on my soul and until Daithi entered, I would sit brooding by the empty fireplace. Uncle Teigue's pockmarked face would rise before my mind's eye and I would blame myself for having abandoned him. Now, like him, I would have to endure the never-ending pain of loneliness, for since Frances had rejected me, what other girl would think me worthy of love? In my despair I would turn to the Bible and read over and over the words of Christ: "And if thine eye offend thee, pluck it out: it is better for thee to enter the Kingdom of God with one eye, than have two eyes to be cast into hell fire."

At times bitterness would engulf me and I would dwell on revenge. Suppose I told Turlough that Frances was O'Conor Don's bastard, would he still want to make her his wife? And what if I told Sir Robert King about Father Bernard and the shrine in Carrick MacDermot? Wouldn't that be a fitting repayment for Turlough's treachery to me? The extent of that treachery might be greater even than appeared, for hadn't Frances warned me about going near the hunt? Did she suspect her gallant of wanting to kill me? Suppose it was Turlough and not Sir Charles Coote who had planned the ambush? No, if that were the case, Fergus would not have shot Brian Dubh. But suppose that the musket ball had been intended for me?

The more I contemplated these possibilities the more certain I became that jealousy was clouding my judgment. Turlough might resent me as a rival but he would hardly have me killed and Frances was too noble-minded ever to marry a man who would stoop to dishonour. Furthermore, it was likely that Turlough already knew about Frances's parentage and that Sir Robert would be more concerned about treason than about religious non-conformity. I was obliged to acknowledge that if I had lost my true love the fault lay in me, not in her.

Thyself thou gav'st, thy own worth then not knowing,
Or me, to whom thou gav'st it, else mistaking ...

How bitterly apt those words of Shakespeare now sounded!

The world around me seemed to mirror my state of mind for even though the weather remained warm, the birds had long since ceased to sing and the cuckoo and swifts had disappeared. Oona, noting my despondency, begged me to visit the shrine but I refused. If my previous visit had not preserved me from evil what could a second visit effect? I would have no more truck with superstition. Lady Eleanor was most solicitous too, asking Bridgeen to cook my favourite dish, colcannon – at that time potatoes were still a rarity in Moylurg – or asking Oona to play for me on the lute. She also washed my hair and showed me how to part it in the middle, the better to conceal my missing ear.

Towards the end of August word reached Moylurg that Brian O'Rourke, chief of the clan and a cousin of Mad Con – the husband of Oona's sister Margaret – had died in the Tower of London. This report cast a gloom over the family, coming as it did hard on the news that the Dublin government controlled by Lords Justice Parsons and Borlase had prorogued Parliament. There were also rumours abroad that His Majesty had gone to Scotland to seek support against the Parliament in London and that the Dublin Puritans were planning a general massacre of Catholics. As if to confirm these evil tidings various omens were reported: a cow had dropped a calf with five legs; the ghost of Bingham had been sighted at Ardcarn; a girl had seen the Virgin in the shrine weeping tears of blood ...

In the midst of this unease Sir Robert King sent for me: Bishop Bedell would be arriving in Abbeyboyle the following week and Sir Robert earnestly requested that I go there to meet him. Not surprisingly, this request caused consternation among my hosts. Cathal Roe, knowing that Turlough was planning to marry Frances, must have feared that I would betray the family out of resentment, yet from what his mother, Lady Margaret, let slip, I gathered that he had borrowed money from Sir Robert and couldn't risk offending him.

Oona was apprehensive too. My refusal to revisit the shrine must have convinced her that I was by now a confirmed Lutheran, though, if the truth be told, I was more an atheist than a Christian of any hue. God had forsaken me in my hour of need and left me defenceless before my enemies. Worst of all, He had caused me to lose the girl I loved, for had I become a Papist, Frances would surely not have spurned me. But it was Daithi who, probably at Turlough's behest, chose this opportunity to attack me openly. Finding my Bible lying on the table at which I was teaching Brian and Terence, he picked it up and remarked, "So this is the poison you're feeding your charges!"

"I am not teaching them that," I spoke calmly, determined to champion what one part of my mind rejected, "and, anyway, since when has the Word of God become poison?"

"The Word of God!" He threw the Bible down scornfully. "The word of that arch-heretic Luther, you mean."

"If you can show me any distortion, then go ahead," I challenged.

"If that Bible contained the true Word of God, then our Bishop would have said so." He ignored my challenge.

"That's a strange answer for a scholar," I observed. "If God gave us reason he expects us to use it, not to accept blindly what some Bishop tells us."

"He didn't give us reason in equal measure," Daithi pointed out, "and I think it ill becomes you to criticize our clergy when your people have stripped them of everything they possessed and driven them like wild beasts into the woods and mountains."

"And what did your people do when they were in power?" I asked. "Look at Bloody Mary in England; look at the Inquisition in Spain and the St Bartholomew Day massacre in France."

"I'm not going to argue about what happened in other countries," Daithi snapped, "but I'll tell you what happened right here in Moylurg during the reign of Bloody Mary's sister, Good Queen Bess: the abbots of Trinity Island and Boyle were taken to your city by Lord Deputy Grey, where they were tortured by having their legs and arms broken and their feet burned and then they were hung, drawn and quartered."

"If the Pope hadn't excommunicated Queen Elizabeth, she'd never have lifted a finger against the Catholics," I averred.

"Wouldn't she?" Daithi snorted. "You have only to look out that window to see the results of Saxon perfidy: Trinity Island desecrated; Innis Mac Nerin desecrated; Boyle Abbey desecrated – that's not mentioning all the churches and convents that have been suppressed and their lands given to Lutherans."

"But doesn't it strike you as strange," I spoke dispassionately, "that people who claim to follow Jesus – who had not even a place on which to lay his head – that people who claim to live according to His example should have possessed so much property?"

"At least the abbeys shared what they had with others," Daithi cried. "Do you think their new owners, like Sir Robert King, will welcome the traveller and minister to the sick and provide learning for the community? No, they will read their Bibles and put guards on their doors and grab everything they can lay their hands on. Don't speak to me of the poverty of Christ for a poor Protestant is as rare in this country as a sober man at a feast."

"That is what the Puritans are trying to change," I said. "They want to return to the simplicity of the early Church; they want to take power away from princes and prelates and give it to Parliament."

"Yes," he scoffed, "provided it's a Protestant parliament. You think your friend Sir Robert is a fine gentleman who wants to help us all – did he oppose Parsons and Borlase when they prorogued the Dublin Parliament? Oh no! And why was it prorogued? Because it might grant the Graces promised to Catholics by King Charles. Do you know that Turlough sold land to Coote so that he could raise money to help pay for those Graces? There were a dozen Catholics in that Parliament, so –"

"What is 'parliament'? Brian interrupted.

"Parliament?" Daithi said. "That's a place where crows gather to decide which cornfield they'll raid next. Your tutor, Charles here, is a kind of crow."

"And you're a kind of jacksnipe," I retorted, "always bleating about the wrongs inflicted on the poor Gaels."

"Come on!" Daithi fumed, raising his fists. "Are you man enough to back up those insults?"

His challenge was so unexpected that I was rendered speechless.

"So you're a coward too," Daithi jeered.

"I have no desire to behave like a ruffian," I countered, aware that Brian and Terence were watching me intently.

"Ha! Spoken like a true O'Flynn." Daithi lowered his fists and proceeded to declaim a satire on the chief of the clann that Aonghus O'Daly had made. This was an insult to my mother's family that couldn't be endured, so I reluctantly raised my fists. Daithi advanced on me, ready to do battle, but before either of us had struck a blow, the master entered.

"Now gentlemen," Cathal Roe regarded me with a twinkle in his eye, "if you can't argue without fighting like cockerels, then say nothing."

"But he can't decide if he's a Gael or a Saxon," Daithi protested. "And that puts us all at risk."

"No, it doesn't." Cathal Roe spoke with quiet certainty. "Now embrace and be friends."

I cannot express how grateful I felt to Cathal Roe at that moment. He was telling Daithi that he regarded me not as a Foreigner but as a man worthy of trust. Daithi and I embraced briefly, at which Oona and Lady Eleanor – who, attracted by the commotion, had just come upstairs – clapped their hands.

"Let's go down to the Hall and we'll drink to the health of these worthy scholars." Cathal Roe took Daithi and me by the arm and ushered us out of the room.

What an evening of talk and merriment we had then! What playing of the lute and reciting of poems and singing of songs! The MacDermots were truly descendants of the Kings of Moylurg and their hospitality was wholehearted and unstinting.

That night I slept badly; maybe it was the wine or maybe it was my fear of what lay ahead. All the people I had failed came crowding round me; accusing me; entreating me; spurning me. Uncle Teigue looked at me out of his pockmarked face, not daring to speak because he felt he had no claim on my affection.

"That's not true, Uncle," I protested. "I'll help you get your lands back."

"It's all right, Charles." He spoke at last. "I won't starve, not while there are strangers to help me." And suddenly he became Cormac, lying on dirty straw in a dark, fetid cell.

"Remember what I told you, Charles." Cormac raised his emaciated arm. "The word! The word! What is written survives. Get all the old learning into books or it will be lost forever ... lost forever."

"What will I write, Cormac?" I pleaded. "I am neither poet nor scholar."

"Write for the glory of God and the honour of Ireland." He turned his face to the wall and dissolved into flame.

My parents appeared to me then. "We don't know, son, whether you're alive or dead," my mother wept. "Come back," my father pleaded. "We won't task you for wasting your talents. If you want to become a poet and chronicler like your grand-uncle Richard, we won't gainsay you."

"I cannot go yet," I cried. "I must visit Abbeyboyle."

A stern Dr Bedell accosted me now. "We are waiting, Charles," he said. "Why do you hesitate? Remember we too are of Ireland: Fergal O'Gara has helped them write their annals and I am translating the Holy Bible for them. The harvest truly is great ..."

"You can take the place of my brother Edward," Sir Robert King encouraged.

"Don't you see that you are only useful to Sir Robert and his friends because you know so much about us and the O'Conors?" Cathal Roe warned. "Don't be fooled by their talk of Edward and the Holy Bible."

"It's your knowledge of Gaelic, not of Latin, he values," Daithi pointed out. "A good spy must be like Brian Dubh, someone who is able to converse with the natives."

"Leave me alone!" I cried. "You are both so full of suspicion, you see evil where there is only good."

"Look at your face then." Daithi held a glass up before me. "Look at your crooked nose and your sand-blind eye and the hole where your ear was. What would Frances think of you now?"

"Frances is of our people as well as of theirs," Dr Bedell pointed out.

"But she's marrying Turlough," Daithi crowed. "She'll never be lured into your heathen fold. Never! Never!"

When he said this, all familiar things slipped away and I was wandering alone through a mountain marsh that quaked at every step. In my terror I called out for help but my words went circling round the empty peaks and returned to burst upon my eardrums with horrid cadences. I drew within the orb of my mind every person who had ever befriended me, including Beibhinn, but they all struggled to get away as if I were a leper. Then in despair I called out to Frances.

"If you stand by me," I pleaded, "I will face any danger, even hell itself."

She seemed to be on the point of joining me but before she could, Turlough's voice rang out, "He killed a man in Dublin!"

"He's not dead," I cried. "Don't listen to him, Frances."

"His memory of his past life is gone." Turlough had changed into Coote, who fixed me with an implacable stare. "That too is a form of death."

"O depraved wretch!" Dr Bedell declared. "Truly man is a wolf to man."

I could see Frances struggling to reach me but some invisible force kept dragging her away. Then I realized that the hosts of heaven had turned against me: faintly at first, then with increasing clarity I heard their muffled, marching feet. My bowels melted with fear. Everything was now spinning around me, forming a great vortex into which I was irresistibly dragged. I felt myself falling down, down through endless space, down from a great happiness that was almost mine, down from the looming shadow of God …

I woke up, gasping with horror.

Next day those of us who had drunk too liberally were as cranky as sacks of weasels and while I was impatiently teaching my charges their English lesson we were interrupted by angry voices from downstairs. Cathal Roe was upbraiding Oona for refusing to be guided by him in some important matter and Lady Margaret was telling her that she should listen to those who had her best interests at heart.

"Are you sure it's my best interests you have in mind?" Oona retorted.

"Quiet!" Cathal Roe commanded. "We've let you have your way far too long. Now, by God, you'll do as you're told."

At this point Lady Eleanor begged him to keep his voice down or the children would overhear him. After that the argument rumbled on, Cathal Roe speaking in tones of bitter reproach, Oona in sullen outbursts, until the banging of the front door brought an abrupt silence.

Despite my attempts to put the unseemly quarrel out of my mind I found it impossible to do so. What did her brother and mother wish her to do that could give rise to such spleen? Was it to end her trysts with Tomás or to stop wearing men's clothes? I set my pupils to writing out a poem from *England's Helicon* while I pondered the question but I was still no nearer enlightenment when Daithi entered to inform me gruffly that Oona was waiting for me in our cabin.

Losing no time, I hurried downstairs and with averted eyes passed through the Great Hall and into the open air. When I pushed open the cabin door, Oona was sitting on a stool by the fireplace, stroking Daithleen, who was gazing earnestly at his mistress.

"Oh, Charles!" She raised her head at the sound of my footsteps and there were tears in her eyes. "What am I to do? They're determined to make me break my vow."

Drawing up a stool beside her, I listened while she poured out the cause of her grief. Sir Robert King had paid Coote the Composition rent owed by Turlough and so averted Turlough's certain imprisonment. Now Cathal Roe wished her to marry Sir Robert, who, ever since his wife's death, had cast longing eyes at her. Sir Robert was being invited to a feast Turlough was giving to celebrate his betrothal to Frances, and Cathal Roe wished her to attend.

"Won't Turlough protect you from any unwanted marriage?" I asked.

"No." The sadness in her eyes deepened. "Turlough is besotted with Frances and will do anything to win our consent to their marriage. Our mother will not bend but if Cathal Roe gives his blessing then Turlough will not oppose my betrothal to Sir Robert."

"You are to be the sacrificial lamb." I made a play on the name "Oona", which signifies "lamb" in Gaelic.

"Oh, Charles," she ignored my poor jest, "I wish Frances had remained faithful to you. Any man who refuses to change his religion, even for the woman he loves, is a man of honour."

"Or a simpleton," I added bitterly.

"I only hope that I will have your fortitude in the struggle ahead." She gazed at me earnestly. "Cathal Roe threatened to throw me out if I persisted in my defiance – what am I to do?"

"Why don't you run away with Tomás?" I said.

She shook her head: "I told you I had made a vow. I will keep that vow even if it brings my death but I fear Tomás may do something rash. Oh, Charles, promise that you'll come with us to the feast – it's being given in the castle on Thursday."

"How do you know Tomás will be there?" I now understood why in recent days so many currachs had been travelling to and from the island.

"I invited him," she confessed, "but that was before I knew Sir Robert would be invited too."

"How can I go?" I objectd. "In Turlough's eyes I would be as welcome as a leper."

For answer she turned on me her tear-reddened eyes. This mute appeal moved me more deeply than words and mingled with my despairing desire to see Frances one last time. Laying my hand on her arm I assured her I would go if her brothers deigned to invite me.

"Cathal Roe will," she declared with a flash of her old spirit, "or else he will go without me."

"I hope I won't be like the guest in the parable," I smiled, "the one who hadn't on a wedding garment."

Chapter 29

ON THURSDAY evening I sat morosely beside Tomás at a long trestle table while the thronged, candlelit hall of Carrick MacDermot rang with laughter and merriment. From the corner of my eye I could glimpse Turlough and Frances at the raised table which formed a T with ours; Lady Eleanor, Cathal Roe and Oona, dressed in the green gown she had worn at the feast at Ballintober, were seated beside them, talking to Frances's mother and stepfather, who occupied the end of the table. At the other end Sir Robert King and his agent, Thomas Hewett, had been assigned places of honour close to Turlough and Frances. Though the gentlemen and ladies were richly attired, Frances, in a gown of purple velvet with white lace collar, glowed among them like the evening star among its radiant companions.

The hall had been swept and dusted for the feast and the bare walls covered with tapestries: the marriage at Cana; the return of the Prodigal Son and, on the wall facing me, Solomon greeting the Queen of Sheba. Tomás had whispered earlier that he had seen these tapestries in Ballytrasna, so they must have been either loaned or presented to Turlough by Patrick French-Fitzstephens. I tried to converse with Tomás but the despair in my heart robbed me of wit and I could only ask foolish questions about the difficulties of transporting wine from Galway. Not that my companion seemed eager to talk; he swallowed his ale in great gulps, meanwhile casting soulful glances at his beloved.

The three dozen or so men and women who shared our table seemed oblivious to our dejection. Most were retainers from Turlough's estate at Cloonybrien but there were also a few wild-looking scullogues in grey frieze jerkins accompanied by their linen-kerchiefed wives and near the upper end, some of the behatted landowners who had attended the *Aonach*. Servant girls and boys carried in piled sciatháns of roast mutton and oaten cakes, huge bowls of troander, pitchers of ale and leather jugs of wine. Fergus, attired in new shirt and breeches, his mouth spread in a wide grin, noticed my half-empty meadar and filled it to the brim – was he pitying me as I had pitied him when he was sitting in the stocks? I gulped the claret, hoping it would numb my anguish.

After we had eaten I saw Niall signalling to the servants to withdraw and Daithi rose. As he did so, Owen, the blind harper who had played for us at the *Aonach*, plucked lightly at his harp. When the hubbub subsided, Daithi broke into a chant, keeping pace with the music. Quickly he ensnared the guests with a golden chain of words. In the manner of the bards he spoke of sharing Turlough's bed, though many other famous poets were in love with the bright-haired warrior of Lough Cé. Turlough had always rewarded him for his poems with lavish gifts: hounds, cattle, mettlesome horses and precious books. Now the noble, open-handed defender of the bards and clerics was about to wed the comely *leannán-sidhe* of Ballytrasna, whose side was as white as river foam, whose hair was as brown as the heather-hen's wing and whose lips were as red as quicken berries. This marriage would bring prosperity and plenty to Moylurg; there would be golden corn swaying in the sun, apples bending down the orchard trees, milk overflowing the pails and flocks grazing the verdant pastures.

"Will the *óinseach* never finish?" Tomás growled.

I glanced covertly at Frances and imagined I could see her blush with confusion – or was it only the glow of the candles on her cheeks? Then a new note in Daithi's ranns made me cock my ear; he was alluding to *Banba*, one of the poets' names for Ireland. Turlough must not let his love for *Banba* betray him into dangerous adventures. Other men had learned to live in peace with the Foreigners: Turlough must follow the example of his father, who was a man of far-sighted wisdom. He would remind him of Fionn Mac Cumhaill who, through excess of pride, had provoked the anger of Cairbre the High King. As a result of this, Cairbre had raised a great army against Fionn and had crushed him at the Battle of Gowra. Turlough must not take offence because he, Daithi, spoke in this blunt fashion; it was his love for the gentle champion of the bright countenance, Moylurg's true prince, the proud descendant of Maolruanaidh Mór, which moved him to such utterance.

"What in hell's blazes is O'Duigenan up to?" Tomás hissed in my ear. "Has his stay at Carrick Mansion turned him into a Teigue-of-Both-Sides?"

"Hush!" I was afraid the nearby guests would overhear him.

"Turlough," Daithi went on, must turn Carrick MacDermot with its ancient walls and battlements into a lime-white palace for the lovely princess who would soon be his wife and with their patronage of bards and clerics, the Rock of the Smooth-flowing Lough Cé would once again become the Oxford of learning of the western world.

As Daithi piled rann on rann, I wondered what Sir Robert and his agent were making of this endless, measured flow of Gaelic. Turlough must have had the same thought, for no sooner had Daithi finished than he thanked him hastily in English, promised him a roan colt, then asked Owen to play *geantraí*, or laughing music, for their honoured guests.

After tightening the brass strings of his harp, Owen plucked at them with his nails, letting loose a ripple of melody such as a summer breeze makes in aspen leaves. I listened like one in a dream to the lively air, contrasting my present misery with the happiness I had known at the feast in Ballintober. A couplet from a poem by Tadhg Dall O'Huiginn came to me:

> My prowess in the banqueting hall
> Has been punished by draughts of sorrow.

When Owen finished amid the acclaim of the gathering, Turlough sent Fergus to him with a goblet of wine. At once the revelry swelled up again, many guests leaving the table to walk about or visit the garderobe. Three or four men approached Daithi, praising his verses as if he were another Virgil. Now that Cormac was in prison my own hopes of writing poems in Gaelic had vanished; I was neither bard nor ollamh but an unfledged scholar who had abandoned his studies.

"Charles." The sound of my name in that soft accent put an end to my brooding. Turning, I saw Frances standing beside me, a look of solicitude on her face. "Have you recovered from your wounds?"

Aware that Turlough was watching, I was grateful for her kindness in talking to me, yet wary of her pity. Did she regard me as she would a pet spaniel that had been mauled by hounds?

"Yes," I heard myself answer. "And how do you fare yourself?"

For a moment I thought regret flickered in her eyes, then she assured me she was happy.

"Here, Charles." She handed me the mermaid necklace. "I have no right to keep it."

Dumb as an ox I accepted the unwanted gift, though my pride urged me to spurn it.

"What are you thinking?" Her expression was bashful.

"I was recalling a sonnet of Shakespeare's." I strove to conceal my hurt. "It's about a gift that was taken back."

"Oh." She smiled uneasily. "God shield you, Charles." And then she was gone.

Pressing the necklace into the palm of my hand, I watched her return to her place by Turlough. As she sat down, Turlough's gaze met mine; then he looked away.

He's a worthier suitor than you, I told myself, aware of his reluctance to gloat over my defeat or his own triumph.

"What did she give you?" Tomás tugged at my sleeve. Wordlessly I opened my fingers.

"A mermaid," he said. "An ill omen."

Too heavy-hearted to rebuke his superstition, I thrust the necklace into my doublet. Then I drained my meadar.

All eyes now turned to the high table where Sir Robert, resplendent in plumed hat and blue velvet doublet, was commencing an address. Speaking in clear, self-assured tones, he commended Owen for his music and recalled how Giraldus Cambrensis, the historian who had accompanied the Normans to Ireland, had placed Irish harpers far above those of Wales, England and France. As for Daithi's poem, he regretted that his lack of Gaelic left him in ignorance of its merits. He had, however, been assured by his dear departed brother, Edward, that the great Spenser regarded Irish bards as worthy of the highest praise, though, like himself, he could only judge their rhymes in translation. He had brought with him one of Spenser's sonnets addressed to his bride-to-be and he begged our indulgence while he read it.

"Go on, you honey-tongued hypocrite, read it," Tomás muttered in Gaelic, as Sir Robert unfolded a sheet of paper.

The sonnet dealt with Phoebus's pursuit of Daphne, in the course of which the gods had transformed her into a laurel tree. Though Sir Robert had not dedicated this recitation to Oona, his admiring glances left no doubt that it was intended for her:

> *Then fly no more, fair love, from Phoebus chase,*
> *But in your breast his leaf and love embrace.*

There was respectful applause when he finished – many of those present having only scant understanding of English. Then, before I could dissuade him, Tomás was on his feet. With drunken plaintiveness, he broke into a Gaelic dirge:

> *Sad is Moylurg tonight,*
> *The lights from cabin doors*
> *Too few and faint*
> *To warm the ghost*
> *Wandering its empty plain.*

It was clear that the unhappy ghost was Tomás, who was pining for his "flower of the amber tresses". Whether Tomás was making up the ranns as he went along I cannot say but from a certain lack of evenness in their composition I inferred he was. Nevertheless, their pathos touched me far more deeply than Spenser's urbane lines. How much more then must they have moved the one to whom they were addressed? As if conscious of this danger, Cathal Roe called on Owen to play "Greensleeves" and the harper complied, then followed it with a lively galliard. When Sir Robert expressed surprise at this show of familiarity with the music of his country, Turlough told him he should thank Mistress French-Fitzstephens, who had often played for them on the lute at Ballytrasna. Emily smiled prettily at this compliment but did not speak.

In such wise the feast continued, Cathal Roe and Lady Eleanor endeavouring to make Sir Robert and his agent feel at home, Tomás and I withdrawing further and further into morose silence as pipes were distributed and the Hall filled with tobacco smoke. When Owen played a rollicksome air he claimed to have learned from the fairies, the common gallants began to jump and prance with their mistresses in the narrow space between the trestle table and walls. Far from reproving them, Turlough smiled his pleasure. Turning to Frances he seemed to press her to join the frolic but Lady Eleanor whispered something and they remained seated.

Wilder and wilder the dancing grew so that I was in constant dread of being knocked prostrate. Then a ripping sound assailed my ear. Two or three revellers losing their balance had clutched at the tapestry of Solomon and Sheba and amid shrieks and curses it fell heavily like a dropped sail. After that Turlough commanded Owen to stop playing, the dancers returned to the table and Niall directed some long-haired bodachs to remove the tapestry. They carried it through the archway leading to the shrine. Was Father Bernard keeping vigil there while we caroused, I wondered.

> *Watch therefore: for ye know not what hour*
> *your Lord doth come.*

No, I concluded, Father Bernard was in all likelihood asleep in some distant corner of the castle.

"Neighbours and … and kinsmen," Turlough's voice broke in on my musings, "I want you all to … to raise your cups." When we had complied, he spoke again, his voice less hesitant, "Let us drink to the health of our honoured guests, in particular to my betrothed, Frances, and to her parents, Patrick French-Fitzstephens and … and his beloved wife, Emily."

Turlough raised his goblet and we all drank. "Now," he continued, I will ask you to drink to the health of our guests from Abbeyboyle, Sir Robert King and his … his *reachtaire*, Tom Hewett."

As I brought the meadar to my lips I wondered if anybody else had noted Turlough's omission of the word "honoured". Sir Robert, at all events, gave no sign of taking offence. Rising eagerly, he called for a drink to "the fairest maiden in all Moylurg, Oona daughter of MacDermot".

I glanced at Tomás. There was the look of a goaded bull in his eyes. "Drink up," I whispered, "or Oona will notice."

Reluctantly he touched the meadar to his lips but did not swallow. As my eyes turned back to Oona and then to Frances, the claret tasted like gall in my mouth. I was about to intimate to Tomás that we should both slip away when Cathal Roe's voice arrested me.

"I will now call on Oona," he was saying, "to drink to the health of the man she likes best in this company."

Foreboding entered my soul. Like a person in a dream I saw through wreaths of tobacco smoke Oona rise slowly, her amber hair framing her wan face. For a moment her eyes were downcast then she gazed defiantly at her brother.

"I drink to the health of Tomás MacCostello," she said in a clear, firm voice.

No sooner had the words left her mouth than Cathal Roe struck her across the cheek with the back of his hand, sending her goblet clattering to the floor. Tomás jumped up but before he could intervene I pulled him back down. "Don't!" I hissed. "You'll only shame her more."

"I'll kill him," he groaned, driving his skean's point into the table. "I'll kill him!"

"In God's name, put that away," I pleaded. "It's all over. Look!"

Cathal Roe was sitting, his bent head clasped between his hands, while Turlough and Frances were whispering together as if undecided what to do. Brushing aside Emily's attempts to comfort her, Oona picked up a small ornamented box and with deliberate fingers took a pinch of snuff. It was obvious that she was trying to hide her tears and my heart went out to her. Turlough was now calling on Owen to play another dance melody but it was Lady Eleanor who resolved the crisis by escorting Oona from the hall.

"Come," I said to Tomás. "We'll go too."

In the general hubbub nobody noticed our departure. As we reached the stair opening, I cast one last glance towards Frances, hoping to catch her eye, but she and Turlough were talking earnestly with Sir Robert. Blindly I followed Tomás down the winding stairs, along passages lit by bog deal torches, past a room full of laughing kernes and out into the coolness of the bawn. A new moon with one yellow rim gazed down fitfully through scudding clouds.

"Charles," Tomás grabbed my arm to keep his balance, "do you see how much they hate me?"

"They don't hate you." I fought to overcome the wine-born nausea threatening my stomach. "Cathal Roe is bitterly disappointed ... his hopes of forming an alliance with the New Foreigners have collapsed like a house built on sand. And as for Oona, she acknowledged you before the whole gathering. What more can you want?"

For answer, Tomás cupped his hands to his mouth and bawled up at the narrow, lighted windows, "Oona! Oona!" Attracted by the commotion, half a dozen long-haired kernes emerged from the castle entrance, brandishing quarterstaffs.

"Be off, you wild Mayo *spalpaire*!" they commanded. "Be off or we'll skull you!"

"Oona! Oona!" Tomás bawled even louder.

"Silence, cur!" A kerne jabbed at him with his quarterstaff.

Backing away, Tomás drew his skean.

"Wait!" I ran between him and the advancing kernes, my right hand raised in a sign of peace. "MacDermot will not thank you if you attack a guest."

My words caused them to hesitate. Quickly I turned to Tomás. "If you wound one of them there will be blood between you and the MacDermots," I cried.

At first he seemed too wroth to heed my warning; then he relented and I led him to the side gate, which was locked. Presently a kerne arrived with the unarmed porter swaying drunkenly beside him.

"The devil take yer souls," the porter growled, fumbling with his keys. "Couldn't ye have stayed above till daylight?"

When the gate clanged shut behind us, we edged our way down to the moored currachs. After clambering into one, Tomás seized the oars and, despite my protests, we were soon heading out into the centre of the lough, the light craft twisting and bucking like a skittish horse. Behind us the castle loomed, massive and dark, except for the lights in the upper windows. Was the girl I loved still sitting beside the Lord of Moylurg, unaware of my absence? A faint sound of harp music came to my ears, sad as the calling of a plover in the vast emptiness of the night. If only we might run on a hidden rock …

The morning Turlough had kept me from going out fishing with the old woman and her savage companion rose from memory. How little did I foresee then that the so-called Lord of Moylurg, riding up like Fionn MacCumhaill on his bay horse, would one day rob me of my heart's treasure? What would have happened if he hadn't arrived and I had entered the currach? Would the old woman have changed shape like the hag Cé who had given her name to the lough? According to Daithi, Cé had turned into a beautiful maiden after being treated kindly by the poet Oisín and had taken him with her to Tír na nÓg.

As these thoughts crossed my mind, the old woman seemed to gaze at me from beyond Tomás's shoulder. Presently her face lost its cunning expression and she was Frances enticing me to swim with her as I had that long-ago afternoon in Lough Fionn. I had only to cast myself overboard and we would sink down together through the hungry waves, down among the silent fish and wavering eels, down to where the starlight died and all pain ceased ...

To appease the powers of darkness I took the necklace from my doublet and tossed it into the lough. There was a tiny splash, then nothing but the creaking of the oars mingled with Tomás's laboured breathing and the slap of waves against the prow. A feeling of desolation engulfed me; I had thrown away a talisman that linked me to Frances. Now there was nothing to show we had once been lovers.

Presently I realized that the currach was drifting. "Why have you stopped rowing?" I asked Tomás.

"I'm waiting till the crow flies home," he said.

"Then we may be here all night," I grumbled, as raindrops began to hiss into the inky waters around us.

"I'm telling you I'm not leaving till that foreign devil does." He shipped the oars.

For what seemed an eternity we sat there in the rocking currach while the sky grew darker and rain soaked our clothing. The image of Simon Peter and his companions on Lake Gennesaret came to me: "We have toiled all the night, and have taken nothing."

Would we too catch nothing except an ague from the cold?

"Aahh!" Tomás's voice roused me. Looking towards the castle I could just discern two currachs with lanterns in their prows heading for the village.

"We'll go now!" Tomás dipped the oars into the water. Pulling with powerful strokes, he quickly drew so near the other currachs that we could distinctly hear Sir Robert's voice warning the boatmen of our approach. To make matters worse, the rain ceased and the re-emerging moon glared down on the loch. Yielding to my entreaties, Tomás turned away, bringing us, by some miracle, safely ashore in the little cove west of the village.

As soon as we had lifted the currach up onto dry land, Tomás pleaded with me to accompany him to Ardcarn, where there was a friend he wished me to meet.

"Who is this friend?" I tried to mask the deadness in my heart.

"Somebody who believes there will soon be a bright day in Ireland." He peered into my face then lowered his voice to a confidential whisper: "Rory O'More himself! Come on, Charles. You and I are men on whom fortune has frowned. Isn't it better to die with swords in our hands than to live without hope and have bodachs and lackeys railing at us?"

"But you have hope," I protested. "You heard what Oona said."

"Yes." Tomás put his arm around my shoulders. "She likes me better than a man almost twice her age. What else could she have said?"

"Frances is marrying a man almost three times her age." I endeavoured to ignore the stench of ale from his breath.

"True," he conceded. "But Turlough is a Catholic – not that I'm saying a Protestant cannot be a man of honour ... but Oona would never ... never ... sell her heritage for a mess of pottage."

"And neither will I." The words came unbidden to my lips. "If I have lost my hope of winning Frances, so be it."

"You won't come with me then?" He took his arm from my shoulder.

"No," I replied in the voice of one speaking from the grave. "I believe that in His own time God will reveal what he wants me to do. Till then I'll watch and wait."

"And what if I were to slit your gullet?" He drew his skean. "After all, you could betray O'More and me to your scripture-prating friends."

This was a different Tomás Láidir, a glowering savage I scarcely recognized – and yet I knew he had killed the wrestler in Sligo and I had seen him crack Donal Bawn's ribs and stab the garron with the very skean he was brandishing now. It wouldn't cost such a man any qualms to murder me – but then my soul inside was already dead.

"Go on!" I did not flinch, though he held the skean to my throat, his eyes blazing like a demon's. "You'll only take what I'm glad to lose."

"Damn you, Palesman!" he shouted. "Damn your black Protestant soul!" and thrusting the skean back into his belt, he turned away without another word.

I stood for a long time watching him stagger off into the shadows; then when the faint thud of hoofbeats told me he was safely mounted, I trudged uphill towards Carrick Mansion.

For a long time I lay on my pallet in the friendless darkness of the cabin, turning over in my mind the events of the night. Once again I had drained the cup of bitterness – and yet my concern for Oona and Tomás had made me forget, if only for fleeting moments, my own unhappiness. The image of the fishermen on Lake Gennesaret returned: "Follow me and I will make you fishers of men."

All at once it seemed that my eyes were opened and I could see that for the past year I had dwelt so much on my own troubles I had hardened my heart to the troubles of others. My father and mother must be grieving over my absence. And poor Cormac and Uncle Teigue ... why had I abandoned them? Begging God's forgiveness for my many transgressions, I finally sank into a dreamless sleep.

When I eventually met Dr Bedell in Sir Robert's library, I knew at first glance that this was the person that Brighid had told me about, the one who would show me the road I must follow. He was one of those rare men who carry with them an aura of inner strength and peace. Maybe it was his calm, penetrating eye, his long, slightly aquiline nose and the bushy white beard descending over his black cassock that created this impression but, whatever the reason, I felt instinctively that this venerable Bishop could see into the inner recesses of my soul. I attempted to speak but immediately broke down, sobbing like a child.

After allowing me to regain my composure, Dr Bedell asked me in fluent Gaelic what was troubling me and I told him about Frances, how I had loved her and how she had rejected me. He heard me out in silence, then reminded me of the words that Virgil had put into the mouth of Anchises, that the body is the cause of fear and desire and that it is only through suffering that engrafted faults are removed from the soul. When the soul is at last purified we are ready for rebirth. Now if a pagan poet had such an insight, how much more should we as Christians perceive its truth? I must, therefore, look on all that had happened to me as part of God's plan for my rebirth.

"For," he continued, "'whom the Lord loveth he chasteneth'. You are being punished, Charles, by the loss of this girl but that is God's way of tempering you for the work he has in mind for you. And I believe that work to be no other than the conversion of the native Irish – no, hear me out."

I was about to object that he must be ignorant of my shameful life in Dublin but his expression convinced me that he knew everything.

"Why do you think that you came to Connacht?" He looked at me earnestly. "Do you not think that it might have been part of God's purpose, like Saul's journey to Damascus? You have gained a familiarity with the language and customs of the Gaels that few of our ministers possess. Why, they believe they can convert the Irish by preaching to them in English – even the University in Dublin has discontinued the Gaelic lectures and Gaelic prayers in chapel that I instituted. What folly! What absolute folly!"

I could see his knuckles whiten as he strove to control his anger.

"They laugh at me for spending my time translating the Bible," he confessed, "and then they wonder why the people cling to their Popish ways. Some of the 'Root and Branch' school even argue that the Irish are not among God's chosen people, that they are excluded from the salvation Christ promised to all – what a grave and terrible error. They forget the words of Isaiah, 'It shall come that I will gather all nations and tongues; and they shall come and see my glory'. Is there any mention there of the English tongue? No, it says 'all tongues' – and that includes Hebrew, Arabic, Gaelic, as well as English. But in their self-righteousness and blindness, our ministers blame the people of this country for their own failure to spread the Word of God. The Gaels are not excluded from salvation – your grand-uncle, Richard Stanihurst, wrote that they are susceptible to good influence, that despite their many faults they are anxious to live righteously – no doubt you can confirm that from your own experiences. There is the same lesson to be learned from the story of St Patrick: he was brought here from Britain as a slave yet he returned to his former captors with the good news of Christ's redemption and they listened and were converted."

He filled a Venetian goblet with water and took a sip and, though there was a jug of wine on the table, I chose to follow his example.

"Charles," his eyes gazed at me unseeing as if he were in a trance, "people like you and me will never be part of the great complacent multitude, rather we will be the leaven that will raise the citizens of this island, whether they be Gael or Norman, Old English, New English, or Anglo-Hiberni – to use your grand-uncle's phrase. I see our descendants as orators, philosophers, artists, poets and, yes, voices crying in the wilderness – men who will take the straight and narrow path rather than the broad and easy one. They will be the men and women who will build a commonwealth of all the people of Ireland and they will take what is best from every tribe in this land and forge one race, one people, who will inhabit a new Jerusalem that will be a light to the nations."

He fell silent, his face still glowing with the splendour of his vision. When he spoke again it was in a quieter voice: "Think of what I have said to you, Charles. Go back to Dublin. Complete your studies then take holy orders: 'The harvest truly is great, but the labourers are few.' Pray for me that my strength will not fail before my work is finished. Now go in God's name, my son."

As I rode back towards the river on Donn, I felt light-hearted with joy. In one of the saddle-bags Sir Robert had given me I carried a dozen apricots, which Sir Robert had charged me to deliver undamaged to the MacDermots as if he imagined them to be the golden apples of the Hesperides, and in the other Dr Bedell's Gaelic translation of the Psalms: "The Lord is on my side; I will not fear: what can man do unto me?"

Sir Charles Coote would soon be escorting me to Dublin where I would have to stand trial but Sir Robert had assured me that both he and Dr Bedell would make sworn depositions on my behalf and that these would weigh greatly with the judge – even if they didn't, the thought of being sentenced to Newgate did not dismay me for I was ready to endure whatever suffering God might send to test my faith.

At the brow of the hill Oona came trotting up on her garron, her amber hair falling over her shoulders.

"You look different," she observed. "What happened?"

I told her about my decision to become a cleric and she confided that she had always thought that, like her, I was more drawn to the life of the spirit than to the life of the flesh. She was sorry that

I would be a parson rather than a priest but then I had been raised a Protestant and it was to be expected.

"The apple never falls far from the tree," she smiled.

Five or six warders lounging outside the abbey stared after us as we passed but, ignoring them, we plunged into the shallow waters of the Boyle and emerged safely on the other side.

Epilogue

THERE IS an incident in Virgil's epic where Aeneas on reaching Carthage sees depicted in a temple the heroes and battles of the Trojan War and he exclaims: "*Sunt lacrimae rerum et mentem mortalia tangunt*" (There are tears in things and man's mortality touches the mind). Now, one third of a century after my return from Connacht, I know what Aeneas felt. Many of the people I met on my sojourn there are either dead or destitute, their world shattered by the Confederate Wars and the avenging sword of Oliver Cromwell.

Dr Bedell, who was imprisoned for a period by Irish Confederates, died just six months after our meeting. Hugh O'Conor was captured in Forty-Two when he and Con O'Rourke besieged Castlecoote. His father, O'Conor Don, having been proclaimed King of Connacht at Carnfree, was defeated near Ballintober in June of the same year by an army under the command of Lord Ranelagh, Sir Robert King and Sir Charles Coote the Younger – who distinguished himself as a ruthless military commander for the Parliamentarians but later changed course and welcomed home our most Gracious Sovereign, His Majesty Charles II. Sir Charles Coote Senior, after a demonic whirlwind of battles against the enemies of Parliament, was shot dead in May of Forty-Two, some allege by one of his own men.

And what of the MacDermots? Turlough raised a regiment and fought for the Confederates to the bitter end. As a consequence, he lost most of his remaining lands in Moylurg and had to accept an English garrison for his castle on the Rock. I do not know what happened to Oona but Sir John Borlase in his history of the Rebellion avers that after the Battle of Ballintober, a soldier pulled a mountero from the head of one of the slain and immediately "there fell down long tresses of flaxen hair, who, being further searched, was found a woman". If this was indeed Oona Bawn, then I grieve for Tomás, who must have surmised that her devotion to Hugh O'Conor led her to this untimely end.

Both Tomás and his brother Dudley distinguished themselves in the Confederate Wars and, afterwards, Dudley went to Flanders where he served as captain in the Duke of York's regiment. On returning home he failed to regain, as he had been promised, his family's lands in the Barony of Costello. Embittered, he became the leader of a notorious band of mounted Pursuers that harried Lord Dillon's tenants. Finally, he was shot and his head was brought to Dublin, where – God have mercy on us all – I saw it myself only seven years ago mounted on a spike above St James's Gate, the empty eyes gazing westward towards Connacht.

And now, to return to my own story: I left Moylurg in September Forty-One in the custody of Sir Charles Coote Senior and after three days riding by way of Roscommon and Athlone, reached Dublin without incident. Immediately I was lodged in Newgate gaol, from which Sir Robert King obtained my release a week later. When I had made my way to Oxmantown, my father welcomed me home like the Prodigal Son and even Thomas, when I had confessed the reason for my flight, forgave me for having taken Nell; my mother and Bridget wept on seeing my marred features, yet they were overjoyed too, for they had despaired of ever setting eyes on me again. They told me that Margaret had married my old school friend John Crofton and was now living in Chapelizod.

My trial was set for the last week in November but in the meantime, as the "prophecy" had foreshadowed, the Ulster Irish rose in rebellion. Thousands of planters were massacred and Dublin made frenzied preparations to withstand attack. Sir Charles Coote Senior was appointed governor and he informed me that in return for enlisting in his regiment, I would be pardoned for my assault on Edmund Devereux. Appalled by his diatribes against Catholics, I refused and was again thrown in prison. At my trial, however, the depositions of Sir Robert King and Dr Bedell swayed the jury in my favour and I was found not guilty.

Thanking God for my deliverance, I resumed my studies. Trinity was almost deserted in those days, Provost Washington and many of the Fellows having fled to England, yet, despite alarms and upheavals, I eventually acquired a Bachelor's degree. Subsequently, in the year Fifty, when the Plague that had broken out in Dublin had carried off my parents, I was ordained a minister.

I will not burden the reader with the details of my life since then. Enough to say I have laboured to the best of my abilities, first in St Audeon's parish, then in St Michan's and now St John's, often in ill health and near despair – the harshness of the Cromwellian settlement and the short-sightedness of our clergy have not been conducive to the spread of true religion among our fellow countrymen. Even Dr Bedell's Gaelic Bible has not been published. Nevertheless, I will continue my efforts, if only because, like St Paul, I am still a prisoner of Jesus Christ.

Like St Paul too, I have never married. My sister Bridget keeps my house, reading the Bible to me, as my sight is almost gone, and acting as my personal secretary. Her kindness to the poor has won their hearts in a way that my preaching of the Gospel never has – and yet, my knowledge of Gaelic has allowed me to enter numerous homes that remain closed to my fellow clergymen.

Over the years I have come to see that, in choosing Turlough, Frances has remained forever the girl with the red lips and bashful smile that beguiled me at the feast in Ballintober. Yet, more and more in dreams she returns in all her morning freshness and it seems that she is on the point of accepting me until something draws her away and then I wake up in such a state of desolation that I can barely bring myself to go on living.

In one recent dream we were alone on MacDermot's Rock. The castle had fallen into ruin and though the sun shone through the trees, briars flourished everywhere. I was at the same time both supremely happy and supremely sad. On waking I composed these ranns in Gaelic:

> *Amid the island garden,*
> *Beneath the tranquil walls*
> *Of castle fallen,*
> *Where olden lives still saddened*
> *The acquiescent air,*
> *Came Frances swinging lightly,*
> *The leaf-veiled sun upon her:*

Bright flowers hung shyly wistful,
Survivors of the briars
Made conscious in their wildness
Of parent blooms well tended
For a princess passed away.

I know that were he alive to read such verses Cormac would censure my disregard for the rules of Bardic poetry but surely Tadhg Dall would understand my yearning for a vision that has vanished, perhaps never to return?

COMPLETED IN THE RECTORY, ST JOHN'S PARISH, DUBLIN, THIS 2ND DAY OF JULY 1674.

KEY DATES

1576   Connacht divided into shires by Lord Deputy, Sir Henry Sidney

1584   Sir Richard Bingham appointed Governor of Connacht

1585   The Composition of Connacht: Gaelic titles and system of land ownership abolished; Sir John Perrot Viceroy

1588   The Spanish Armada; Brian O'Rourke of Brefni shelters survivors

1591   Brian O'Rourke hanged in London

1592   Trinity College, Dublin founded by Elizabeth 1

1594-1603 Rebellion of O'Neill and O'Donnell ("The Nine Years War")

1595   Red Hugh O'Donnell reinstates Conor MacDermot as chieftain of Moylurg

1596   Bingham replaced as Governor of Connacht by Sir Conyers Clifford

1599   Hugh O'Conor knighted by the Earl of Essex in July; First Battle of the Curlieu Mountains in August: government forces under Clifford defeated by Red Hugh O'Donnell, Conor MacDermot and Brian Oge O'Rourke

1601   O'Neill and O'Donnell defeated at Kinsale (3 Jan 1602 new style)

1602   Second Battle of the Curlieu Mountains: government forces defeated by Rory O'Donnell and Conor MacDermot

1603   Elizabeth 1 dies; O'Neill surrenders to Lord Deputy Mountjoy; James VI of Scotland becomes king of England as James 1

1604   Sir Arthur Chichester appointed Lord Deputy

1605   The Gunpowder Plot; Sir Charles Coote appointed Provost-Marshal of Connacht

1607   Hugh O'Neill and Rory O'Donnell leave Ireland ("The Flight of the Earls")

1608-10 The Plantation of Ulster

1612   Bishop Conor O'Devany hanged in Dublin

1613-15 Chichester's Parliament – Calvagh, son of Sir Hugh O'Conor Don, loses to Sir John King in bid to represent County Roscommon

1616   Shakespeare dies; Hugh O'Neill dies in Rome

1617   Sir John King is granted the lands of Boyle Abbey; Brian Oge MacDermot is granted some of his ancestral lands, including Carrick MacDermot, and Sir Hugh O'Connor Don receives a new grant of Ballintober. Tadhg Dall O'Huiginn dies

1617-20 "The Contention of the Bards"

1620   The Pilgrim Fathers sail to America on the *Mayflower*

1625   Charles 1 becomes King of England

1626	Dr Boethius Egan, a Franciscan, appointed Bishop of Elphin
1627	Charles I offers Irish Catholics concessions ("The Graces") in return for subsidies; William Bedell appointed Provost of Trinity College, Dublin
1628	Oliver Cromwell represents Huntingdon in the English House of Commons
1629	Florence O'Mulconry, founder of Irish Franciscan College in Louvain and Archbishop of Tuam, dies in Madrid; William Bedell appointed Bishop of Kilmore
1632	Wentworth (Lord Strafford) appointed Viceroy
1633	Wentworth arrives in Ireland
1634	Charles I repudiates "The Graces"
1635	Wentworth visits Connacht to lay foundation for a plantation scheme – commission sits at Boyle in July
1636	Annals of the Four Masters (*Annála Ríoghachta Éireann*: Annals of the Kingdom of Ireland) completed; Brian Oge MacDermot, Lord of Moylurg, dies in Athlone
1637	Sir Robert King's brother, Edward, drowns in a shipwreck in the Irish Sea; Milton writes his elegy, "*Lycidas*"
1638	Scots revolt against Charles I
1639-41	Last Irish parliament in which Catholics sit (save 1689); Sir Robert King represents Boyle
1640	Don Eugenio (Owen Roe) O'Neill wins praise for his defence of Arras; Archbishop Laud imprisoned in Tower of London; Strafford arrested in November
1641	Strafford executed in May; Irish Rebellion begins in October; planters massacred in North; Rory O'More defeats government forces at Drogheda; Roscommon gentry meet in Ballintober at Christmas and take oath to support the king and maintain the Catholic faith; Con O'Rourke and Hugh O'Conor besiege Castlecoote – O'Conor captured (1642 new style)
1642	Civil War begins in England; Battle of Ballintober: Irish under Calvagh O'Conor Don defeated by Parliamentarians under Lord Ranelagh, Sir Robert King and Sir Charles Coote Jnr. Sir Frederick Hamilton captures Sligo – its inhabitants massacred. Owen Roe O'Neill arrives in Ireland; Bishop William Bedell dies
1645	Archbishop Laud is executed for treason; and Muiris O'Mulconry ("The light of poetry"), who assisted the Four Masters for a month with their Annals, dies

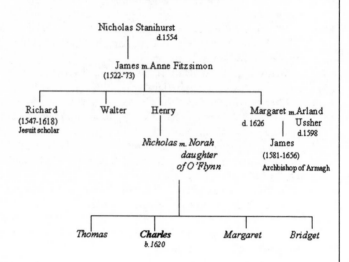

The Stanihursts of Dublin

Nicholas Stanihurst
d.1554

James m. Anne Fitzsimon
(1522-'73)

Richard
(1547-1618)
Jesuit scholar

Walter

Henry

Margaret m. Arland
d. 1626

Ussher
d.1598

Nicholas m. *Norah*
daughter
of O'Flynn

James
(1581-1656)
Archbishop of Armagh

Thomas

Charles
b.1620

Margaret

Bridget

Note:
Names of fictional characters are in italics.

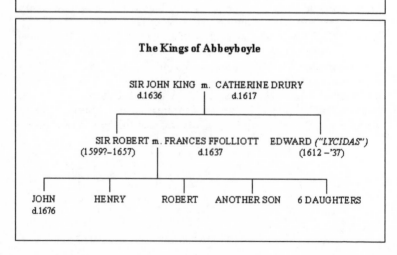

The Kings of Abbeyboyle

SIR JOHN KING m. CATHERINE DRURY
d.1636   d.1617

SIR ROBERT m. FRANCES FFOLLIOTT
(1599?-1657)   d.1637

EDWARD *("LYCIDAS")*
(1612 -'37)

JOHN
d.1676

HENRY

ROBERT

ANOTHER SON

6 DAUGHTERS

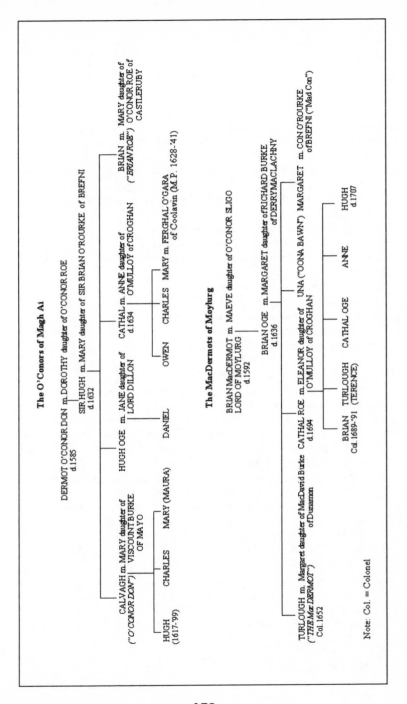

The O'Conors of Magh Ai

The MacDermots of Moylurg

Note: Col. = Colonel

GLOSSARY

Aurea mediocritas: The golden mean

Ave Maria, Pater Noster, Salve Regina: Hail Mary, Our Father, Hail Holy Queen

Baptizmo te in nomine Patris et Filiis et Spiritus Sanctus: I baptize you in the name of the Father and of the Son and of the Holy Spirit

Carpe diem: Seize the day, i.e. enjoy the passing moment. *Horace, Odes, 1, xi, 8*

Dominus vobiscum: The Lord be with you

Hoc est enim corpus meum: This is truly my body

In medias res: Into the midst of things, i.e. in the middle of the action

Ipso facto: By that very fact

Mirabile dictu: Wonderful to relate

Omnia bona bonis: To the good all things seem good

Pax vobiscum: Peace be with you

Pro tempore: For the time being

"Procul o procul este, profani" conclamat vates, "totoque absistite luco.": "Away, far away, you unhallowed ones," cries the prophetess, "and be gone from all the grove." Virgil, *Aeneid*, vi, 258-9

Quem di diligent adolescens moritur: He whom the gods love dies young

Requiescat in pace: May he rest in peace

Sine qua non: Without which not, i.e. an indispensable condition

Superanda omnis fortuna ferendo est: It is given to us to overcome every kind of fortune, i.e. whatever fortune may be ours, we can rise above it [by enduring it]. Virgil, *Aeneid*, v, 710

Talibus orabat dictis arasque tenebat: Thus he prayed, and held (laid his hands on) the altar. Virgil, *Aeneid*, vi, 124

Tempus edax rerum: Time that devours all things, i.e. Time destroys everything

Ultima Thule: Farthest Thule; any far-off, unknown region

No entiendo. ¿Hablan ustedes castellano?: I don't understand. Do you speak Castillian?

A ghrá: Love; darling

Aonach: A fair

Ard-rí: High king

Beannacht Phádraig agus Bhríde ort: The blessing of Patrick and Brigid on you

Blas: Accent

Bodach: A churl; lout

Bodhrawn (*bodhrán*): A dimwit; dullard
Bonnyclabber (*bainne clabair*): Thickly curdled milk
Bulcaan (*bolcán*): Fiery spirits; a raw whiskey-like poteen
Callow (*caladh*): A river meadow; wet grassland
Camán: A hurley stick
Chun a fháil amach: In order to find out
Coarb: The abbot of the founder's monastery or principal abbot of a
    monastic federation
Creaght (*caoruigheacht*): A herd of cattle with its keepers
Crios: A girdle; belt
Crobhdhearg: Redhand
Croimbéal: A moustache
Cúl: A goal
Dia duit a Shéamuis: God be with you, Seamus
Duan: A poem
Duileasc: Dulse, an edible seaweed
Eric (*éiric*): A fine or compensation
Fág an bealach! : Get out of the way! A war cry
Fáilte roimh: Welcome
Fainic! : Beware!
Fear leighis: A doctor
Fubún! : Shame!
Geocach: A strolling musician or singer
Gallowglass (*gallóglach*): A foreign warrior; a Scottish mercenary or his
    descendant
Garron (*gearrán*): A small horse, sometimes called a "hobby"; a gelding;
    a nag
Girseach: A girl
Glib: A fringe of hair over forehead; loose tress of hair
Goirm thú! : Bravo! A term of approval
Go mbeannaí Dia dhuit: May God bless you, a greeting
Go raibh mait agaibh: Thank you
I do chló féin: In your own shape or form (*An bhfuil tú i do chló féin
    arís?*: Have you recovered completely?)
Kesh (*ceis*): A crossing made of sticks and branches; a wattled causeway
Kish (*cis*): A wicker container; basket
Leannán-sidhe: A fairy lover or sweetheart
Lóipínigh: Ragamuffins; dirty, poorly dressed people
Miodoge (*miodóg*): A dagger
Moy Mell (*Magh Meall*): The Pleasant or Happy Plain, one of the Celtic
    heavens
Ní thuigim: I don't understand
Óinseach: A fool
Ollamh: A man learned in poetry, law, history etc.
Pishogues (*piseoga*): Superstitious practices or beliefs; witchcraft; sorcery

Pookawn (*púcán*): A small open boat with a mainsail and jib
Praiseach: Porridge; a mess
Quicken tree: The rowan tree
Raiméis: Nonsensical talk; nonsense
Rann: A verse; stanza
Reachtaire: A man in charge of a noble household; chief steward
Rince fada: Long dance, a type of traditional dance
Róisín Dubh: Little Black Rose, a poetic name for Ireland
Sasanach: An Englishman
Sciathán: A wickerwork tray
Scullogue (*scológ*): A farmer; yeoman
Sheugh (*seoch*): A dyke or drain, especially an overgrown one
Shleeveen (*slíbhín*): A sly, cunning person
Sidhe (*sídh*): A fairy; one of the Tuatha De Danann; the mound where
    they lived
Síol Muireadaigh: Descendants of Muiredach Muillethan, especially the
    O'Conors
Skean (*scian*): A knife
Sliotar: The small hard ball used in hurling
Smacht: Control; discipline
Soc: The nose of a ploughshare
Spalpaire: A big strong fellow; a loudmouth
Spéirbhean: A sky woman, i.e. a beautiful woman; a goddess
Stracaire: Ripper; tearer
Súgán: Straw rope
Tír na nÓg: The Land of the Young, one of the Celtic heavens
Tráthnóna breá, buíochas le Dia: A fine afternoon, thank God
Turlough (*turlach*): A lake that comes and goes, depending on rainfall
Uí Briúin: Descendants of Brian, son of Eochaid Muigmedon
Ullagone (*olagón*): Wail; lament
Usquebagh (*uisce beatha*): Literally, "water of life"; whiskey

BIBLIOGRAPHY

Books in Irish

An Seabhac. *Tóraidheacht Dhiarmada agus Ghráinne*. Baile Átha Cliath:
Cómhlucht Oideachais na hÉireann, Teór., 1939.
Beaslaí, Piaras. *Éigse Nua-Ghaedhilge*. Baile Átha Cliath agus Corcaigh:
Cómhlucht Oideachais na hÉireann, Teór., n.d.
Ní Chinnéide, Mairead agus Clíodna Cussen. *Bainne Na Bó: Bainne agus
Bánbhianna in Éirinn ó thús Aimsire*. Baile Átha Cliath: An Gúm,
1986.
Ó Cadhlaigh, Cormac. *An Fhiannuidheacht*. Baile Átha Cliath: Oifig an
tSoláthair, 1947.
Ó Ciardha, Séamus agus Domhnall Ó Conalláin (eagarthóirí). *Aenéis
Bhirgil, Leabhar VI*. Baile Átha Cliath agus Corcaigh: Comhlucht
Oideachais na hÉireann, Teór., n.d.
Ó Conchúir, M.F. *Úna Bhán*. Conamara, Co. na Gaillimhe: Cló Iar-Chon-
nachta, 1994.
Ó Donnchadha, Tadhg (Torna). *Filidheacht Fiannaigheachta*. Baile Átha
Cliath agus Corcaigh: Cómhlucht Oideachais na hÉireann, Teór.,
1933.

Books in Irish and English

Bergin, Osborn. *Irish Bardic Poetry*. Dublin: Dublin Institute For Ad-
vanced Studies, 1970. [It contains poems from the "Book of O'Conor
Don", written in Ostend, 1631.]
Carney, James. *Medieval Irish Lyrics* with *The Irish Bardic Poet*. Port-
laoise: The Dolmen Press, 1984.
Knott, Eleanor. *Irish Syllabic Poetry: 1200-1600*. Dublin: Dublin Institute
for Advanced Studies, 1974.
Irish Classical Poetry: Filíocht na Sgol. Cork: Mercier Press, 1960.
Mac Enery, Marcus. "*Úna Bhán*". In *Éigse: A Journal of Irish Studies*.
Vol. 4: part 2, 1944.
Ó Muireadhaigh, Réamann. "*Marbhna Ar Mhuiris Mac Torna Uí Mhaol-
chonaire*". In *Éigse: A Journal of Irish Studies*, Vol. 15: part 3, 1974.
Ó Tuama, Seán and Thomas Kinsella. *An Duanaire 1600-1900: Poems of
the Dispossessed*. Portlaoise: The Dolmen Press i gchomar le Bord na
Gaeilge, 1981.

Pearse, Pádraic H. *Dánta Gríosuighthe Gaedheal* ("Songs of the Irish Rebels"). In Desmond Ryan (ed.), *The Collected Works of Pádraic H. Pearse*. Dublin, Cork, Belfast: The Phoenix Publishing Co., 1932.

Biographies and Family Histories

Bourke, Eamonn. *Burke: People and Places*. Co. Clare: Ballinkella Press, and Castlebar: De Burca Rare Books, 1984.

Boylan, Henry. *A Dictionary of Irish Biography*. Dublin: Gill and Macmillan, 1978.

Clarke, Aidan. 'Bishop William Bedell (1571–1642) and the Irish Reformation'. In Ciaran Brady (ed.), *Worsted in the Game: Losers in Irish History*. Dublin: The Lilliput Press, 1989.

Dictionary of National Biography. Oxford University Press, 1973.

Forristal, Desmond. *Seventeen Martyrs*. Blackrock, Co. Dublin: The Columba Press, 1990. [Chapter 6 gives an account of Bishop Conor O'Devany's life and death.]

Holden, Anthony. *William Shakespeare: His Life and Works*. London: Little, Brown and Co., 1999.

Lennon, Colm. *Richard Stanihurst: the Dubliner 1547-1618*. Blackrock, Co. Dublin: Irish Academic Press, 1981.

Levi, Peter. *Eden Renewed: the Public and Private Life of John Milton*. London: Macmillan, 1996.

McCallen, Jim. 'The Costello Era'. In *Stand and Deliver: Stories of Irish Highwaymen*. Dublin: Mercier Press, 1993.

Mac Dermot, Betty. *O'Ruairc of Breifne*. Manorhamilton: Drumlin Publications, 1990.

Mac Dermot, Dermot. *Mac Dermot of Moylurg: The Story of a Connacht Family*. Manorhamilton: Drumlin Publications, 1996.

Mac Lysaght, Edward. *Irish Families: their Names, Arms and Origins*. Dublin: Allen Figgis, 1972.

O'Conor, Rev. Charles. *Memoirs of the life and writings of the late Charles O'Conor, of Belanagare, Esq. M.R.I.A.* Dublin: printed by J. Mehain, 1796.

O'Conor Don, Rt Hon. Charles Owen. *The O'Conors of Connaught*. Dublin: Hodges, Figgis and Co., 1891.

O'Conor, Roderick. *A Historical and Genealogical Memoir of the O'Conors, Kings of Connaught*. Dublin, 1861.

O'Faolain, Sean. *The Great O'Neill: a Biography of Hugh O'Neill, Earl of Tyrone, 1550 –1616*. Cork: Mercier Press, 1970.

Shuckburgh, E.S. (ed.). *Two Biographies of William Bedell, Bishop of Kilmore*. Cambridge University Press, 1902.

Wedgewood, C.V. *Oliver Cromwell*. London: Duckworth, 1962.

Bardon, Jonathan and Stephen Conlin. *Dublin: One Thousand Years of Wood Quay*. Belfast: The Blackstaff Press, 1984.

Boydell, Brian (ed.). *Four Centuries of Music in Ireland*. London: BBC, 1979.

Brady, Ciaran and Raymond Gillespie (eds). *Natives and Newcomers: the Making of Irish Colonial Society 1534-1641*. Blackrock: Irish Academic Press, 1986.

Colum, Padraic. *A Treasury of Irish Folklore*. New York: Crown Publishers Inc., 1954.

Corish, Patrick J. *The Catholic Community in the Seventeenth and Eighteenth Centuries*. Dublin: Helicon History of Ireland, 1981.

Curtis, Edmund. *A History of Ireland*. New York: Barnes and Noble, 1961.

Danaher, Kevin. *Irish Country People*. Cork: Mercier Press, 1966.
In Ireland Long Ago. Cork: Mercier Press, 1967.

Emania: Bulletin of the Navan Research Group, Number Five. Belfast: Dept. of Archaeology, Queen's University: Autumn, 1988. [This issue focuses on Rathcroghan.]

Frazer, Sir James George. *The Golden Bough*. New York: The Macmillan Co., 1947.

Gantz, Jeffrey (trans.). *Early Irish Myths and Sagas*. London: Penguin Classics, 1981.

Gillespie, Raymond. *Conspiracy: Ulster Plots and Plotters in 1615*. Belfast: The Ulster Society for Irish Historical Studies, Queen's University Belfast, 1987.

Gillespie, Raymond and Gerard Moran (eds). *A Various Country: Essays in Mayo History*. Westport: Foilseachain Naisiunta Teoranta, 1987.

Gormley, Mary. *Tulsk Parish in Historic Maigh Aí: Aspects of Its History and Folklore*. Printed at Roscommon Herald, Boyle, 1989.

Greene, David H. (ed.). *An Anthology of Irish Literature*. New York: The Modern Library, 1954.

Gregory, Lady Augusta. *Gods and Fighting Men*. New York: Charles Scribner's Sons, 1904.

Grose, Francis, Esq. F.A.S. *The Antiquities of Ireland*. London: S. Hooper, 1795.

Jackson Knight, W.F. (trans.). *Virgil: The Aeneid*. Harmondsworth: Penguin Classics, 1964.

Kelly, Blanche Mary. *The Voice of the Irish*. New York: Sheed and Ward, 1952.

Kilgannon, Tadhg. *Sligo and Its Surroundings*. Sligo: Kilgannon and Sons Ltd., 1926.

Madigan, Michael, SVD. *Donamon: A History of the Castle and its Owners*. Roscommon: The Divine Word Missionaries, 1997.

Mattimoe, Cyril. *North Roscommon – Its People and Past*. Printed at Roscommon Herald, Boyle, 1992.

MacDonagh, Bernard. *The Spanish Armada: Illustrated Account of Francisco de Cuellar Story*. Sligo: The Sligo School of Landscape Painting, n.d.

McDonnell-Garvey, Maire. *Mid-Connacht: The Ancient Territory of Sliabh Lugha*. Manorhamilton: Drumlin Publications, 1995.

McDowell, R.B. and D.A. Webb. *Trinity College Dublin 1592-1952: An Academic History*. Cambridge University Press, 1982.

McGarry, James P. *The Castle of the Heroes – on Loch Key*. Printed at Roscommon Herald, Boyle, 1965.

McGreevy, Rev. John, D.D. "The Diocese of Elphin in 1637". In *Roscommon Historical and Archaeological Society Journal*, Vol. 2: 1988.

MacLysaght, Edward. *Irish Life in the Seventeenth Century*. Dublin: Irish University Press, 1969.

Moylurg Writers. *Boyle: the Origins; the Buildings; the Times*. Printed at Roscommon Herald, Boyle, 1988.

Murphy, Gerard. *Glimpses of Gaelic Ireland*. Dublin: C.J. Fallon Ltd., 1948.

O'Connor, Frank (trans.) "To Tomaus Costello at the Wars". In Frank O'Connor (ed.) *A Book of Ireland*. London: William Collins and Co., 1959.

O'Corrain, Donncha. *Ireland Before the Normans*. Dublin: Gill and Macmillan, 1972.

Ó Fiaich, Tomás. "Republicanism and Separatism in the Seventeenth Century". In *The Republic: A Journal of Contemporary and Historical Debate*, No 2: Spring/Summer 2001.

Ó hÓgain, Daithi. *Myth, Legend and Romance: An Encyclopaedia of the Irish Folk Tradition*. New York: Prentice Hall Press, 1991.

O'Suilleabhain, Sean. *Irish Folk Custom and Belief: Nósanna agus Piseoga na nGael*. Dublin: The Cultural Relations Committee of Ireland, 1967.

Roscommon Historical and Archaeological Society Journal, Vol. 1: 1986.

Sharkey P.A. *The Heart of Ireland*. Boyle, Co. Roscommon: M.J.Ward, 1927.

Vallely, Fintan (ed.). *The Companion to Irish Traditional Music*. Cork University Press, 1999.

Wilson, John Dover. *Life in Shakespeare's England*. Cambridge University Press, 1911.

Wheeler, H.A. and M.J. Craig. *The Dublin City Churches of the Church of Ireland*. Dublin: A.P.C.K., 1948.